Also by A. E. Hotchner

The Dangerous American
Papa Hemingway
Treasure
King of the Hill
Looking for Miracles
Doris Day
Sophia: Living and Loving
The Man Who Lived at the Ritz
Choice People
Hemingway and His World
Blown Away

Praise for the work of A.E. Hotchner

Papa Hemingway

"Part Boswell, part Euripides, Hotchner has written a greatly detailed and very loving book of memoirs."

- New York Times Book Review

"Ernest Hemingway himself comes on stage ... Make no mistake about it; this is a tragedy in the classic sense — the fall of a giant ... It is hard to imagine a better biography."

- Life Magazine

"As a feat of reportorial portraiture it seems to me absolutely brilliant and on the same level with Truman Capote's In Cold Blood ... Mr. Hotchner deserves to be compared not only to Capote but to Boswell."

- New York Times

King of the Hill

"Mr. Hotchner has written a lovely book ... the situations arouse humor as well as sympathy."

- Publisher's Weekly

"A good, amusing and startling book, told by a craftsman."

- Los Angeles Times

LOUISIANA PURCHASE

A Novel

A.E. HOTCHNER

VIRGINIA PUBLISHING CO.
ST. LOUIS

Virginia Publishing Company
4814 Washington Blvd.
St. Louis, MO 63108

ISBN 1-891442-00-7

First hardcover edition 1996 by:
Carroll & Graf Publishers, Inc., New York, NY

This book is dedicated to my forebears
who came from Austria, Poland, Hungary, and Ireland,
all of whom became Americans.

Acknowledgments

The author is indebted to Elizabeth Curren, Betsy C. Fentress, Maureen Zetlmeisl, Prof. Howard Miller, and especially Coralee Paull, the diligent researchers who tracked down much of the source materials for this book. Also, the author is grateful for the generous cooperation of the Historic New Orleans Collection, the Missouri Historical Society, and the Director of the Palace of Versailles. The author also thanks Jody Rutherfurd for her help and support.

The episodes depicted in the book are rooted in actual historical events, as are most of the characters, although there are contractions of time and, in a few instances, several characters have been amalgamated into one. But the book itself is based on the history of that time, the last half of the eighteenth century, when turbulent and chaotic events in the Midwest severely challenged the resiliency of the human spirit.

Yet, Freedom! yet thy banner, torn,
    but flying,
Streams like the thunder-storm against
    the wind.

—Lord Byron,
    Childe Harold's Pilgrimage

VERSAILLES,
1750

One

MADAME DE POMPADOUR had just stepped into her morning bath when the king sent for her, a most unusual occurrence. In the ten years that she had held the title of *maîtresse en titre*, Louis XV had not once varied from his daily routine when they were both in residence at Versailles. Nor had she varied from hers.

On awakening in his private bedroom, the king would invariably be helped into his dressing gown by his valet, and, escorted by the First Gentleman of the Bedchamber, he would proceed across the Council Room to the Royal Bedchamber where he supposedly had spent the night. It had been the bed chamber of his great-grandfather, Louis XIV, and its furnishings had been precisely maintained as it was on the day the old monarch died: the royal canopied bed, two tapestried armchairs, a dozen folding stools, a table with a lapis lazuli inlaid surface, a decorative screen, a crystal chandelier, Savonnerie carpet, and a clock embellished with precious stones. Louis XV's morning ritual was to lie down on the royal bed for a few minutes, to satisfy the formality of the public *lever*, then rise and attend to his toilette. He was first shaved by the royal barber who afterwards bathed his face with a soft sponge dipped in cold water and alcohol.

Attendants then brought him his breakfast which consisted of black coffee and fruit. After saying a prayer, the king was dressed and wigged by his valets after which he would go into the Council Room where he received ministers and ambassadors who presented state matters. At the conclusion of this brief ceremony, which the king barely tolerated since he was much more interested in affairs of love than in the affairs of state, he would ascend the small private staircase connecting his private bedchamber to the apartment of Madame de Pompadour. The two of them usually had lunch by themselves, a simple lunch consisting of a light soup, chicken wings, a savory. The king greatly enjoyed Madame de Pompadour's wit and gossip, and she was as much his mistress for her sexual companionship as for her conversation, her panache as a hostess, her flair for dancing, singing and performing, her skill at card playing (one of the king's passions), and her remarkable talent for maneuvering the intrigues of Versailles' courtesans to conform with the king's wishes.

But she cleverly kept this maneuvering so unobtrusive as to disguise its existence. Her graceful beauty and the captivating manner in which she sang, played the clavichord, danced, and created new and exciting décor, belied the strong-willed woman who was the buffer between the king and the thousand nobles who lived at the palace with their entourages. Often she was able to affect the king's edicts, to determine who was in and out of favor, even what laws should be promulgated, for the king had little interest in politics and state matters. His was a life of sensual enjoyment: hunting, card playing, elaborate costume balls, epicurean banquets, luxurious costumes, and promiscuous carnality to augment his regular erotic relationship with Madame de Pompadour.

Louis XV had acceded to the throne of France when he was five years old. His father, mother, brothers and sisters had all been murdered by the evil Dr. Fagon who eliminated the entire royal household in the incredibly short span of two weeks by administering bleedings, emetics, purges and other arcane ministrations. When Louis XIV was afflicted with gangrene, Dr. Fagon's only treatment was several glasses of asses' milk every day which did nothing to restrain the gangrene that slowly encompassed the old king's body and finally killed him after a reign of seventy-two years. The only reason that Louis XV escaped the mortal fate of the rest of his family was because his royal nurse, the duchesse de Ventadour, spirited the child out of the palace and hid him until a regent took over.

When he was fifteen, the young king was married, by arrangement, to Marie Leczinska who had been selected by Cardinal Fleury. She was the twenty-two-year-old daughter of the king of Poland.

Louis saw her for the very first time at the altar. Louis XV was a handsome youth with a strong, well-formed physique, and the court gossips spread the word that on his wedding night Louis proved his love for his bride seven times over. Marie was no beauty, but she had a pleasant mien and the king was patently in love with her. During the first twelve years of their marriage they produced ten children, but only seven daughters and one son survived. By then Marie Leczinska had become a stodgy, plodding middle-aged bore who dressed frumpily, avoided having sex with the king, and surrounded herself with a coterie of some of the most tedious, dull-witted members of the court of Versailles.

It was no wonder, then, that the king installed a succession of official mistresses. The *maîtresse en titre* who preceded Madame de Pompadour was the duchesse de Châteauroux who died of pneumonia in 1745 at a relatively young age. She was fiercely aligned with the duc de Richelieu and together they controlled all aspects of life at Versailles. Through the duchesse, a vain, beautiful, vindictive, ambitious woman, avariciously devoted to the accumulation of wealth, the duc de Richelieu was able to dominate the king who was thirty-four years old at the time of the duchesse de Châteauroux's death.

When Madame de Pompadour became the King's new *maîtresse en titre,* however, she wanted no part of Richelieu's attempt to establish a partnership with her similar to the one he had enjoyed with the duchesse. Madame de Pompadour, whose married name was Madame d'Étoiles when she left her husband to assume her royal position, had schemed all her life to become the first bourgeoise to rise to this exalted position; she was not about to cede any of her coveted prestige to the conniving duc. She had nurtured this obsession to become the king's mistress ever since the age of nine, when she had been told by a fortune teller that one day she would reside at Versailles and "reign over the heart of a king."

Jeanne-Antoinette Poisson was her maiden name, and after spending a year at a convent in Poissy, she had received an intense and varied education: she had been taught to dance and sing by Jéliotte, a star of the Comédie-Française; the renowned dramatist, Crébillon, had tutored her in drama, and she was able to recite entire plays from memory; she was a knowledgeable botanist, expert in the fine nuances of gardening; she painted, performed admirably at the clavichord, engraved on enamel, gold, and precious stones, collected exotic birds, and had a sound understanding of virtually all forms of art; in addition, she ran her household with a well-organized, exquisitely original touch, a virtue that was not lost on Louis XV when she became the mistress of his court.

In a letter to a friend, a member of the court wrote: "Not a man alive but would have had her for his mistress if he could. Tall, though not too tall; beautiful figure; round face with regular features; wonderful complexion, hands and arms; eyes not so very big, but the brightest, wittiest and most sparkling I ever saw. Everything about her was rounded, including all her gestures. She absolutely extinguished all the other women at the court, although some were very beautiful. Her whole person was halfway between the epitome of elegance and the first degree of nobility."

After installing her as his official mistress, the king considered it unseemly, under the circumstances, for her to retain her married name; he lost no time in bestowing upon her an ancient title, long dormant: Marquise de Pompadour.

From the outset of her incumbency at Versailles, the duc de Richelieu resented her presence and did everything in his power to thwart her liaison with the king, but despite his powerful position as First Gentleman of the Bedchamber, he found Madame de Pompadour unassailable. In fact, she soon usurped those functions that the duc had previously monopolized. It was she who now counseled the king on who should be appointed ministers and generals, and who should be demoted or dismissed. She determined which diverting, witty members of the Versailles court should be invited to the king's soirées for gossip and card playing (the king himself made the after-dinner coffee), and whereas the duc used to be the king's source of gossip and amusing stories, now it was Madame de Pompadour who delighted His Highness with spicy court gossip and ribald stories she recounted from the *Gazette Scandaleuse* sent to her daily by Berrier, a lieutenant of the Paris police, a friend from her pre-Versailles days. As a matter of fact, many aspects of her previous life fortified her position at the court, especially her experiences in the theater. Her participation in amateur productions had resulted in friendships with many authors, playwrights and composers, and she lost no time establishing her own little theater at Versailles to entertain the king.

This was particularly rankling to the duc de Richelieu who for years had been in sole charge of *Les Menus Plaisirs,* a specific list of pleasurable distractions that constituted the main preoccupation of life at Versailles. The resident nobles and their entourages, three thousand or more, while in residence at Versailles were removed from the cares and distractions of managing their estates, so that

Versailles became a sealed capsule wherein the denizens were totally immersed in the sybaritic activities of *Les Menus Plaisirs.*

For many years the duc's entertainments had been unvaried: the Comédie Française and the Comédie Italienne each performed once a week, repeating their limited, staid repertoires, and the king either attended them unenthusiastically or not at all.

Madame de Pompadour, however, who had earned a reputation as one of the finest amateur actresses and singers in France, brought fresh, new theater to Versailles. In the Ambassadors' Staircase she constructed what she called the *Théâtre des Petite Cabinets,* an intimate jewel of a theater designed by Boucher and Perot, which only seated twenty spectators and became the most sought-after event. Madame de Pompadour was able to assemble remarkably talented actors, singers and dancers from among the nobles and their retinues, and she chose the finest musicians for her own small orchestra from the king's royal band.

The first play Madame de Pompadour presented was Molière's *Tartuffe* in which she played the lead opposite a very talented young nobleman, Guy Laroule, who lived at the court. He had a tall, sinewy body, a resonant voice, and dense chestnut hair that framed strong features dominated by the intensity of his blue eyes. Beside his left eye was a short, heavy scar, a trophy from a royal tournament which Laroule, one of the court's most accomplished swordsmen, had won.

In the ensuing entertainments, *Le Préjugé à la Mode* by La Chaussée, and Dufresny's *L'Esprit de Contradiction,* Madame de Pompadour and Guy Laroule again performed together as they did in all the productions, both dramatic and musical, that she presented. They were particularly lauded for their performance in the three-character opera, *Erigone et Bacchus.* Madame de Pompadour prevailed upon many of her pre-Versailles friends to write original plays and operas for her theater; Voltaire, for example, wrote *La Princesse de Navarre* that combined ballet, song and comedy, and an opera, *Le Temple de Gloire.* Madame de Pompadour and Guy Laroule's triumphs only intensified the duc de Richelieu's resolve to denigrate Madame de Pompadour who in all his years at the court was the only person who had successfully defied his Machiavellian authority. The duc was an elegantly handsome man, fifty or so, whose unctuous charm, wit and intelligence cloaked his underlying nefariousness and corruption. He easily seduced ladies of his choice and just as easily charmed their suspicious husbands. He was accustomed, without exception, to having his own way, even with the king. For years he schemed to contrive some way to weaken Madame de Pompadour's seemingly impregnable position with the monarch. Madame de Pompadour was aware of Richelieu's machinations; spies in surreptitiously placed positions kept her informed of the duc's activities. But now, as she stood face to face with the king and the ominously smirking duc, she suspected that Richelieu had plotted against her in some way that her spies had not foretold.

"I regret to disturb you at so early an hour, Madame la Marquise," the king said.

"It is of no moment, Your Grace," Madame de Pompadour replied, increasingly disturbed by the duc's posture which now radiated smugness suffused with anticipatory gloating.

"The First Gentleman of the Bedchamber and I have been discussing our problems in the Louisiana Territory in North America," the king continued, "and it is our conclusion that certain vital areas should be in closer alignment with us. I am speaking specifically of the territory of New Orleans. There are numerous plantations in the vicinity that are not producing. Is that not correct First Gentleman of the Bedchamber?"

"Yes, Your Majesty, either they lay fallow or else they are worked and the proceeds do not properly go to the Crown."

Madame de Pompadour was searching desperately for some linkage between the New Orleans situation and herself but she was mystified, although she knew very well that the duc was about to spring his trap.

"We have instructed the Duc de Richelieu to draw up a list of reliable, qualified gentlemen to whom we would cede those plantations that most needed attention and my purpose in summoning you, my dear Marquise, is to inquire as to your appraisal of one of those gentlemen whom the Duc has nominated."

Madame de Pompadour now looked directly at Richelieu who could no longer contain an overt smirk of satisfaction.

"And just who would that be, Excellency?" Madame de Pompadour inquired.

"Guy Laroule," said the duc. "Since you have been so *intimately* connected with him in your theatricals, we felt that you could best inform him of His Highness' decision."

Hearing the duc's intonation of the word *intimately,* Madame de Pompadour understood immediately what plot he had hatched and why it was bound to succeed. She should have known that the duc had his own spies.

"Is it a request, Sire," Madame de Pompadour asked the king, "to be acted upon at Guy Laroule's discretion?"

"No, dear Madame," the king replied, "it is a command. I trust you will be able to find an adequate replacement who can perform with you in your most enjoyable presentations."

"Your Highness," the duc interjected, "I have already found a more than adequate replacement—the Duc de la Vallière assured me he has had theatrical experience in recitation and voice."

"Is he not a trifle too advanced in age?" the king inquired.

"With age comes experience," the First Gentleman of the Bedchamber replied.

"Would the Duc de la Vallière be satisfactory, Madame?" the king asked Madame de Pompadour.

"I am familiar with the Duc de la Vallière's abilities," Madame de Pompadour responded in clipped words. "I appreciate the First Gentleman of the Bedchamber's interest in my theatrical presentations but as it is an activity far afield from his pursuits, I think it best that I attend to the selection of the players."

"As you wish, Madame," the king said, casting a bemused sidelong glance at the duc whose face imperceptibly registered Madame de Pompadour's rebuff.

"With your leave, Sire, I shall return to my quarters."

"Yes, of course," the king said. "We shall lunch after the Council of Ministers."

With an abrupt nod to the duc and a graceful curtsy to the king, Madame de Pompadour quickly glided from the room.

As she hurried along the secret passageway connecting her apartment with the king's, Madame de Pompadour was flushed with feelings of embarrassment, anger and fear—embarrassed that she had been obliquely chastised, angry toward the conniving duc, and fearful lest the king's action presaged a diminution of his intense feelings for her. And there was something else: an overlay of guilt that involved Guy Laroule, for in fact he was more than a fellow performer on stage, and she wondered how much Richelieu actually knew about his relationship with her and how much he had told the king.

As she arrived at the stairs at the end of the corridor, two of her servants were in attendance at her lift chair, ready to raise her up the stairwell to her apartment. She settled into the chair and the servants rotated the levers that elevated the chair to the top of the steep, winding staircase where Madame de Pompadour's lady-in-waiting attended upon her; she hurried into her small apartment which consisted of only three rooms—a drawing-room with Verbeckt's carved wainscotting, a small study, and a bedroom with an alcove. The apartment faced north, with a panoramic view of the statues and their surrounding flower beds. In contrast, the king's private quarters, although called the *Petits Appartements,* consisted of fifty rooms and seven bathrooms, but he much preferred staying in Madame de Pompadour's small suite which was cozily and elegantly furnished.

She resumed her morning bathing ritual that the king had interrupted. As her maid, Madame du Hausset, helped her into her bath, her mind turned to the evening's costume ball. The king loved these elaborate balls which, in keeping with the Versailles tradition started by his grandfather, were open to the general public provided the celebrants were properly attired and that the men had swords at their waists. Even this requirement was not a deterrent, for there were enterprising palace personnel at the entrance who, for a fee, provided swords for the occasion. What the marquise was thinking, as Madame du Hausset rubbed her shoulders with scented pomades, was not about the enjoyment of the ball but about how her dear friend, Guy Laroule, would receive the unexpected royal transfer to Louisiana.

Madame du Hausset now brought the marquise a bowl of her morning elixir, prescribed by her physician, Dr. Quesnay: a truffle and celery soup, and a cup of hot chocolate laced with triple vanilla and ambergris. The prescription called for Madame de Pompadour to consume this royal repast five times a day. Although she had stopped short of revealing to Dr. Quesnay the truth about the condition she wanted treated, she nonetheless induced him to prescribe this diet which the physician assured her would "heat the blood." Madame de Pompadour ate little else other than her prescribed tonic and she was convinced that it was slowly improving her condition, a condition she had revealed to only one person—Guy Laroule.

In the course of their theatrical undertakings, the marquise and Guy had developed a deep and trusting relationship, intimately identifying with each other's emotions, both on and off the stage. There was an openness and honesty about Guy that inspired Madame de Pompadour's trust. It probably accounted, in large measure, for their success on the Versailles stage. And it was this trust that induced the marquise to confide in Guy the brooding secret that cast a pall over her otherwise brilliant and enjoyable life as the king's mistress.

"Guy," she said one evening, after they had been rehearsing in her apartment, "I am quite worried about my . . . my position with the King."

"Why, how can that be?" Guy said. "His Majesty obviously adores you. He would not have a meal or dance a gavotte without you. Worried?"

"Our relationship is wonderful in many ways," the marquise said, "but the King is of Bourbon lineage and thus very hot-blooded, but alas I am of a much milder temperament and no match for his desires. I am the reigning mistress and I am a good mistress at the luncheon table, the theater and the dinner parties, but I am not a good mistress of the bed which, to a Bourbon King, matters most of all."

"You refuse the King?" Guy asked, incredulously.

"No, of course not, but I am not good in bed because I am *acting* response rather than actually *feeling* response. Oh, it is not the King's fault—he is virile and enjoys sex immensely—no, alas, it is my own lack of temperament which manifested itself long before, when I was married. I long to please the King—I adore him—but he thinks I'm fearfully cold, I know. I would give my life to please him."

"But has he told you this—that he thinks you are cold?"

"Not in so many words. And I do believe he likes me in many ways, but last night, as you know, it was very warm and he preferred to sleep on the couch rather than in bed with me, on the pretense that the couch was cooler. As a result, I have been depressed all day. Oh, Guy, I am terrified of losing him. He is so manly, so active, and I am so frail, and I bring him no sexual passion. Perhaps it was all the miscarriages I have had since I became *maîtresse en titre* that have robbed me of sexual feelings—no, I can't ascribe it to that because right from the beginning I have pretended to feel that which I didn't feel."

"But he continues to have sex with you, does he not?"

"Yes, but . . ."

"Has he ever complained about your lack of response?"

"No, but . . ."

"Then you have imagined . . ."

"No, I have not imagined. If it were not for the Parc aux Cerfs . . ."

"Ah, then, you know about his secret little villa in town."

"I know only that young girls are maintained there for the King's sexual pleasures."

"Well, I hear they are mostly low-class women who come for the money and do not know that the man they service is the King."

"But what are they told?"

"That he is a wealthy noblemen from Poland, a relative of the queen. The gossip is that he performs to excess, and the royal physician has cautioned him to slow down. But I hear that the King feels that it is perfectly all right to have sex as often as he likes as long as he uses no aphrodisiacs. What he doesn't seem to realize is that change is the greatest aphrodisiac of all."

"And yet, despite all those girls at the Parc aux Cerfs, he still has sex with me virtually every day. But how can I, inhibited as I am, be worthy of his lovemaking when he has his pick of all those voluptuous girls?"

"All you need know, Madame, is that despite these young voluptuaries, you must still arouse him or else he would not come to your bed every night and have sex with you."

There was a pause now while Madame de Pompadour poured the tea that had been left cooling on the table before them.

"It is my feeling, my dear Reinette," Guy continued, using the childhood sobriquet her family had invented for her after the fortune-teller's prediction, "that you are ascribing an unrealistic importance to the King's sexual desires. In the palace, making love is not of great importance; there is much sexual activity outside the bounds of marriage with the knowledge of both husband and wife. It is just another activity—not a matter to be overemphasized, the only restriction being that the wives of noblemen should not indulge with footmen or princes of the blood. In my view, the King attaches more importance to your companionship as a raconteur who can make him laugh and titillate him with the latest Paris scandals, to your eye for decoration and architecture, to your exquisite culinary skills, and most especially to your theatrical talents—you should see his rapt expression when you are singing—I dare say if the King were asked his preference amongst his principal passions—playing cards, hunting at Fontainebleau, sex and palace diversions like the costume balls, he would be hard put to name one over the others. Your concern over your sexual placidity fictitiously magnifies his feelings which, I assure you, are perfectly sated with you as his bed partner."

"If only I knew how to respond in a way to please him and excite him."

"What do you mean?"

"I mean I have never really felt aroused nor have I ever climaxed, so I have no way of knowing how to pretend in a manner that pleases him. Is that not important to a lover's ego—that a woman be sexually overcome by his manliness?"

"Yes, for some men."

"Is it important to you?"

"Well . . . I like reciprocity of pleasure, if that's what you mean."

"Guy, I have a very intimate question to ask you—it embarrasses me and I would not ask it if I weren't so desperate—could you inform me about a woman's response—how it truly is—you are a fine actor . . . perhaps you could . . . oh, this is too embarrassing . . . it is not a thing to ask you."

"No, no, do not be embarrassed—I understand your predicament. I would say, yes, that it is possible to discuss the subject and to demonstrate reactions as I have experienced them. We can rehearse as if we were staging a scene for the theater. Just as it is not necessary to kill a person to simulate murder, so we should be able to create a believable illusion of sexual response without having actual intercourse. If that doesn't succeed, only as a last resort we can have sex but solely for its theatrics, as a demonstration. But I think we need not go that far. We shall rehearse as we do any of our scenes, only I shall be director as well as actor."

"Oh, Guy, how splendid that you are so sympathetic to my plight. I worry so, I have such anxiety. I have been on a special diet that Dr. Quesnay prescribed to heat my blood, but I fear it has accomplished little. If I am rehearsed in the right responses, then perhaps I shall bring the King more pleasure."

Two

THIS WAS, THEN, the first of several occasions when Guy and the marquise simulated sex as teacher and pupil. Finally being able to release her long-repressed confession about herself had a somewhat liberating effect on Madame de Pompadour. Although she never achieved with the king more than a mild feeling of response, she succeeded in producing the sounds, body movements, and expressions associated with a fully aroused woman; in her lovemaking with the king she definitely felt benefited by the acting lessons she received from Guy Laroule and by Dr. Quesnay's elixir.

It was obviously this rapport with Guy Laroule that the duc de Richelieu and his informants had twisted into an accusation that Madame de Pompadour was being unfaithful to the king. As she sat at her dressing table, applying her subtle cosmetics, the Marquise was imagining the sly, crafty way the duc had insinuated—he never directly dealt with such accusations—to the king that Guy Laroule could better serve the royal household by being sent to the far reaches of New Orleans.

Acting on an impulse, Madame de Pompadour rose from her dressing table and crossed the bedroom to the fireplace where, with the assistance of Madame du Hausset, she found a small opening in the wall behind the painting of the Hermitage at Compiègne which hung over the hearth. The adjoining apartment belonged to the Marquise d'Épénais, a pompous, bilious woman whom Madame de Pompadour invariably avoided. As she studied the small opening, she could picture the Marquise d'Épénais with her ear pressed against the opening, hearing sounds and snatches of conversation which she reported, with embellishment, to her dear friend, the duc de Richelieu.

"Madame du Hausset, please instruct the palace maintenance staff to repair the fissure in this wall at once," Madame de Pompadour said. Within the confined walls of Versailles, eavesdropping and other forms of espionage were commonplace, and the marquise was annoyed with herself for not having taken precautions against this kind of malicious intrusion.

Now, however, she had no time for reprisal, for she had to concentrate on the serious problem which the duc had created for her; her options, she decided, were few: either try to persuade the king to change his mind about Guy, or accede to the royal order and inform Guy that his pleasant existence at Versailles, where he had lived for most of his adult life, had come to an end.

The more she thought about her first option, the less inclined she was to embrace it. If she came on strong on behalf of Guy, that might reinforce the notion that he was indeed her lover. And, obviously, Madame de Pompadour could not tell the king the truth about the intimate matter that she had confided to Guy. Also, the marquise did not want to run the risk of compromising her current projects that were very dear to her heart. Work was currently in progress on ten new châteaux which she was having constructed in various regions of France. In addition, furniture, tapestries, crystal, china, rugs, jewelry, and gowns were all being made to her designs and specifications at enormous cost, and she was determined that nothing should interfere with their fruition.

Besides, if the marquise were to accede to the king's request without a murmur of dissent, it would demonstrate that she was emotionally indifferent to Guy Laroule. No, on reflection, that was definitely the course she must follow; better to suffer the loss of Guy Laroule than the loss of her way of life.

"Madame du Hausset," she said to her maid, "do you intend to be at the masked ball this evening?"

"Yes, Madame."

"And what costume do you plan to wear?"

"I shall come as Little Bo Peep—I made it myself."

"I should like to trade costumes with you. We are the same height, and there should be no problem."

Madame du Hausset was astonished. "But, Marquise, it is quite a simple costume without adornment. Only the mask is silk, whereas your Diana is bejeweled and sequinned and composed of the finest cloth."

Madame de Pompadour was at her writing desk, scribbling a note. "Take this to Monsieur Guy Laroule. Deliver it *only* to Monsieur Laroule. It is not to be handed to anyone else, not even his valet. Understand?"

"Yes, Marquise, of course." Madame du Hausset hurried off, mystified. It was Madame de Pompadour's plan that her anonymous costume would cloak her identity and permit her to have an unobserved meeting with Guy who, after receiving her note, would know to search for Little Bo Peep among the hordes of people who, that night, would pack the ballrooms and dining rooms of the great palace, even crowding into the queen's private bedroom.

Guy Laroule had been born at Fontainebleau where his father was Chief Huntsman of the Forest. His mother was a lady-in-waiting to the queen, in charge of her wardrobe. Since the queen had little or no interest in clothes, other than that they adequately protected her from drafts, Madame Laroule's role was far from demanding. But her lethargy matched Madame Laroule's own disposition which in turn complemented the queen's stodgy existence. Guy seldom saw his mother, and when he did, they had virtually nothing to say to one another. His mother would concentrate on her needlepoint, exhibit no curiosity about her son's life, and answer his futile attempts at conversation with as few words as possible.

But Guy did have a good rapport with his father, an ebullient, hearty man who was fond of good wine and always maintained at least two mistresses in the *Gros Pavillon* wing where he lived. Hunting stags in the adjacent forest of Bière, a huge, wild expanse, was one of the king's passions. In season, he often came to Fontainebleau with Madame de Pompadour, accompanied by an assemblage of noblemen, including Guy Laroule who was indisputedly the court's finest huntsman. His father had started taking Guy into the forest to shoot birds when he was but five years old, and not only was his shooting skill remarkable, but he also had a prodigious knowledge of the habits of the quarry that he hunted, whether birds, wild boars, or stags. In fact, he was the only huntsman who could go into the dense forest for the express purpose of bringing back a brace of rare, tiny *bécasses,* which was the king's favorite delicacy, and never fail to return with the little woodcocks swinging from the muzzle of his shotgun.

Guy's proficiency with his sword matched that of his marksmanship, and these attributes, plus his theatrical talents, made him very popular among Versailles' most coveted cliques. He was also admired for the originality and boldness of his dress; he was virtually the only courtesan who dressed in doeskin, not in the crude style of hunters but in sophisticated dress that styled the doeskin along the lines of accepted court fashion. He was sought after by many of the most beautiful women of the court, both married and unmarried, but his private life was so discreet that even the most proficient of the court's gossips had no succulent revelations about him.

As a youth, Guy had been well educated by the court's tutors, and two plays which he had written were performed in the Versailles theater with Madame de Pompadour and Guy in the leads. Subsequently, his plays were given performances in Paris at the Opéra Comique. Guy's apartments at both Versailles and Fontainebleau featured skins and head trophies of his hunts, but his pied-à-terre in Paris, where he went infrequently, had been decorated by an interior designer in a traditional manner.

Guy had never been beyond the region encompassed by Versailles, Fontainebleau and Paris, nor had he any desire to leave that circumscribed area. There were innumerable opportunities to travel with groups of his friends to England and Italy, but Guy declined all these invitations.

When Madame du Hausset appeared at his door with Madame de Pompadour's note, Guy considered her switch to Little Bo Peep amusing and not the least foreboding. He himself had designed a costume of skins and furs to indicate that he was Thor, the god of war; he was particularly pleased with the fierce face presented by his mask. Guy liked the king's costume balls because of their theatricality, and he looked forward, as usual, to enjoying himself.

Versailles was ablaze with the light from thousands of candles and torches. The roof, the porticos, the balconies, the balustrades, the walkways, the gardens, the fountains all gleamed with an undulating amber brightness. Carriages crowded the approaches; the vast Hall of Mirrors was so thronged with people that they could not reach the large banquet tables heaped with turkeys, fresh salmon, trout pâtés, filets of sole, boars' heads and mountains of cheese, pastries, and fruit. Indoor fountains ran wine in place of water. The Hall of Hercules, the Chamber of Venus, and the Chamber of Diana also had sumptuous buffets, and musicians to play for dancing. The Chamber of Mars was set up for gambling. All the crystal chandeliers were festooned with roses and carnations. Poor families came with their children, even their dogs, and those who could reach the buffets gorged themselves and filled their pockets with food to take home with them.

The Queen's Staircase was massed with people inching toward the Queen's Antechamber, her reception room and her bedchamber. The queen, of course, was not present but this didn't deter the curious who wanted to see how their queen lived.

The preponderance of the people, however, were elegantly costumed and masked, and it was not too long before those who had come for the food and to gawk, began to depart, leaving the crowded Hall of Mirrors to the aristocrats and their friends. The king always made a late entrance at every ball, each time trying to be more spectacularly costumed than the time before. On this occasion, the king's fancy turned to fashioning costumes to resemble yew trees patterned after those in the garden outside; the lower part of the costumes represented the base of the tree, while the upper costume copied the trunk to which branches were attached. It was difficult to maneuver in these costumes, but the king and the six noblemen he had enlisted as accompanying "trees" entered single file and then grouped together like a copse in the forest.

While the king was enjoying himself with his fellow trees, Guy was trying to locate Little Bo Peep among the dense throng of shouting, laughing, drinking, jostling celebrants. Finally he saw her, near the entrance to the Chamber of Plenty. She was holding her Bo Peep shepherdess' crook aloft as a beacon to guide him to her. They settled together on a banquette just inside the chamber's portal. Neither unmasked.

"Why did you give up on being the beautiful Diana?" Guy asked.

"So as not to be recognized. Everyone knew about my costume. Now they will think that Madame du Hausset is me and I, in turn, can have this anonymous conversation with you."

"You sound very serious."

"What I'm about to tell you *is* serious. The King, prodded by our dear friend, the duc de Richelieu, has come to a decision about you that is most upsetting."

"What have I to do with Richelieu?"

"He is getting at me through you. You know what enemies we are."

"And how do I figure in this?"

"The Duc knows how much you mean to me and he has convinced the King that you and I have had a dalliance."

"But that's absurd."

"Regardless, the King has decided that you should leave the court."

"Leave Versailles?"

"Yes."

"What about Fontainebleau?"

"There, too. In fact, you must leave France."

"And go where?"

"New Orleans in Louisiana."

Guy looked at her, shocked, disbelief in his eyes.

"Oh, I'm so sorry, Guy. If I thought I could overcome this I would, but this afternoon the King's courier brought me all the papers to give to you."

"What papers?"

"Your travel arrangements, a generous stipend for expenses, and the charter for the plantation which has been bestowed on you by royal edict. And you will get an annual pension."

"A plantation? Has the King gone mad?"

"The King, I'm afraid, has gone jealous, something I would never have believed."

"I know absolutely nothing about farming or anything else that has to do with a plantation. Perhaps I should speak to him . . ."

"No, Guy, don't humiliate yourself—I promise you he will not grant you an audience. His order is irrevocable."

"And just when am I scheduled to depart?"

"There is a ship leaving in two weeks."

"Two weeks! How can I possibly prepare myself in two weeks?"

"There is a positive side, Guy."

"Nonsense."

"Yes, there is. You are being given a large tract of land near New Orleans which has the reputation of being a little Paris. Over there you can become important and wealthy. Here, what life is there for you? You do not have a title or land of your own, or any official standing in the King's court. You will never be on the Council of Ministers and you are not trained for the military or any other government service."

"Reinette, you must speak to the King on my behalf. I cannot be banished like this to the swamps of Louisiana. I hear there are savages there. It is not a life for me."

"But, Guy, the life you are going to embark upon is not just New Orleans. France owns all of Louisiana, all the territory that follows the great Mississippi River all the way north. We have forts and trading posts all the way up to the Great Lakes. There is another great river that joins the Mississippi in the north. We have reports that most of the marvelous furs we now receive here come from the Indians up there and then are brought down the Mississippi to New Orleans. Think of the possibilities! The Louisiana Territory is almost as big as all of France and you will be there to take advantage of it long before anyone else. And you go there with the stamp of authority of the King of France upon you."

Guy appeared not to be listening to anything Madame de Pompadour was saying. "Reinette, if there is any meaning at all to our friendship, you must intercede with the King for me. You are the only one who has his ear—we all know what power you have. He appoints generals and ministers from your lists. It is said that it is you who decided that France should enter the war between Prussia and Austria in support of Austria because of your friendship with Maria Theresa. Surely with such power as you have over the King, you can induce him to reverse himself about me. I will give up performing with you in the Petit Théâtre. I shall vacate my apartment here and only live at Fontainebleau, and if that doesn't satisfy the king, I shall move permanently to my apartment in Paris. You must intercede for me. If I am banished to Louisiana it will be nothing less than a death sentence."

"Guy, my dear Guy, why can't you understand that I cannot jeopardize my position with the King. I adore him. He is my whole life. I sympathize with your fear of the unknown. This royal life here and at Fontainebleau are all you know. But your apprehension is unfounded. You are still young enough to start a career. I cannot. This is my career, my life. I am not his official mistress just to service the King in bed. I have a destiny. As you point out, I am here to run France. The King does indeed depend on me for advice. I am more in control of the affairs of state than he is. And you too must rule your own destiny. When you get to New Orleans, Guy, do not settle for the same dilettante life you have here. There will be great opportunities. It is a new country. Anything is possible. Do not stand around waiting for windfalls—climb the tree and take what you want. That is what I did. For years, I schemed how to become *maîtresse en titre.* Then, after I achieved it, I took hold of what I wanted. I love you, Guy, I do. I know you are hurt. You think I am sacrificing you for my own ends. But, in all honesty, there is nothing I can do . . . or want to do. That sounds selfish, does it not? Perhaps I am. I want to keep what I have. Please try to understand. I care about you, Guy. I will do everything I can for you, save asking the King to change his mind. That I cannot do."

The dense milling crowd was oppressing them, pushing against their legs, surrounding their banquette from all sides like ocean swells pounding against a sandbar. The room had become suffocatingly hot. Guy could feel sweat rivulets running down his body. He wanted to say something hurtful to Madame de Pompadour but he was too drained to conjure up words. He felt betrayed. And helpless. How many times he had cornered stags who had come to the end of the hunt, encircled by the hounds, at bay, panic in their eyes? And now he was at bay, his mouth dry, blood in his eyes, drawing difficult, deliberate breaths, a siphoning force within him drawing off his strength, constricting him, negating the inner resolve that he had always relied upon when pressed. Now in its place was a feeling akin to death.

At bay.

THE VOYAGE

Three

THE DOCK AT LE HAVRE was bustling with passengers and commodities arriving for the large-bellied, four-masted schooner anchored there, *La Gironde,* destination New Orleans. Under the command of Captain Albert de Vauberci, the ship had twice made the crossing to Nova Scotia but this was her maiden voyage to New Orleans.

Guy arrived in his carriage around eleven o'clock accompanied by his manservant, Claude Reynaud, and his closest friend, Philippe de Lorraine, whose father was the duc de Lorraine, the king's exchequer. Since early boyhood, Guy and Philippe had been inseparable friends, both raised at Versailles, sharing tutors, a passion for hunting, swordplay, and amorous amusements amply provided for by the ladies of the court. Although Guy had many friends who would gladly have given him a farewell party had they known about his departure, Guy only told Philippe about the king's edict. After the initial shock, Guy's reaction was one of embarrassment; he felt disgraced, as if publicly adjudged guilty of a crime and banished to New Orleans as punishment. That he had been invested with a large plantation and a royal stipend did not assuage the condemnation he felt at being banished from Versailles. The passing days intensified his sense of insecurity, in fact, fear, at having to leave the safe, familiar, contained Versailles world he had inhabited all his life. The scene that unfolded before him on the dock only heightened his misgivings.

A stream of horse-drawn carts was arriving at *La Gironde*'s gangplank and unloading human cargo, men and women recruited from the prisons of France, most of them under protest, preferring to serve their sentences in dismal prisons rather than risking the hazards of an unknown country. Shackled to each other, they were being pushed and prodded up the gangplank and into the hold where detention areas would restrain them during the three to four months of the crossing.

A large wagon drew up carrying a group of young girls in the care of several nuns, girls who had been collected from houses of correction in Paris. Marriages had been arranged for these girls with sailors living in New Orleans. The nuns had provided each girl with a dowry for her provisional marriage consisting of two coats, two shirts and undershirts, six headdresses, and other personal items intended to facilitate these nuptials.

In other carts, contingents of thieves, murderers, and prostitutes were arriving, cursing and damning the authorities who struggled to force them onto the ship. At an aft gangplank, livestock was being loaded: goats, sheep, chickens, geese, pigs, horses, mules, as well as cases of wine, barrels of brandy, cheeses, and other foodstuffs that could endure the long months at sea. A six-wheeled wagon drawn by four dray horses containing a variety of household furniture, including pianos, harps, and ornate garden fountains, the latter destined for the governor's mansion were also being unloaded.

A few carriages discharged high-born ladies coming to join their husbands, as well as other aristocrats who elected to go to New Orleans to escape serving sentences in the Bastille or Fort l'Evêque, sentences imposed for such indictments as "attacked the guard at the Comédie with a drawn sword," "killed his adversary in a duel," "caught poaching," and even one charge on the manifest that the accused "took a bow from the archer's hand." An attractive middle-aged woman, arriving in an ornate fiacre that bespoke her aristocratic status, had been charged with being "outrageously impious." Her uncle was commander of the garrison stationed at the fort in New Orleans.

"You have quite a complement of fellow travelers," Philippe remarked. "It should be anything but a dull crossing."

"Yes, quite likely," Guy replied bitterly. "I can see myself cavorting with the prostitutes and murderers down in the prison galley."

"But what about these others—that lady mounting the gangplank, holding up her skirts?"

"My mother's age. We can have a jolly time discussing her rheumatisms."

"But you will eat and drink well—even geese for your foie gras."

"Presuming I survive three months on this floating torture chamber."

"It will do nothing for you to be sullen and resentful. There are gentlemen to play cards and discourse with at meals. Why don't you try to concentrate on whatever alleviates a dreadful situation?"

"You are telling a man who wants to die to whistle a merry tune. Let us say that I will survive this abominable crossing—which I doubt—am I not ill equipped to run a plantation where I shall have to raise crops, get them to market, and be in charge of all the workers who work there? Slaves. Indians. These cutthroats who are on this boat. I tell you, Philippe, my only hope is that I am washed overboard on this crossing. I am too much of a coward to take my own life, but I will welcome divine intervention."

"I shan't argue with you, for we both know that you will survive both the crossing and your life in New Orleans. I hear New Orleans is quite like Paris. I know you too well, Guy. I have seen you all too often in the jousting tournaments, nimbly extricating yourself from perilous challenges, then rising to overcome your adversary. You will do that in New Orleans."

"Philippe, please, no more of your unctious bromides. 'Overcome my adversary'—what rubbish! Louisiana is my adversary—the King of France is my adversary—the thieves and murderers of New Orleans are my adversaries—this looming plantation is my adversary—look at it . . ." Guy produced a map that had been delivered to him by the king's Minister of Territories and spread it out in front of Philippe. "Am I to overcome all this by my swordplay? Shall I skewer the King, the Governor of Louisiana, and an assortment of criminals with my trusty sword and roast them over a fire?"

"Now that you mention your sword, I have a going-away present for you—you have always admired the matched épées my father gave me, and I am happy to bestow them on you to remind you of me while you are away."

"No, that's too valuable a gift."

"The more valuable the gift, the more valuable the friendship. I shall miss you, Guy. Versailles will not be the same for me without you."

The two friends embraced; Philippe would have said a final few words but was interrupted by an explosion of noise erupting from the dock. A group of women, chained two-by-two, with telltale fleurs-de-lis tattooed on their arms and shoulders, were being herded onto the gangplank of *La Gironde* by several armed soldiers when the snarling women turned and attacked the soldiers, kicking, scratching, and biting them, beating them with their chains. A melee of screaming, cursing bodies was flailing and falling all over the dock, a few rolling into the water. The women appeared to be gaining the upper hand over the outnumbered soldiers, but the soldiers, bloodied and scratched, their uniforms ripped, opened fire on the women, killing several and wounding a score or more. The fracas subsided as suddenly as it had started. The soldiers tossed the dead women back into the wagon, along with those who were too badly wounded to travel, while a couple of deckhands washed down the blood-slickened gangway.

The voyage to Louisiana, which ordinarily took three months, lasted all of five months, the crossing beset with unfavorable winds and storms of unprecedented ferocity. Guy's cabin, which was on the upper of *La Gironde*'s two decks, was no more than eighteen feet in length and about seven feet wide, barely able to accommodate a narrow bunk and a washbasin. There were two small portholes, about twice the size of Guy's hand, but he was seldom able to open them because of the turbulent waves that swept the decks. Only two days out of port, the first violent storm struck unexpectedly, ramming the ship against a rock, violently jolting the cargo and passengers, but thanks to the sturdy construction of *La Gironde*, it was not seriously damaged. It was then, however, that the winds became contrary, turning head-on against the plunging ship, creating such turbulence that anything not battened down was pitched precariously every which way rendering all the passengers, without exception, violently seasick. For two days, Guy stayed in his narrow bunk, suffering, it seemed to him, as he had never suffered before, praying that some divine force would snuff out his life.

One of the worst tempests came howling at the ship out of the northeast and savaged it so ferociously that most of the fowl, the goats, and the pigs that were on board to furnish fresh food during the voyage, were killed, either from smothering or from being pounded against the walls of their enclosures. Their carcasses had to be thrown into the sea, and for the rest of the voyage, there was nothing to eat except rice cooked in water, salted beef, fatty bacon, which Guy found inedible, and beans seasoned with lard since there was no butter on board. In fifteen days, plodding against the contrary winds, *La Gironde* made little progress, advancing only as far as it should have gone after three days. At the end of the first month, the supply of drinking water had diminished to the point that each person aboard was rationed to one pint a day.

Whenever the weather permitted, Guy wrapped himself in blankets and slept on deck in an area protected by an overhang of the bridge; he often carried a plate of the daily gruel there and ate alone. On days when the weather drove him from the deck, he ate at a designated table in the cramped dining area that he shared with a Monsieur Trémencourt, a businessman from Rouen. Despite the torments of the crossing, Monsieur Trémencourt was ebullient over the prospect of his impending life in New Orleans. He had a satchel filled with publications, provided by the Compagnie des Indes, which owned *La Gironde* and had considerable holdings in New Orleans and its vicinity; these publications covered the Mississippi, the Territory of Louisiana, particularly New Orleans, all of them describing life there in glowing terms. On those occasions when they dined together, Monsieur Trémencourt assailed Guy with glowing accounts of the existence that lay before them.

"You say you are going to run a plantation," Monsieur Trémencourt said, extracting a pamphlet from the attaché case which unfailingly accompanied him, "well, just read here about the soil and the climate. Perfect for raising succulent peaches, pears, apples, all this fruit, the arbors fed by rushing streams. Every kind of vegetable you can imagine. And the game? Here's the list—look here, wild ducks, venison, pheasants, snipes, woodchucks, on and on. You will think you are back in the forests of Fontainebleau. As for the fishing, read this account—one day's fishing expedition and look what they netted." He drew another pamphlet from his lode. "And no need to worry about servants and workers—plenty of Indians and Negro slaves—just look at these prices! You can buy a top-notch African slave, not one of the lazy variety from the Indies, for a month's wages you would pay a worker in France. And you'll get his wife and children for no extra. The girls make wonderful concubines—here's an account by a plantation gentleman who has two of them in residence. Oh, it will be a glorious life—you are unreasonably apprehensive."

On another occasion, Monsieur Trémencourt located Guy, who was huddled against the wind on the deck, and gave him a printed treatise put out by the Company of the Indies that dealt with the discovery of seemingly inexhaustible veins of gold and silver that could be harvested by simply sifting the bottoms of lakes and rivers, and especially the mud of the Mississippi which, according to the treatise, yielded gold in prodigious quantities. "And now, my dear fellow," Monsieur Trémencourt said, pointing to a particular page, "here is the most startling thing of all. In this area here, which you see shaded with slanting lines, the fields are covered with a unique plant which grows only there, nowhere else. The dew that accumulates in the cup of its flowers eventually hardens into a glistening nodule so that when the petals drop away, voilà! There is a diamond perched atop the stem."

At first, Guy was amused by Monsieur Trémencourt's enthusiasms, but eventually he wearied of them. "May I ask you, sir," he said one evening when the seas were so turbulent they had to hold their plates against their bodies to eat, a method they had appropriated from watching the crew members, "the Company of the Indies sells shares, does it not?"

"Yes."

"And you have purchased some?"

"Yes, and so have several others among the passengers."

"But outside of these brochures put out by this Indies company, have you had any corroboration of these remarkable claims from anyone who has been to Louisiana?"

"Well, no, but the Compagnie des Indes has an impeccable reputation . . ."

"But if New Orleans is so desirable, then why is the hold of our ship filled with some of the worst riffraff culled from the streets and prisons of France? Why is it not filled with persons like you, anxious to fill their coffers with gold and silver and diamonds gathered among the flower petals?"

"It is because I am in on the very beginning of this incredible opportunity. When word spreads around, when the world becomes aware of people like me who have become millionaires many times over, then the rush will be on. It is because I know an official with the company that I have these valuable reports."

"Well, now, Monsieur Trémencourt, if life promises to be as re-

warding as you describe, would you not like to purchase a plantation not far from New Orleans, favorably situated on a river whose
soil will undoubtedly produce all these agricultural wonders you
have spoken about? I would be prepared to negotiate with you at a
very good price for this sizable tract I now own."

"Oh, I would, Monsieur Laroule, I would, believe me, I would
jump at the chance, but unhappily, I have invested almost all my
money in Indies' stock, and what little remains I must live on while I
garner New Orleans' riches."

"I understand, but after you have accumulated sufficient gold and
diamonds, you may want to consider my offer. I am not attracted to
a life cultivating the soil of a plantation, no matter how plentiful the
crop, so here's my address in case owning a plantation appeals to
you once you are a millionaire."

"I'll certainly keep that in mind. I can see that, considering the life
you come from, you'd be much happier in New Orleans, which
everyone agrees is a diminutive Paris. Not just the Company of the
Indies—*everyone!* Here, look here, I have sketches of New Orleans,
and as you can see in this sketch, you could just as well be looking at
a neighborhood on the Left Bank."

After this discussion, Monsieur Trémencourt never again proscly-
tized about the delights of New Orleans, perhaps apprehensive that
Guy might, while on the subject, make another effort to sell him his
plantation.

Four

DURING THE ENDLESS, repetitive, tedious days of the crossing, several of the passengers made efforts to socialize with Guy, inviting him to join their card games and dining tables, but he politely declined all invitations. In his mind he was enduring an unwarranted punishment on this hellion of a ship; he would allow nothing to interrupt his self-pity. For the better part of each day, he relived separate moments of his life at Versailles: the costume balls, the wild boar hunts, the elaborate dinners, the musicales, especially the last concert in the music room when a six-year-old boy named Amadeus Mozart had excited everyone with his exquisite performance at the piano; but in his grieving nostalgia for the life he would never be a part of again, Guy's reveries about the plays in which he performed with Madame de Pompadour predominated. The day before his departure, he had met the marquise for the last time in the Temple de l'Amour on the grounds of the Petit Trianon, Louis XV's recently completed tribute to his mistress and their shared love for farm animals. Hen coops and pigeon houses adjoined the château, with housing for cows and sheep pens in a small adjoining garden. The grounds were laden with trees, shrubs and flowers, many varieties from other countries, a profusion of flora never before seen in France. At a fierce gallop, Guy rode his favorite stallion to his rendezvous with Madame de Pompadour, crossing the open fields, then

through the forests that stood between Versailles and the Petit Trianon, emerging on the pathway and across the stream that led to the
Temple de l'Amour, a stately pavilion surrounded by twelve ornate
columns which rose from a bed of lilacs and laburnum. Madame de
Pompadour was already there, reading the latest poems sent to her
by Voltaire. A Limoges tea service was set on a small table before
her, along with petits fours and a large silver tureen of native strawberries cultivated under the direct supervision of the king.

Madame de Pompadour rose and came to the steps of the pavilion
to watch Guy tether his white-sweated horse. As Guy came up the
steps, she took his hand and led him to the tea table.

"Don't let us be sad," she said. "We have never been sad together,
so at this last meeting, let us be as gay as always. May we?"

She poured the tea, and they ate the plump, succulent strawberries, chatting amiably as if rehearsing a scene in one of their plays.
Without preamble, however, the marquise suddenly said, as if it
were simply part of the stream of their inconsequential chatter, "I
suppose you know, Guy, that I have been in love with you. Not in
the same way I love the King, but in some ways . . . did you know
that? Did it ever occur to you?"

"Of course. But I respected the restraints we had to observe."

"I suppose it became obvious to others. That was our undoing.
One can be blameless, but it is the perception that counts. I regret
now that we . . . I think that with you I could have . . . No, no, I
must not talk about it. It is cruel to confess this on the eve of your
banishment. But it is a frustration."

"Shall I ever see you again?"

"Not likely."

"If the King were to die . . ."

"The King is fifty-two and of good stock. Do not forget that Louis
XIV lived to be over eighty years old."

"I had many fantasies about us."

"Tell me."

"After performing a romantic scene with you, afterwards, I
would, in my imagination . . . fantasize."

"That is why we interacted so well as performers, wasn't it?"

"Of course. I relished the intimacy of our rehearsals."

"How will it be without you, Guy? I try to imagine it. Last night I
was so distraught with contemplation of the void you would leave in
my life that, on impulse, I mentioned your name to the King."

"In what way?"

"How difficult it was finding a replacement for you. That good actors do not grow like the strawberries."

"And what did the King say?"

"That whoever the actor was didn't matter much, because all eyes were always on me."

"That's true."

"Nonsense. And you know it. I am only as good as my fellow actor allows me to be—and you, dear Guy, were the perfect partner. I will miss you, oh, in so many ways. That I kiss you good-bye now is very painful. I feel an ache here in my wishbone, a sharp pain that will be a long time going away, maybe never."

"May I request a memento, a keepsake?"

"Anything."

"That small ring with your crest on it."

She took it off and gave it to him.

"I shall wear it on a chain around my neck. My talisman. That way, you will accompany me wherever I go."

She put her arms around him, rose on her toes, and kissed him on the lips, at first lightly, and then forcefully, letting him feel the intimacy of her tongue, her breath quickening, her fingers thrusting into his back.

Abruptly, she broke away from him. "You must go now, my sweet Guy. The King arrives within the hour, and it would not do for him to see you here."

Confused and aroused, Guy looked at her longingly for the last time. Then, hurrying down the steps, he quickly mounted his horse and galloped furiously away along the pathways of the Petit Trianon.

Five

CAPTAIN DE VAUBERCI had intended to put in at the Canary Islands to take on water, but the wind was so perverse *La Gironde* had to be rerouted to the island of Madeira, off the African coast, which belonged to the king of Portugal. The captain saluted the islands with seven shots from one of his four cannons; the nearest town responded with five shots and with a small boat which carried a party of four welcoming officials. *La Gironde* lay over for a day while her store of water was replenished, and she shored up her pantry with local food: lemons, dried fish, bread, salad, preserves, and tree-ripened fruit in abundance. Unfortunately, there was no poultry to acquire although the town's mayor did present the captain with a splendid ram.

Guy spent his day ashore wandering by himself through the fruit-heavy orchards and the narrow streets of the old village, Pistola. He ate lunch at a small café that served local wine and fishcakes. The owner of the café, whose wife did the cooking, had caught the fish early that morning. He also waited on tables. Guy was fascinated with the simplicity of this kind of life, in stark contrast to the complex Versailles existence to which he had been accustomed. It occurred to him that perhaps he should jump ship and live here in these unpretentious, sympathetic surroundings. He certainly had enough wealth to live for quite a long time in this simple village where he could build a house to his liking. On the rises beyond the town, he could see dense forests where good hunting was likely. Although he had fished only in the rivers and streams near Fontaine-bleau and Versailles, the prospect of deep-sea fishing appealed to him. He thought now about a monastic life in this small village, free of the responsibilities the plantation posed as well as intricacies and intrigues he would surely have to face in New Orleans.

The hour approached to board the ship and Guy's resolve began to weaken. When the small launch brought him back to *La Gironde*, he faced the moment when he would have to pack and disembark once and for all, he faltered, a kind of paralysis setting in. As he sat on his bunk, his head in his hands, he said aloud, "You are a coward, a damn coward. What do you believe in? Who are you? You may as well throw yourself overboard. Who do you care about? Who cares about you? If you should jump overboard, who will miss you? Nobody."

Leaving Madeira, heading now across the open expanse of the Atlantic, the wind was favorable for two days and good progress was made, but on the third day the wind reversed itself and swung against the ship which bucked and rolled and struggled to make headway. Two hundred leagues from Madeira the ship's lookout announced the sighting of a pirate ship, probably from the Barbary Coast. The captain had had the foresight to rehearse the crew and passengers in a pirate drill so that now everyone went immediately to their battle stations. The crew manned and loaded the four cannons. The captain took up a position on the poopdeck with Monsieur Trémencourt beside him, both armed with shotguns. The ensign, also armed, stationed himself on the bridge, with Guy as his assistant. The second captain was on the forecastle with two of the other armed passengers. Several women were positioned on the bridge, next to a stockpile of cartridges which they were to distribute when the men started to fire their weapons.

The pirate boat circled *La Gironde* several times, assessing the ship's defenses, but the presence of the four cannons and the armed men at their stations evidently discouraged them and they left.

When *La Gironde* reached the equinoctial line of the tropics, the weather turned suffocatingly hot and humid. The wind did veer favorably for a few days before again altering to a perverse direction. A second pirate ship approached while *La Gironde* was virtually wallowing, but it, too, was discouraged after viewing the firepower that would confront them.

But a threat more ominous than the pirate ships suddenly struck—a vicious storm agitated the seas so violently that it was impossible to stay in bed unless lashed down with ropes. The ship groaned and staggered under the pounding of the mountainous waves which thundered against the ship's decks, striking with such force as to crack the glass of the portholes. It was impossible to move inside the ship without being pitched against the walls and down the stairs. The violent sea drove Guy from his niche on deck, and as one turbulent day turned into another he berated himself for not having followed his impulse to leave the ship for a life of serenity on Madeira.

Severe heat and pummeling seas also wrecked havoc in the overcrowded hold of the ship. Not in good health to begin with, many of the wretches who had been crowded in there succumbed; their corpses was carried up to the deck and pitched over the rail. By the time the ship would eventually reach New Orleans, two-thirds of the people in the hold would have perished.

The situation on board brightened, however, when the gale-force wind did a sudden about-face and propelled the ship at great speed in calmer seas toward the island of Santo Domingo, where, eventually, *La Gironde* mercifully dropped anchor at the Quay St. Louis.

La Gironde stayed at Santo Domingo for five days to make repairs to the damage caused by the storms, and to replenish supplies. The governor hospitably invited the captain of *La Gironde* and its favored passengers, Guy among them, to dine at his mansion, serving them a banquet that rivaled a dinner at Versailles. All the furnishings came from France, and the menu, featuring the classical cuisine of the mother country, was prepared by French chefs. The evening with the governor, whose lovely wife and daughters were dressed in modish Paris gowns, raised Guy's spirits for the first time since his banishment. He danced with two of the daughters and drank more than his share of the exquisite Burgundy and Cognac.

The five days passed quickly, and once again, when *La Gironde* was ready to sail, Guy was tempted to abandon ship and stay in Santo Domingo, but while he vacillated, the ship eased away from the quay and resumed its journey to New Orleans. The governor's daughters, one of whom was infatuated with Guy, were on the dock to see them off. The governor had sent departure presents for all his guests: barrels of sugar, kegs of wine, and brandy.

Now that the route would take *La Gironde* through the Straits of

Florida and into the Gulf of Mexico, the expectation was that the passage would be calmer, but such proved not to be the case. The first day, the seas were indeed placid and the wind correct, but on the second day, the ship was becalmed and then a brisk contrary wind arose that made it difficult to stay on course. After the short respite on Santo Domingo, Guy's feeling of despair intensified as he kept to himself in his starboard niche in the crook of the bridge. Life in the Governor's Mansion, although not nearly as elaborate as Versailles, nonetheless rekindled Guy's longings for the world he had been forced to relinquish. The orchestra that had played the music for the gavotte, the beautiful theater whose performers had entertained them with an operetta, the seductive perfume of the daughters who flirted and teased, quite like the ladies of the court, all evoked now-painful emotions.

The winds increased, further slowing the progress of *La Gironde*, and then came the insistent and unpredictable currents of the Gulf of Mexico, which were at cross purposes to the wind. The ship rolled fitfully in the chaotic seas, making little progress, the heat now more intense than ever. The crew continued to bring up corpses from the hold and pitched them over the side with no attempt to confer on them even a snatch of prayer.

On the day that the distant banks of the American mainland were sighted the swiftness of the currents augmented; winning the tug-of-war with the winds, they began to push *La Gironde* off course, forcing it toward a spit of land identified on the captain's chart as White Island. The captain desperately maneuvered his sails, trying to avoid the island, which was reputed to be inhabited by savages who tortured captives and engaged in a ceremony that forced their hostages to drink their own blood. But as the ship drew ever nearer to the island, its course was abruptly halted by a sandbar that held it fast in its grip. Under the captain's command, the crew frantically raised and lowered sails, attempting to dislodge the vessel, but *La Gironde* did not budge. A sounding revealed that it had sunk about five feet into the sand.

Concerned that the White Island natives might spot the beleaguered ship, the captain decided to lessen its weight in an attempt to float it free. He ordered the four cannons removed from their mounts and lowered into the sea. That done, the ship's ballast, which included rocks, lead ingots, and large scraps of iron, was also thrown overboard. When even this did not suffice, the captain considered jettisoning all the passengers' traveling chests, which would have stripped Guy of the last of his possessions. At the last moment, however, the captain changed his mind in favor of casting off all the barrels of sugar, each of which weighed about three hundred pounds. The ship rose a notch, but not enough to free her. The crew searched the deep hold and located more ballast, mostly heavy chunks of iron, which were cast overboard, as were one hundred and three barrels of brandy destined for the governor of New Orleans and for the officers of the fort overlooking the harbor. Captain Vanberci even ordered the members of the crew to sacrifice their own individual barrels of rum and brandy. Still the ship held fast. As evening approached, as a last resort the captain lowered the ship's launch and dinghy, loaded them with crew members and the two anchors along with their attached ropes in an attempt to pull the ship backwards. The sailors strained at their oars, churning up the sandy water. The passengers on board leaned over the railing, egging them on, as slowly, inch by inch, the ship began to struggle against the sand, finally freeing itself and riding clear.

After that, one of the ship's officers, the sounding line in his hand, stayed in the dinghy ahead of the ship until it had safely returned to deeper water. But to circumvent the sandbars, *La Gironde* had to go nineteen leagues off course so that the days of additional sailing plus the ever-oppressive heat again put water in short supply; once more it had to be rationed to a daily pint per passenger along with the customary bottle of wine. Some of the passengers bartered their wine for water, but Guy, gaunt and dispirited, seemed indifferent to the heat, perhaps inured by his sense of withdrawal, as if he were no longer affected by what was happening to him.

For fifteen days, the wind blew in the same direction as the powerful currents, dead-on opposed to the ship's progress. In order to maintain his position and not lose ground, the captain was forced to lower the anchor several times a day to avoid being pushed backward.

Eventually the wind abated, although the contrary current remained strong, but the judicial use of his sails enabled the captain finally to sight land which turned out to be the uninhabited island of St. Rose. The crew went ashore in the sloop and dug holes off the seashore which produced several barrels of fresh water that were brought back to the ship. *La Gironde* rode at anchor off St. Rose for three days until the winds turned strongly in its favor.

Several days later the boat reached Dauphin Island, where they picked up a local captain who steered them to Balize, just west of the entrance to the Mississippi. It was five months to the day that *La Gironde* had left Le Havre and arrived here, the last stop on its Atlantic journey. But more obstacles were yet to come, for to reach New Orleans, the Mississippi had to be navigated in small boats, called pirogues, made from the trunks of large trees that had been scalloped out; each pirogue carried several passengers with their luggage, but the pirogues were precarious, more unstable than canoes, and were known to roll over easily depositing passengers and luggage alike in the muddy water. A flotilla of large pirogues were now approaching, each capable of transporting sixteen passengers; these would be loaded with the miserable passengers remaining in the hold who had survived the crossing.

Guy shared a small pirogue with Monsieur Trémencourt and Madame Jocelyn Breton whose husband was a major in charge of the New Orleans garrison. They sat atop their traveling chests that were secured in the well of the pirogue, placing them in a precarious position above the gunnels. The sun was blisteringly hot, but they were warned to move as little as possible so as not to disturb the fragile equilibrium of the boat. Madame Breton prattled aimlessly about her husband's exploits in the military, while Monsieur Trémencourt continued to extol the approaching New Orleans bonanza, neither listening to the other, and Guy trying not to listen to either one of them.

The swift, choppy river ran from Balize to New Orleans for only thirty leagues but it took six days to navigate that short distance, with hardships worse than those suffered on *La Gironde*. What complicated this leg of the voyage was the necessity of setting up camp along the shore each evening, an hour before the sun went down, so that there would be time to prepare supper and make up sleeping pallets before swarms of voracious swamp mosquitos called maringouins attacked. This vicious insect was usually joined by the frappes d'abord which were larger and more menacing than the maringouins; both inflicted poisonous bites that easily became infected. Sometimes the latter's dense swarms formed a black wall of attack so solid that it looked as though it could be cut by a knife. The insects would completely cover a person's body from head to foot giving the appearance of being wrapped in tar paper; many victims had died from such pervasive attacks.

The only defense against the mosquitos was to pitch protective pallets before dark. By sticking bent canes in the muddy ground around a mattress, the crew created a cradle they then covered with a large piece of porous linen in such a way that the maringouins and frappes d'abbord could not find an opening to get at the occupant. Guy and the other passengers slept with their clothes on and were obliged to enter a pallet before sundown, remaining there until first light drove the attackers away. Twice violent downpours in the night soaked Guy; his mattress almost floated into the river. The mornings after the storms, the pirogues advanced very slowly since they were just as waterlogged as the mattresses.

The banks along the entire length of the river were overgrown and impenetrable with no sign of cultivation. The adjoining forests teemed with animal life: serpents, adders, scorpions, alligators, vipers, and wildcats. But although they often came close to the pallets at night, they did not actually attack any of the occupants. Torrential rains and dank humidity induced colds and inflammations among the passengers, some of whose faces and legs began to swell. Madame Breton's legs swelled so badly she had to be carried ashore from her pirogue each night and helped onto her pallet. During the night, she often cried out in pain when she moved her legs, her cries like that of a wounded beast.

NEW ORLEANS, 1752

Six

Guy's pirogue arrived in New Orleans early in the morning. His once-elegant clothes were now streaked with mud. There were tears and rips where thorns and brambles had caught the brocaded fabric of his tunic. He had no idea where his plantation was located, nor how he would get there.

According to the papers which accompanied his royal grant, the plantation had been in the possession of a Monsieur de Sévigny, who had cultivated it, but title had reverted to the Crown during the preceding year on Monsieur de Sévigny's death. No indications in Guy's papers of entitlement mentioned any persons who should be contacted, only that it was called the Diderot Plantation, and a map was included that chartered its location. For Guy, whose life had revolved around a circumspect world of orderly events to which one simply responded, a predictable world without challenge or uncertainty, the prospect of arriving in a strange place where he was unknown had, for the first time in his life, made him fearful.

As the sailors unloaded his traveling trunks onto the dock, Guy inspected his depressing surroundings. As far as his eye could see, the quay was covered with islands of rusted ballast, pitched there by arriving ships, and with refuse and garbage, most of which came from the many taverns that catered to arriving sailors and dockworkers. A carriage approached and stopped where Monsieur

Trémencourt stood with his luggage. A gentleman, who was obviously a friend of Monsieur Trémencourt, descended from the carriage and greeted him heartily, while the driver and footman loaded his chests onto the carriage's roof. As they drove off, Monsieur Trémencourt waved to Guy, but he did not inquire if he had transport. All along the quay, people were arriving to meet the pirogues' passengers. Even the derelicts, however few remained, were herded into carts and taken to public shelters.

When the dock was finally stripped of all activity, Guy became aware that a cart drawn by two large mules, which had been there all along, was now approaching him. The cart was painted bright red. The driver, who wore a buckskin vest with a fringe of blue beads, was wearing a straw hat with a pointed crown. The cart was crudely constructed, with bumpy wheels, but the mules, who wore straw hats matching that of the driver, were sleek and well-fed, their harness in good repair.

The cart stopped in front of Guy. The driver descended, tipping his straw hat. He was a tall, graceful, black man with a curious complexion and a luminous sheen to the heavy muscles of his exposed arms. His smile was as wide as his face, and his hands the size of melons. He looked to be no more than thirty.

"Suh! I note your arrival and welcome you on 'half o' the royal city of New Orleans!" He made an elaborate bow, this time doffing his straw hat. "I note that you are the last of the landing parties," he continued, "and I inquire of you as to whether you may require some assistance with your trunks. Have no concern, suh—you can deal with me without fear of the Code Noir, since, as you see here, I am a free Negro." The man drew an abused blue paper from his pocket and handed it to Guy. "I also have a work permit for my cart and mules as this yellow paper will 'test." He handed Guy another well-worn document, frayed at the creases. "That is my name, Tricot, and, as you can see, suh, I am authorized to carry passengers and commodities of all descriptions."

"Then you were a slave?" Guy asked.

"Oh, yes, suh, born here on Trépagnier Plantation twenty-four years ago. Mother, father, slaves, two brothers, and a sister also."

"Then how did you manage . . . ?"

"I, myself, had been sold at twelve years of age for twenty dollars to Monsieur de Siavet, a friend of Monsieur Trépagnier, to labor at his plantation, planting indigo. I lived in the slave quarters with other boys and never saw any of my family again. But then, at thirteen, I was working in the field when I see smoke in a great cloud rising from the little house where the Mademoiselles were schooling. Three Trépagnier daughters. I ran fast as legs would carry me to the little house where now many flames appear going skyward. As I open the door, there is so much smoke I cannot see, but I crawl on the floor and find the Mademoiselles all coughing and choking and crying and holding each other. Then all of us crawling, I lead them out of the house and away just as the burning roof goes crashing and everything burn."

"Anyone hurt?"

"Just a little, except for Monsieur, the tutor."

"What happened to him?"

"The fire burned him up as it burned the timbers."

"You are a hero."

"It was because of this that Monsieur Trépagnier applied for papers that I become what we call a free person of color. The Governor signed the papers and that is who I am. Monsieur Trépagnier hired him a new tutor and built a new schoolhouse where I was included with the demoiselles. I learned to read and write and add figures and to speak proper Creole and not like a slave speaks. I still live on Trépagnier Plantation, but I have no obligation to work there. I can freely ply my trade."

"Are there many of you free slaves?"

"Not many, suh. Perhaps one hundred."

"In all New Orleans?"

"Yes, suh. We are almost all of mixed blood. The Government prefers those of mixed blood."

"And you are of mixed blood, too?"

"Yes, suh. When my parents were purchased by Monsieur Trépagnier, my mother, who was light-skinned, as am I, was chosen by him to grace his bed. Monsieur Trépagnier likes Negro ladies of light color. At present, two mulatto ladies reside in the main house."

"Then Monsieur Trépagnier is your father?"

"By fact, yes, but by law, my father is the Negro slave who is married to my mother."

"And how many Negro slaves are there?"

"In all New Orleans, perhaps two thousand."

"And what number of white people?"

"It is told thirty-two hundred. But Indians—ah, Indians—they go and come so very much, no one can say."

"Are there Indian slaves?"

"Yes, but they are not desirable. The men work badly in the fields, and the women are not cheerful."

"Well, Tricot, I certainly would like to hire your services to transport me and my chests to Diderot Plantation—are you familiar with it?"

"Diderot? No, suh, but there are many, many plantations . . ."

"I have a map."

Tricot studied the map briefly, sounds of recognition escaping him. "Suh, I know just about where this location is—we can reach it by the river road."

"Is it far?"

"Not to exceed an hour. Do you visit friends?"

"No, it is mine by royal grant."

"Oh, suh, how splendid to possess one's very own plantation from the hand of the King."

"We shall see."

"See what, suh?"

"Whether it will be splendid."

Seven

THE ONLY ROUTE ACCESSIBLE to the plantations was the Tchoupitoulas Road which ran alongside the river. It was a narrow dirt roadway, deeply rutted by wagon wheels, with occasional small clearings to allow carriages going in opposite directions to pass each other. Tricot's cart was drawn swiftly by the two mules, but lacking springs to cushion the jolts of the high wooden wheels, it rode hard. A low levee, dotted with willow trees, ran alongside the Tchoupitoulas Road; during the high water season, long keelboats, barges, and ungainly flatboats called "charlands" would come down the Mississippi from the north and make fast to the willows while discharging their cargoes. The owners of these huge flatboats would then abandon them at the dock, rather than face long and often fruitless efforts to try returning them against the strong Mississippi current. When the spring and summer floods receded, leaving the charlands high and dry, dock scavengers would then take them apart and sell the wood for building purposes and for fuel, leaving unusable pieces of the boats to rot amid the clutter on the docks.

After a while, the levee gave way to vast open spaces where the plantations were located, one after the other. As he passed by, Guy had a panoramic view of their mansions, outbuildings, and crops. The Negroes laboring in the fields, planting, harvesting, pruning, were a large disciplined work force. Plantation after plantation were surrounded with hedges of oranges, orchards, and well-tended flower gardens. As they passed the sumptuous Livaudais Plantation, its manor house screened by cascades of delicate gray moss draped from the trees, Guy asked Tricot to halt briefly to better view the beauty of the twin-gabled mansion and its surroundings. Until this moment, the word plantation meant nothing to Guy, other than an expanse where crops were grown. He had no idea that the mansions, the gardens, and the fields would be so attractive, so inviting: the Trépagnier mansion with its columned portico and twin chimneys; the Ormond Plantation, its mansion distinguished by ten columns bisected into upper and lower porticos, and pigeonniers at both flanks of the house; the Parlange Plantation with its vast fields of indigo.

"Suh, I have had the honor to have entered this Parlange manor," Tricot said, "and it is of a beauty I will not soon forget. Marquis Vincent de Termant, a most distinguished gentleman, is its owner, and like you, received it as a grant from the French Crown. All the furniture is from France, and the Marquise de Termant dresses in fine clothes from Paris. I am the one who has brought these packets from the boats when they arrive. That is how I know. Yes, suh, one who inherits a grant from the Crown leads a very princely life. You will see, now you are a plantation owner."

For the first time since he left France, a sense of anticipation stirred in Guy. He became curious about Diderot Plantation and whether its architectural efflorescence would equal the mansions passing before him. I hope it resembles this Parlange mansion, he thought, surrounded as it is with a striking assemblage of oaks and cedars, decorated with shards of moss that darken the atmosphere. I would like my house to have these same open galleries supported by these graceful colonettes. Guy also admired a pair of octagonal plastered pigeonniers with wooden finials that stood apart from the house. If Diderot Plantation does not have pigeonniers, then I will have them built, he thought. He was amused by the way his new-found proprietary attitude was predominating now over his former distress.

The cart continued its journey past the plantations, some as grand as the Rienzi mansion, others more modest. Tricot had never been this far along the Tchoupitoulas Road which accounted for the fact that Diderot Plantation was unknown to him. The road began to narrow even more, the roadside vegetation growing denser and higher, to the point that it was like traveling through a roofless tunnel. After an oblique turn to the right, where the road parted from the river, Tricot halted his mules and consulted the chart Guy had given him.

"Ah, yes, certainly, look, suh. It is a plantation somewhere along this stretch. We now should be on the lookout for it."

As the road took its new direction, the terrain became marshy, with meandering pools of water connected by bog vegetation and dense moss draped from the bare branches of trees it had killed. The cart stopped abruptly, the mules rearing at the sight of what appeared to be a log lying across the road. Tricot spoke to the mules soothingly, calming them, then reached back and took a hickory staff from the cart. As Tricot walked toward the log, Guy realized that the log was in reality an alligator whose body covered the entire width of the road. Guy dismounted and took hold of the reins in case the mules, who were still shuffling nervously, decided to bolt. Tricot approached the head of the alligator, keeping himself distanced from its tail, and then suddenly lashed out with his stick, striking the animal behind his head. The tail lashed furiously from side to side, stirring up a balloon of dust, but after another whack on its head, the alligator lumbered forward into the swamp and disappeared.

Shortly after that encounter, they came upon the plantation. The approach was so overgrown with vegetation that it was difficult to follow its course, but Tricot assured Guy that this kind of overgrowth was to be expected when a plantation was not occupied for any length of time. When the path took its final turn, revealing the plantation itself, Tricot pulled up, shocked at what he saw. The panorama before them was unrelentingly black: the black of fire that had burned to the ground what had been a majestic mansion, its charred remains suggesting the outline of the house; the black vista of what had been dark blue fields of a luxurious indigo crop; the black stumps of trees whose leaves and branches lay in ashes around them; black, black, black, everywhere—the slave quarters, the pigeoniers, the barns, the flower and vegetable gardens, a child's playhouse—all scorched, all a rubble of black tombstones. In one stroke, all of Guy's tentative expectations were destroyed.

Without speaking, Guy and Tricot dismounted and walked slowly around the desiccated grounds; there was no sign of life. Nothing there to attract birds, insects, animals, an arid graveyard, not even a weed able to penetrate the charred crust of the land.

As they approached the far side of the territory, they came upon the repugnant sight of five scorched bodies: two adults, and the smaller remains of three children, quite likely the plantation owner, his wife, and their children. Tricot examined the remains, but found nothing that had not been consumed by the fire.

Having seen more than he could bear, Guy sat down heavily on a boulder, one of the few things the raging fire had not destroyed, and tried to make sense out of the predicament he was in. Obviously, the plantation had to be abandoned, but if he went to live in New Orleans, what would he do for a living? The resources he had would last awhile, but what would happen once they were gone? I am fit for neither trade nor profession, he thought. That has not been my way of life. I could not even acquire a prosperous wife, since I've been told there's a severe shortage of women in New Orleans, prosperous or otherwise.

"Do not despair," Tricot said.

"What?"

"Yes, of course, at this moment, to see this . . . this horribleness, it seems hopeless, but it is not, not hopeless."

"Who would do such a thing? To burn all this, to murder the family . . ."

"I would think the Chickasaws. This is what they do. But not the plantations up here. Not until now."

"Who are the Chickasaws?"

"A tribe of Indians who cause the most trouble. Very fierce. They make treaties; their chief says nice things with much smiling, then they pretend to go away but they come back by night. They burn and steal and kill. Look, you see here at the head of this body, gone at the top, the skull here? They have taken it as a prize. All these bodies, same thing. Chickasaws are vicious people. Of course, I do not know for sure, but I believe all of this is the ugly work of the Chickasaws."

"But why would they do these terrible things? Just hate?"

"No, suh, for commerce. Probably one hundred slaves were on this plantation. Chickasaws take them away and sell them for very much money."

"People would buy Negroes from Indians?"

"No, it does not happen like that. Chickasaws sell the slaves to a white slave broker who sells them to buyers."

"But to sell a slave, don't you need papers? Proof of ownership?"

"Oh, yes, but the broker makes up new papers, with official seals. There is no problem with that."

"But the slaves—do they not reveal what happened?"

Tricot shook his head in wonderment at Guy's naiveté. "Ah, suh, I can see you are not familiar with the ways of slaves. If such a slave were to say anything about the happening here, he would be lashed and put in isolation irons, or worse, perhaps beheaded and his head put on a pike. No, the slaves that were here are now . . ." Tricot sighted something that caught his attention. "Look yonder there, at the end of the field, there's a rise of smoke, do you see? And it is white smoke, not black. Someone is probably cooking."

The hut from which the smoke was emanating was constructed of a hodgepodge of scavenged materials covered with a clumsily thatched roof. There was a doorway, but no door; windows, but no panes or shutters. There were two deerskins stretched across the dirt floor. Against the rear wall was a bed that consisted of a straw-covered pallet raised from the ground by flat-topped rocks at its four corners. At one of the windows stood an Indian who was stirring an iron pot over a small fire. The Indian was very old, his face severely wrinkled, his braided hair turned starkly white. He was of medium height, copper-colored, and emaciated. He wore a jacket of fringed buckskin and mitassis, a kind of scalloped leggings of a different skin, perhaps bleached alligator, and a necklace of small shells.

His back was to the door. Without turning his head, he said to Guy and Tricot, who stood in the doorway, "Good day, gentlemen. Come in." He spoke perfectly accented French. "I must stir this ragout lest it burn. Will you join me? I have plenty since I captured a large hare this morning."

The only weapons in the hut were a bow and a quiver of arrows, hung on the wall, and a double-tipped spear which stood in the corner, so Guy surmised that one or the other accounted for the hare.

In the middle of the room, there was a crude table composed of several planks laid on top of pillars of stacked rocks. The old Indian carried the pot to the table along with three tin plates onto which he ladled his ragout, chunks of hare surrounded by turnips, carrots, beans, corn, and potatoes, in their own juices, the hare's blood flavoring the sauce.

"The vegetables are fresh—I borrowed them from a neighboring garden last night. Does the dish please you?"

"Very much," Guy answered. "I have not eaten since yesterday, so it is most welcome."

"Who are you and why are you here?" Tricot inquired.

"I am here because I lived here for twenty years before the Chickasaws attacked us. My name is Franchmastabbia. I was master of the gardens here for Monsieur de Sévigny, the owner whose body and those of his wife and children lie yonder in the ashes. I wanted to bury them, but Choctaws do not bury their dead in ground that has not been consecrated."

"This is Monsieur Guy Laroule, who is the proprietor here now, by Royal Grant."

"I suspected as much. Would you like more ragout?"

"Yes, please. It is the first good food I have eaten in months."

"I am flattered, sir."

"What happened when the Chickasaws attacked?"

"They came in the night without warning. A great army of them on horses, many with firebrands, with which they set all the buildings afire. And then they set upon the indigo fields, the gardens—all my beloved flowers and vegetables—the poultry houses, killing all the chickens, turkeys, rabbits, ducks, and in the pens, the pigs and lambs. But the worst was setting their torches to the barns, with the cattle and sheep trapped inside. I still hear all the animals screaming in terror. They took all the horses and rounded up all our slaves, one hundred and ten, and some of them took the women and young girls into the manor house where they raped them, and then tortured and killed them, all of them, in a frenzy. They were drinking taffia and yelling Chickasaw war chants. It was then that they took their torches to the house and burned it down to the ground with all the dead bodies inside. They took all the wine, the brandy, and some valuable things from the manor house before they burned it. Then, with the animals screaming and the fire roaring everywhere, they rode away with the male slaves in their capture. Only the men fetch good prices on the market. I, myself, was saved only because when I first heard them and saw the fire, I hurried into the cold chamber that is below ground where we store food. I heard the pounding of their horses overhead, but they did not discover my hiding place. Surely as a Choctaw, they would have killed me on sight. It is they who paint all Indians with a bad name. Oh, monsieur, you should have seen the three young daughters of Monsieur de Sévigny. They were beautiful little angels, picking flowers in my gardens, always laughing, playing games, dancing on the lawn. . ."

The three men ate the rest of their meal in silence, the Indian's account of the massacre confining them to their own thoughts. Franchmastabbia's thoughts revolved around the little girls, seeing them in his mind's eye not as small angels cavorting on the lawn, but seized by a group of barechested Chickasaw, their faces painted with blue spirals, lines, and crisscrossed patterns against a vermillion background. They had scars on their bodies accented with red slashes, gaudy trinkets around their necks, and glass-beaded bands around their foreheads. Pendants hung from their ears and noses. On their heads they wore their prized helmuts of tall, many-colored plumes which framed their faces. He could still hear the shrieks of the little girls who struggled fiercely as the Chickasaws carried them into a small storage shed where their pitiful cries tore at the heart of the night. And then the silence, the terrible silence. Franchmastabbia was reliving the moment when, cowering in his underground hiding place, he stuffed his fist in his mouth to stifle the sound of his weeping. Even though he knew that at the time there was nothing he could have done to save them, nevertheless he felt guilty for not having tried, for not having sacrificed himself. "My guilt is that I am still alive and the others died," he said aloud, but, deep in their own thoughts, neither Guy nor Tricot responded.

Triggered by the Indian's account of the massacre, Tricot was reminded of what happened to his younger sister. She, too, was beautiful and graceful, and her voice, extraordinary. In the evenings, when she would sit outside the slave quarters and sing, most of the Negroes gathered around her, sometimes adding their own voices if they knew the song. When Leander, that was her name, was twelve, and on the verge of becoming a woman, her small breasts just developing, the plantation manager, an atrocious bully and drunk, came to the slave quarters one night with a repugnant looking man, fifty-odd years old, greying stubble on his chin, a soft belly sloshed over the belt of his breeches. The manager called out Leander's name. She stood, head bowed, before the two men, who reeked of the liquor they had been drinking.

"What do you think?" the manager asked.

The beefy visitor inspected Leander as he would a head of cattle on the market. He squeezed her legs and all around her torso, fingered her small breasts, pulled back her eyelids to better inspect her eyes, put his hand between her legs.

"I don't know, she's skinny."

"Well, damn it, Farley, fatten her up. She's certified a virgin mulatto, what more you want?"

So the sale was consummated and the manager said, "Come on, Leander, you're now the property of Mr. Farley."

She asked to get her things, but Farley said in a loud, coarse voice that he didn't want her wearing those nigger things and he would dress her up the way his mulatto woman should look. It was then that Leander turned to Tricot, then ten years of age. "Please," she said to him, her eyes begging, "please."

But Farley took her firmly by the arm and pulled her away before Tricot could respond. He never saw her again. Later on, after the fire, when Tricot had been liberated from his slave quarters, as he sat in the little schoolroom with the master's daughters, he often thought about Leander; it bothered him that he was living so well while, as he imagined, his sister was being brutalized by the repulsive drunkard who had bought her.

As for Guy, he was trying to overcome his pervasive depression and focus his attention on how to solve the bleak situation in which he now found himself. I sit here, he thought, grateful for a dish of rabbit stew cooked by an old Indian. These are the only two people I know here—a slave with freedom papers and an ancient Choctaw. The plantation I own is worthless. I do not have an introduction to a single influential person in New Orleans—in fact, no names, no letters of introduction to anyone, influential or otherwise. I have a goodly amount of capital in my possession—considerably augmented by a box of gold sovereigns delivered to me dockside in Le Havre by Madame Pompadour's equerry—but unless I invest it in something—purchase a business of some sort, perhaps—I will simply use it up, and then what? I could, perhaps, function in some government position, but for that I would need the recommendation of the Crown, and I do not think I can look to Louis XV for that.

As he became increasingly desperate, Guy considered bribing the ship's master to return him to France without noting his presence on the manifest. With forged papers he could go to live in some remote region of France where he could learn to plant a vineyard or raise cattle. But if somehow he were identified and it became known that he had returned to France in contravention of the king's orders, the consequences to him would be calamitous. A refrain from a duet he had sung with Madame de Pompadour, one of Louis XV's favorite melodies, insinuated itself into his dismal thoughts:

What a joy to awaken to another day,
What a joy to know I have you.
What a joy that the world is moving my way,
And whate'er we want to do, we do.

As if reading his thoughts, Tricot said, "It is not as bad as you may think, suh."

"What?"

"I know the situation looks bad, but the fact is you are the owner of all this."

"All what, Tricot? Blackened fields, houses burned to the ground, corpses to bury, charred animal carcasses everywhere—what do I have? Misery. I am without shelter, carriage, servants, food, drink, companionship—I have neither friends nor foes."

"All the better for a clean start, since there are neither friends to borrow from you nor foes to take from you."

"What about the Chickasaws?"

"No, master," the Indian said, "once the Chickasaws attack like this and plunder everything, they do not return."

"Suh, the fields can be plowed and seeded and sprouting by spring—is that not true, Franch?—I cannot pronounce all your name. You grew things here. . . ."

"Yes, of course, indigo is an easy crop. It likes this soil—we can get it ready in a fortnight."

"But what do we use for plows? For horses and mules? The plantations we passed all had many slaves working in the fields. I have none."

"Ah, suh, you have but to go to New Orleans where all the things you need are purchasable. It is a city bursting with everything. I know the markets, where the best mules are—the big strong ones that come down from Missouri on the long boats—the best bargains in slaves, in plows, a special place for fowl and other animals, and with my freedom papers, I am allowed to bargain on your behalf."

"And where will I live?"

"I will take you to the office of Monsieur Charles Grotesquieu, who is an architect of whom I have heard mention."

"And how do you come to know such an eminent man?"

"Oh, suh, I do not know him, I only know *of* him. But I assure you, with proper compensation he will be pleased to accept you as a client."

"Perhaps you would look favorably upon my humble services,"

the Indian interjected. "I know planting, both crops and flowers, and, as you can see, I can function in the kitchen until you have proper cooks. I have also secret methods for influencing the rain and the sunshine, and for stopping floods."

"And while all this is happening, where will I stay?"

Tricot thought about that, looked toward Franchmastabbia, who said, "Here, Master."

"What? In this miserable shack?"

Tricot said, "We can scrub it clean and fix it all up for you. There are pheasants, wild turkeys, and all manner of fowl and fish around here. I, myself, am a very good cook of alligator tail—have you ever eaten it?"

"No, Tricot, I'm afraid I would not salivate over a dish of alligator tail."

"It will surprise you. A delicacy, suh, cooked as I do it, with peppers and tomatoes. There are many surprises in the woods and waters around here."

"There is also a terrible stench," Guy said.

"That is the urine and droppings of the alligators," the Indian explained. "There are many in the marshes around here because no one has been here to keep them away. It is something we can manage. Then the air will be sweet."

"Tomorrow I can bring carpenters, free slaves like myself," Tricot said, "to put in a door, windows, and a floor. I have whitewash for the walls and ceilings. In New Orleans you can buy rugs and dishes, candles and lanterns, a bed, an armoire, linens, et cetera. In two weeks time, the carpenters will build you a small house where you can live until the plantation house is finished."

Tricot's words should have stirred some hope in Guy that the situation could possibly right itself, but the devastation around him was too discouraging. Having led a charmed and protected life, free from adversity and challenge, the enormous undertaking that faced him now seemed far beyond accomplishment. Especially since the messengers of hope were a quasi-slave and an ancient Indian.

"I suggest, if I may, suh," Tricot was saying, "that you spend the night at an inn in New Orleans, where you can bathe and eat properly, and then in the morning, we can go about our chores early."

The suggestion appealed to Guy, not just because of the prospect of a decent night's lodging, but also because he was curious about whether New Orleans was indeed the little Paris Monsieur

Trémencourt had described on the ship. Guy packed a bag, leaving his chests in the Indian's cabin, and as the mules began the return journey to New Orleans, Guy actually did feel somewhat better than he had on arrival.

Eight

THE CITY OF NEW ORLEANS was first inhabited by eighty convicted salt makers who were deported from France for evading the tax levied on their product. Designated as the new seat of government in Louisiana, the city had been built on land that extended from the banks of the Mississippi to a huge interior lake, later named Pontchartrain, a stretch of land that the Indians, who had first named the river, Misi Sipi, or "great water," had used as a portage for their canoes and supplies. It had taken the French four years to clear the heavy stands of cypress trees and the impenetrable vines and brush, and to lay out the streets and docks of the new city, named in honor of Louis Philippe, duc d'Orléans, a dandified libertine who was regent of France. Since Nouvelle Orléans was below sea level, extensive levees had to be constructed.

The frame houses were built on the squared streets were bricked between their posts, roofed with cypress shingles; most of them had rear courtyards with flagstone pavements. The houses were flush with the banquettes, or sidewalks, but in the forty-five years of the city's existence no attempt had been made to cobblestone the dirt streets. As New Orleans' reputation grew, people of quality—engineers, businessmen, aristocracy—had emigrated from France, bringing with them the trappings of their affluent lives. They built grander houses with ornate *galeries,* or balconies attached to their second stories, a virtual necessity in the subtropical, stifling heat of the summers.

The turning point for New Orleans, later called its Golden Age, occurred in its twenty-fifth year, when Pierre-Cavagnal de Rigaud, marquis de Vaudreuil, arrived from Paris as the new governor. He was a man of patrician birth, married to a sophisticated, wealthy woman fifteen years his senior. They packed their ship to the gunnels with the finest furniture, carriages, clothes, wines, crystal chandeliers, grand pianos and other luxurious objects. They were soon followed by considerable numbers of their friends and acquaintances, aristocrats who also brought with them their treasured possessions. The advent of these aristocrats and people of means allowed the marquis to establish a court devoted to pleasure, a hedonistic succession of dinners, masked balls, gambling soirees, theater presentations, musicales, and similar events, in conscious imitation of Versailles. The marquis built an extravagant mansion befitting his lofty position, where he often entertained with sumptuous dinners served on plates of gold, and where especially commissioned plays and operas were performed.

On their way into the city, Tricot was regaling Guy with stories about the grand marquis and his formal balls with their masked and costumed participants. Tricot dwelt at length on the Mardi Gras, instituted three years previously by the marquis, an unrestrained period of revelry and debauchery preceding the start of Lent. By the time Tricot's cart reached New Orleans, Guy anticipated a city as elegant as Paris, the streets busy with ornate carriages, the sidewalks filled with people wearing doublets and robes of damask, velvet, and silk, but unfortunately, that was not, to his dismay, the city he came upon.

The unpaved streets were a foot deep in mud; the black, clinging muck adhered to the hooves and the legs of the horses, and to the large number of dogs and hogs that roamed unattended. Between the streets and the banquettes were open ditches which were, in fact, the city's sewer system. The combination of the open sewage and the defecation of the dogs and hogs produced an overpowering stench. As the mules strained to move the cart through the clinging mud, Guy observed the endless number of taverns and saloons, one right after another, not elegant places, just serviceable establishments (or so it seemed in passing) dispensing alcoholic beverages. Some had signs outside announcing that gambling at cards was permitted. There was also a notable number of gaudily dressed ladies, black, white, and mulatto, who walked slowly along the banquettes in front of the saloons. If this is little Paris, Guy thought, then I am Louis XIV.

Tricot stopped the cart in front of an inn which, under the sign of a robust rooster, identified itself as Le Coq Hardi. Tricot took Guy's bags from the cart and followed him into the dim interior of the inn. A group of men were drinking noisily at the bar. The air was redolent with their tobacco smoke which blended with the aromas coming from the kitchen where the evening's meal was being prepared. Guy obtained a room and made arrangements to meet up with Tricot at nine o'clock the following morning.

Guy had intended to walk around the city after dinner, but after three glasses of claret and a heaping bowl of fish chowder, it was all he could do to get himself back up the stairs to his room. The bed was swaybacked with prominent lumps in the mattress, but the turbulent months at sea and the agony of the day dropped Guy to the bottom of the well of his being where he slept deeply and undisturbed.

Nine

TRICOT ARRIVED AT Le Coq Hardi early the following morning; he tied his cart to a hitching post outside the inn and waited in the reception room while Guy consumed a breakfast of gingered pineapple, coffee, and rolls in the dining room. Tricot stood patiently near the door, for as a free man of color he was permitted to enter the inn, but not to sit down.

"The carpenters are hard at work at your plantation," Tricot informed Guy as the cart got underway, the mules straining and slipping in the foot-deep mud as they had the day before. "Would you first, perhaps, desire to visit the slave market? There is a fresh shipment, arrived only yesterday."

As Tricot guided the cart along the muddy street, trying to avoid the foraging hogs and cesspools heavy with the dung of the horses and pigs, he acted as a tour guide. "You will note the houses to your right, suh, are mostly eight feet above the ground, set on posts which are filled between with bricks made here from Mississippi mud. The upper part of the houses are of cypress log, which is the tree the most plentiful. Over there, where you see those three men tied onto that wheel, they are thieves who will most likely be hanged for all to see later in the day."

"And those women in the stocks?"

"They are girls of bad conduct. Ah, the women here, suh, are a vexing problem. Even the married ladies, even the ones with titles, they are not faithful to their gentlemen. The Governor likes a good time, much dancing, banquets, wine, entertainment, and the ladies and gentlemen enjoy bedding each other. But those girls there are probably girls of commerce who are not properly sponsored, or maybe help themselves to money of their customers that wasn't theirs."

"They, too, will be hanged?"

"Oh, no! They will likely spend the day on the wheel in the hot sun, then receive a dozen lashes and be let go. Women here are in very short supply, so, of course, no woman ever would be hanged, no matter what her crime. Not even Negro women or mulattos. Mulatto women are highly prized by white gentlemen."

The cart had left the center of New Orleans and was now moving along the quay that ran beside the Mississippi. There were mounds of rubbish and rotting fish thrown there by arriving and departing ships. From the look of it, the quay had never been cleaned, except for the rotting fish that scavenging birds, cats, and dogs carried away. There were several large ships tied up at the dock, the brig *Eliza* from Philadelphia, the ship *Valour* from Liverpool, England, the brig *Moses Gill* from New York, and the *Eliza Trice* from Nova Scotia. There were also smaller ships bound for Havana, Pensacola, and Natchez.

As the cart traversed the quay, Tricot took a clipping from the *Louisiana Gazette* and handed it to Guy. It was a prominent advertisement that had appeared the previous day:

IMPORTED FROM AFRICA
In the Ship "Sarah"
Henry Kennedy, Master
A Cargo Upwards of
100 CHOICE YOUNG HEALTHY NEGROES
Consisting of Men, Boys, Women, and Girls
The Sale of Which Will Commence on
Board Said Ship on Monday,
the Twentieth Instant
and Continue Each Succeeding Day
(Sundays Excepted) Until
the Whole Are Disposed Of.
For the Conditions of Sale Apply to
James Moss, Jr. at Madame Chabot's
or to John McDonough, Jun. and Co.

There was also an advertisement by a broker named Paul Laver-see, of thirty-four Negroes from the Gold Coast aboard the schooner *Sukey*, and another by the brokers Chew and Rolf, of sixty-eight young Congo Negroes on the brig *St. Lorenzo*.

"I think it best we get our slaves from Master Kennedy," Tricot said. "It is known that his Negroes are authentic Africans, whereas the *Sukey* and *St. Lorenzo* are sometimes suspicioned of secretly mixing in West Indian Negroes and presenting them with forged certificates as Africans."

"But why the preference for African Negroes?"

"Because West Indian Negroes are poor workers and they practice voodooism. An African slave can be trained more easily. I assure you that Monsieur de Sévigny buys all his slaves from Master Kennedy. They cost a little more than the West Indian Negroes, but Monsieur de Sévigny, who does not part with money easily, says they are worth it."

The *Sarah* was a large, ungainly vessel in need of paint, and Master Henry Kennedy was a large, ungainly man in need of a bath. He had only the index finger on his left hand, his nose was crooked to the right and there was a lattice of scars across his forehead.

"You're in great good fortune, Monsieur Laroule," he boomed, "in that you are the first to arrive, and so you have first choice of these magnificent Negroes that I have handpicked in Africa. There is not a finer buy in this port, rest assured. Hurry them up here, boys," he bellowed to his crew. "We have a purchaser to hand."

The hatch door swung wide and a file of Negroes began to emerge and assemble on the deck. The men, naked to the waist, were in their early twenties, the women between fifteen and eighteen years of age. There were a few young boys and girls. All of them were bare-foot.

"Finest group this year," Master Kennedy was saying, "all well fed, certified no disease or germs. The females clean, the boys able to do men's work, the young girls all guaranteed virgins. To what use do you seek them, Monsieur Laroule?"

"To work his plantation," Tricot answered. "And there is need of women to cook and to tend the manor."

"Are these families?" Guy asked.

"No, not at all," Master Kennedy answered. "Our purchasing agent in Africa assembles the best he can find and we take our pick from them. What quantity are you seeking?"

"That depends," Tricot said.

"On what?"

"On the bargain you give us if we buy in quantity."

"Twenty or more?"

"Yes."

"A hundred and twenty-three dollars for the males, eighty dollars for the females, forty dollars for the boys, and ten dollars for the girls. And the five mulattos—look at them—are they not beautiful? Can you imagine better for your bed, Monsieur Laroule? A bargain at a hundred and sixty dollars. They sing, dance, all certified without disease or any bodily improprieties. You there. . . you. . . yes, you—do your dance for Monsieur Laroule."

The summoned young woman hesitated and Master Kennedy, speaking an African dialect in a harsh voice said something to her that set her to dancing. She was a strikingly handsome young woman, lithe, graceful, but while she danced her face was expressionless.

"Buy twenty of the men and I will sell her to you for fifty dollars. You want to inspect her? Take her to my cabin."

Again Kennedy spoke to the woman in an African dialect. She stopped dancing and began to walk toward the captain's cabin.

"It won't be necessary," Guy said.

The captain stopped the mulatto, directed a puzzled look at Guy.

"I would like to confer with Tricot for a moment." Guy walked to a far corner of the deck, Tricot following.

"I have no stomach for this," Guy said, in a low voice. "I find picking over these people as I would beef at the butcher's totally repugnant."

"But you need servants, suh, or you cannot run your plantation."

"I realize that. I'm not saying I don't have to buy some. I'm simply saying I cannot personally go from one to another of these slaves and examine their hands and teeth and feet and prod them and poke at them. . . . I want you to do it."

"I, suh? It is a great responsibility. One cannot be sure from this brief inspection that the slave will be a good worker. Then I am to blame. I have seen Monsieur de Sévigny administer lashes across the back of his slavemaster because he recommended two slaves who stole from the master and ran away."

"Did they find them?"

"Oh, yes, of course. The army has special soldiers with dogs who track runaways. They were both hanged and their heads displayed on pikes."

"Well, I assure you, Tricot, there will be no lashes if the slaves you buy turn sour. How many would you say I need?"

Tricot considered this. "I would say for now thirty male slaves and a few of the women."

"All right. Choose thirty of the males and five of the women, but no girls or boys or mulattos."

"But suh, I should point out that it is not easy to buy a mulatto in New Orleans, and this one of the captain's is desirable and at a very good price."

"What makes you think I must have a mulatto?"

"Every plantation owner has at least one mulatto. Even the married ones. Two is more usual."

"Do not buy the mulatto."

"All right, suh, as you wish. But I should tell you that it is expensive to use a lady of the street and you cannot be sure of her . . . well . . . health . . . With your own mulatto, you can have her whenever you want without payment and you know she has a healthy condition."

"I'd prefer to seduce the Governor's daughter, if he has one," Guy said.

"He does, suh, but she is fat with pimples and a voice that scares away the gators."

"Then I shall be celibate and turn all this into a religious experience."

"As you wish, suh."

"So for the time being, Tricot, we will buy the thirty slaves and see how we do. A condition of the purchase must be that Captain Kennedy keep them for a week or so while we put up some kind of shelter for them."

"Oh, suh, do not worry about how they will live—they can sleep on straw pallets in the field, and we can feed them *gru* and cornbread until the kitchens are ready."

"What is *gru?*"

"Corn that is ground into meal and boiled in an iron pot called a *gru*. It is in great quantity, and very inexpensive."

Guy stood to one side as Tricot discussed the slaves with Captain Kennedy who said he would be pleased to hold the purchased slaves for a fortnight if he received a payment of fifty percent of the purchase price in advance, the other fifty percent to be paid on delivery of the Negroes. Guy maintained his aloof position while Tricot carefully made his selections, closely inspecting each slave's body, observing them as they responded to the captain's commands to walk, to squat, to jump, to lift each other.

In condoning this process, Guy felt that he was being a traitor to his own perception of the rights of individuals. Toward the end of his Versailles residency, Guy had been reading and studying the writings of the British philosopher, John Locke, and a French philosopher, the Baron de Montesquieu. Both men espoused the belief that all persons were entitled to certain natural rights that could not be infringed by government laws. Locke especially stirred Guy's empathy with his compelling belief that life, property, and freedom of thought, speech, and worship were man's inalienable rights. Locke felt that in the conflict between public liberty and the "divine right of kings," that "natural rights," which included property and personal liberty, could not be usurped by government, monarchial or otherwise. Locke made compelling assertions that divine right rested not with kings but with the people themselves, and that no government had the right to interfere with an individual's freedom. Revoking that freedom from any group of people was, according to Locke, repugnant. Locke pointed out that although the Greeks believed that the people must rule, they had no provision for protecting the rights of minorities. It is for that purpose, Locke reasoned, that governments exist in the first place. Guy openly agreed with Locke and when Louis XV heard about these debates among his noblemen, he issued an edict to the French parliament: "In my person only does the sovereign power rest. From me alone do my courts derive their existence and their authority. To me alone belongs legislative power. By my authority alone do the officers of my court proceed. Public order in its entirety emanates from me." To emphasize this pronouncement, Louis abolished parliament and dispersed its members. "I think the king is right," Voltaire stated. "Since it is necessary to serve, I had rather do so under a lion of good pedigree than under two hundred rats of my own kind."

Locke's theories had a deep impact on Guy's own beliefs. His most trusted servant was a Moor who had been with him since he was a boy. Guy treated him as he did all the other servants at Versailles, paying him the same wage and giving him the same privileges as the others. The writings of Locke and Montesquieu were being widely read at Versailles, but only Guy and a few others endorsed them, usually in heated debate with the overwhelming majority of noblemen who argued that a society could only function with those who were privileged being served by those who were not.

But now, faced with the necessity of acquiring slaves in order to survive and start his plantation, Guy found his capitulation to the system repugnant, a bitter pill to swallow.

When the thirty men and five women had finally been chosen, Guy paid the captain with a gold sovereign and received conditional bills of sale for each slave.

On their way to the cart Guy said that he wanted to pay the slaves a daily amount, to make them feel they were a part of Diderot Plantation. "A man at Le Coq Hardi told me that the average wage for a white worker is fifty cents a day, so let's say we pay them two dollars a week."

"Oh no, suh!" exclaimed Tricot, who was shocked at the suggestion. "That would not be permitted."

"By whom? They are my property. What I do with them is my business, is it not?"

"No, suh. Not where slaves are concerned. Do you not know the *Code Noir?*"

"The Black Code? No, what is that?"

"I carry it with me in my portfolio. You can read it while we are on our way to see Monsieur Chiribon about carriages. Here you are—the *Code Noir*—an edict of Louis XIV and, as you can see, it was issued at Versailles in 1724. It is the law here, suh, very strictly enforced. No one can alter it in any way. Just last year, the overseer of Forestière Plantation was charged to be a Protestant and the governor confiscated all the slaves of the plantation for his personal use and sentenced the overseer to a year in jail and then to be sent up the river to Natchez unless he converts to Catholicism while in jail."

"Are you a Catholic, Tricot?"

"Oh, yes, suh, it is forbidden to be otherwise."

On the way to the carriage-maker, Guy studied the document handed to him by Tricot, which read as follows:

Code Noir

Louis, by the Grace of God, King of France and of Navarre, to all present and to come, greetings. The Directors of the Company of the Indies having represented to us that the Province and Colony of Louisiana is considerably established by a large number of Our subjects who use slaves for the cultivation of the lands. We have judged that it behooves our authority and our justice, for the preservation of this colony, to establish there a law, and certain rules, to maintain there the discipline of the Catholic Apostolic and Roman Church, and to order about what concerns the state and condition of the slaves in the said Islands, and desiring to provide for this, and to make known to our subjects who inhabit there and who shall settle there in the future, that although they inhabit climes infinitely remote, We are always present, by the extent of our power and by our application to succor them. We have said, decreed, and ordered, the following:

ARTICLE I orders that the edict of 1615 be applied to Louisiana, and that all Jews who may have established their religion there be expelled within three months, under penalty of confiscation of body and property.

ARTICLE II orders that all slaves in the province be instructed and baptized in the Catholic religion.

ARTICLE III forbids the exercise of any other religion than the Catholic.

ARTICLE IV forbids marriage of whites with slaves, and concubinage of whites and manumitted or free-born blacks with slaves, and imposes penalties.

ARTICLE V enacts that children born from the marriages of slaves shall belong to the master of the mother.

ARTICLE VI forbids slaves belonging to different masters to assemble in crowds, by day or by night, under pretext of weddings or other causes, either at one of their masters' or elsewhere, and still less on the highways or secluded places, under penalty of corporal punishment, which shall not be less than the whip and the fleur-de-lys; and in case of repetition of the offense and other aggravating circumstances, capital punishment may be applied, at the discretion of the judges. It also commands all subjects of the King, whether officers or not, to seize and arrest the offenders and conduct them to prison, although there be no judgment against them.

ARTICLE VII orders seizure of goods that are offered for sale by slaves without permission or mark.

ARTICLE VIII authorizes slaves to give information against their masters, if not properly fed or clad, or if treated inhumanely.

ARTICLE IX orders slaves disabled from working by old age, sickness, or otherwise, to be provided for by their masters, otherwise they shall be sent to the nearest hospital, to which the masters shall pay eight cents a day for each slave, and the hospital shall have a lien on the plantations of the masters.

ARTICLE X declares that slaves can have nothing that does not belong to their masters, in whatever way acquired.

ARTICLE XI Any slave who shall have struck his master, his mistress, or the husband of his mistress, or their children, so as to produce a bruise or shedding of blood in the face, shall be put to death.

ARTICLE XII Outrages or acts of violence against free persons committed by slaves shall be punished with severity, and even with death if the case requires it.

At R. Chiribon et Fils, Guy purchased two carriages and four horses: an ornate manor carriage for social use, and a "working carriage" for such chores as going to market. The manor carriage horses were a nicely matched pair of bronze geldings with a well-mannered gait and good configuration. The other pair were dray horses that could be used for heavier work.

After Chiribon et Fils, Tricot took Guy to a farm shop located in the section of New Orleans where bricks were baked in giant kilns and sawmills cut cypress logs into boards. At the farm shop, Guy purchased the plows and other farm equipment that Tricot recommended. He also bought four mules to work the plows. These mules, brought down by longboat from Missouri, were twice the size of local mules and much better suited to pull the heavy plows through the fields.

Not far from the farm shop was a barn where a free slave, a friend of Tricot's, sold farm animals which he raised. Guy enjoyed selecting the poultry, hogs, cows, and other farm animals that were to be delivered as soon as proper fencing was put in place and a barn erected. The free slave, whose name was Eleander (he rented the farm from a white landowner named Pierre Cudahy), offered Guy and Tricot a lunch of fresh ham, eggs, and biscuits made of wheat flour, but served Guy and Tricot at separate tables, as the law required.

The afternoon was spent at the gunsmith's. The proprietor, Monsieur Ribaut, a gaunt, bald, stick of a man, enjoyed discussing firearms with Guy who was obviously very knowledgeable about hunting guns. He was able to inform Monsieur Ribaut about certain guns being produced by Versailles gunsmiths that had new features Ribaut had not yet heard of. Ultimately, Guy purchased a variety of hunting guns, some suited for birds, others for larger game; he also included several guns that would be effective in defending the plantation against attack. By the time the guns and ammunition had been assembled, the afternoon was all but over.

"May I suggest, suh," Tricot said as they returned to the cart, "that you sleep another night at the inn. Tomorrow we can visit Monsieur Charles Grotesquieu, the architect. On the way to pick you up this morning, I took the liberty of informing his office of your visit tomorrow. It will probably take many hours. Is that satisfactory?"

Guy said it was.

"Now, suh, on our way back to the inn, we will pass by The Governor's Mansion. Would it please you to stop and present your card to his majordomo? It is the proper thing for a plantation owner to do on arrival. Versailles has probably advised Governor Vaudreuil about you in the last royal pouch, and he will expect you to announce your presence to him."

That evening, after a dinner consisting of oysters, roasted swan, a mutton chop, pickled eggplant, and yams cooked in coals, accompanied by a bottle of Burgundy, Guy went to see a play at the Cap-Français Theater along with a German traveler, Herr Ulrich Reininghaus, he had met at dinner. The theater was located on the second floor of a small wooden building located on St. Peter Street between Royal and Bourbon. The theater was long and narrow with a raked pit. Toward the front of the pit were two tiers of boxes, the upper tier reserved for people of color. Toward the back of the lower tier were two special boxes, one at the governor's disposition, the other reserved for patrons who could afford the steep price of the tickets. The Cap-Français was a far cry from the theaters Guy had frequented in France. The scenery was perfunctory and showing wear, and the number of candles and torches used to light the stage was woefully inadequate. But the play, *Eugénie,* was well received because the performers, a company of French actors who had come to New Orleans from Santo Domingo, were first-rate.

After the play, Herr Reininghaus, who often came from Natchez to New Orleans on business, suggested a visit to Madame Carondelet's gambling establishment where a great variety of games of chance were in progress: coq, pontalba, canne, monte, primera, lans quenet, dice, hoca, biribi, faro, and basset. There were also several billiard tables and a lively bar well stocked with as good an assortment of liquors as any comparable Paris establishment. Crystal chandeliers enlivened with candles were suspended from rough rafters, and the floors were completely carpeted with luxurious furs fitted so closely together that the boards were not visible. The gamblers, mostly men, were well dressed and played for high stakes.

Herr Reininghaus went straight to the faro table, purchasing a sizable amount of chips, but Guy contented himself with touring the room and observing the various games in progress. At Versailles Guy had played cards but those low-stake games were designed for social intercourse, not for big winnings. Guy's tour of the tables eventually brought him back to Herr Reininghaus's faro game; the German was perspiring profusely, his face flushed with the excitement that comes from wagering high stakes.

After watching him lose a particularly large wager, Guy unobtrusively left the room and returned to the inn. This new life I've been thrown into is enough of a gamble, he thought, without involving any of my precious capital. Back in his room he added up what he had spent so far, and it came to a sobering sum. Now there will be the architect's fees and the cost of rebuilding, furnishing the house, and buying plants, feed, food for the slaves, and God knows what else. I, who never gave a second thought about taking risks, I am now running scared.

Ten

ARCHITECT CHARLES GROTESQUIEU was a man of more than ample proportions, with a fleshy nose on which perched a gold-rimmed pince-nez and under which sprouted a luxurious moustache. He smoked a meerchaum pipe which he snatched from his mouth when his Rabelaisian laugh frequently erupted. Although not trained in the law, he wore a brown barrister's wig and a waistcoat of brocaded silk.

"What shall it be, Monsieur Laroule? A house of grandeur and beauty? The Trianon? Fontainebleau? Malmaison? Would you like to outdo the Governor, put his little shack to shame? I am afraid I cannot quite give you Versailles but believe me, we can be grand, grand, grand! If you want something different, I have here the plans for the Czar's palatial hunting lodge in St. Petersburg. I am cosmopolitan, Monsieur Laroule, I can give you a Venetian palazzo or a Chinese pagoda, a Rhine castle or a Provence château. I am a builder of dreams, Monsieur Laroule, a builder of dreams."

Amused by Monsieur Grotesquieu's architectural fantasies, Guy remarked that obviously he had not seen the charred wasteland that was all that remained of Diderot Plantation. "Oh, yes, I have indeed seen it," Monsieur Grotesquieu replied. "This morning, bright and early."

"Then how can you offer me . . . ?"

"The phoenix, Monsieur Laroule, the phoenix—I am a magician of the ashes. Just tell me about your dream house, I shall wave my architectural wand, and presto!"

Guy said his only dream was to have a plantation house in the manner of the Parlange and Ormond mansions. Perhaps not so large, since he had no family. . . .

"At present," Monsieur Grotesquieu interrupted, "but when you have a wife, five children, two mistresses, relatives from France . . . I do not like to build additions, Monsieur Laroule. They are distortions, distractions, disturbances of the original beauty of the house. Symmetry! Symmetry above all! No, sir, better to plan copiously than to wear a tight corset. Now I have been working on this new design which features six columns across the façade with a second-story portico running along the entire front of the house with a carved balustrade. Dual chimneys, four fireplaces, gabled roof, six French doors opening onto the lower veranda—look at it—is this not a thing of consummate beauty?"

"It is indeed a splendid house . . . on paper," Guy said, "just what I had in mind. Only one thing, I would like to have the house balanced by two wings, joined at the roof with walkways in between. I think wings give the house better balance."

"Yes, yes, wings make the house fly." The architect began to sketch wings onto the drawing of the house. "So what we will have is the central part of the house, with four rooms on each floor, arranged in a square. It will be built with a heavy cypress frame filled in with mud, moss, and bricks, then lathed and stuccoed over. All the timbers will be morticed, tenoned, and pegged together. The wings will each have four rooms with fireplaces, but they will be all brick with no cypress. There will be covered galeries between the wings of the house. The main level will have rounded columns of plastered brick, but the colonettes on the veranda above will be of cypress carved by an Indian of my acquaintance who is truly an artist. In this area behind the house, we will build slave cabins—how many slaves do you own?"

"I am starting with thirty. . . ."

"You will have triple that within the year. So, let us say, thirty slave cabins in a semicircle back here." He indicated the cabins with an arc of Xs. "Then, to the side here, will be the stable, a meat storage house, and the incarceration chamber."

"The what?"

"The jail."

"Why would I need a jail?"

Monsieur Grotesquieu looked at him quizzically. "How else will you punish the Negroes when they get out of line? Now, if I may pass out compliments to myself, you will note that nowhere in the drawing for the house is there a completely vertical or horizontal line. Soft edges, roundings, a very fluid design, a romantic concept, if you will. And the colors will also be soft and romantic. The walls of the manor will be a lemon-yellow color, as will the second floor of the wings. All the shutters will be a pale green, the pillars a creamy white as well as the downstairs of the wings. As soon as my workers clean up the site, we will get started."

"You understand that I need these buildings as quickly as possible," Guy said. "I have slaves arriving in a fortnight."

Monsieur Grotesquieu plucked his pipe from his mouth as he exploded with a gust of laughter. "Your slaves will survive, Monsieur Laroule, whether their grandiose quarters are ready or not. If I may ask, have you ever built a home before, Monsieur Laroule?"

"No."

"You will find it a more pleasant experience than you now anticipate. All right. Down to business. I require a substantial payment of earnest money to seal our undertaking. I will then put into motion one of the most joyful experiences of your life."

It was late afternoon by the time Guy left Monsieur Grotesquieu's office. As Guy came through the street door, he was pleased to see a grinning Tricot sitting at the reins of the new town carriage. The glistening brown geldings looked even more beautiful than they did at the stables where Guy had previously seen them.

"There is time to visit the markets before returning to the plantation," Tricot said, "if you would like to do so in order to see what foods and commodities are offered for sale."

The markets and commercial shops occupied a large area near the quay, which gave them easy access to ships, longboats, canoes, and rafts discharging their cargoes. Guy had not expected the variety and the amount of produce and goods offered for sale. He was also assailed by the stench of the rotting fish and produce strewn on the docks, and by the malodorous interiors of the food markets that had no ventilation and seemingly no system for removing refuse. But the quantity and variety of the foodstuffs were impressive. Stalls in rows as far as the eye could see, offering mounds of peas, wild beans, sweet potatoes, apples, figs, pineapples, several varieties of rice, peaches, watermelons, corn, eggs, wild peppers, chocolate, milk, eggplants, squash, onions, pumpkins, and, in addition, many other vegetables and fruits indigenous to Louisiana which Guy had never seen before. There were other stalls in the marketplace crowded with hanging game: swans, wild geese, wild turkeys, rabbits, pheasants, doves, chickens, quail, partridges, water hens, teals, and other wild ducks.

The redolent fish stalls offered an even greater quantity and variety of fish: perch, pike, sturgeon, eel, carp, crab, crayfish, shrimp, salmon, oysters, rays, and many local varieties, like the brill, unknown in France. Beyond the fish stalls was a large section of the market devoted to meat, the mainstay of the New Orleans diet. Wild oxen, venison, pork, veal, beef, lamb, mutton, and great slabs of buffalo beef, prized by Creole palates, were in great abundance. Fresh pork and beef cost five cents a pound; butter, nineteen cents a pound; a jug of milk, eleven cents; a barrel of kidney beans, three dollars seventy-five cents; and sugar, which was imported, twenty-one cents a pound. Although Guy had no knowledge of the cost of foodstuffs, Tricot assured him that by Paris standards these foods were great bargains.

There were also shops in the market that offered imported items: anchovies, prunes, almonds, vermicelli, Cuban cigars, quality rum, Veracruz white sugar, coffee, tea, furs, olive oil, laces, jewelry, silks, brandied fruits, sausages, pickles, raisins, liqueurs, wines, whiskey, and cognacs.

Shops adjacent to the market specialized in household effects such as cypress and walnut chairs, beds and wardrobes, horsehair mattresses, walnut consoles, card tables, fauteuils and rocking chairs upholstered in leather and scarlet velvet, mirrors, pictures, linens, down quilts, embroidered cloths, porcelain, silver, tapestries, backgammon boards and tables, silver candlesticks, bathtubs of copper, glassware, English hardware, and cotton goods.

"As you can see, suh," Tricot said, "when the mansion house is completed, there is no problem to furnish it with fine objects. And when your kitchen is ready, the market will provide you with whatever your stomach desires."

On the way back to his carriage, Guy said, "Tricot, you have been a godsend to me, coming here as I did, knowing no one, knowing nothing about the city or the customs, and I thank you for your help. I would like it very much if you would become the overseer of my plantation. Your salary would be generous, and I would include quarters for you in Monsieur Grotesquieu's plans. I assure you that in France I always treated my servants very well, and I think you will find that I am a good person to work for."

"I do not doubt it, Monsieur, but I cherish my position as a free person, and although I have had offers of employment, I have preferred to be on my own. But, of course, I would be pleased to help you get started. You are a most gracious person."

"I do not in any way wish to compromise your freedom. I would give you the same conditions as white overseers on the other plantations. Has there ever been a Negro overseer?"

"No, suh, not to my knowledge. And there may be problems. A person of color, as I am, being in authority over white persons, especially Creoles—even the slaves would resent me."

"I see no problem in it. I will back your authority in every way."

"Thank you, suh. Your confidence in me is tempting, but the pull of my freedom is also strong."

"Well, then, think about it. That you will work for me for the time being is what is important. I will pay you whatever you charge people now for what services you provide, with a bonus—is that agreeable?"

"More than agreeable, suh."

Eleven

IN THE WEEKS THAT FOLLOWED, the land was cleared of its charred rubble, the bodies were blessed and buried, the slave quarters hastily constructed, and the fields furrowed and planted with indigo seed. At first, Guy's response to all this activity was as a spectator, detached, going the rounds as an observer. But the turning point occurred on the day Monsieur Grotesquieu came to inspect the construction of the foundation being laid for the manor house. As the sun fell and the light began to wane, Monsieur Grotesquieu approached Guy, who had been watching, and invited him to return to New Orleans with him to dine at a private club of which Monsieur Grotesquieu was a charter member.

"Let us ride together in my carriage," Monsieur Grotesquieu said. "It will return you here after dinner."

Settled back for the ride, Monsieur Grotesquieu offered Guy a pinch of snuff and discussed a myriad of details related to the house, the garden, the marketing of indigo, the best way to handle the slaves, social life in New Orleans with the emphasis on which invitations to accept and which to avoid, the bank of preference, the most astute lawyer, if needed, the deplorable state of medical treatment. "There isn't a doctor in New Orleans who has an honest certificate on his wall. They are all imposters who have never studied medicine nor even apprenticed to a doctor. They put on white coats and hang a leeching cup on a chain around their throats, but they know far less about anatomy and treatment than the bumpkin who milks my cows. There isn't a single surgeon in all New Orleans. Will you believe that? Not one. If an operation is needed, one must return to France on the first ship out of port, and pray to make it without dying en route."

Monsieur Grotesquieu also heaped scorn on the heads of what he referred to as New Orleans' predatory and unfaithful women. "The women here are extremely ignorant as to the means of securing their salvation, but they are very expert in the art of displaying their beauty. There is so much luxury that there is no distinction among the classes so far as dress code is concerned. The magnificence of display is equal in all. Most of them reduce themselves and their family to the hard life of dining at home with nothing but sagamity to eat, but flaunt themselves at parties in robes of velvet and damask, ornamented with the most costly ribbons. They paint and rouge their cheeks to hide the ravages of time, and embellish their faces with small black patches."

Monsieur Grotesquieu's club, La Bagatelle, was located in a narrow house of his design on Royal Street. Since he was president of the club, Monsieur Grotesquieu was received with appropriate ceremony and escorted to the most desirable table at the windows. After a decanter of Scotch whiskey had been placed on the table and a toast proposed to the future of the new house, Monsieur Grotesquieu eased his corpulent body against the back of the cushioned banquette on which he sat, and through the lens of his pince-nez, fixed Guy with a squinted eye.

"I have observed you closely today, Monsieur Laroule, the way you go from watching the slaves in the field, to observing the construction men, to strolling past the Indian who plants the gardens, to visiting the horses, round and round you go, but you are aloof, that's the key word, Monsieur Laroule, *aloof*. My God, man, this is *your* plantation, *your* new château-to-be, but you act as if it belonged to someone else and you were a visitor. Have you ever planted a seed, Monsieur Laroule? No? Ever walked behind a plough, fed hogs, cooked a fish over a fire? You should *experience* them, then you will better know how to deal with your people who do these things. *Belong*, Monsieur Laroule. Aloof is no good. Feel the palm of my hand—just feel this—that's a callous, and it came from working in my gardens. I have no crops, I am not rich enough to own a plantation, but when I first moved in, I worked everywhere around my house to *experience* what it was like. Of course, now I wouldn't be found dead with a hoe in my hand, but I know how to run my place. When a slave makes an excuse for not doing something, I know I was able to do it, so therefore he can do it. I have twenty slaves and six Creole employees, and I am the taskmaster of them all. And so must you be. Otherwise, you court disaster. This is the only life you have at the moment, is it not? I'd say you better seize your opportunity, or—poof!—it will ride right past you, and you will never be able to catch it. Be involved, Monsieur Laroule. Get callouses on your hands. They are badges of honor. When you shake a man's hand, he will respect that callous."

In the days after the dinner with Monsieur Grotesquieu, Guy gradually became more and more involved with the plantation's renaissance, having come to realize that Monsieur Grotesquieu was right, that his future depended upon the success or failure of the Diderot acreage. To his surprise, Guy soon discovered that he derived physical satisfaction in handling a plough behind a pair of strong-haunched mules, in guiding the heavy, ungainly plough along the planting lines. He felt an aesthetic pleasure from inhaling the musty smell of the fresh, black earth as the plough's blade churned the inner soil up to the surface. Indigo is a fast-growing plant, and the emergence of green shoots so soon after sowing seeds in the soil was a source of wonderment and satisfaction to Guy, who had never before worked the ground or even paid much attention to the meticulous gardens of Versailles. He felt both a kinship with and a proud proprietorship of the rows of tiny emerging plants, thin lines of young green against the ebony soil. He confronted his challenges: overseeing the rebirth of the plantation, facing everyday problems that related to matters foreign to his experience and temperament, goading others to perform beyond their limitations, adjusting to his rather primitive, unadorned living conditions, forcing his body to toughen to the physical demands imposed on it, and, above all, psychologically having to disassociate himself from the languid, rather dissolute life he had led at Versailles, and involve himself with the stark life which now faced him, shorn of all the indulgences which had been handmaidens to his existence.

Franchmastabbia had come to him the evening he returned in his new carriage, anxious to know whether or not Guy had decided to keep him as overseer of the gardens. "It would be very dangerous of me to have to leave here and reveal myself," the Indian said. "Either the Chickasaws or my own people, the Choctaws, would kill me.

The Chickasaws because they are sworn enemies of us Choctaws,
and the Choctaws because I renounced them."

"Why did you do that?"

"Because they are stupid, cruel. Are you familiar with Choctaw
customs? The babies are white at birth, but mothers cover them with
bear oil, bake them in the sun to turn them brown, then flatten the
heads of their boy babies by putting heavy bags of sand on top of
them, altering their skulls into all types of different shapes, believing
this makes them beautiful. That is why the Choctaws are called
flatheads. They are lazy and filthy, dirt caked on their bodies which
turn the color of soot. Worst of all, they are cowards. Choctaw
women and girls do most all of the work. Such a tribe is not a place
for Franchmastabbia, a civilized man, master of gardens, a man who
can influence the rain and the sun."

With Franchmastabbia in charge of planting, and Tricot, who had
agreed to be the overseer, in charge of running the plantation, Guy
was able to pay close attention to the construction of his mansion.
Charles Grotesquieu came twice a week in an elaborate brougham,
drawn by a team of magnificent Arabians, to cast his wary eye on
construction details, demanding perfection.

The slaves posed constant problems. Many of them, despite Master Kennedy's assurance, were in need of medical attention, but since
there were no doctors available, treatment was a combination of
Franchmastabbia's tribal remedies and Tricot's knowledge of what
his previous plantation owner had prescribed for his slaves. In addition to the slaves' medical problems, animosities rose between slaves
who came from African tribes that were antagonistic to each other.
And there were violent clashes between male slaves vying for the few
women, clashes that Tricot mediated by strictly confining the women
to their own quarters. Male slaves who violated this segregation
were given ten lashes and remanded to the newly built jail for a
period of time imposed by Guy on Tricot's recommendations.

Two weeks after his arrival, Guy received an invitation from Governor Vaudreuil to attend a ball at his mansion. For the occasion,
Guy made an appointment with Maurice Castellon, who was, according to Monsieur Grotesquieu, the only tailor in New Orleans
who knew how to clothe a gentleman's body. Guy chose a black
fabric, piped with silver, that Monsieur Castellon, who had been
apprenticed to the renowned Maison Beaumont in Paris, tailored to
perfection.

Governor Vaudreuil, the "great marquis," had made a determined effort to re-create the ambience of Versailles by surrounding himself with a coterie of devoted, magnificently uniformed officers, and by investing his court with an aura of pomp and ceremony. Modeling himself after Louis XV, he devoted his life to the visceral pleasures of dining, card-playing, and dancing in the setting of elaborate balls. Although he had issued an edict forbidding masked balls in public places, no such restraint was imposed on his own masked affairs.

To finance his elaborate lifestyle, the great marquis and his wife controlled the only liquor shop where soldiers and officers were permitted to buy alcohol and drugs. On their way to the Governor's Mansion, Tricot described the situation to Guy. "The drugs, of course, are very bad for the soldiers, and there are always a hundred, two hundred, in the hospital. There are sixty officers or more, the elegant ones who surround the Governor, but they never set foot in the barracks, so filthy, so repulsive, you can not imagine. There is no duty required of the soldiers who can do anything they want so long as they drink at the Governor's liquor store. They carry out of it wine and spirits which they resell to the Negroes and Indians at profit. Everyone knows about this, but, of course, it is a vice no one tries to stop because it is the great Marquis' own venture. Liquor supplies are purchased by Madame Vaudreuil, who also sells other merchandise she forces merchants to buy at prices she fixes. She keeps in her very own house every sort of drug sold by her steward—I know, I have been sent there to buy some by the master of my plantation—if the steward is away, Madame Vaudreuil will herself measure the requirements and betakes herself to the ell. The Marquis is not ignorant of this, for it is a source of much income for him."

As Guy's carriage approached Governor's Mansion, the dark night became illuminated by hundreds of firepots which had been placed along the driveway. The doors of the mansion had been removed, and the front of the house was ablaze with the glow from five hundred wax candles. The costumes of the guests were extravagant and elaborate, the women favoring rich embroideries, silks, and mousselines trimmed with taffeta, lace, or gold sequins. Compared to the fashions in vogue at Versailles, these costumes were gaudier and more vulgar, but they did create a festive, buoyant atmosphere. Headdresses of aigrettes, elaborate displays of jewelry, and rouge provided further embellishments.

What forcibly struck Guy as he dismounted from his carriage and entered the mansion was the vast number of servants in attendance, more, it seemed to him, than serviced the vastly larger Versailles. Of course, the rooms at Governor's Mansion bore no resemblance to the magnificence of Versailles, but they were richly furnished. The dinner, which preceded the ball itself, was limited to seventy-five guests who were seated at tables of fifteen; fifteen servants were in attendance at each table, each assigned to a single guest. The marquis greeted the guests as they arrived in the large, high-ceilinged state dining room with its canopy of crystal chandeliers. On being presented to the governor, Guy was impressed with his elegance and noble bearing, a tall, smiling man, with gracious gestures and no outward vestiges of arrogance. Half the guests were masked, the other half, like Guy, prefered to reveal themselves. Governor Vaudreil wore a thin gold mask across his eyes, which was so slight as not to mask him at all.

Dinner, which was served on solid gold plates, was an endless succession of succulent dishes prepared by French chefs, alternating fish, fowl, and game. The courses were presented dramatically, and the wines offered by the sommeliers were of exquisite vintage. A stringed ensemble played softly at the far end of the room.

Guy's dinner partners were both masked, one a middle-aged, portly lady, with an ill-fitting wig, the other an attractive, younger woman, whose eyes, startling blue, were all that Guy could see of her face, which was covered by a mask sequinned with flecks of gold and silver. She had a richly modulated voice, and a light, trilling laugh; she wore a gown of blue silk with a single black pearl on a gold choker adorning her neck. Warmed by the wine and the splendid food, a far cry from his plantation cuisine, Guy realized how long it had been since he had been in the company of an attractive woman; the perfume, the enticing laugh, the luminous eyes, the swell of her breasts above the low bodice of her gown.

After dinner, the guests were escorted to the ballroom where an additional four hundred guests had been invited for dancing and gambling. Guy's dinner partner accompanied him to the ballroom, her hand resting lightly on his arm. As the music started, she turned to him and they started to dance without the customary invitation and acquiescence.

"Is it not warm behind your mask?" Guy asked.

"Is that your way of asking me to remove it?"

"I should like to see who you are."

"I am an ugly hag who only goes to balls when her face can be fully covered. Otherwise, you would not be dancing with me."

"Your eyes are not those of an ugly hag."

"My only virtue. That is why they are on display."

"Do you realize it is unfair to dance with a gentleman who is fully revealed while you are an enigma about whom I know nothing? We have shared a table for two hours, but I do not even know your name."

"You may call me Avril."

"Is that your name?"

"No, but it is a name you can call me."

"Are you married?"

"May I show you a new step? We dance so divinely together that I think we should enlarge our repertoire."

As they danced, Guy fascinated by his nebulous partner whose small, delicate hand held firmly onto his, a lieutenant, wearing an ornate dress uniform, approached them, causing them to pause.

"Monsieur Laroule, forgive this intrusion, but the Marquis de Vaudreuil would be honored to receive you at the conclusion of your dance. I shall accompany you. Thank you."

The lieutenant withdrew.

"Well, Monsieur Laroule, a private audience with the great Marquis—there must be some intriguing things about you which you have not told me."

"All right, I shall reveal all—this is really a human mask I am wearing—underneath I am an old man with a repulsive face."

"Then we are perfectly matched."

"Perfectly."

The music stopped, ending the quadrille, and the lieutenant approached.

"May I have the pleasure of dancing with you again later on?" Guy inquired.

Without answering, she turned and walked away as if, in responding to the governor's request, Guy was rejecting her.

The governor received Guy cordially. "I suppose, Monsieur Laroule, that after Versailles our humble party is a pitiable affair."

"Not at all, Your Excellency."

"I am pleased that you have joined our community, for, as you may know, I am partial to the theatrics which are regularly performed in my theater here. Have you seen it? Well, I shall have Lieutenant Masson give you a tour. I know of your prowess in acting and singing—I am sorry to say we do not have very good voices. Perhaps you will have time to perform for us—it would please me greatly."

"I would indeed like to perform, but I have not brought music or scripts with me."

"Oh, we have all that. And an excellent orchestra, if I say so myself. Sets, costumes, all that—splendid, truly splendid. But the performers—ach! Herr Gutfreund, who has come here from the Munich Opera, is a tenor whose notes flutter off key like a pheasant in a cornfield. Unfortunately, I do not have a Madame de Pompadour to offer you for your duets, but perhaps you will find one or two of our ladies with an acceptable voice."

"You know more about me than I had anticipated."

"We know all about you, Monsieur Laroule, but it is no matter. Neither my wife nor my mistresses sing."

Angry shouts from the opposite side of the ballroom interrupted their conversation. The volume of the commotion increased as the music stopped, and dancers began to shout at one another. What had occurred was that the elder son of the governor, who disliked French quadrilles and danced them badly, had several times during the course of the evening succeeded in having English dances substituted, which he danced better. Since no one objected to these few substitutions because, after all, he was the governor's son, he decided to assert himself even further. After seven French quadrille sets had already been formed, and the dancers had begun to move to the music, the governor's son had shouted to the orchestra in a commanding voice, "English quadrille!" The astonished and angered dancers had shouted back, "French quadrille!" thus creating the resulting ruckus now disrupting the ball. When the son commanded the orchestra to stop playing, which they had, that infuriated the dancers even more. The shouting and shoving matches escalated. As Guy made his way across the crowded floor, the military guard that had been stationed outside the mansion was ordered into the ballroom to restore order, and the soldiers appeared with fixed bayonets and drawn swords. At the sight of the guards, the tumult, if anything, doubled. When the officer in charge ordered his men to ready their guns to fire, the women began to flee in panic; but the men, whose numbers were rapidly augmented by others from the gambling rooms, stood their ground. Grenadines lined up on one side, gamblers and dancers on the other, all ready to fight, the guards aiming their guns, the men standing firm.

Vaudreuil attempted to push his way through the crowd to restore order but could not make any headway, and his voice was lost in the pandemoniun. Guns, bayonets, and swords were now lined up against swords, chains, and tabletops. Guy found himself trapped in the space between the two warring groups, swords and guns on either side of him. More in self-preservation than in heroics, he grabbed a gun, leaped on top of a table, and fired once into the ceiling. The explosion stunned the crowd into silence.

"Step back, all of you!" Guy shouted. "Are we going to kill our defenseless women and ourselves over a dance? Put down those guns! Put those swords back in their sheaths where they belong!"

The guardsmen lowered their guns, but a few of the dancers continued to brandish their swords.

"You, there," Guy shouted, "sheath those swords."

All but one complied.

"Monsieur, put your sword away, or if you are so anxious to use it, I shall give you immediate answer outside here."

The swordsman gave Guy a long, hard look, then slowly returned his sword to its sheath.

"Now, as for the dancing, I see there is a small ballroom beyond this one. Let us divide up—those wanting to dance the English quadrille can go there—all other dancers can dance the French quadrille here. Let us have peace."

Guy hopped down from the table as the crowd began to disperse and the music resumed for those dancing the French quadrille. Guy looked for Avril, but she was nowhere to be seen. He searched for her in the ballroom where they were dancing the English quadrille, and in the gambling rooms, but he never found her. On the other hand, all of New Orleans society had found Guy. He had unwittingly introduced himself to everyone in spectacular fashion, and from that evening on he would be on nearly all the invitation lists.

When he belonged to the Versailles Court, Guy's existence centered around the social events which were the palace's lifeblood. Now, however, although he was receiving invitations to virtually every significant social event in New Orleans, Guy found that he had lost his interest in socializing and preferred staying on his plantation and attending to its needs. It was thrilling to walk along the paths among Franchmastabbia's newly planted flowers and shrubs, and through the burgeoning fields of indigo. Guy would visit the slave quarters

on horseback in the evening and talk with the Negroes as they sat
outside their cabins to escape the hot, humid interiors. When he first
made these visits the slaves were suspiciously taciturn, but in time
they accepted his good will and talked openly with him. The slaves
who came from interior tribes spoke only their own dialects, but a
few of those who had been captured along the African Gold Coast
and British East Africa, both controlled by the British, and French
West Africa, were able to make themselves understood in English or
French. They acted as interpreters for other slaves in their groups.
Guy himself spoke English well enough to communicate with the
Negroes from the British territories, in particular a slave from the
Gold Coast named Nemo who was fast becoming the leader of the
group.

Tricot was helpful in educating Guy about his slaves, helping him
to understand the primitive life they led in the African villages they
came from, the inferior role of the women, the disdain the men had
for female children, the cruelties they inflicted on each other, the
process whereby a leader was chosen and how he wielded his power.

"A slave's daily life is governed, some by ritual," Tricot explained,
"but most by superstition. There is a superstition about everything
that happens. It is important that you know of these so you can
understand these people better. I have written down here a list for
you of some of them, not all. To record all of them would take a
very big book."

He handed his list to Guy:

It is bad luck to fall down on Monday.

It is bad luck to have three candles burning in one room.

It is bad luck to leave a chair rocking. You will die within one year.

To break a mirror foretells seven years bad luck, unless you throw all
the pieces into a running stream.

If little children put their arms over their heads when sleeping, you
should lower them, for they are calling down misfortunes on their
heads.

To pass a child through a window makes a thief of him.

You must always burn and not throw away your hair; for the birds
will take it for their nests, and you will become insane.

If you have a sore on the tip of the tongue, it is a sign you have lied.

If a man cannot make a fire burn, it means that he shall have a drunken wife.

It is bad luck to spit in the fire, as it "dries up your lungs" and then you die.

If you throw salt after a stranger leaving your house he will never return.

A picture falling from the wall tells of death.

If you lie on a table, it means that you will die and be laid out on one before long.

To keep a dog at home, cut a small piece from the end of his tail and bury it under the front steps.

To keep a cat at home rub its two front paws in the soot of the chimney.

If a woodpecker knocks on the house it is a sign of death.

Never sweep out the house after sundown, for you will sweep someone's soul out of the house with the sweepings.

When you drop your comb, if you put your foot on it your wish will come true.

To kill a spider makes it rain.

To hang a dead snake up in a tree makes it rain.

To kill a frog and not turn it on its back makes it rain.

If the rain falls while the sun is shining it is a sign that the devil is whipping his wife.

Blue jaybirds are evil spirits; on Friday they go to hell to report to the devil the bad things that happen in the world.

To cure warts, rub it with a green pea; then wrap it in a piece of paper and throw it away; the person who picks it up will get your warts. Or, you must count the warts carefully, and then tie as many knots in a string as there are warts, and bury the string; as the string rots the warts will disappear. This is a sure cure.

To cure rheumatism: heat an iron pot red-hot; into this, throw three live frogs; the grease which cooks out of them should be saved and used to rub the painful part of the body. This is a sure cure.

Many old people have the gift of healing. They can cure pain by rubbing with their hands. The way they achieve this power is as follows: catch a live mole and rub him to death between your hands; if the mole bites you, it is certain that you will never be a healer, but if you succeed in crushing it to death before it harms you, you will have the power of healing.

As a result of his visits with the slaves and Tricot's instructions, Guy began to empathize with the miseries of this human chattel. Having never had any contact with the underclass in France, this was a new experience: humans without hope.

It was this growing empathy that probably accounted for Guy's reaction when one morning Tricot came to him with a Negro who had obviously been subjected to severe bodily punishment. He was naked except for a dirty loin cloth, and his upper body was a hatchwork of bleeding whip cuts. His left eye was a bloody pulp and his face severely bruised and swollen.

"He throws himself upon your mercy, suh. He is a slave who has run away from the Duroux plantation, which is several plantations up the road from here. Monsieur Duroux is known for his cruelty to his slaves, and this one wishes to tell you his story."

"Yes, of course—what language does he speak?"

"He is from the French Congo, but he speaks a dialect that fortunately I am able to understand but would not suit your ear."

"Then you can translate as he speaks."

Through badly swollen lips, the slave painfully recounted his experience:

"Because I was unable to do the work assigned to me, I was brought to Monsieur Duroux for an explanation. I swore to him that I had done my best, but that my strength was insufficient for the labor imposed upon me. He set four men upon me. They threw me to the ground, stripped me naked. Duroux himself applied the whip. He struck me again and again until I lost consciousness. One eye was put out by a blow from the butt of the whip.

"He ordered the four men to take me far enough from his dwelling so that my cries would not disturb his rest at night. There I was bound to a tree. In my nakedness I was a prey to the mosquitoes which settled upon me in swarms. I remained there for two days and two nights without food or water.

"My brother, who had made an attempt to soften Duroux's heart, was tied naked to a tree nearby. In this position, standing with his back to the tree with his body exposed to the sun, he presented a pitiful sight. His body was covered with blood and was black with flies and mosquitoes. He was released at the end of thirty-six hours, but he died the following day.

"At times there have been as many as fourteen men, naked and tied to stakes in the sun on the beach. Duroux walks up and down before them, prodding them in the softer parts of their bodies with his sword, enough to draw blood. I was untied this morning. I have run away.

"Please, Master, if you have any pity in you, please, sir, allow me to stay here with your slaves."

"It is a serious offense to commandeer another man's slave," Tricot warned. "There are criminal penalties."

"Take him to the slaves' quarters and let the women wash his wounds and rub on his body whatever balm they have for healing. And they must clean and cover the cavity from which his eye is missing so that infection will not occur."

The slave bent to his knees in gratitude and attempted to kiss Guy's boots, but Guy took his arm and, raising him, turned him over to Tricot.

"Perhaps it would be better if you sent him to the slave council in New Orleans . . ."

"No, they would simply return him to Monsieur Whatever-his-name-is."

"Duroux."

"Who would kill him. No, do as I say."

"It will have consequences, suh."

"Most everything does."

During the afternoon of the following day, while Guy was in one of the indigo fields, three men on horseback came swirling into the unfinished courtyard of the plantation and demanded to see Monsieur Laroule. When Guy approached, one of the men dismounted and addressed him.

"You are Monsieur Laroule, the proprietor of this plantation?"

"I am."

"And I am Bernard Duroux. One of my slaves has run away, and he was last seen in this direction. Have you, by chance, seen him? A slight fellow, stripped, very black, without size or sinew."

"Yes, I have."

"And do you know where he is?"

"He is here, receiving medical attention for the severe wounds you inflicted upon him."

"Whatever his condition, he is my property, and I demand that you relinquish him."

"I will not dispatch a man to his death," Guy said. "I am not an executioner."

"He is not a man, he is a slave. And what I do with him is my business, not yours."

"You are wrong, Monsieur Duroux. His life is now on my conscience, and I do not see that it benefits you to take him for the sole purpose of killing him."

"One can tell that you are new here, Monsieur Laroule, and quite naive. The purpose is to hang him in front of the other slaves so that they will never even think of running away."

"That reason does not persuade me. I repeat, I will not send a man to be killed."

"Then you refuse to return my property?"

"Under these conditions—yes."

"I suppose you are aware that makes you a thief."

"Call me whatever you will."

"I do not tolerate thieves, Monsieur Laroule, and I demand immediate satisfaction to address your insult."

The other two riders swung down from their horses, one of them handing Duroux a sword which he pulled from its scabbard. Duroux was a muscular man, rather stocky, but from his movements it was apparent that he was quick and light on his feet.

"This is your choice, Monsieur Laroule, return my property or subject yourself to the wrath of my sword."

Without a word from Guy, Tricot had gone to Guy's temporary house and brought back two swords for Guy's selection.

"I must inform you, Monsieur Duroux, that I am an accomplished swordsman and I think you would be better off settling this matter in a judicial manner, but I am aware of how you treat your slaves, so if you are intent on dueling, I am pleased to oblige you."

By way of an answer, Duroux raised his sword and assumed a rather dramatic dueler's stance. The two men touched swords, Duroux immediately lunging at Guy's midsection, Guy easily eluding the thrust. Then, with a dexterity Duroux had probably not encountered before, Guy flashed his sword from side to side, a dazzling whir in Duroux's eyes, upended Duroux's sword, and stingingly slipped his own into Duroux's side, just the point of it, entering his flesh only a fraction of an inch, but causing a cascade of blood to redden the bodice of Duroux's silk shirt. Duroux's reaction was to drop heavily on the seat of his trousers, clutching his wounded side as he emitted a series of high-pitched groans.

"I only pricked him lightly," Guy said to Duroux's accomplices. "He is quite able to journey back to his place."

Duroux's companions helped him into his saddle, and one of them, mounting his own horse, led Duroux's horse by its reins, while Duroux, slumped in the saddle, continued to whimper.

This fleeting incident had a profound effect on Guy's relationship with his slaves and workers. That he had risked his life to protect a black man canonized him in their eyes. And when word of the duel reached New Orleans a day or so later, the legend of the stranger from the Court of Versailles would be further enhanced.

During the course of constructing the plantation house, it became a ritual for Monsieur Grotesquieu to inspect the progress every Wednesday and then return with Guy to New Orleans to have dinner at his club. The two men had developed a fondness for each other to the point that the Wednesday dinners continued after the mansion was finished; in fact, Monsieur Grotesquieu nominated Guy for membership in his club and, despite a long waiting list of applicants, Guy, with the hearty endorsement of the club's president, was expeditiously approved.

"I have never owned anything," Guy told Monsieur Grotesquieu at dinner the day following the episode with Monsieur Duroux. "What I possessed at Versailles was at the sufferance of the King, so that it was not my possession at all. As witness my banishment. I had no control nor responsibility. I was a participant in events I did not originate or control. But now all that has changed. The slaves are beholden to me. The crops, the animals, the food, all beholden to me. It is as if I were mayor of a little village, which probably accounts for my reaction to Monsieur Duroux. I was completely surprised by my defiance in that I did not back down from his challenge. It is as if a stranger inside me had awakened and pushed aside the man I was. If he becomes too pushy, this inside fellow, I trust you will let me know."

"I'll do better than that," Monsieur Grotesquieu said, "I'll push him right back where he belongs."

Twelve

THE FIRST REHEARSAL for *Le Père Indien,* written by the Comédie Française playwright, Le Blanc Villeneuve, took place at the governor's theater. Joined to the rear of his mansion, it had its own entrance. The governor had sent his personal carriage to fetch Guy for the rehearsal, which had been arranged after a visit to Diderot by the director, Vincent Portameux. It had not been easy to persuade Guy to perform. The specter of going back on the stage, which had been his undoing with Madame de Pompadour, was one that disturbed Guy. Not only that, his way of life now was so far removed from the frivolous existence he had led at Versailles, that he felt a void in that part of him that had once enjoyed the make-believe of performing. The esprit of the Versailles palace, particularly the cameraderie of the group of players, the intimacy of his rehearsals with the marquise, conspired to motivate him on the stage. Now he was being asked to perform with strangers who, he had been told, had nebulous talent. But in the end, the persistence of Monsieur Portameux induced Guy to acquiesce, primarily because he was aware of the importance to a newcomer of having good relations with the governor.

There were ten players in *Le Père Indien,* four of whom had singing parts. Guy was assigned the lead role, that of an explorer, and as he was introduced to the other members of the cast, he was arrested by the sight of the beautiful woman who was to play opposite him. "Monsieur Laroule, may I present Comtesse Mai de Villars du Breuil. She will sing the part of the Indian princess."

As Guy bent over her outstretched hand, he held her eyes with his, aware of a familiarity that he could not immediately fathom. His long, puzzled look caused the comtesse to laugh, and that gave away her identity: the startling blue eyes, the trill of her laughter.

"Comtesse," Guy said, releasing her hand that he had touched lightly with his lips, "I believe I once saw you in a wonderful performance as Avril at the ball, did I not?"

"Yes, but my performance that evening left much to be desired."

The face that had hidden behind that mask was now mocking him, a face delicate, yet strong, the lips well-defined and full, her eyes sapphires on the white velvet of her skin.

"Quite a coincidence, isn't it?" Guy asked.

"Not at all, Monsieur Laroule. The Governor placed me at your table so that we could become acquainted before performing together."

"And if I had decided not to perform?"

"The Governor . . . and I . . . would have persuaded you."

The comtesse displayed an assurance bordering on vanity, obviously fostered by the adoration of men who had been mesmerized by the combined allure of her small curvacious body, her striking face, and the vivacity of her personality.

She read her lines adequately, without too much animation, which was to be expected at first rehearsal, but she fully projected her singing, a lilting lyric soprano, easily scaling the top notes, looking Guy directly in his eyes as they practiced their duet, her fluted voice nimbly embellishing his strong baritone.

The director, who had suffered through several untalented, off-key tenors and baritones, was ecstatic in his praise of Guy's performance. "Ah, Madame la Comtesse," the director effused, "what a pleasure it is that we finally have a partner for your exquisite voice."

"We will be better once we get to know one another," the Comtesse du Breuil responded. "Perhaps you will lunch with me tomorrow, Monsieur Laroule, and devote the afternoon to rehearsal. We have but ten days to get ready."

"It would be a pleasure," Guy replied.

"We can experiment with harmonies," she said. "I believe that harmonies are most important—do you agree, Monsieur Laroule?"

"By all means."
"To accommodate each other."
"Precisely."
"So that the voices are as one."
"Yes."
"I am so glad we see eye to eye."
"We do, indeed."

The Comtesse Mai de Villars du Breuil lived in a white-gabled house with gold balustrades, not far from the governor's mansion. The house had originally been built by the chief official of the Compagnie des Indes but when the official resigned and fled the country amid allegations of fraud and chicanery, the house had been sold at auction and bid in by the comte, who had arrived in New Orleans to assume the post of Minister of Finance, accountable directly to the king, not to the governor. Louis XV wanted more income from New Orleans; the comte, by increasing taxes and levying royalties on the illicit slave trade, was able to provide the desired monies. But the comte had carefully avoided encroaching on the governor's personal revenue from his liquor and drug monopolies, the accommodation uniting them in friendship.

The comtesse, dressed in a flowing white gown that accentuated her beauty, received Guy in a small downstairs sitting room where two servants served a simple luncheon of foie gras and crayfish, accompanied by an extraordinary white Burgundy. For most of the lunch, the comtesse enlightened Guy about previous productions at the theater and the roles she had performed. After lunch, she led Guy to the music room. "I do not play the piano very well," she said, "but I thought it preferable that we have our first rehearsal alone so that no one hears our mistakes but us."

Guy sat on the piano bench beside her as they tentatively went through the first of their duets, a love song that embraced the explorer and the Indian princess.

"What do you think?" the comtesse asked.

"A nice blend, I think, but now we should try to sing with more passion. We sound like we were singing a hymn in church."

The second time around was much better, the comtesse moving closer to Guy on the bench as she sang, both of them singing out, letting their voices embrace each other, and by song's end, they achieved a lovely harmony. As the song concluded, pleased and exhilarated, the comtesse reached her lips up to Guy's and kissed him lightly, then kissed him again, this time her arms embracing him. The passion of the song had induced a physical arousal to which Guy responded. The comtesse slipped from her gown as they moved to a nearby chaise and wordlessly coupled themselves as naturally as they had coupled their singing, the comtesse guiding Guy inside her, both of them still hearing the song, moving to its cadence, a different duet played to the same music, the rhythm reaching a slow crescendo, now sounding a different music, climaxing at the same moment.

Every afternoon, for ten days, they lunched, rehearsed, and made love, invariably in the music room. On the third day, while coupled to his body, moving to his rhythm, the comtesse impetuously began to sing the love song from *Le Père Indien*. Guy responded, and although their quickened breathing affected the duet, the song nonetheless heightened their sensuality as they paced themselves to climax precisely as they sang the final erupting notes.

During these afternoons, there was little discussion about their personal lives nor any avowals of love. When Guy asked the comtesse about the security of their daily sessions, she replied that there was nothing to be concerned about.

"Your husband?"

"Least of all my husband."

"What do you mean?"

"He has his own 'friends.' "

"Oh, yes, the custom here—mulatto mistresses."

"No—mulatto misters."

"Then you can have no children with him?"

"Only by immaculate conception."

The performance of *Le Père Indien* before the governor and two hundred of his invited guests, including Monsieur Grotesquieu, was a triumph. The ten days of intimacy infused their performances with a cohesiveness and a sensuality that had the governor on his feet, leading the bravos of seven curtain calls.

At the dinner that followed the performance, the governor gaudily toasted the performers as "two rare gems in the diadem of the theater," and presented them with statuettes of pelicans fashioned out of Limoges crystal.

After dinner, while Guy danced a French quadrille with the comtesse (the governor's son was not present), he said, "It feels strange not to have a rehearsal tomorrow."

"Perhaps there will be another show to perform in a month or so.
I shall speak to the Marquis."

"And lunches?"

"Whenever we have rehearsals."

"Not until then?"

"What would be the point of it?"

"Quite right."

"I hope we have two good parts again. I enjoy rehearsing."

The following Wednesday, when Guy dined with Monsieur Grotesquieu, the architect mentioned how much he had enjoyed the show.
"I had no idea you were so accomplished," he said. "And the comtesse was never in better voice."

"She performs frequently?"

"Yes, she dotes on theater."

"Tell me about the Comte."

"A charming thief. He steals the Crown blind, but Versailles is so
far removed, it has no clue what is happening here. The Governor
knows, but he steals so much on his own, he can hardly point a
finger at the Comte."

"I understand that the Comte is partial to his own sex."

"Who told you that?"

"The Comtesse."

Out came the pipe. "Hah! She neither knows nor cares. Sex to the
Comtesse is but another stage performance, whereas the Comte pur-
sues sex as a policeman chases a thief. Men, women, mountain
goats, name it, the Comte will bed it. That is, any and everything
except the Comtesse. He was quite drunk here one night—he's a
member—and when someone mentioned the Comtesse—she had
just acted in something or other—the Comte took off in a diatribe
against her. Terrible stuff. 'The witch with the poisoned vagina'—
that kind of thing. How was she with you?"

"She threw herself into it."

"Into you, you mean."

"That, too."

"She tried to seduce me once when I came to her house to discuss
an addition to their carriage house."

"What happened?"

"I said I never have intercourse with anyone who is paying me for
my architectural services since it might adversely affect my fee."

"But if they offer you payment for seduction?"

"That is a different story, but I would starve trying to make a living that way."

Two weeks after Guy rescued Pierre Deroux's battered slave, he died. Guy and Tricot did everything they could for him, but there was no way to abate the infection in his eye socket. A doctor was brought from New Orleans (the only one who would consent to treat a slave) but all he did was sprinkle some antiseptic powder over the open wound. Franchmastabbia mixed a potion of herbs with the poison sacs of wasps which he applied while burning dry jasmine, but that, too, was ineffectual. The slave was buried in the cemetery plot that had been staked out at the farthest corner of the plantation; already two other slaves who had suffered from serious afflictions when they arrived, were buried there.

Thirteen

AFTER HIS EPISODE with the comtesse, Guy realized that that kind of mindless intrigue was redolent of the gossip, backbiting, sly fornications and frivolous politics of Versailles which had become an anathema to him. After *Le Père Indien,* he never again performed on the governor's stage despite many entreaties from the great marquis. Nor did Guy accept any of the scores of invitations for social functions to which he was invited, preferring to isolate himself on his plantation and devote his time to harvesting his first indigo crop.

Ever since he supervised the planting of the seeds, Guy had been studying the history of the indigo plant and the procedure for processing it. He knew that the blue dye extracted from the plant had an ancient past, having been used in Egypt and India as far back as 1600 B.C. Textile producers in Europe considered the Louisiana indigo among the most desirable on the market, and by studying the economics involved, Guy ascertained that at the going market price of one dollar per pound, he could turn a substantial profit. But he also knew that the process for removing the dye from the plants was complicated and not without risk. With Monsieur Grotesquieu's help, Guy found an experienced indigo dye-maker, a Creole named Sylvestre, whom he hired at twelve dollars a month to supervise the construction of the shed for the processing of the plant.

Guy participated in every phase of the indigo's processing, often working alongside Sylvestre, Tricot, and the dozen slaves who had been chosen to work in the shed. When the work wagon arrived to cart the barrels to the docks, Guy and Tricot followed the big dray into the city and watched the barrels as they were off-loaded, weighed, and stowed aboard the brig *Avenger* for the long voyage to England. Guy's indigo weighed in at a thousand pounds, and it occurred to him that the draft for one thousand dollars which he now had in his pocket was the first money he had ever earned. He felt too good to return to the plantation and eat his customary solitary dinner. This was an occasion to savor. He decided to walk the relatively short distance to the club and arranged for Tricot to pick him up later that evening.

It was a splendid twilight. The humidity had abated somewhat and a brisk breeze off the gulf was discouraging the mosquitos. Guy was rather surprised that at this particular moment he began to think about Madame de Pompadour and their last farewell at the Petit Trianon. He knew now that she was the only woman he had ever truly loved, even though that love was never fully consummated. He missed her at this very moment when he wished to share his good fortune. She would have genuinely rejoiced in his accomplishment, elated that he had overcome brutal obstacles and arrived at this savored moment. Of all the women he had ever known, his mother included, the marquise had cared the most about him. That is true love, he thought, not impetuous passion, not responding synthetically to another's trials, misfortunes, and victories, but a deep, abiding involvement with your beloved.

He turned onto Burgundy Street, passing the shuttered shops: the apothecary with clumps of medicinal herbs on display in its window; the saddler with the sign of a tin horse out front; the shoemaker, his window filled with boots guaranteed to withstand the mud and the rain; the fabric and bedding merchant; the spirits shop; the notary with a window sign:

Documents and Other Written Matter Read Aloud
Letters Written
Signatures Affixed to Documents
Documents Notarized

The notary shop was always crowded with customers since only a small proportion of the citizenry could read and write. Most of the twelve hundred whites in New Orleans had little or no education; in particular the middle-class French Creoles relied on their vigor, neatness, and good looks to get by. It was said that a Creole's boredom increased as his opportunities for escaping it narrowed. This craving for excitement accounted for the abuse, sarcasm, gossip, and quarreling that permeated their relationships with each other. They were also notorious liars. Both sexes reveled in gaudy clothing which they wore while indulging in their two great passions, drinking and dancing, especially the Creole women. But they could not be bothered with the discipline of schools and formal education, many of them not able to write their names. They were slothful but intelligent, often solving problems by guile and subterfuge rather than facing them head-on. Their unique solution to the problem of the muddy streets and banquettes, for example, was not to repair the streets, but to bypass them in the rainy season by going across the rooftops.

Guy's path now took him to Dauphine Street, bustling with inns, boarding houses, hotels, dance halls, and a succession of taverns, some of them crude saloons, others disciplined and attractive, still others raucously alive with dancing and gambling. Tavern owners were divided between Creoles and Acadians, also called Cajuns. The Creoles ran noisy establishments where the favored drinks were red wine, usually claret, often cut with water drawn directly from the Mississippi, and a crude cheap rum distilled from sugar cane, called *taffia*. The Creole taverns resounded with music and dancing and bursts of inebriated song.

The Acadian taverns, on the other hand, were frequented by those who preferred drinking in a more subdued atmosphere. These taverns featured gambling and a wider assortment of liquors, including a new drink, which a New Orleans druggist, A. A. Peychaud, first dispensed as a tonic at his apothecary shop on Toulouse Street. It was composed of cognac and a concoction of Peychaud's invention, which he called "bitters" which the tavern served in a double-handled cup called a *coquetier*. Many English-speaking travelers had trouble pronouncing the word which they eventually distorted to "cocktail." By either name, the drink was gaining popularity at Acadian bars.

The Acadians, whom the Creoles regarded as their inferiors, were thrifty, industrious people who had been driven out of the Canadian province of Acadia, or Nova Scotia, by the British. Their French ancestors had emigrated to the province from the northern coast of France as settlers in the early 1600s and regarded the territory as their own. But when the British acquired Nova Scotia a hundred years later and demanded that they adopt British customs and laws, the Acadians refused; the British ultimately deported the entire population of seven thousand, dispersing them among their American colonies after driving them from their homes which they burned to the ground. A small contingent of these Acadians arrived in New Orleans, where they opened taverns and sought work as farmers. Some years later, a much larger influx of Cajuns would come to New Orleans from Baltimore and settle in the bayous and prairie lands.

Guy walked slowly past the taverns, enjoying the various stages of merrymaking which he observed through the windows and open doors. He was tempted to go in and join the revelers, but he knew that as an obvious outsider he would not be welcome in their midst. As he passed the Cajun Bon Vivant tavern, he heard a commotion emanating from a small alleyway between the buildings. Angry voices. Cries. A burly man, a woman, and a boy, the man enraged, belt in hand attempting to lash the boy whom the woman was trying to protect. The boy, who appeared to be about twelve years of age, was trying to get at the man, attempting to grab his arm. The man, bellowing curses at the woman as he fought her off, was able to whip his belt across the back and legs of the boy who shouted at him defiantly.

"Get away, you bitch, you bitch!" the man yelled as he shoved the woman forcefully against the wall. Then, with the flat of his hand, he struck the boy in the face, breaking his hold on the belt.

"Stop, stop, Henri," the woman screamed. "He's cut, stop, stop!" She regained her feet and hurled herself at the man as the boy continued to flail away at the man's arms, trying to divert his blows, the man's powerful arms fending him off and the belt again going whack! whack! whack! against the boy's body.

Guy, at first transfixed by the sudden brutal panorama, now started into the alleyway, intent on intervening, when an employee, wearing a white work apron, appeared at the tavern's sidedoor.

"Monsieur Boustique! Monsieur Boustique!" he called out several times, finally getting his attention. "You are wanted at the bar. It is urgent."

The man called Boustique was breathing heavily. He stared at the disheveled woman and the boy. "You both stay right here. I will deal with you when I come back."

As soon as he departed, the woman went to the boy and inspected his bruised face and the red welts swelling up on his legs and arms where the leather belt had landed. "Hurry, Rémi," she said, "we must leave before he gets back."

"But he will just follow us back home," the boy said.

"Not until later. Maybe by then he will calm down."

"I could kill him," the boy said, "for what he did to you."

"Does it hurt badly?"

The woman now became aware that Guy was nearby. She pulled the boy toward her as though facing another threat.

"Madame, I have witnessed this attack. If you and the boy desire safe haven, I would be glad to provide it."

"Why, thank you, monsieur. Thank you, kindly. But he is my husband, and I am bound to handle this as best I can. It is not the first time . . ."

"I cannot understand a father attacking his son so brutally," Guy said.

"He is not my father," the boy said bitterly.

"My son's father is dead," the woman said. "Come, come, Rémi, we must leave before he reappears."

"May I assist you?"

"Thank you, monsieur, but our calèche is just down the street."

"If you wish, I shall accompany you."

"Yes, thank you."

The woman moved gingerly, hurting from the blows to her back; the boy, despite his own wounds, assisted her. Guy offered to help, but the two of them seemed to be managing by themselves. Guy did aid both of them to mount their wooden calèche, its wheels metal-rimmed, a rather primitive conveyance. Guy took his handkerchief from his pocket and bound it around the boy's arm, where blood was trickling from an open cut.

"Madame," Guy said, "if you and the lad find yourselves needing assistance, I am at your disposal. Here is my card. Please call on me if ever you have need of me. What I have seen is revolting. You should not be subjected to such brutality."

"Thank you, sir," the boy replied, "my mother and I are most grateful to you. *Au revoir.*"

The woman snapped the reins and the horse responded, pulling them slowly through the muddy street, the boy sitting close to his mother, his head leaning against her shoulder.

By the time he reached La Bagatelle, Guy's euphoria had evaporated in the wake of the scene he had just witnessed. He feared for the well-being of this brave woman and her courageous son. Perhaps I should go back to that tavern and have a talk with that Cajun brute, Guy was thinking. How else will he be deterred from continuing his assaults on them? A rage like his is not easily quelled, but if he knew he would somehow have to be accountable to me . . . then again, I have no right to be asserting myself in something that I'm not a party to. "Monsieur, just who are you? This is my private life and it has nothing to do with you. Get out of my tavern and do not meddle in my business." I'd better give it some thought, Guy cautioned himself as he walked into the club. There may be special laws about husbands and their dominance over their wives.

Monsieur Grotesquieu was not present, but Guy was pleased to see that two gentlemen whom he knew through Grotesquieu were at the bar: the Baron de Bastrop, who owned a 30-square-mile tract to the north, and the Marquis de Maison Rouge, who had a tobacco plantation on the Ouachita River. Both men were bachelors, one a widower, the other disinterested in marriage. By tacit agreement while in the club, no one was to speak a word about business or politics. They welcomed Guy enthusiastically and the baron poured him a generous glass of Scotch whiskey from a bottle on the bar. There was a man sitting at a table alongside the bar whose face was vaguely familiar to Guy, but he could not place where he had seen him before. As Guy conversed with the baron and the marquis, he was suddenly aware that the man had approached and was standing at his elbow.

"Monsieur Laroule? It appears you do not remember me."

He was an expensively dressed man with a diamond ring on one hand, a large ruby ring on the other, and a gold-and-pearl Moor's head stickpin in the bib of his jabot.

"Your face is familiar, but I just can't place it . . ."

"I will give you a clue—*La Gironde.*"

"Monsieur Trémencourt!"

"The same."

"How different you look!"

"The mark of affluence, Monsieur Laroule. Clothes make the man."

Guy had forgotten Trémencourt's penchant for clichés.

"So, Trémencourt, it looks like you found a field of those diamond flowers you described."

"No, all those promises of the Company of the Indies, as you yourself now know, they were all lies; the gold and silver on the bottom of the lakes and rivers, the flowers that produced diamonds from their stems, the life here in New Orleans like the boulevards of Paris—the stock has become worthless. John Law, that thief, has fled, and I lost all my investment."

"Then how did you . . . ?"

"A most felicitous occurrence—will you have another drink? Barman, the same, please. Well, this is what occurred. Quite by accident. I had a friend here—the one that you saw pick me up at the dock—François Azor, very well connected. Not long after my arrival, he took me hunting—pheasants, ducks, whatnot, a large preserve he owns up north. Don't ask me where, I am atrocious on geography, but about an hour away. Anyway, we are hunting—he is a very good shot and I am not—but I am walking along and I see these strange rocks all over the ground. I know something about minerals, so I look at these rocks and I see they have heavy black veins in them from which I cut a sample with my knife—lead. Heavy with lead. So I make a deal with François on the spot—fifty-fifty. I bring in tools and workers and we dig down for a sample and, sure enough, a month later, right there, a first-grade lead deposit. Do you know the value of lead? In quantity, better than gold, better than silver, easy to dig, costs nothing to mine the ore, out comes the lead. Every army in the world needs Trémencourt lead—well, not just mine, but lead, lead, lead. I have three hundred slaves—three hundred! Four mines now and as fast as it comes up, it gets processed, zuk! zuk! zuk! Nothing to it—into the ships and away, cash at the dock. What a business! Nothing to feed, nothing to water, nothing to spoil! I am selling *rocks*! What to do with all the money, that is the only problem. I am into bear grease—a very big market here, used for cooking. And now furs. The Indians here bring me furs, I pay in geegaws—beads, bracelets, mirrors, ribbons, kettles, muskets, and whiskey, yes, whiskey. I have an arrangement with Madame Vaudreuil, the Governor's wife; she gets two pelts a bottle, I get six pelts. It's a very good arrangement, but the weather here is too hot for furs; they fall apart. But up north, ah, the Indians there are wonderful hunters, the fur much better quality farther up the Mississippi—that's the place to go. Keep it in mind. Now what about you, Laroule, your plantation—you still want to sell? How much? I wouldn't mind a plantation—Trémencourt Plantation—sounds nice. How much?"

Guy told him about his travails at the plantation, but that he was now happy there and it was not for sale. During dinner Trémencourt, who had bribed his way to membership, regaled Guy with accounts of some of his other investments: slave smuggling from the Indies ("Governor Vaudreuil gets a percentage, so I don't have to worry"); wine imports from France; sugar and tobacco imports from Cuba. He described his luxurious life: a harem of quadroons; a mansion of sixteen rooms (no, he didn't use architect Grotesquieu); four imported carriages; a stable of purebred horses; a personal tailor from Paris; a musician in residence to play piano, clavichord, and harp during meals; a tutor to teach him English; another instructor to teach him dancing ("I have two left feet"); a chef hired away from one of the best restaurants in Paris. "I will invite you to my next soirée, the best table in New Orleans, elegant guests. I will lend you one of the quadroons for the evening. Have you ever had sex with a quadroon? Oh, you are missing out on something. Sex with one of my quadroons is like being borne up to heaven on a golden chaise."

"I prefer the other direction."

"Either way, she will transport you there. All of this, everything, imagine, because I picked up a rock while hunting pheasants."

Fourteen

TWO DAYS AFTER the upsetting incident at the Bon Vivant tavern, a handsome woman presented herself at the gate of the Diderot Plantation, inquiring for Monsieur Laroule.

"How different you look," Guy said, on receiving her. "How is your son?"

"He is fine, thank you. He has a very resilient body . . . and mind. He is a remarkable boy, if I say so myself."

"And did your husband . . . what was his name? Boustique?"

"Yes, Henri Boustique."

"He is an Acadian?"

"Yes. He did not return to the house that night. He came back only yesterday, but he speaks to neither of us."

"All the better, I would say."

"It will be like this until the next unpleasantness."

"He beats your son?"

"He resents him, especially because Rémi will not take his name. He keeps the name of his father, Riveau. Rémi adored his father, Lieutenant Robert Riveau—he commanded a detachment at Fort Rosalie located upstream in Natchez Territory. The commander of Fort Rosalie was a certain Captain Shepard, who was, to put it simply, power crazy. The things he did to the Indians! He declared as his own a plot of land near the fort that was the Indians' sacred burial ground and temple. It was his plan to evict the Indians, dig up the cemetery, and turn the land into his personal plantation. He planned a great feast and a celebration for the event, but my husband warned him to be on guard, that the Indians were angry and might attack. Captain Shepard rejected the warning and went ahead with the celebration. The Indians came, bearing gifts for Shepard, and in the field, in front of the fort, they played a spirited lacrosse game between two of their best teams. Most of the garrison troops and their families, seven hundred of them in all, came out to watch the game, which suddenly broke off, as the Indians seized concealed weapons and attacked, slaughtering all the spectators and then invading the fort, killing all those who were inside, including my husband. Shepard was captured, but the Sun Chief decreed that he did not deserve to die a proper death inflicted by warrior braves, but a miserable death at the hands of the tribe's crippled dwarf, Little Snake, who gleefully battered Shepard to death with a wooden hatchet. Rémi and I escaped the massacre because Rémi was in bed with the measles. To this day, my son has the delusion that somehow he might have helped save his father."

"It is always difficult to be a survivor. A strange kind of guilt."

"He's a very grown-up boy, but we had a hard time after Robert was killed. It is not easy here for a widow with a young son. We were without means, but the Ursuline nuns allowed us to live in their convent. That is how I originally came to New Orleans, one of the *filles à la cassette*—that's what we were called—casket girls—because we each came with a little chest filled with our clothing. Many girls of questionable character had been shipped over, but the government needed proper girls to marry the reputable men who had settled here. The French authorities chose young girls from reputable middle-class families who had good character and housewifely skills. I was one of those chosen. We were brought here by the Ursuline nuns, who first settled here forty years ago, to live in their convent. During the day, qualified men were allowed to visit us under the supervision of the nuns. At night, we were confined to the convent. When a man asked to marry a girl he had chosen, he first had to be approved by the nuns, and then we girls had the right to turn down his proposal if we wished. It was in this manner that I met Robert Riveau, who visited me many times before he asked for my hand. He was a handsome, considerate man, a wonderful father." She fell silent while she thought about him. "He read poetry." After another pause, she said, "After his death, when the Ursulines heard of my

plight, they offered to give Rémi and me a room in the convent. I
went to work for Sister Xavier, who is a pharmacist, a most remarkable woman. She provides medicines for the King's hospital, which
she compounds from strange plants and herbs that she grows. I
helped with those. Medicine is in terribly short supply here, and her
concoctions are desperately needed. The best thing about living at
the convent was that Rémi was able to attend school there. The
convent school is the only one in New Orleans. Parents either send
their children to France to study or hire tutors. Rémi goes there to
this day, and he has been educated very well. It was a satisfactory
life, but I knew I couldn't continue to live in a room in a convent
and properly raise a son of his age. Two years ago, after a Sunday
mass, a man came up to me and Rémi and introduced himself—it
was Boustique. He said he had seen us for several weeks at Sunday
masses and asked if we would give him the pleasure of having a
coffee with him. That's how he came into my life. It's hard to believe
now, but he was charming and acted like he was very fond of Rémi.
He said his first wife had died on the journey from Nova Scotia and
lamented that he had never had any children. I did not love him, but
when after several months he proposed marriage, I had to consider
Rémi's best interests. Boustique had a comfortable house, and I mis-
takenly thought he could fill the role of a father and a companion
for me. And at first he was—but not for long . . . not for long . . .
I suppose it started when he wanted Rémi to change his name. *Ordered* Rémi to give up his father's name. Rémi would not. His father
had taught him to stand up for himself. He's just twelve, but he has
convictions. I do not know why I am telling you all this. I am sure
you are busy and this cannot be of interest to you. I only came to
return your handkerchief and to thank you. But, you see, it has been
a long time since I have been able to talk to anyone." She attempted
to restrain her tears.

"I am glad you came," Guy said. "I have often wondered, yesterday and today, about you and Rémi after that unfortunate occurrence—whether you were all right. Boustique is certainly a brute of a
man."

"Yes, but he is also clever. He has an arrangement with all the
other tavern keepers to fix the price they pay for wine at public sale
and how much they charge for drinks in their taverns. That way,
nobody reduces the price and all of them make rich profits." She
rose from her chair.

"Oh, how remiss of me," Guy said. "May I offer some tea or coffee, perhaps?"

"No, thanks, I must be getting back."

Guy accompanied her to the calèche, which looked even shabbier in the bright sunshine. Guy helped her up the carriage step into the driver's seat.

"Oh, my goodness," she exclaimed. "I almost forgot to give you your handkerchief. My son asked me to thank you."

"I want you both to know that you have a friend in me."

"Thank you, Monsieur Laroule. We are sorely in need of friendship."

Fifteen

Monsieur Grotesquieu, not without difficulty, persuaded Guy to have a soirée to celebrate the completion of his plantation house. Not that Guy was not pleased with the house, quite the contrary, but it was his recently developed aversion to social functions that was now influencing him.

"It is my best work," Grotesquieu said, "and it is a home you should be proud of—so for those two reasons you should invite some people and have a joyous affair. It may be the only house you will build in your lifetime. As for me, I doubt I shall ever design a better one. Look at the austere lines, the delicate slope of the wings, the carved balustrades, how it sits there like a house on a throne, reigning over the entire plantation."

Guy invited Baron and Baroness de Bastrop, the Marquis de Maison Rouge with a lady of his choosing, Monsieur Trémoncourt and a few other members of La Bagatelle, the Governor and Mrs. Vaudreuil, several government people Guy had met in the course of establishing the plantation, the contractor and his wife, and after some hesitation, Comte and Comtesse Villars du Breuil, the latter invitation influenced not by a desire to resume relations with the comtesse, but by Guy's curiosity about the comte.

Originally, Franchmastabbia was to perform the Choctaw ritual of exorcising all evil from the new abode and blessing it with good fortune, but the old Indian had been ill for several days and was not up to the task. Nevertheless, the house was given its due in a series of toasts proposed by Grotesquieu, the Baron, and Monsieur Trémencourt, who carried on too long but amusingly about all the houses he had built and lost. Guy's kitchen produced a spectacular dinner that featured both a roasted suckling pig and a wild boar, along with several spicy Creole dishes previously unknown to the guests. With Grotesquieu's help Guy had found a remarkable vintage Bordeaux at the shop of a wine merchant who was a client of Grotesquieu's. The house glowed with the yellow undulating light of a thousand candles caressed by a gentle evening breeze.

The guests stayed late, the music remained lively, and all agreed on departure that this was the best housewarming they had ever attended. As the last of them left, Guy was happy that he had staged the party and that the house had turned out so well. It had been a most rewarding adventure, choosing door pulls and chandeliers, bedposts of mahogany and divans of red velvet, mirrors and desks, armoires and rugs, stoves and washbasins. Tricot interrupted his reverie.

"Sire, I am sorry to intrude, but I have discovered that Franch is in serious trouble. I think you'd better come."

The air in Franchmastabbia's hut was humid and fetid. There was a single candle burning at his bedside. The old Indian lay on his back, breathing with difficulty, the top of his head covered with a cloth bedcap. Guy picked up the candle and held it close to Franchmastabbia's face. What he saw repelled him. Both sides of the Indian's face were covered with huge, connected, pus-filled blisters, some of them leaking their yellow liquid along the craggy gulleys of his old face; his eyes were almost swollen shut, pustules on their lids; his hands and wrists, and the exposed part of his neck were also covered with pustules, his face and neck swollen to twice their size. His features were so disfigured by the swelling as to be almost unrecognizable.

Tricot tapped Guy on his arm and handed him a large, white linen napkin. "We had best tie these across our noses, suh. He has the black pox, and it is dangerous to breathe in."

They stood there, two masked figures in the pale light, both of them stunned by the tragic sight of Franchmastabbia's impending doom. Guy knew nothing about the disease; in fact, had never heard of it. "Is there a remedy?" he asked.

"Not the black pox, suh, no, I do not think so. We used to be pierced with a needle with a dab of the pox to prevent it, but it is no longer allowed."

"Why? Who would want to stop the injections?"

"The Church. They said it was a sin to put disease into the body."

"Would it help Franchmastabbia? An injection?"

"No, once you have it, there is nothing you can do."

Franchmastabbia groaned aloud, and his eyes flashed open for a second as he gasped for breath. Dried vomit was splattered on top of his blanket. He appeared to have a high fever. Placing his fingers carefully to avoid the pustules, Guy took the Indian's wildly thumping pulse. Franchmastabbia began to emit a rhythmic sound, a raw rasp that struggled to free itself from his enlarged throat.

"There must be a doctor who can help," Guy said.

"There is a Doctor Voigord who, they say, treats the pox. He runs the hospital for lepers at the Bayou Gate on Metairie Ridge."

"Would he be there now, do you think?"

"Yes, suh, he lives there."

"With the lepers?"

"Yes, he is very religious about lepers, Christ, and the Bible."

"Quick, then, hitch up the horses."

Franchmastabbia heard their voices, but he could no longer see out of the slits of his eyes obscured by pus that had oozed into them. To his fevered, disoriented mind, the voices belonged to his father and his brother, Tingenbill, who had been killed years ago during a buffalo hunt. But in his delirium, he could hear his father telling Tingenbill that it was Franchmastabbia's arrow that had killed him. Even now his father's words echoed in his memory.

"*No, brother, no,*" pleading in his feverish delusion, pleading not to blamed, but the father was stern, wrathful. "*You, Franchmastabbia, you brother-killer, may the Chickasaws take your scalp. You killed your own brother, your own flesh and blood.*" Begging his brother for forgiveness, now finally admitting it, "*yes, yes, it was my arrow, I didn't see you, I was aiming at the buffalo, there was a tree there, father, forgive me, father, father . . . I have lived with this sin so long a time, but I loved him, why can you not hear? My brother, I loved him!*"

It was almost daybreak by the time Guy found the doctor's house and returned with him to the plantation. During the ride back, whipping the horses, the carriage careening along the unfriendly road, Guy asked the doctor what he could do for Franchmastabbia.

"I do not know how far the disease has travelled," the doctor replied. "You say there are large pustules, so I will lance those and drain them and then apply a pomade of my invention all over the pustulated areas to try to stop their discharges. Most critical are the nose and throat. If the pustules form there, they can cut off breathing and swallowing. There is probably a high fever—I have an elixir for that. The black pox is very difficult because it attacks the whole body, not just one area. So we must do many things at the same time to best the clock."

"Tell me the truth," Guy said, "is it always fatal?"

"Not necessarily. In medicine, there is no such word as 'always.' "

Upon entering Franchmastabbia's hut, it was immediately apparent that Dr. Voigord's services were not needed. Franchmastabbia had managed to put the muzzle of his shotgun under his chin and pulled the trigger with his toe. Most of his head was missing. There was a message scrawled almost indecipherably on the wall above the bed. "Please bury me as a Choctaw," it said.

The following day, Guy went into town to inquire about how to arrange for a Choctaw burial, but at the coroner's office he was faced with a different problem.

"You say a suicide, the Indian was a suicide?" the coroner asked.

"Yes."

"Are you aware that that is a crime?"

"No, but what difference? The man is dead."

"Ah, yes, but the corpse must be indicted, tried, convicted, and sentenced before I can proceed."

"Proceed to what?"

"To deliver the corpse to lie rotting and bleaching among the offals, bones, and refuse of the butcher's stall. That is the law. Do you have the corpse at hand?"

"No, it is at the plantation. I will deliver it tomorrow."

"Very well."

That night, with Tricot's help, Franchmastabbia's body was loaded into the work carriage and taken to the Choctaw tribe on the Tombeckbee River. Guy presented the chief with an assortment of beads and a bottle of taffia before requesting burial for Franchmastabbia. Guy watched as two tribesmen constructed a scaffold of forks and poles twelve feet high on which they placed the corpse. The chief explained that the body would remain in place until the flesh putrified and slipped off the bones.

"We will then bury the flesh in our graveyard and put the bones in a box which will be placed in the Bone House along with all the other dead warriors."

Sixteen

MADAME BOUSTIQUE and her son came in the middle of the night, knocking frantically on the door of the manor house.

"Please excuse us, monsieur," Madame Boustique said, "but we are in peril, and you kindly offered . . ."

"Come in, come in." Guy, in his nightrobe, opened the door wide and lit a torch.

"I think he is following us," Madame Boustique said. "The boy, he is after the boy."

Guy looked at the boy who had a purpling bruise spreading on the left side of his face.

"Henri came home late from the tavern, drunk as he always is . . ." She was too upset to continue. "You tell him, Rémi."

"He told me this morning to have a fire burning in his bedroom—I forgot."

"You do not share a bedroom?" Guy asked the woman.

"Not for a year. He is punishing me, he says, because of a ball we went to—I consented to dance with a man he does not like."

"That night he threw her out of the carriage on the way home, in the dead of night, and made her walk home," the boy said. "I tried to jump out to help her, but he grabbed me. He is very, very strong."

"Tell me about tonight," Guy said.

"He barged into my room, awakened me from sleep, and began to yell and beat me," Rémi said.

"We managed to get out of the house when he went down for a drink," the woman said.

"He said he was not finished with me," the boy said. "I had my knife ready. If he had come back . . ."

"We slipped out of the house the back way, but he heard us hitching up the carriage. I let our other horse out of the barn so we had a head start, but he will catch it and come after us."

"Does he know you came here?"

"He saw your card the other day on my bureau."

"What did you tell him?"

"I said you were . . ."

Three violent thumps on the door interrupted her. Guy led mother and son into a room and told them to lock the door.

The assault on the front door was repeated. Guy opened the door, holding the torch before him. Henri Boustique stood glowering at him, slapping a riding crop across the palm of his left hand.

"I have come for my wife and son," he said.

Guy did not answer.

"I know they are here. That is my calèche outside."

"The boy you call your son, but who is not your son, has been severely beaten."

"He is being punished, which is no bloody business of yours."

"A boy being brutalized is my business. I have given them safe haven here. They will only leave here on their own volition."

"Own volition be damned," Boustique shouted, whacking his crop against the side of his leg for emphasis. "Either they come out, or I am coming in to get them."

"No, Monsieur, you are not. This is my house, and I do not permit trespassing."

"And I do not permit kidnapping. I am in my right to enter and redeem my property!"

"Your presence here is a trespass in itself. You have not been invited onto my property and you are hereby charged to remove yourself."

"The hell, you say!" Boustique shouted as he started to bull his way forward toward Guy who stood in the doorframe, but before Boustique could make his move, a strong arm grabbed him by the back of his coat collar and propelled him backwards.

"Monsieur Laroule said you were trespassing," Tricot said.

"Now, sir, your choice is, you can leave voluntarily or you can leave under escort. Which will it be?"

Boustique shook his powerful shoulders free of Tricot's grasp. "What it will be is your hide," he said to Guy. "I demand satisfaction for this outrage."

"You shall have it. Just name the time and place. I have matched foils—we can settle it right now, if you like."

"What! You think I am crazy letting you choose the weapons? Because, I suppose, you are a fancy swordsman. It will not be foils."

"Muskets, then."

"Muskets neither."

"What do you propose?"

"You will hear from my second tomorrow, and you tell that wife of mine that after I am done with you, her and the boy are going to catch a heavy load of hell from me. What I have done to them before is going to be child's play compared to what is going to happen to them now."

"Tricot, get him out of here. He contaminates the air."

"Do not touch me, nigger," Boustique said as he started to leave. "Christ, a Versailles fairy and a nigger—what a combination!"

The following day, Boustique's second, a heavy, full-bearded man dressed in a black leather jerkin and beaded Indian pants tucked into high leather boots, appeared at the door of the manor house and demanded to see Guy.

When Guy appeared, he said, without preamble, "Tomorrow afternoon, four o'clock, at Indian Pass. Boustique will meet you for an alligator pull."

"What is that?"

"Ask an Indian. Be there."

With that, the bearded giant, whose name was Loup, turned, swung himself up on his horse with amazing lightness for such a heavy man, and rode off.

"Alligator pull? That is what he proposes?" Tricot said when Guy asked him about it. "Well, suh, that does not fit us very well. It is an old Indian duel, tug-of-war over a pit with an alligator in it—or several alligators."

"What are you saying, we are on opposite sides of a pit, trying to pull each other into the pit to give the alligator a good dinner?"

"Yes, suh, the rope is tied around your waist so you cannot let go.

One man is certain to be fed to the alligator. Not so good for you because Boustique is shorter than you, which means closer to the ground, and he weighs more."

"That means we have to be smarter and quicker. What kind of terrain will it be?"

"Probably dirt, perhaps muddy."

"Then we need good footing. And we need practice. Get a stout rope and get a pit dug. Then you and I will rehearse the tug-of-war. It is important that Madame Boustique and the boy hear nothing of this or they might go back to him for my sake. But before you do anything, I want you to go to the blacksmith with my hunting boots."

"But suh, your boots should go to the shoemaker."

"No, what I want is the work of a blacksmith."

When Guy and Tricot arrived at Indian Pass the following day, Boustique and five of his cohorts were already there, smoking, passing a bottle around, enjoying themselves. The first thing Guy checked was the condition of the ground—a muddy, slippery surface. Then Guy walked over to the pit which was eight feet deep, eight feet wide, and twenty feet long. There was shallow water in the pit and an immense alligator, his head resting on the surface of the water. Alongside the pit was a coil of one-inch hemp rope. Boustique got to his feet and walked to the pit opposite Guy. The bearded Loup came forward, carrying two grappling hooks.

"All right, here is how it is. We each start eight paces from the pit, the rope tied around our waists—we tie your rope, your second ties ours. Each second has one of these hooks to use if his man gets pulled into the pit. Dr. Levallière is here if needed for an emergency. The alligator has not been fed for three days. Good luck."

Guy sat down on a tree stump and changed his boots to the pair the blacksmith had prepared for the occasion. He took off his jacket and his waistcoat and donned a pair of thick, pliable leather gloves. Tricot tested his grappling hook. Loup uncoiled the rope, tossing it across the mouth of the pit. He wound it once around Guy's waist and securely knotted it. Tricot did the same with Boustique. Loup then measured eight paces on each side of the pit, drawing a line on the ground with the side of his boot. Guy and Boustique took their places as their seconds stationed themselves with their grappling hooks on their respective sides of the pit, ready to snare their man the moment he might be pulled into it, snatching him to the surface before the alligator could trap him in its jaws. Guy wound a loop of rope around each of his gloved hands, his left hand farther down the rope than his right. As Boustique gripped his end of the rope, it stretched taut between them.

Dr. Levallière said, "Gentlemen, I shall be the starter. I will count three and go. Are you ready? All right, then: one—two—three—go!"

Both men immediately strained against the rope, trying to get an early advantage, but neither gave an inch. It was apparent that they were evenly matched and that ground could only be slowly gained by steady, relentless force. Boustique now had both heels of his boots dug into the muddy surface; this kept him from slipping, but to move he would have to raise his feet, and in that instant he would become vulnerable. Guy had his feet solidly planted, but he was not back on his heels, which made him slightly more mobile.

For five minutes it was a standoff, each man slanting backward, arms bent, the rope looped around his hands. Boustique did not wear gloves. As the severe strain began to tell on them, both men began to emit guttural sounds; veins in their necks became distended; sweat broke out on their faces and arms. For eight minutes, neither man budged, but then, imperceptibly at first, Boustique's boots began to slide forward, just a fraction of an inch, but Guy picked up on it for he had kept his eyes on them. Now he could feel the movement in the rope as he took a short step backward, his feet firm in the muddy surface, his arms and legs straining to increase the pull on Boustique, urging himself to tug harder, harder, keep Boustique's boots sliding forward, not let him set himself.

Watch his heels, he told himself. *If he tries to move a heel to brace himself, pull harder, keep him off balance, watch the heels, do not let him dig in. He is slipping, I can feel the rope giving, more leg, I need more leg, bend more, put your back to it! My arms are getting tired. I must keep them bent but they are straightening, he is so damn strong. God, my arms are going—if they straighten out I might lose my grip on the rope, I have got to hold on and keep him slipping, slipping, slipping, until I get him close to the pit, then just as we practiced it, one—two, he will be in the pit. But my arms hurt at the elbow, the pain in my shoulders, he is damn strong, did I give on the rope there? No, I will not give in! Come on, legs, save me, keep on pulling him, there! Good! He slid again, and again, pull in the slack, he is sliding forward now, pull back, dig in your boots, pull, pull, pull. . . .*

"No, God damn, no!" Boustique shouted as his boots slid on the slippery surface. Then, with a mighty heave, he checked his slide and pulled Guy's progress to a halt. Feeling the impetus swing toward him, Boustique, relying on the strength of his upper body, began to move Guy, straightening his arms, intensifying his exertion.

The pendulum of attack swung back and forth; Guy losing ground, then regaining it; Boustique starting to slide forward, then savagely exerting his powerful arms to stem the slippage. Another exchange, and then both men began to tire, their legs cramping, their arms numb, pain across their foreheads, their backs cracking under the strain, and yet neither gaining the upper hand.

Guy was praying for a second wind, a sudden rejuvenation that would override his weakening and give him the burst of power necessary to pull Boustique into the pit. *Two feet, if I can move him two feet, I will use the one-two, now I will do it, now when he thinks I am finished, now when he least expects it, all I have left, plant my legs, a sudden fierce pull. Now!*

Summoning up what remaining strength he had left, Guy moved the tiring Boustique forward, the slipping boots giving ground. *Now, now is the time for it. One!* Suddenly he let the rope go completely slack as Boustique reeled backward, losing his grasp, *Two! Jerk the rope forward, run with it, before he can grasp it. Pull, run, dig in hard, pull, pull, pull . . .*

Boustique hurtled forward, grabbing at the rope, but it was too late. As he was propelled into the pit, both Loup and Tricot simultaneously hooked him with their grappling poles, pulling furiously to try to keep him from the alligator's lightning-quick jaws, up, up, the body clear of the water, clear of the thrashing alligator, all but Boustique's right arm. As his body swung clear, his right arm hung down, not clear. The hungry jaws snapped with a sickening sound, slicing the hand off at the wrist as cleanly as a knife cutting bread, the spurting blood staining the slimy water. But as Loup's grappling hook pulled Boustique away from the pit, a curl of the rope, now slack, wound around Loup's leg. Boustique's counterweight precipitously jerked him over the edge of the pit. The voracious alligator immediately attacked and clamped him in its jaws, dragging him beneath the roiling water, there to devour him.

Dr. Levallière ran to assist Boustique, opening his medical bag as he ran, quickly removing a tourniquet and winding it around Boustique's arm below the elbow, twisting it, tighter and tighter until the compressed blood vessels cut off the supply to the wrist and the torrent of blood gradually abated. The men rushed Boustique into a carriage and drove him at high speed toward Royal Hospital.

Guy sat down heavily on the tree stump, his tunic drenched with sweat. He took off his boots, the ones the blacksmith had put the iron spikes in, and put on his dress boots. He did not feel victorious. He did not feel that virtue had been served. He just felt bone-tired.

In the reddened muddy water of the pit, there was no sign of Loup, not even a vestige of his clothing.

Without informing his mother or Guy, Rémi left school early and went to see Boustique at Royal Hospital where he was in the general ward. When Rémi appeared at Boustique's bed, they looked at each other for a minute or two without speaking. Boustique had a heavy padded bandage wrapped around the stump of his right wrist which was elevated in a sling.

"I want you to know I am sorry this happened to you," Rémi said, finally. "I came to tell you that I forgive you for the terrible things you did to my mother and me. I hope you heal all right. I am glad we are not together anymore, but I am not glad this bad thing happened to you."

"I blame your mother for this—if she had not run away. . ."

"Do not blame us, Monsieur Boustique. What happened was God's will."

"What? That an alligator ate my hand? God's will?"

"It is your right hand, is it not? The one you struck us with."

"Nonsense! If you had not run away . . ."

"I came here to try to make peace with you, to forgive you, to ask you to now let us live our lives as we wish to. I am sorry that God punished you, but maybe now everything will be all right."

"You'd better go now."

"I just wanted you to know how I felt."

"So now I know."

"Have you no compassion in your heart?"

"Tell your mother I will not bother her again."

"All right."

"Or you."

"Thank you."

"Is that enough compassion?"

Seventeen

M<small>ARIE</small>-T<small>HÉRÈSE</small> B<small>OUSTIQUE</small> was an unadorned woman who wore simple clothes, neither rouge nor powder, her chestnut, auburn-flecked hair unfashionably pulled tautly along her temples and piled into a bird's nest. She was petite, a little over five feet, but her body, disguised by the loose-fitting clothes she wore, was full-breasted and curvacious. On her left cheek, just above her upper lip, was a small birthmark that gave the illusion she was wearing one of the beauty patches so favored by the high-styled ladies of New Orleans. Her hands were extraordinarily beautiful. She carried herself with a graceful dignity, but she did not affect any of the modish gaits and slouches in vogue. She spoke in a susurrant voice; her smile illuminated her face.

When she heard about the duel between Guy and her husband, she was both appalled and guilt-stricken, but Guy was able to persuade her that she had no accountability for the tragic event which Boustique had brought on himself.

"What I hope," Guy had said, "is that you and Rémi do not attach some savior role to what I did. I want to be your friend, not your benefactor. Most of all, I do not want gratitude. What we do for each other is rewarding to each of us in different ways.

She took one of his hands in hers, turned it palm up to expose the row of raw blisters where the rope had burned through Guy's gloves. "And this is your reward?"

"Yes. After the blisters heal, my hands will be that much tougher."

Marie-Thérèse had been called Thérèse by her first husband, a name which Rémi, as a little boy, had pronounced "Trace," and that continued to be his name for her instead of "mama." At first, Guy had addressed her as Madame Boustique, and she called him Monsieur Laroule, but after a week Guy suggested that they drop the formalities; from then on, he called her Marie.

Guy was just as direct about their staying in his house. "I realize you feel awkward remaining here as guests, but let us be practical. You and Rémi have nowhere to go, although probably the Ursulines would take you in again. But, as we both know, that is not a proper place to raise your son. You have no funds nor any prospect of any. Certainly Boustique will not provide for you or the boy. I, on the other hand, have this big house, all these unoccupied rooms. I have no one to supervise the kitchen, the laundry room, the gardens—you could be very helpful."

"And what about your accounts and ledgers?"

"I have an office here . . ."

"What I mean is, who maintains them?"

"Well, I do, as best I can."

"I ask because I am organized and good at managing. I can certainly oversee these domestic things you indicate, but I am also good with sums and accounts. When I worked for Sister Xavier, I did all her bookkeeping for her pharmaceuticals."

"Good! I am abysmal at all that, and I will gladly turn it over to you. So now, you see, you are no longer a guest, but a participant."

"And Rémi can do chores. He is quite strong, and he feels at home here."

For the first time in his life Guy felt that he had a real home. No longer did he eat alone or spend his evenings alone, or go to concerts and plays by himself. Under Marie-Thérèse's direction, the cooks prepared more varied and much-improved cuisine; the neglected gardens were restored to the bloom they had when Franchmastabbia was alive; and the house was decorated with the drapes, curtains, bedspreads, and other furnishings that Guy had not as yet procured.

For someone who had never been around children, Guy was surprised to discover how much he enjoyed his relationship with Rémi. Guy even liked to discuss homework with Rémi, especially when it related to the writing of essays. He taught Rémi basic swordsmanship, took him hunting, practiced shooting at targets with bow and arrow. When he went to New Orleans, Guy occasionally brought back a small present for the boy, a pocketknife, a spinning top. As for Rémi, Guy brought back memories of the father Lieutenant Riveau had been. No longer did Rémi dread going home to the cruel house of Henri Boustique, oppressed by the rules imposed upon him and by Boustique's badgering. Nor did he have to suffer the indignities Boustique heaped upon his mother. When Guy and Marie-Thérèse were together at the dinner table, or going over the books, or walking in the garden, Rémi hopefully tried to detect signs of familiarity between them; but unfortunately they were very proper with one another, even when Guy invited Marie-Thérèse to accompany him to the opera or to a rare social event. On those occasions Rémi would force himself to stay awake until they came home, hoping for a show of affection, but invariably they would simply bid each other good-night, his mother thanking Guy for a delightful evening, and then, as Rémi observed by peeking through the doorcrack, they would each go to their respective bedrooms without so much as a touch of their hands.

One afternoon when Rémi came home with a little present for his mother, Guy discovered the remarkable coincidence that it was her birthday as well as his own on that day; he was even more astonished to learn that they were the same age as well. They celebrated with a festive dinner and a bottle of champagne; in wishing each other a happy birthday, they politely kissed each other's cheeks, but there was not the slightest sign of affection Rémi desperately wanted to see.

But it was happening. Imperceptibly. When Guy invited Marie-Thérèse to accompany him to the governor's command ball in honor of the anniversary of Louis XV's coronation, she said that regrettably she would have to decline for she did not have an appropriate gown. During her marriage to Boustique, he was opposed to "putting on airs with fancy dresses and rouge."

"Then we will have to come to an understanding," Guy said. "What you do here merits compensation. I have been meaning to discuss this with you. Not only have you personal needs, but there are also Rémi's needs to consider."

"A salary? I would not think of it. You provide us food and lodging and . . . more than that . . . a *home*. That is more compensation than I can ever earn."

"All right, then. Let me explain from my point of view. Going to a ball or a concert is not something I like to do by myself. It is as much for my sake as for yours that I invite you."

The following Wednesday, when Guy went into New Orleans for his weekly dinner with Monsieur Grotesquieu, he also went to the finest couturier in the city, a woman who had once had a fashionable boutique in Paris. Unbeknownst to Marie-Thérèse, Guy had brought along one of her dresses to provide measurements for the couturier who also provided a wig, shoes, and a gold necklace with a garnet pendant. On the night of the governor's ball, when Marie-Thérèse came down the stairs to meet Guy in their living room, she was beautiful in a way Guy had never witnessed before. All of the Versailles beauties he had known, including Madame Pompadour and also the recent comtesse, were artfully painted and groomed with their beauty enhanced by skillful practitioners, whereas Marie-Thérèse was naturally beautiful, without enhancements. The gown, fortunately, suited her, highlighting the lines of her body; the white wig modest but attractive, the garnet lying precisely in the cup of her throat. She had applied cosmetics sparingly, just enough to enhance her delicate features, a slight dusting of rouge beneath her cheekbones, her eyelids subtly accentuated, a subdued ruby sheen on her lips. Guy had not realized until that moment how truly attractive she was.

She smiled at him and said, "You have made me feel beautiful."

"And you are."

"No, I am not, but for the first time in years, I can enjoy the illusion."

When they returned from the ball that evening, there was a moment of hesitation when they were saying good-night, when they both looked deep into each other's eyes, moving closer together, but they were interrupted by Tricot, who brought dread news:

"The slaves—four of them—have come down with the black vomit. We have taken them from the others, but it is very contagious."

"What is the 'black vomit?' " Guy asked.

"Yellow fever," Marie-Thérèse replied.

"Yes, suh, the mosquitos carry it. It is very deadly."

"I suggest you move all the slaves out of their quarters," Marie-Thérèse said to Guy, "and let them sleep outside on the ground, if need be. All cooking should be out-of-doors over wood fires. If it catches on, yellow fever can wipe them all out. Keep them out of this house. I will do the cooking and cleaning. We cannot take the risk."

"I have already taken precautions, suh. We have distributed a clove of garlic and balls of camphor for every slave to keep on his person. Tar is being burned in and around the cabins. All the slaves and all the cabins are being sprayed with hartshorn and vinegar. They are the best medical treatments. We will spray the slaves every day from now on."

After he had gone, Marie-Thérèse said, "Can you imagine that New Orleans doctors prescribe such pathetic remedies? All superstitious nonsense. You may as well tell them to avoid black cats. All the more reason not to consult a New Orleans doctor when you are sick. Believe me, Guy, there is no remedy except to pray. There was an outbreak of the black vomit three or four years ago. I lost the only good friends I had here—two wonderful women—terrible deaths. If you contact yellow fever, God is the only physician who can cure you."

Eighteen

THE PLANTATION PROSPERED. In addition to the indigo crop, Guy had been persuaded to plant wax trees and sugar cane in a far section of the property that the slaves had cleared of trees and undergrowth. The cane was relatively simple to plant, but complicated to harvest and process. To begin with, the cane stalks were laid six inches deep in shallow trenches. Sprouts pushed up from the eyes and the joints of the cane which was cultivated in rows, the same as other crops. When harvested, the cane would be taken to the mill where three iron-sheathed cylinders, two of them set against the third, were turned by circling mules. The canes, tied in small bundles for greater compression, were given a double squeezing while passing through the mill. The extracted juice trickled down a trough into the boiling house while the flattened stalks, called *bagasses,* were taken to sheds to dry for later use as fuel under the coppers and stills.

Guy also planted candleberry trees to produce wax for candles. The twigs of the trees were cut into small pieces and put into a vat with a framework at the bottom which allowed the *lessive* poured over them to drain through. After a couple of hours, the fatty part of the twig gradually separated and fell to the bottom of the vat, producing a sediment which, when cool, became a loaf of greenish wax of fairly firm consistency from which the candles were made.

Preoccupied with his three crops, Guy paid little or no attention to events occurring beyond the confines of the plantation. The French and Indian War raged in the north as the French desperately tried to defend their territory in the Ohio Valley in order to preserve an essential link between their colonies on the St. Lawrence and those on the Mississippi. During this conflict, the French Government virtually abandoned New Orleans, giving it little or no money, or military to protect it. To guard the city against violent raids by bloodthirsty Chickasaws intent on scalps and booty, the governor built a four-foot high fence around the entire city. It was also a means of stemming the tide of runaway slaves. The governor had invited Guy to attend an emergency council meeting to deal with the crisis caused by the war, but Guy, concentrating on his plantation's activities, politely declined the invitation.

At first it was believed that Rémi had come down with a cold that worsened over the course of several days. His face was flushed, his eyes teary, his nose congested, his lips scarlet, and he was running a temperature. Marie-Thérèse kept him in bed and applied poultices to his sore throat, but when Rémi began to vomit as his fever mounted, Guy set off to fetch Dr. Voigord.

By the time Guy went to New Orleans and returned with Dr. Voigord, Rémi's condition had undergone a precipitous change. His fever had disappeared, in fact dropped considerably below normal, his skin had become cold to the touch and had acquired a lemon-yellow tint. Dr. Voigord examined Rémi quickly and shook his head. "My dear people, I have the burden of informing you that your son has yellow fever."

Marie-Thérèse gasped, her hand flying up to her mouth. "Oh, my God. Are you sure, Doctor? He does not have black vomit . . . when my friends had it . . ."

"Yes, yes, I am very sure. His vomit will blacken as blood seeps into it."

"But you say yellow fever," Guy said, in a constricted, fearful voice, "but he has no fever. His skin is cold."

"Precisely. It is the second and dangerous stage of the disease. Here, feel his pulse—it is very slow and feeble."

"Is there medicine . . ."

"Yes, I will give you some purification powders, but to be honest, they have little effect. It is a dread disease, very contagious. You should both be careful. Cover your faces. The *vomito negro* mosquitoes are brought to port by the ships from the West Indies, and it is their sting that causes the trouble. Rémi must drink plenty of liquids to replace what he vomits, or he will dehydrate. That is one way the disease kills. Also try to keep his nasal ducts and throat free of phlegm and clear his eyes every few hours. Someone should be with him at all times. The next three or four days are critical. I will return if you like, but there is little I can do. Such a fine lad."

Guy escorted him to his carriage. "Doctor, I want to know—is it possible to recover from this?"

"Yes, it does happen."

"How often?"

"Perhaps . . . oh . . . I would say, one out of ten."

Guy and Marie-Thérèse took turns keeping vigil at Rémi's bedside. Every four hours throughout the day and night, they spelled each other, each time bringing fresh pitchers of water, but Rémi was so inert it was difficult to induce him to drink. It seemed that all life had gone out of his cold body, his breathing was shallow and irregular, his eyes closed against the opaque liquid that seeped from his lids.

On the third night of their vigil, Rémi's condition took a sudden, frightening turn. His temperature climbed rapidly, and he began to perspire. Marie-Thérèse pressed her fingers against the side of his throat where his racing pulse thumped heavily against her fingers. Rémi began to thrash about, calling out indecipherable phrases, a jumble of guttural sounds and words, pulling at his throat, not responding to his mother's questions, uncontrollably delirious. Marie-Thérèse ran down the hall to Guy's room and burst in on him without knocking. He had been asleep but awoke when he heard her running steps in the hall.

By the time they reached his room, Rémi was in full delirium, screaming incomprehensible invectives, his arms flailing at some unseen menace, his face scarlet and sweating.

"Help him, oh, please, Guy, help him," Marie-Thérèse implored.

Guy got into bed with Rémi and wrapped his arms firmly around the boy, pinning his flailing arms against his body and restraining him from moving. Remi struggled furiously to free himself, his eyes wide open in terror, his tongue fiery red, Guy straining to keep the boy, imbued with the strength of his delirium, from breaking his hold on him. Marie-Thérèse, haunted by the deaths of her two friends, helplessly watched the frenzied struggle, softly murmuring, "Do not hurt him, oh, do not hurt him."

Rémi tried to bite Guy's restraining arms, but Guy constantly maneuvered to keep his arms away from Rémi's mouth, all the while speaking soothingly to him, trying to pacify him, trying to penetrate his fevered brain to touch some chord that would counter his hallucinations. But the struggle continued, the boy fighting his demons, Guy maintaining his grip on his burning body while trying somehow to coax him out of his delirious state. Although Guy knew nothing about the disease, he instinctively felt that Rémi might recover if he passed this crisis. But the boy's resistance, his insistent strength, was challenging. Two hours, then three, the struggle continued unabated. But in the fourth hour, Rémi's angry cries began to taper off; he struggled less against Guy's grip and the fire of his skin began to cool off. Gradually, Rémi's resistance receded, and finally his body went limp; his eyelids closed over his frightened eyes as the storm of the delirium spent itself. Guy released the boy from his aching arms. He felt Rémi's pulse, which had quieted down, and nodded to Marie-Thérèse who came to the bed and also felt her son's pulse to reassure herself. She stroked Rémi's forehead, pushing back his damp hair. As she did, Rémi opened his eyes. He saw his mother's face leaning over him and Guy's face beside him. "I feel . . . I am . . ." he managed to say, then, totally exhausted, he fell into a deep sleep.

Quietly, Guy got up and covered the sleeping boy. For several minutes he stood side by side with Marie-Thérèse, watching Rémi, both of them slowly permitting themselves the hope that he was out of danger. The realization that her son had possibly overcome a death she had been preparing herself to face, released Marie-Thérèse's restrained emotions and finally overwhelmed her. Guy put his arm around her as she wept and buried her face against the warmth of his chest.

The boy continued to sleep peacefully. It was finally safe to leave him. Guy and Marie-Thérèse left the room and softly closed the door. They walked down the hall to Guy's room and wordlessly entered his bed. When their bodies touched there was the illusion that they had been long lost lovers at last reunited. Marie-Thérèse had never surrendered so much of herself to a man. She kept no reserve. Nothing for herself.

And Guy knew, from the moment he entered her body, that he was on a voyage from which he would never return.

Nineteen

IN THE SPRING, Guy was out in the field, busy with the indigo harvest, when Marie-Thérèse came to tell him that several men had come to see him, one of them having identified himself as Sheriff Claude Lèche. Guy was hard pressed to complete this harvest, having lost half of his slaves to the yellow fever epidemic that had swept through the cabins. On arriving at the manor house, Guy was perplexed to see that one of the men waiting for him was Bernard Duroux. Why would Duroux make a complaint so long a time after their duel? And, besides, he had only pinked Duroux with his sword, certainly not a serious offense.

"Monsieur Laroule," the sheriff intoned, "I am here to inform you of a document that Monsieur Duroux here has just brought back from Versailles, signed by His Majesty, Louis XV." The sheriff unfurled the paper he had been holding in his hand and proceeded to read from it: "Royal Proclamation. May all men know, that a Royal Charter granted to Guy Laroule conferring title to a tract of land in New Orleans known as Diderot Plantation is hereby revoked and shall henceforth be considered null and void and without purpose. Be it also known, that on this day I hereby confer all right, title, and interest to said Diderot Plantation on Bernard Duroux of New Orleans, with the understanding that a tithe of his income from the operation of the plantation shall henceforth be forwarded to the Crown. By Royal Edict, His Majesty, Louis XV."

For a moment, Guy was too stunned to react. "That cannot be," he said.

"I assure you, monsieur, this document is official," the sheriff replied.

"But . . . but I have built this house, the slave quarters, all this planting. There was nothing here, the land had been ravaged."

"The law is," the sheriff said, "that title acquires all buildings affixed to the land. You may remove the slaves but not the buildings. All livestock, carriages, furnishings, clothes, and supplies are removable."

"But I have crops . . . I would like time to go to France and . . ."

"That is not possible, monsieur. The law is that the plantation must be vacated within thirty days."

"But how could I possibly get to Versailles in thirty days? There must be a way to delay . . ."

"I assure you, monsieur, there is not."

"The work and money I have put in here . . . I cannot believe . . . I shall consult an attorney."

"Whatever you wish, monsieur, but if the premises are not vacated within thirty days, I shall have to evict you."

Duroux was thoroughly enjoying his moment of triumph. "You drew first blood," he said to Guy, "but I draw last blood."

After reading the proclamation for himself, Guy's first reaction was one of anger. He had invested most of his funds in the plantation, which was finally beginning to produce income, and he was damned if he would let them strip him of everything that was rightfully his. The thought of surrendering the manor house, on which he had squandered so much attention and which he loved, yes *loved*, the first really meaningful possession he had ever had, of handing it over to that miserable Duroux, that smirking, repulsive man, whose sadistic torture had killed the slave Guy had tried to save.

And, now, when I have finally found a woman I love, a boy who is a son to me, a feeling that I have created something here that is truly the life I was meant to live, how can I let them end it when it has just barely begun? But how can I stop them in the face of that piece of paper signed by the King? Proclamation. What a deadly word. How could Madame de Pompadour let this happen? But, then, she may not have known of it. If I could get word to her I am sure she would come to my rescue. Even if it comes later, an amended proclamation, what a pleasure it would be to throw Duroux off my land.

But in the meantime . . . the meantime . . . His anger subsided and was replaced by a feeling of hopelessness, the way he felt the day he arrived in New Orleans. *Where shall I go now? What do I say to Marie-Thérèse and to Rémi? This has become their home and it is cruel that they have to leave it so soon, especially for the boy who has been without a true home most of his life. I am so fond of him. And Marie—I am so accustomed to her body beside mine every night, sweetly, lovingly beside mine, her soft whispers confiding to my ear, and her lovely cheerful face at breakfast. Her wise counsel. Her expertise at our finances. Yes, our finances. They are my family and it is ours now, not mine. I do not take her love for granted, and yet I have come to expect it, to need it. I have had many women in my life, but I have never been loved, not loved in this way by a woman who cares about how I feel, how I think, and how I can bring more happiness in my life. I am suffused with happiness. And the boy, too, genuinely likes me, as I like him; in fact, come on, say it, I love him.*

After the night we struggled and he fought his way out of death's grip and I held him and felt him making his good fight, screaming at death, flailing at death, willing himself to live, the resolute courage of this lad, is it any wonder I have come to love him? The way he is with me, inquisitive, respectful, playful, dependent, so happy that his mother and I are together, that we are all together.

I will spare her the bad news as long as I can, she has had enough. I shall first see if there is some way that I can postpone or prevent this eviction. I am certainly not going to take a sheriff's word for it—a sheriff who was probably bribed by that bastard Duroux.

Guy did not mention his predicament to Marie-Thérèse. Instead, he went to see Grotesquieu at his office. After Guy gave him the proclamation to read, Grotesquieu immediately closed the door to his office and told his secretary not to disturb him.

"The way I see it," Guy told him, "my only hope is to delay the forfeiture and try to get word to Madame de Pompadour. This was probably done behind her back, arranged by that snake, Richelieu. I have put most of my fortune in the Diderot Plantation, and I must do everything I can to save it."

For the only time since Guy knew him, Grotesquieu was at a loss for words, so painful was it for him to tell Guy what now he must hear. He took off his pince-nez, polished them, then slowly filled his pipe and took his time lighting it. "I take it you have not been following events at Versailles?" he said finally.

"Versailles? No, I have been preoccupied with events at the plantation. Of what events do you speak?"

"It is no wonder you have not heard. I hear that Monsieur Tinerais, who prints the broad bills, is going to start a newspaper next year. It is difficult to be au courant without a newspaper."

"Do not keep me in suspense, André—what is it about Versailles?"

"I think it best that I read to you a letter that I have received from my old friend, Comte Dufort de Cheverny, for whom I once designed a château in Normandie when I lived in France."

"I know the Comte—he had an apartment at Versailles."

"Precisely. A confidant of the King. He writes: 'The tragic news at the palace is that Madame de Pompadour has died . . .'"

"Oh, no! Died? She was a young woman . . ."

Grotesquieu resumed reading. " '. . . died by piece work, if one may so express it. Her whole system was disordered since she abandoned her milk diet. To please Louis XV, she had resumed eating normal foods. She grew thin, she coughed, she had terrible palpitations during which her heart seemed to jump. She wept and groaned, 'My life is a fight.' She colored her cheeks, masked her thinness (for she had fallen away to a skeleton), covered her wrinkles with powder. Her whole system was failing, and the change of life came to put her at the mercy of the slightest trouble. She did not know whom to trust; she dismissed her doctor, Quesnay, and gave herself over to the quacks. On the 28th of February, she had a hemorrhage of the lung which she survived, and a Mass of thanksgiving was celebrated. But on the 7th of April, 1764, she collapsed at Choisy and by order of the King was transported to Versailles, although, according to inviolate tradition, only a member of the royal family is permitted to die in a royal palace. For the last few days of her life, the King hardly left her room. She could not breathe lying down, and sat in a chair, wearing a dressing gown over a white taffeta petticoat; she had a touch of rouge on her cheeks and always smiled at everybody. Not one word of complaint passed her lips. When the doctor said she was dying, she asked the King if she ought to confess; she was not very anxious to do so, as it meant that she would not be able to see him again. However, he said that she must. He bade her a last farewell, and went upstairs to his own room. A priest came. She said to those of us in the room, 'It is coming now, my friends; I think you had better leave me to my soul, my women, and the priest.' She told her women not to change her clothes as it tired her and was no longer worthwhile. The priest made a movement as if to leave the room; she said: 'One moment, Monsieur le Curé, we will go together,' whereupon she died.

" 'The King ordered all the funeral arrangements. It was six o'clock on a winter evening in a veritable hurricane. The will of the Marquise contained a request that she be buried in the Church of the Capucines, Place Vendôme, where she had prepared a magnificent mausoleum. The King took the arm of Champlost, his principal valet, and, when he reached the door of his room, made him close it behind him as they sat outside on the balcony. He maintained a religious silence as the procession passed along the avenue. Despite the bad weather and the bitter air, of which he seemed insensible, he followed it with his eyes till the last bit of the funeral cortège vanished from sight. Then I entered the room. Two great tears rolled down his cheeks and he said these few words to me: "That is the only respect I am able to pay her. The Marquise will not have fine weather for her journey." ' "

Grotesquieu put the letter back in his desk drawer. Guy sat motionless, his head bowed, aggrieved. She was frail, yes, but too young for death.

"I regret having to bear such intolerable news," Monsieur Grotesquieu said.

"She was a lovely woman. Too ambitious, perhaps . . . profligate . . . but wonderfully creative . . . and . . . good to me."

"But alas, gone to eternity. Without Pompadour to protect you, you see, Duroux was able to deal for your plantation. I hear there is a new *maîtresse en titre*, named Madame du Barry, a hard woman eager for wealth. I would say your only hope of a postponement lies with the Governor, who likes you. Throw yourself on his mercy. Who knows? Politics and weather are two things no one can really predict. But let me just say, Guy, that if a month passes and you do not succeed in gaining a postponement, I have an unoccupied house on my grounds, quite a nice house, and you are welcome to stay there."

*   *   *

Guy boldly presented himself at Governor's Mansion without first arranging an appointment as protocol required. After a short wait, the governor's equerry returned to announce that the governor would see him forthwith. In his note, Guy had explained that he was requesting this impromptu audience due to an emergency.

The young officer led him into the study, where the governor, a tall, thin man, plainly dressed, with the air of a public functionary, awaited him.

"Come in, Laroule, come in," the governor said heartily. "You come at a propitious moment. May I present Louis Billouart, Chevalier de Kérélac, who has just arrived to succeed me as Governor. I am on my way to be the new Governor of Canada. Do you like the theater, Kérélac?"

"Yes, indeed I do." He had a high-pitched, nasal voice.

"Ah, good. Laroule is a first-class actor and singer. Perhaps you will sing at the Governor's inauguration party, Laroule? What do you say?"

"I would be delighted."

"I shall be contacting you," Kérélac said.

"What was it you wanted to see me about?" Vaudreuil inquired. "I am hard pressed to be ready for the ship's departure tomorrow, but if it is something brief . . ."

"Well, thank you, Your Honor, but I did not know of your departure. I will not trouble you."

"Fine. I appreciate your consideration, Laroule. I bid you farewell," he extended his hand, "and wish you every success with your plantation."

"Thank you, Governor," Laroule said, shaking his hand, his face grim. "May you have a good journey."

Twenty

IT WAS AFTER MASS the following Sunday that Guy told Marie-Thérèse about the eviction. They were in a small chapel where they had gone to light a candle in front of a shrine to the Virgin Mary. They were seated now, facing the shrine and the banks of burning candles.

"Realistically, I do not believe that I can do anything in one brief month to prevent our eviction," Guy said. "It is a cruel turn for you and Rémi, you have suffered more than enough. I thought you would be secure in our life at Diderot, but now I bring you a future no more certain than your past."

"You bring us a future with you, Guy. That is all the future we need. Where we live, how we live, matters not."

"We can move to the house Grotesquieu offered, but I will no longer have an income nor even a thought of what enterprise I can substitute. I can move all the plows, the mules, the farm equipment, but I no longer have the means to purchase a plantation, even if one were available. And now that Vaudreuil is departing, I do not have access to whatever concessions I might have induced from him. Bleak is the word, Marie, bleak."

She reached over and took his hand. "Do not worry, Guy, we are going to have a fine life."

Guy smiled at her, lovingly. "And just how can you be so sure?"

"I went to see Madame Renée last week . . ."

"Ah, yes, the fortune-teller you told me about."

"I do not like the word 'fortune-teller.' It rings of quackery and foolery. She is a serious prognosticator. Two weeks before you came into our lives, when I was in the depth of despair, Madame Renée told me that you were about to appear."

"I? She identified me? By name?"

" 'Here in the tea leaves,' she said, and she showed me the configuration, 'is a man of noble birth, tall, agreeable to the eye, a man of means and principle, who will come forcefully into your life and drive your husband away.' She stirred the tea leaves some more and said, 'I am sorry to tell you, I see your husband in blood, probably dead.' "

"Then you were expecting me?"

"Yes, as I now expect us to have a fine life."

"Because Madame Renée told you so?"

"No, because I love you and Rémi loves you, and that is as fine as life can be."

"Marie, I was going to wait a bit longer, but here with the Virgin Mary as our witness, I ask you to marry me. I have found out one can get a divorce in Natchez. I do not need a fortune-teller to tell us that we are, indeed, going to have a fine life together."

Marie's grip on his hand intensified. "Guy, I love you in every way a woman can love a man. I love the way you look, the way you talk, the way you are with Rémi, the way you think, your fearlessness, your bravery, call it what you will, the way you make love to me, but, alas, I cannot marry you."

"Why? Why not?"

Marie nodded toward the statue of the Virgin. "Because of her."

"I do not understand."

"I am a devout Catholic, Guy, and I would never go against the Scriptures. As long as Boustique lives, my marriage to him cannot be dissolved. We were married in the Church, before God, and my covenant is with God."

"But what Boustique has done to you and the boy—does God approve?"

"If I were to divorce and marry you, we would not be married in the eyes of God. And by divorcing I would have sinned."

"And by living with me now, do you not sin?"

"No, in so doing, I do not break a covenant with God. I will live with you happily, forevermore, but I cannot marry you."

"And how will you be named? Madame Laroule, or Madame Boustique, or perhaps revert to Madame Riveau?"

"No, I am Madame Boustique, and that is how it will be."

"Then everyone will know that we are not man and wife. What will they think of you?"

"Guy, my darling, I long ago gave up caring what other people think. They care about such things much less than you think—those with scruples may eventually be won over, or, if not, they are the kind of people we do not care about. When I first began to keep the plantation's books and had to deal with purveyors who shorted us or overcharged us, they were appalled that a woman was broaching such things with them. 'Let us speak to Monsieur Laroule about it,' they said. 'No,' I replied, 'you have me to deal with.' And they did. Grudgingly, at first, but eventually I was treated equally. That is how it is, Guy. We live our lives as best we can, and people accept us or they don't. Do you not agree?"

"Yes, of course. As a Catholic myself, I know that you are right. But I would like to have children with you. What about that? Will you have no children with me?"

"I will . . . I am . . ."

A puzzled look crossed Guy's face. "What did you say?"

She put her face close to his and smiled. "I am."

"Our child?"

"Yes."

He eased her forward and they both knelt before the Virgin, their hands clasped; they bowed their heads and silently prayed for the child and their new life, whatever it might be.

"Marie, may I marry you now? A marriage arranged between the two of us? Our own personal vows, with the Mother of God as our witness?"

"Yes, Guy. Let us marry."

"I, Guy Laroule, do pledge to you, Holy Mother, that I take Marie-Thérèse as my wife, to love and to cherish, and to protect, as long as I live."

"And, Holy Mother, I, Marie-Thérèse, do take this man, Guy, as my husband, to love and cherish as long as I live. And, Holy Mother, in the name of love, please forgive us our transgressions."

The house on Monsieur Grotesquieu's property was too small to accommodate all the furniture from Diderot Plantation but it was comfortable, and there was a small adjoining cabin for Tricot. Guy gave his slaves and livestock to Grotesquieu, who stored Guy's farming equipment in an unused ramshackle barn situated in a remote corner of his property.

Weeks passed as Guy tried fruitlessly to solve his predicament. With Grotesquieu's assistance, he canvassed properties that could be acquired but they were either too expensive or the soil had been worked out. He had discussions with the owner of a sugar plantation, Etienne de Boré, who had discovered a method for boiling sugar cane syrup to make it granulate. But Monsieur de Boré had extravagant expectations for the future of his granulation discovery, and the investment he required to become his partner was far beyond the diminished capital that Guy possessed.

On another occasion, Guy asked for and was granted an appointment with the new governor, Kérélac, the purpose being to determine if there was some government function that Guy could perform.

"Perhaps there may be in the future," the governor had said, "but for the time being, to ensure a smooth transition, I shall retain all of Governor Vaudreuil's people for this year. But I shall certainly keep you in mind."

One night, as Marie-Thérèse and Guy lay languidly in their bed after having made love, she said, "Darling, I know you are not enamored of Madame Renée, but would you please visit her with me for a consultation?"

"Madame Renée?"

"I told you about her phenomenal ability to analyze tea leaves."

"Oh, yes, I recall—the fortune-teller."

"Please do not call her that. She is not some itinerant gypsy who pretends to get messages from her tarot cards. Nor is she a clairvoyant who does abracadabra with a crystal ball."

"So she does abracadabra with tea leaves. What's the difference? I cannot believe that my destiny lies in a bowl of tea leaves."

"All right, then. Make fun of me if you will. There is a mystery to life that can only be addressed by certain people with special powers. But if your mind is closed, I shall not make another attempt to open it."

Having had her say, Marie-Thérèse separated from him and rolled over to her side of the bed. He attempted to make up to her, but she refused to say anything further. Not even good-night. It was their first quarrel.

* * *

The following day they went to see Madame Renée. She was a mountainous woman with a triple chin, confined to a wheelchair because her legs could no longer sustain the weight of her body. Her face was quite beautiful, however, and her voice had a lyrical lilt to it, almost as if, when she spoke, she was singing. She did not live in a gloomy, cobwebby, bat-ridden hovel as Guy had anticipated, but in a small, brightly painted house, profuse with flowers and canaries in cages.

"Have you ever had a consultation before, Monsieur Laroule?" she inquired.

"No."

"I sense some skepticism on your part."

"I am not sure . . . well . . . yes, some."

"I hope to make you a convert."

For the next half-hour, she prepared the tea-reading, first selecting a pinch of nine different leaves from boxes on the table. After placing the leaves in a silver bowl and arranging them in a certain pattern, she poured hot water over them and studied the leaves as they reacted to the scalding. Twice she stirred the leaves with a gold fork. Then, with her obese arms folded across her breast, she leaned forward, and with her face only inches above the surface of the bowl, she studied the contents intently. Minutes passed. Finally, she said, "You have had a serious reversal, Monsieur Laroule." More minutes passed. "There is much happiness here, also. A contradiction. Happy, but unhappy. I do not see desperate, but you are hard pressed. Perhaps money and commerce, as far as I can tell. But there is a solution. Would you like to see it?"

Guy rose from his chair and went to look over her shoulder. She pointed with her gold fork to a line where the leaves had separated. "Just here. That is where you cross over to a new life. The leaves over here are agitated—that means opportunity. But then here, you see, the leaves lay flat and tranquil."

She fell silent again as she peered fixedly at the leaves. Guy returned to his seat and watched her face; her frowning, rouged, round-cheeked, pretty face changed expressions as she received emanations from the leaves.

"It is a strange message I perceive, Monsieur Laroule. It seems that your future lies in your past."

"I do not understand."

"Nor do I, but that is what the tea leaves are telling me."

"My past? I cannot return to France if that . . ."

"No, not that far back. Here, you see, your recent past. There is something here . . ." She poked at the leaves . . . "Not too long ago . . ." She pulled her head back and looked at him. "That is all I can tell you. Examine your recent past, Monsieur. There is something of importance there."

On their way back, Guy admitted to Marie-Thérèse that he was indeed impressed with Madame Renée, but he felt that the vague message was not helpful. "My future, she says, is in my recent past, but ever since I have arrived in New Orleans I have concentrated exclusively on the plantation. My future is certainly not in that. Even if Duroux dies, the plantation goes to his heirs and does not revert to me. You and Rémi are both in my past and in my future, but I am sure that is not what she means. My future is my past. It is like one of those disturbing incidents in a dream that you recall on awakening and spend a day trying to interpret. That is the vexation of soothsaying—questions without conclusions."

A few weeks later, while awaiting Monsieur Grotesquieu for their weekly dinner at the club, Guy again encountered Trémoncourt in the bar, looking even more prosperous.

"Come, Laroule, join me in celebration, yet another. Life is a daisy chain of celebrations. Who would have thought I am a *force,* Laroule, a *force.* I have just concluded an arrangement with Cuba, only yesterday disembarking from Havana, whereby all tobacco will be shipped to my company; *all tobacco,* Laroule, I am the tobacco king, the cigar czar. New Orleans tobacco is so inferior, unacceptable, but Cuban tobacco à la Trémencourt—nirvana. Do you smoke? This is a cigar to treasure—a Sampassas. Here you are, light up. And barman, open a proper champagne for us.

After several self-congratulatory toasts to his new-found tobacco eminence, Trémencourt paused to inquire about Guy's plantation. "How does it go, Laroule? I am about to acquire a plantation for myself, not to plant, God forbid having to look after crops that may wilt or succumb to insects. I only harvest rocks, as I told you, but living in a plantation mansion intrigues me—lord of the manor—that appeals to me."

As Trémencourt paused to down his glass, Guy told him briefly about his misfortune.

"Well, then, you're well out of it, Laroule, be thankful, it is hard work with a pittance return. Why do you not consider what we discussed when I saw you last?"

"I do not recall. . ."

"Furs. Do you not recall I told you there was a gold mine, so to speak, in trading furs acquired up north? The Indian tribes there, I told you, are great hunters and their pelts far superior to anything we get here. Up the Mississippi, where it meets the Missouri, I hear all these wonderful stories about the furs. I would send an expedition, but there is no one I can trust. I will make you a proposition, Laroule. You are hurting—no plantation, no prospects. Partners, fifty-fifty. I will finance, you will organize and go up the Mississippi, find a place where we can establish a fur post. I, myself, do not have the time because of all my ventures, but this can be lucrative, Laroule, *lucrative*—better than tobacco, better than slaves, better even than lead—furs—furs that we buy with trinkets: foxes for beads, beavers for blankets, otters for mirrors and knives."

"But who owns the land up there?"

"France, of course. We own all of it, all the way up to Canada. Do not worry, there is no one way up there to oppose us. A few army posts along the way. I know, I have studied it. I have seen the furs; some trickle in here on the keelboats. Magnificent. Lustrous, thick, gorgeous, not like here, weak from the heat. What do you say, Laroule? Do you know the demand in Paris and London? A set of rich pelts brings in more than a whole shipment of tobacco. What do you say?"

"Going up the Mississippi against the current would be very difficult."

"Of course, of course, that is the saving feature. It certainly is difficult, that is why no one attempts it. And costly. Boats, crew, supplies, all that, costly. My money, your time, fifty-fifty."

"But I have just married . . ."

"Take her along. 'The weaker sex.' Hah! They are stronger than we are by far. I refer to fortitude. And braving the elements. What is there to keep you in New Orleans? Nothing. Do you really enjoy living here with its filthy climate, swarms of mosquitos, the stink of the streets, the lazy Creoles? What is there to keep you here? What do you say?"

"I will speak to my wife about it."

"Yes, yes, do that. Adventure, Laroule, nothing ventured, nothing gained. I will lunch with you a week from today. Is that enough time? If not you, I have others I will approach. It is a venture whose time has come. We will be the fur kings, Laroule, you and me. Co-kings. See you next week."

He drained his champagne and hurried off just as Grotesquieu was entering the club. At dinner, Guy regaled Grotesquieu with Trémencourt's proposal and asked his advice.

"Very risky business, Guy. That is a long way to go. He risks money, you risk your life, not an even exchange."

"But do you think he is right about the furs—that there is an avid market for them?"

"I have no doubt about it. Furs are all the rage. But what about Marie-Thérèse and Rémi?"

"I would take them with me."

"Up the Mississippi? Have you ever been on the river?"

"Yes, when I came here."

"But that's down here where it joins tributaries. It's quite different when you move out of these waters. A strong, unpredictable current flows down from the Great Lakes. You would be going against the current all the way in a boat weighted with cargo. Worst of all, you could not use sails."

"Why not?"

"It is a broad river, but not broad enough to navigate with sails, and for the most part, the wind blows north to south."

"You make it sound forbidding."

"All treasure is forbidding, Guy, or it would not have such high value. Look how deep one must dig for gold and how hard it is to find it. And diamonds. Not to mention emeralds and rubies."

"Trémencourt brought out that old cliché, 'nothing ventured, nothing gained.' "

"True. But it can also be 'everything ventured, nothing gained.' I do not believe that others have not tried. You can be sure they have tried and failed. Hostile river. Hostile Indians. Hostile surroundings. Think it through carefully, Guy; there is no virtue in being impetuous."

To Guy's surprise, Marie-Thérèse was receptive to the idea of leaving New Orleans, although somewhat suspicious about the fur-trading expedition. "I do not see that there is anything to recommend New Orleans to us now. We all have bitter experiences to forget. Rémi and I would love to leave here. I dread being in the same city as Boustique, passing his tavern, even having to worship in the same church. I have no friends here. I wish there were a school for Rémi other than the convent. I have such a wonderful new life with you, I would dearly like to start it in a new place we could call our own. But as for the fur proposal . . . I am not so sure. . . . Do you trust Trémencourt?"

"It really is not a question of trust. If he does not provide the funds, obviously I shall not go. It is a question of him trusting me."

"But if you have trouble, which I am sure you will, will he support you?"

"Well, I guess that is part of the risk."

"You know what just occurred to me? Madame Renée said your future is in your past—she could have been referring to Trémencourt and when he first talked to you about this."

"You are right. If this is to be my future."

"How long does it take to go up the Mississippi?"

"I have no idea. I need to find out many things if we decide to proceed. What kind of boat? How does one make progress against the strong current with no sails? How many miles are we talking about? How much of a crew? How about supplies and equipment? A thousand questions to answer. But the first question is: Are we tempted? It would certainly be a new life, but with a baby on the way now . . ."

"Guy, let us say we are tempted enough to seek some answers. What alternative do we have? To become permanent wards of dear Grotesquieu? Yes, I would say we are tempted, baby included."

Twenty-one

TRICOT KNEW A MAN, now retired, who for years had been the master of a Mississippi flatboat that transported freight, mostly livestock, from Kentucky to New Orleans. He was a heavy-set, once-muscular man, a Creole, who received Guy's bottle of whiskey with thanks, immediately pouring cups all around.

"Well, I can tell you, hauling upriver is a buster. Where you say you want to go, clear up to where the Missouri joins in? Whoo-eee, that's a piece, maybe four months, maybe five. You understand about riverboating?"

"No, not at all," Guy said. "I want to go up there with eight or nine men and supplies, food, tools, clothing, materials like wood planks, the things I would need to build an outpost."

"The river is a bitch, monsieur . . ."

"Laroule."

"Laroule. Coming down you can ride the current, and a damnable current it is, and sometimes you can catch a breath of wind in a square sail. I come down from Louisville in four weeks, but going back, three to four months. You understand there is all kind of obstructions, dangers, and calamities lying in wait; snaps and bars, waterfalls without warning, whirlpools and eddies. I was once caught in a whirlpool that twirled us so strong all the crew became dizzy and could not pole us free. We smashed against a rock and stove in one side. Had to swim to make shore. Lost the boat and twenty head of cattle. Current really thunders around the big rocks, the Grand Tower, Cornice Rock, Devil's Bake Oven, the Devil's Anvil, the Devil's Backbone, the Devil's Tea Table—you can tell from the names ole Lucifer has got control on the Mississippi. Then there's the extreme crooked bends of the river so you have to go back and forth, back and forth. Going all the way up to the Missouri, I would say a boat would have to crisscross the Mississippi about four hundred times. On a good day you can make maybe fifteen miles, but sometimes we made so little headway at the end of the day we would look back, and what did we see? The place we started from. Then there's rapids, sandbars of quicksand, and cave-in banks, but the worst of all is uprooted trees, some adrift, some stuck to the bottom, called snags, either planters or sawyers—places like the Devil's Raceground and what is called the Council of Snags—dead trees stickin' up out of the water so thick it is like a forest. So you add to all this warpath Indians ambushing you and pirates waiting to rob you, floating ice in the winter, lightning storms in the summer—I tell you, Monsieur Laroule, it is not a trip for the faint of heart. But if you are stuck on it, then you better get yourself the best boat and best patroon you can find."

"What kind of boat would that be?" Guy asked.

"Well, for going down river, what I was on, the best is the flat-bottom—it can carry fifty tons of cargo. But for going upriver, you get yourself a keelboat made of straight yellow poplar hammered together with wooden pins of seasoned white oak. You be sure they do not bring in old boards, it only takes a couple of rotten boards to give way in the rough water, and you find yourself going right down to the bottom."

"What will such a boat cost?"

"Expensive. A good flatboat will run you about seventy-five dollars, but a keelboat I would say goes at something like a hundred and thirty-five dollars. But getting the boat is the easy part. What's hard is finding a good patroon to captain your boat. You have to be careful—get the wrong man, he can steal you, wreck you, abandon you—just steer you into shore and walk off, leave you stranded. I seen it done more than once. So you be careful to land the best patroon you can find, and I would say you better get a Kaintuck, not a Creole."

"What is a Kaintuck?"

"The American ones who bring the boats down from the north,

mostly Kentucky fellows. That's how they are all called, wherever they come from. These patroons are the roughest, toughest, biggest two-fisted men you will ever see, and they can drive a crew who are also big, pugnacious men, drink and fight too much, but they can pole, rope, cordel, warp, and bushwhack your boat up that river."

"What is all that?"

"That is how you get upriver, by pole, rope, pushing, pulling—we have our own ways—but what they say, a keelboater is half horse, half alligator. Four, five months of physical hell, but these keelers are the only fellows who can do it, so it will cost you dearly, eleven dollars a month for a good keeler, and maybe twenty dollars for the patroon. Now, about the patroons. Give them your hand, accost them with a bold air, taste their whiskey, and you win their hearts. But a little too much reserve or haughtiness offends them instantly and draws upon you torrents of abuse if not a personal assault, so proceed carefully. Only four patroons I would recommend: Mike Fink, James Gerty, Bill Sedley, and Mike Wolf. First thing you do, see if any of them is in port, then make your deal *if* they will take you upriver. Mostly they bring in a flat and go back by the Natchez Trace, but you take yourself to the Swamp, on Girod Street, that is where they will be if they be in port."

"There is a swamp?"

The old patroon laughed. "No, no, not a real swamp, that's just what it is called. A whole section there, along Girod Street, that is where the keelers and flatters hang out when they are in town. Drinking, gambling, fighting, roistering, womening, so bad there, even the police will not go in. No, sir, so watch your step, and your pocket. Dress down. No watch, no jewelry. Bring a bottle like you brought me. Now if I had a choice, my number one would be Mike Fink. He spells it 'Miche Phinck,' sort of his joke, but do not be put off by that. He was a scout in the French-Indian War afore he took up keelboating. He is big, but he does not look belligerent. Hah! Do not let his looks deceive you. He has a round, pleasant, handsome face, fine strong teeth, with a very fit and muscular torso. He's known as the Snapping Turtle. First time I met him was at Mother Colby's Boarding House in the Swamp. That's where he and most of the other patroons stay. I get introduced and he says to me, he says, by way of introduction, 'I can out-run, out-hop, out-jump, throw down, drag out, and lick any man in the country. I'm a Salt River roarer. I love the women and I'm full of fight.' Never saw a man drink like he does. They tell me he can drain a gallon of whiskey into him in twenty-four hours without affecting his speech or conduct. I believe it. Another thing about Mike, he has never been hurt in a fight, and he has had plenty. One of his men told me the secret was nature had give him solid, bony sides instead of ribs, so there is no opening for knives, bullets, or dirks to penetrate. He is also a great shooter. I once seen him make his woman place a tin can between her knees, up near her crotch, at thirty yards away he plinked it pretty as you please.

"If Mike is not around, then go for Bill Sedley. These patroons will get your boat upriver if they have to kill the crew to do it. But Tricot, you cannot go with him. You know how they are about Negroes."

"I know. I have this scar across my forehead to remind me."

"They do not have Negroes up where they come from and they sort of look on them the way they look on animals they hunt."

"But Tricot can show his papers," Guy said. "He's a freed slave."

"Won't make a difference to them since none of them can read."

No matter that he had been forewarned, Guy was nonetheless unprepared for the roiling streets of the Swamp. Some drunken groups roamed Girod Street singing river songs, some were brawling, rolling around in the dirt of the street, committing mayhem on each other; still others, stiff-legged and awkward in their drunkenness, were trying to capture the evasive hogs and chickens that roamed in their midst. Giant street torches flared at intervals, painting the night with deep shadows and flamed patches, a roistering hell partially illuminated.

Guy approached a river man, drinking from a bottle of wine, who was more spectator than participant. "Excuse me, sir, but do you know if Mike Fink is in town?"

"Mike Fink! You betcha, he's in town," the man responded, speaking with a thick Kentucky accent unintelligible to Guy, who knew some English, but not *this* English. "Came to town, and afore a cat could wink an eye he's had galore of drinks, but instead of turnin' nigger he's a good old hoss and splits everything with his friends and even skyes a copper to see who'd get his last chaw o' 'baccy; it'd shore be harder'n rowin' up Salt River to find a cleverer parcel o' fellers 'n Mike and them keelers. I never seed so many niggers in all my born days as they is here. Thicker'n black bugs in spiled bacon ham, and gamblers, thieves, and pickpockets skitin' about the street like weasels in a barnyard. Mannee, it did beat all—how that woman I had put on the fixin's. Made her look right smart, but she had no business acting so fofarrow for she was jist a yaller gal. She was makin' meat all right and doing it slicker'n greased lightnin'. The eyes she was makin' 'd bamboozle a dead Injun into thinkin' she was awful fond o' him but she was only waitin' her chance to lift that keeler's plunder. Might fetch a greenhorn or a flatter, but it'd shore be harder 'n climbin' a peeled saplin' heels uppard to count any coups on an old dyed-in-the-wool keeler. Yes siree! If you lookin' for the world's best keeler, you take yourself inside that door, Mother Colby's Boarding House, facin' you, big as Cave-In Rock, red-feather heisted, you find Mike Fink, give 'im a bottle and he'll greet you kindly."

Fortunately, the man pointed to the door he was talking about, for he could have just as well been speaking Swahili, so little of his speech did Guy understand. He thanked the man and proceeded across the street, carefully avoiding colliding bodies.

Mother Colby's Boarding House belied its name. Anyone remotely resembling a Mother Colby was nowhere to be seen. The entire downstairs of the house was a bar with small tables tightly arranged around it right up to the wall. River men sat drinking at the tables, served by an assortment of attractive barmaids, who skittered about bearing drinks on small, round trays which they held high above their heads as they squeezed between the tables. They wore identical costumes that featured tight white blouses that exposed most of their breasts, and short black skirts without undergarments. All the girls were young and white. Probably, thought Guy, girls who were part of that maniacal bunch that boarded my ship at Le Havre.

The only Negroes in the place were an elderly fiddler, his hair gone white, who played ceaselessly, and a drummer who deferred to the fiddle. It was obvious that the barmaids were available, on payment to a cashier who sat at the foot of the rear stairs, for visits to the rooms above. The men were noisy, but compared to those in the street, relatively contained—at least for the time being.

Upon entering, Guy found a room so thick with tobacco smoke, it was like looking through frosted glass; at first he had trouble distinguishing anyone. But as his eyes adjusted he saw at a nearby table a man who fit the description of Mike Fink. He wore a red shirt, fringed buckskin trousers, a multicolored sash tied around his waist, a deerskin vest with a beaded mosaic on its panels, and a blue surtout down to his knees. In the band of his broad-rimmed hat was a prominent red feather.

Guy hesitantly approached his table. "Excuse me, sir, but are you Mike Fink?"

"Who wants ter know?" Mike said with a thick Kentucky twang, at the same time reaching out and relieving Guy of the whiskey bottle in his hand.

"I am looking for someone to captain a boat upriver for me and I am told he is the best."

Mike poured whiskey into all the cups on his table. "You see all them red feathers in this here room? Every man of 'em is a patroon but they's nary one of 'em can hold a candle to Mike Fink. But buckin' up that damn river, that don't appeal to me. You got the add-verse current and a straight-on wind. You can have a square sail, but you almost never get a wind blowin' up your backside when you're headin' north. And handlin' a keeler's a damn sight worser than a big flatter that slicks down the current."

A huge, disheveled man, well over six feet, suddenly loomed in front of Mike Fink and began to spew a tirade at him. "Dig the wax outta your ears, Fink, and lissen what I gotta say. This is *me*, and no mistake! Billy Earthquake, Esquire, commonly called Little Billy, all the way from North Fork of Muddy Run! I'm a small specimen, as you see—a ramote circumstance, a mere yearling, but cuss me, if I ain't of the true 'imported breed,' and can whip any man in this section of country! Whoop! You hear me, Fink, all you pissy-sissies with your red feathers. Won't *nobody* come out and fight me? I haint had one for more than a week, and if you don't come out, I'm fly-blowed before sundown, to a *certingty!* So come up to taw!"

"May be you don't know who Little Billy is? I'll tell you: I'm a poor man—that's a fact—and smell like a wet dog, but I can't be run over! I'm the identical individual that grinned a whole menagerie out of countenance, and made the ribbed-nose baboon hang down his head and blush! Whoop! I'm the chap too, that towed the *Broadhorn* up the Salt River, where the snags were so thick that a fish couldn't swim without rubbing his scales off!—fact, and if any body denies it, just let 'em make their will! Cock-a-doodle doo! Maybe you never heard of the time the horse kicked me and put both his hips out of jint—if it ain't true, cut me up for catfish bait! W-h-o-o-p! I'm the very infant that refused its milk before its eyes were open, and called for a bottle of old rye! W-h-o-o-p! I'm that little cupid! Talk to me about grinning the bark off a tree!—'taint nothing; one squint of mine at a bull's heel would blister it! Cock-a-doodle de-doo! Oh, I'm one of your toughest sort—live forever, and then turn to a white oak post. Look at me, I'm the *ginewine* article and I can chaw more tobacco and spit less, and drink more whiskey and keep soberer than any other man in these localities! Cock-a-doodle-doo! You too yaller to fight Fink? You be sportin' a yaller feather, not red."

"Excuse me," Mike said to Guy as he stood up, and so quick nobody saw it, he landed one punch to Billy's jaw and toppled him slowly, all six-feet-three of him, like a giant pine tree felled by a woodsman's axe. Then Mike resumed his seat and poured himself a fresh whiskey as a couple of men dragged Billy's inert body away.

"How fer up you fixin' to go?" Mike continued as if nothing had happened.

"Up to the Missouri River."

"Trek that fer cost ya twelve dollar a month a man, double fer me. Plug Mackay here be second pilot. Say hello, Plug. And Dirk Kettlehorn, this one here, he be dancer, fiddler, and cook."

"Fiddler? Dancer?"

"The spirit, Frenchy, grub feeds the belly, but gotta have music 'n dance to feed the spirit. Four months out there on the river gotta have us some lively time. I got me a good crew here, ship out with eleven men . . ."

Fink grabbed the wrist of a passing barmaid, a tall, long-legged girl with black hair down to her waist. "Hold up there, Zizi, got me a stack of coins here." He dug some coins out of his trousers' pocket and stacked them on the edge of the table. "Watch this here magic, Frenchy," he said to Guy. "Zizi the magician will make them disappear. Show 'im, Zizi."

Zizi gave Mike a big smile, circled the coins, then raised one of her long legs, swung it over the corner of the table, straddled the coins, and snatched them up with her vagina. Mike and the others whooped in satisfaction. "God damn, but that's the best bar act I ever seed," Mike said. "You ever see anything top that, Frenchy?"

Guy wanted to tell him not to call him Frenchy, but then again they were getting along so well. Mike continued, "Girl's gotta purse like a steel trap. Treat you to a roll upstairs with her, Frenchy. Guaranteed she'll snatch you like you never been snatched afore."

A red-feathered patron at an adjoining table was now summoning Zizi to perform the same act on a stack of coins that he had put on the corner of his table. His crew was watching her with intense anticipation as once again she swung one of her long legs over the stack and trapped it. She had only gone a few steps, however, when she abruptly screamed in pain, dropped the tray she was carrying, and tried desperately to release the coins. The patroon and his crew were convulsed with laughter, holding on to each other in their hysterical merriment. "We've warmed them up for ya, Zizi," the patroon shouted through his laughter.

"They put a flame to the coins," Plug Mackay, the second pilot, explained.

"Let's put a flame to them," Fink said, as he and his crew charged the other group, knocking them off their chairs and spilling them onto the floor. Within seconds the entire bar erupted, as if on some prearranged signal, a free-for-all as fists pounded, bottles smashed on skulls, table legs ripped off to become clubs. Screaming barmaids tried to escape the carnage while the barman brandished his musket to no avail; brass knuckles, knives, dirks, and devil's claws started to appear. And through it all, the old fiddler continued to play, accompanied by the beat of the unruffled drum.

Twenty-two

With Grotesquieu's help, Guy assembled eight men—two carpenters, a blacksmith, two ex-soldiers, a scout who had lived with the Indians, a fur trapper, and a cook—who were destined to remain with Guy as a cadre to help him establish the fur trading post once they found a suitable site. Their salaries ranged from twenty to twenty-six dollars a month.

Mike Fink found a keelboat to his liking that cost Guy a hundred and eighty-six dollars. It was seventy feet long and ten feet in beam, with a shallow keel, sharp at both ends. It would draw about two feet of water when loaded. The middle of the boat was occupied by a cabin with an inside clearance of six feet. A cleated footway ran all around the gunwales, eighteen inches wide, which the crew needed for poling the boat. In the bow were seats for rowing. There was a high mast amidship. At the stern was a long steering oar extending twelve feet beyond the boat. The capacity would be somewhere between thirty to thirty-five tons. There was a one-pound cannon mounted on each side of the boat; the cannons were an additional cost, as were the poles, hawsers, and other equipment. Mike Fink demanded two months' pay in advance for himself and his men.

"Gettin' the supplies is up to you, Frenchy," Mike said, "but you better lay in some good victuals. We're not goin' to subsist on fried turds and cattle beans. Lay in some good flour, not that mealy crap

from Cuba, salt pork, plenty tobacco, twelve barrels o' whiskey—
that's the fuel that makes my men run—and some nice plump hens,
geese, turkeys, pigs, only thing no white horses or cows, got that?
Posolutely no white horses or cows."

"Why so?"

"Not unless you want us to go under. Bad, bad luck, Frenchy, and
I won't put a toe aboard if I see 'em on deck."

"Mike, I would prefer not to be called Frenchy."

"What the hell, you ashamed o' where you come from? Christ,
I'm called a Kaintuck, but why not, I'm from Kentucky and proud of
it. No place on the universal 'arth like old Kaintuck; she whips all
out-west in prettiness. You might bile down cr'ation and not get
such another state out of it."

"It's just—I don't like to be called that."

"Really? What name you want?"

"Monsieur Laroule."

"Well, that's a pretty stiff name for close livin', but what the
hell—long's you load in the whiskey and pay salaries on time I'll call
you anythin' you like. Let me tell you somethin' about meself you
prolly don't know. I may be freewheelin' and a head-basher, but
when I hire on with you, I am loyal to the last drop of me blood. I
will stick by you come what may come, and I expect you to live up
to your end of the bargain, clear?"

It took days to assemble all the provisions they would need for so
long a trip and for setting up the outpost once they got there. In
addition to the items Fink had enumerated, Guy bought lumber,
tools, salt, muskets, ammunition, wine, rope, knives, a variety of
food, boxes of trinkets for Indian trading, seeds, animal traps, medicines, blankets, raingear, a seemingly endless stream of items arriving at the dock where the new keelboat was tied to the trunk of a
willow tree.

Thus far, keeping careful receipts, Guy had paid for all this from
his own funds, which were running low. It was imperative to receive
Trémencourt's funds, but only after leaving a half dozen messages at
his office did Trémencourt finally respond. During lunch, Guy
briefed him on the state of readiness of his expedition and gave him
a written accounting of what amounts were owed to him. Guy also
indicated how much capital would be needed for the future of the
project. Trémencourt went over the submitted figures carefully, then
returned the list to Guy.

"We have a problem," he said.

Guy said nothing.

"This certainly looks like you are well prepared, and I have no doubt that you will succeed in trading for furs with the Indians, but how will you bring them into New Orleans?"

"How? By flatboat down the Mississippi. It is only a three or four-week journey downstream."

"Yes. But then?"

"What are you getting at, Trémencourt?"

"I have been informed that you cannot bring furs into New Orleans without a charter. That is probably why no one has done it."

"But can we not get a charter?"

"It must be granted by the Crown, a Royal Charter. Otherwise the furs will be confiscated by the customs agent without compensation."

Guy stared at Trémencourt as he contemplated this unexpected turn of events. "Let me see if I understand you. You induced me to undertake this project. I have advanced almost all my own funds relying on you to compensate me. Now you tell me we cannot go forward."

"Not unless we obtain a Royal Charter to procure furs on His Majesty's Louisiana property up north."

"And how do we obtain such a charter?"

"Obviously from the King."

"Who is at Versailles."

"Precisely."

"And that is the only way?"

"Yes."

"What about the Governor?"

"He does not own Missouri."

"You are saying one must go to Versailles and personally implore Louis XV to grant this charter?"

"Yes, the King or someone who has his ear. Richelieu, perhaps, or the new *maîtresse en titre*, Madame du Barry, who, I am told, is very accommodating if she is properly induced."

"Can you arrange that?"

"Alas, I have no palace connections. But that is your forte, is it not?"

"But I am forbidden to return to France."

"Then we are at an impasse and must abandon the project."

"And the funds I have expended?"

"Try to recover as much as you can."

"It is not just, Trémencourt, that you induced me to spend all this money and effort, and then wash your hands of me."

"It is a situation over which I have no control. I am a business-man, Laroule. I invest for profit. If I were to give you a thousand dollars, I would expect two thousand in return. But if we have a warehouse full of beautiful furs we cannot sell, then neither of us profits. Do you understand? I can sell my lead. I can sell my tobacco. That is why I invest in them. Bring me a charter signed by the King, I am prepared to finance you." He looked at his watch and rose from the table. "I regret I have an appointment. . .."

It did not take Guy long to discover that the outfitted keelboat and all the supplies he had purchased could not be returned. According to custom, all sales were done deals. And when Guy intimated to Mike Fink that there was a possibility that the trip might be post-poned, Mike replied that whether they went upriver or not was immaterial as long as they were paid for the agreed period of time. "You kin postpone the trip, but you cain't postpone payin' Mike and his men. You catch my drift?" is the way Mike put it.

Guy discussed his predicament with Marie-Thérèse, who sug-gested that they talk to Grotesquieu about it. "He seems to have an extra set of eyes inside his head that sees solutions."

"Sometimes it is prudent to suffer a small loss to avoid a large one," Grotesquieu observed after Guy had told him about Trémencourt's defection. "How much does this expedition mean to you, Guy? I mean other than problematical money and profits."

"It has come to mean a great deal. To go someplace of my own choosing and establish something where nothing exists—that would give me a sense of renewal. And for Marie-Thérèse and Rémi, it would be a fresh start to a new life. I have confidence that I can succeed. I have dealt with many Indians since I have been here, and I think that I can establish a good relationship with them. Oh, I know that some of those tribes up north have a reputation for cruel bellig-erence, but I have had dealings with the Chickasaws here, and I honestly think I have a way with even the most bellicose chieftains. And I like furs, per se. I like the adventure of hunting and trapping. I would like living again in a place where there is a change of seasons, where one sees spring awaken and snow fall. I have never felt a sense of belonging here in New Orleans. I am an outsider and I shall always be an outsider. Marie-Thérèse and I have discussed this and she feels as I do. I think it is our destiny, André, to make our way far up there where we can create a life of our own. And besides, what is my future here? Thanks to your sufferance, we have a roof over our heads, but how do I earn a living? Singing itinerant songs on street corners while Marie-Thérèse passes the hat?"

"Give me a day or two to think about your problem," Grotesquieu said. "The way I see it, there are three components—you need financing, you need a Royal Charter only obtainable at Versailles, and you need extraordinary luck against punishing odds. Perhaps I can help with the first two, but as for the latter, that is best handled by divine intervention, with which I have negligible influence."

Three days later, Grotesquieu knocked at Laroule's door and inquired whether it was a convenient time for a visit. At the moment, Guy was helping Rémi with his homework which was shoved aside as Grotesquieu joined them at their table. Marie-Thérèse came down from an upstairs bedroom.

"I have assembled a consortium of people to provide the capital you need," Grotesquieu said. "Baron de Bastrop, the Marquis de Maison Rouge, and I will each contribute five hundred dollars with the understanding that you will repay seven hundred from profits, if you have any."

"That is very kind of you, but I fear I shall require somewhat more than that to establish an outpost with permanent structures."

"There is another investor who matches our total contribution."

"And who might that be?"

"The Comtesse Mai de Villars du Breuil."

Guy was stunned.

"She did not even ask me about repayment. I simply said you had a financial problem and she said, 'How much does he need?'"

"No conditions?"

"None, other than she would like enough beaver pelts to make a coat. No mention of interest, profit, nothing. Very chic of her."

"Who is this Comtesse?" Marie-Thérèse asked.

"We performed in an operetta when I first arrived here."

"Should I be jealous?"

"Only if the past bothers you."

"If that is all there is to it, then I shall try not to be jealous."

Grotesquieu continued, "As for your concern about not being able to return to France, I have carefully read the Royal Proclamation you gave me and I find nothing to stop you. Let me read this sentence to you . . ." He pinched the bridge of his nose with his gold-rimmed pince-nez: " 'Be it known that from this date henceforth, Guy Laroule ceases to be a resident of France, but by Royal Edict is granted legal status as resident of New Orleans, Province of Louisiana.' Now in my opinion, there is nothing in that edict to bar you from *visiting* France as long as you do not attempt to settle down and become a *resident*. Do you not agree? If you arrive with a *passe de voyage,* which you can easily obtain at our passport office, there should be no problem. So now, you have the money to finance your trip and nothing to stop you from returning to Versailles to obtain a fur charter, but as I see it, you still have one remaining problem for which I see no solution. You know the old saw—a man cannot be in two places at the same time. How can you go up the Mississippi for furs and at the same time sail across the ocean for permission to sell the furs? That is a conundrum beyond my solution. But I leave you to reflect on it. Perhaps you can think of something clever."

"Well, I could postpone the trip to France, although I do not know how long I will be upriver."

"Yes, and I must warn you, we hear rumblings that Louis XV may cede New Orleans and Louisiana Province to his first cousin, Charles III of Spain."

"Why would he do that?"

"Because it is costing him a fortune to maintain us—several million a year. You had best get your charter before Spain takes over, if it does."

After Grotesquieu's departure, dinner was served, but no one spoke or ate very much. In fact, the only sound in the room was the sonorous ticking of the hall clock.

Finally, Marie-Thérèse said, "Let us go sit near the fire." The depressing silence was now more bearable with the warm glow of the flames on their faces.

"The worst part is," Guy said finally, "that I cannot take their money to pay my expenses if I do not go. That means to compensate Mike Fink and everybody else, I will be wiped out. Then what will we live on?"

"I can work at the brick ovens," Rémi said. "Many boys work there."

There was no further conversation before they said good-night to Rémi, who went up to his bedroom. Marie-Thérèse and Guy lingered for a while in front of the fire; after a few futile attempts to make conversation, they, too, went up to their bedroom.

About an hour later, when they were in bed but not yet asleep, they heard a tentative knock on their door, then Rémi's voice: "Are you asleep?"

"No, Rémi, come in," Marie-Thérèse said as Guy lit a taper on his bed table.

The boy came in and sat on the edge of the bed beside his mother. "I have been lying in my bed thinking about what Monsieur Grotesquieu said—that a man cannot be in two places at the same time. But I think I have a way to solve it—now do not say no right away because that's what you will think at first, but I really think it will work. Here goes: Guy goes to France to get the charter, and Tricot and I will go with the boat upriver to find a place for the outpost."

Guy laughed. "You are right, Rémi, the answer is no."

"But why? You say you have the great Mike Fink and his crew to handle the boat, so for however long it takes to get there, what is there to do but keep an eye on everybody? Tricot is good at that, he was in charge of all the workers at the plantation, was he not? And I . . . well, sure, yes, I am only a boy, but I am almost thirteen and tall for my age, and I know more about things than you may think. When you go through bad times and have to deal with bad people, you learn a lot."

"But darling Rémi," his mother said, "being on a boat with those terrible river men is no place for a young boy."

"But Mother, I am not a *young* boy, I am an old boy. I know how to take care of myself. I can handle a gun and a knife, as you well know, and I can read and write and add sums and speak three languages which none of those men can do, and that gives me an advantage—I mean, it will make them feel inferior to me. I know, I have seen grown-ups react that way. And with Tricot behind me, since he also reads and writes and is so big and powerful. . ."

"I am afraid your mother is right," Guy said. "This is not an expedition that a boy and a Negro . . ."

"Listen," Rémi persisted, "what is it you want done? You want a boat to take eight workers and supplies to some place up the Mississippi where the Missouri River flows into it, is that right? Then you want these men to build a couple of shelters where we can stay while we wait for you. Why can't Tricot and I do that? From what I hear, if you come up the Natchez Trace on horseback or carriage, it is a lot faster than the river, and you will probably join us not too long after we get there."

"I think it might work," Marie-Thérèse conceded, "if I go with them."

"Out of the question," Guy snapped. "Four months on that boat is no place for a pregnant woman."

Rémi went around to Guy's side of the bed and knelt down so his face was on a level with Guy's. "You have taught me a lot, Guy. How to hunt, how to handle a musket, a sword, tie knots, lots of things, and some things I already knew, like fishing, catching gators, and cooking Creole."

"Mike Fink and his men are very bad about Negroes," Guy said. "They would make it miserable for Tricot."

"Not if it is all settled before we go. You can talk to them. And you have seen how Tricot takes care of himself. Don't worry about that."

"And what am I to do," Marie-Thérèse asked, "while you go up the Mississippi with Tricot and Guy goes to Versailles?"

Guy took her in his arms. "And you, lovely lady, will stay here, take care of your growing baby and wait for me to come back to both of you."

Twenty-three

MIKE FINK AND HIS MEN were busily at work on the boat when Guy approached with Rémi and Tricot. "Good day, Mike," Guy said, speaking English. "May I converse with you for a moment?"

"Go ahead, converse," Mike said, while continuing to work on the connection of the steering pole.

"This is my son, Rémi, and this is Tricot. They are going to be accompanying you on the trip."

"Don't concern me one way or t'other long as they don' get in the way. We got close quarters and we cain't be trippin' all over a passel o' outsiders."

"They will not be in the way, but Rémi will be in charge with Tricot's assistance."

Mike stopped work very deliberately and slowly turned his head around to look at them. "What say, a boy an' a nigger *in charge?*" His voice was rising. "With *me* aboard, *they* are in charge?"

"Of course, I do not mean the running of the boat. Obviously, you are the master of the vessel. But Rémi is in charge of *my* interests, acting on my behalf."

"That's your affair. I only care 'bout gettin' the boat upriver and gettin' paid, y'understan'?"

"Fine. Now about Tricot here . . ."

Mike Fink had resumed working on the tiller.

"I know you are unaccustomed to having to deal with Negroes, but he is a free slave, he has papers, and I ask you not to call him nigger."

"Well, what the hell is he, then? He's black as a slab o' coal an' his hair is frizzy an' if that don' make him a nigger, I don' know what does."

"No, it does *not* make him a nigger, which is a word decent people do not use. Perhaps they do up where you come from, but not on my boat. Not by you or your men. His name is Tricot, and that is what he will be called. Can we agree on that?"

"Hell, I'll call him anythin' you like. Don' mean a damn to me. Call him white if you want."

"All I ask is you treat him same as everyone else aboard."

"Well, long as he keeps to himself and knows his place, won' be a problem."

"His place is to handle things for me along with Rémi."

"I don' know what you're riled about," Mike said. "Look to me like he's big enough to take care of hisself."

"He is."

Mike stopped work and walked up to Guy. "Now we got this small-potato stuff out of the way, let me tell you what *is* important. We gotta move outta here damn soon or by the time we get up north there'll be ice on the river, an' the last thin' I want bumpin' my ass is hunks of ice knockin' holes in the hull. We're just about set to go, so Friday the boy and the nig . . . an' Tricot better be here bright an' early for shovin' out. One more thin'—you gotta name? Law is, boats gotta have a name."

"What do you think, Rémi? How about the *Marie-Thérèse*?"

"I was thinking the same thing."

Mike handed Guy a piece of paper and a sliver of charcoal. "Here, put it down so we get it right."

Guy handed the paper to Rémi, who wrote his mother's name in block letters.

"Who that?" Mike asked.

"My mother."

"Let's hope she brings us luck."

Two policemen approached the boat. "We are looking for Mike Fink," one of them said. "You Mike Fink?"

"I may be."

"We have a warrant here for your arrest. Put out your hands to be bound."

"What the hell for?"

"For causing a riot and injuries, and for destroying property at Mother Colby's Boarding House."

"Me! Was I the one put the torch to those coins and scalded that poor girl's pussy? The hell I was!"

"You tell all that to the magistrate. Put out your hands."

"The hell I will."

Both policemen drew their guns. "Perhaps I can be of assistance," Guy said. "May I see that warrant?"

"You want to look this over, Mike?" Guy asked, knowing full well that Mike could not read.

"Naw, you read it, Frenchy."

Guy took his time reading the document. "Have you read this warrant?" Guy asked the policeman who had presented it.

"Well, no . . ."

"Have you?" Guy asked the second policeman.

"We do not have to read anything," the second policeman said. "That is not our job. We just arrest."

"Well, for your information there is nothing here about arresting Mr. Fink. Only to serve him with this warrant. Look for yourselves."

"You read?" one of the policemen asked the other.

"No, what does it say?"

"I ain't a reader either."

"So it is just a misunderstanding," Guy said. "Nothing about arresting him, just to serve this paper on him. It says here he is to be in court two weeks from today. That sit well with you, Mike?"

"Absolute—two weeks from today, I be there."

The policemen looked at each other and shuffled their feet, perplexed as to what to do next. "Well, guess we better take that paper back to headquarters . . ."

"But you have served it on Mike who must now keep it in his possession until he goes to court."

"What do you think, Jack?" the one policeman asked the other.

"I guess we done our duty."

"Yes, I guess so."

They walked away indecisively.

"Was that the truth you told them?" Mike asked when they were out of earshot.

"My advice is to lay low until you shove off."

Rémi was now reading the document. " 'Arrest and bind the accused by the wrists, and deliver him forthwith to the Bourbon Street jail.' ''

"Thanks, Frenchy," Mike said. "You got a favor coming to you."

"Then my favor is to do what I asked about Tricot."

"Not to 'nigger' him."

"Yes. And treat the boy decently."

"You got Mike Fink's word on it and when Mike Fink gives his word it is like comin' down from God hisself."

Guy departed for France hurriedly, with scarcely enough time to pack. What happened was that Grotesquieu had an unexpected visit from his old friend, Captain René Forestière, commander of the French naval frigate, the *Piémontaise,* which had put into port briefly and was destined to leave for France the following morning. Grotesquieu had asked Forestière to take Guy along even though it was against regulations to carry a civilian passenger on a French warship. But Forestière had a reputation in the navy as a maverick and he lived up to it, saying of course he would take Laroule if he could be ready to board the launch at six o'clock the following morning. The *Piémontaise* was a well-equipped warship, carrying thirty-six nine-pound cannons and rigged to make the crossing in under three months. With a crew of a hundred and twenty, there would be no need to be on the lookout for pirates.

Marie-Thérèse and Rémi accompanied Guy to the quai where a launch, manned by four *Piémontaise* sailors awaited him. Guy took Rémi to one side to talk to him privately. "You are brave to take the boat upriver, Rémi, and I am proud of you. Your mission is to find us a high place where we will not be flooded as New Orleans is. These are rough men you are with, but do not ever back down from them. Confront them, let them know you are not to be bullied, but at the same time, do not provoke them, just keep a steady temper and always remember that every day that they work hard moving the boat, you are that much nearer to your destination."

"Do not be concerned, Guy," Rémi said. "I will try to make a friend of Mike Fink. I don't think he is as tough inside as he pretends to be on the outside."

"Every Sunday say your prayers and read from the Bible with Tricot. I am so sorry to have to send you on this mission—a boy to do a man's job, but I do have confidence in you or would not let you do this. I am very fond of you, Rémi. You are my true son even though I did not conceive you. I would like to adopt you legally, and maybe I can arrange it when I get back. I shall join you with your mother just as fast as I can. I embrace you." For a moment, they held each other tightly, then Guy moved to where Marie-Thérèse was waiting. "It will be a fast trip, darling. I will be back before you know it. I have left you ample funds in the bank, and Grotesquieu will be looking after you. It is hard to believe that by the time I return our baby will be almost ready to make its debut. We must think of a name, girl and boy."

"I shall study English with Sister Annette while you are gone, and when you are back, I shall speak as well as you."

A sailor approached from the launch. "Pardon me, sir, but we should be shoving off."

Guy took Marie-Thérèse in his arms, conscious of her stomach against him. "This is a delicate time to leave a woman, forgive me, but I hope it is the last time we are apart. I love you, Marie-Thérèse, and I am already missing you." He kissed her tenderly.

"Take care of yourself, Guy. Do not take a chance of being arrested—if you see there will be trouble, just leave and come back. We will somehow manage, we three . . . I mean, four." She reached her lips up to his, then took his arm and walked him to the launch. They looked at each other one last time before Guy stepped onto the launch, and the sailors rowed briskly away.

The following day, Marie-Thérèse bade farewell to her son. When she saw her name on the bow of the keelboat, she asked Mike Fink to take it off. "I am superstitious about such things," she said.

"But we gotta have a name, Madame," Mike said. "It's the law of the sea."

"All right," she said. "Rémi, what about we name the boat *L'Espérance?*"

"I think that is a nice name for this particular boat."

Tricot said a polite good-bye, telling Marie-Thérèse not to worry, that he would look after Rémi; and Rémi, feeling self-conscious with the men on board watching his departure, kissed her lightly and mumbled that he loved her before striding up the gangplank, which was immediately withdrawn as the men in the bow began to row away from shore.

Marie-Thérèse stood on the quai for a while, watching the long slender craft slowly disappear, her mind not yet adjusted to the fact that the only two people who mattered to her had now slipped away on rather perilous missions. Rather than sad, she felt empty, and a bit light-headed. She had a nagging feeling about those two cannons on the sides of the boat; they seemed so solitary and futile, and yet their very presence suggested a hostile force to be combatted.

As she mounted the carriage to be driven back to the house, she was aware of a draining loneliness, akin to how she had felt those many years ago when she had left her parents' comfortable home in Rouen to board the ship that brought her here; the loneliness she had felt those first days with the Ursulines with no one to relate to, unsure of her future, apprehensive. Of course, now in her body she carried an embryonic life and that was reassuring, but this incipient family was so new, uprooted before it was rooted, perhaps it was only an illusion, a passing phenomenon destined never to reappear. As she looked out the carriage's window at the landscape of broken willows, a pervasive sadness filled her and slow tears ran down her cheeks.

I am a woman loved by, and in love with a splendid man whose baby I carry; I have a son who gladdens my heart; so why do I weep? Are they sad tears or tears of joy? Does it matter? Oh, yes, it matters. I am not a widow who has lost her husband to the sea and her son to the river, no, I am a bountiful woman who sheds joyful tears for my love, my baby, and the fine life that lies ahead of me, almost within my grasp.

But she turned her face from the window and covered her eyes with her hands, as tears, both sad and joyful, moistened her palms.

ON THE
MISSISSIPPI

Twenty-four

Rémi's first night on the river was scary. He was the only one allowed to sleep in the cabin which was filled with those supplies that had to be kept dry; everyone else slept on deck. Rémi had just fallen asleep when he was awakened by a terrible grunting noise and banging just beneath him. He rushed out on deck and reported it to Mike Fink, who was sitting on the cabin roof, smoking. It made him laugh. "Now, sonny, don't get flustrated—that thar's only the catfish and perch swirlin' around. They's thicker 'n hailstones in an ice storm. The river's plumb full of fish but mostly they's not good eating. The catfish are siza whales, but boney as hell, 'n the buffalo fish, sturgeon 'n perch are rotten tastin'. But us boatmen don't much like fish, so we don't put out no lines."

Rémi had no idea Louisiana was so enormous. He thought it was just the territory around New Orleans, but Mike Fink showed him on the map how the river winds up north with Mississippi and Tennessee on the starboard side and Arkansas on the portside, followed by Kentucky and Illinois on the starboard and Missouri on the portside, all of it contained in the area called the Louisiana Territory which ran from New Orleans all the way to the Great Lakes.

"Where we're headin's," Mike told Rémi, " 'bout twelve hundred miles up the Mississippi. We'll be lucky to make ten or twelve miles a day, reason being that the Mississippi is obstrupery crooked, with big bends make us go sideways 'stead of straight ahead. Today was forced to go along the neck of a fifty-four-mile bend, but we only went five miles forward. Current bucks us, so we try to stay close on the shore where it's not so strong, but then we're riskin' the bank caving in, so we keep to the banks that slant backwards, not forwards."

Mike explained that the water sometimes washed away the bottom of the bank so that huge hunks of land suddenly fell into the river; if a boat was underneath, it could be wiped out. Mike had seen it happen. Mike had counted three hundred and ninety-five bends in the river up to where the Missouri flows into it, which is where he was now headed.

In all his rough years, Mike had never found himself in the company of a boy, and although at first he regarded Rémi as an annoyance, he slowly came round to enjoying their relationship, answering his questions, seeing the river anew through Rémi's incredulous eyes, even protecting him from the bullying of his crew. Mike knew he would never have a family, given his roisterous life, but this filial interlude intrigued him and softened his gruffness.

Sandbars, islands, and logs were all over the river. A crewman stood in the bow at all times to watch for these obstacles, especially the sandbars and logs. The crewmen had names for everything. They told Rémi to watch for a sandbar called General Hill's Left Leg because of its odd shape. What they called Patty's Hen and Chickens was a group of small islands and one big island. A really bad turn in the Mississippi was called Devil's Elbow, and Muscle Shoals got its name because of how hard they had to work to get around it.

There were several methods for moving the boat up the Mississippi, the most common was "fernensting" which was accomplished by the boatmen setting their poles on the bottom and pushing off. These poles were about twenty feet long, tipped with iron at one end and a button at the other. In order to put their entire weight on the pole, the boatmen placed the button against a thick pad on their shoulders, then leaned forward and crawled aft on their hands and toes the length of the gangway that ran all along the top of the gunnels. These boatmen all wore red shirts, which identified them, and they were the toughest, most muscular men Rémi had ever seen. Their shirts were heavy with sweat and blood stained; they had huge callouses on their shoulders where the poles were placed. Mike stood on top of the cabin from where he operated the tiller that steered the boat. He gave commands so that the boatmen moved in unison. When he ordered, "Stand to your poles!" the men would arrange themselves in two files, one on each runway, facing the stern, with their poles "tossed" ready for action. At the command, "Set poles!" the men lowered their poles to the river bottom. When Mike called out, "Down on her!" the men put the buttons against their shoulders, bent the pole down, and walked aft, pushing the boat upriver under them. When they reached the stern, Mike would shout "Lift poles!" at which the men turned and ran forward while trailing their poles in the water. It was this maneuver that gave the gangway its name, the running board. When a log was encountered, the men would poke the spike ends of their poles into it and push the boat around it—a maneuver known as a "reverend set." When he wanted the men to release the log, Mike would yell, "Throw your poles wide and brace off!" Then to back away, "Set poles! Back her!" and the crew would give it a mighty heave.

Mike explained to Rémi that more dangerous than floating logs were the ones known as planters and sawyers. These logs had their root ends fixed in the river bottom with the free end pointed downstream. The planter was a log that laid like this under the surface and speared the boat that struck it. The sawyer was a planter with a free end that bobbed up and down with the current. The sawyer could be spotted, Mike explained, because it breaks the surface, but there were "sleeping sawyers" which were the most dangerous because they did not bounce up and down but suddenly rose up when a boat passed over them; they could stave in the bottom of a boat. Mike pointed out many disabled boats on the river sunk by planters.

When the river was too deep to use the poles, the next thing Mike did, if he could get to the shore, was referred to as a "cordelle." The cordelle is a tow line several hundred feet long with one end fastened to the top of the mast and the other end held by a boatman on shore. To keep the boat steady, there was a short rope called a "bridle" tied at one end to the bow and the other end to a ring through which the cordelle was passed. To get to the shore the crew either waded in or, if too deep, they swam with Plug McKay, the second pilot, leading the way, the end of the cordelle between his teeth.

The men on shore then pulled the boat forward. As Mike steered, the men on shore sometimes had to cut a path with their axes to get through thick brush and other hindrances. They also had to be on the lookout for snakes, many of which were poisonous, and they always carried guns in case of Indian attacks.

But when the shore was too thick with brush and rocks to penetrate, or when the cliffs abutted the water, they had to perform a maneuver called "warping." A skiff was kept on board for this purpose. Two men in the skiff would carry one end of the cordelle upriver and fasten it to a tree. That accomplished, the men in the bow of the keelboat hauled it forward by pulling on the rope hand-over-hand up to where it was fastened. The cordelle was then untied and again taken forward by the skiff and fastened to another tree upriver, and so on. This was the hardest and slowest method to move the boat which could only travel about six miles upstream on warping days.

Bushwacking was still the easiest way to propel the boat forward. This method involved grabbing a branch from the vegetation on the banks, walking aft to the stern, releasing the branch, then repeating the same maneuver, over and over. If all else was ruled out, the men could use the oars and row. But the trouble with rowing was that the boat had to be in deeper water away from the shore where the current was strong. Whatever method was used, it was very hard work; every hour Mike yelled "Rest!" and the crew got a few minutes off. That was when they received a "fillee," a drink of whiskey dispensed into cups by Mike from a keg on deck. The boatmen drank the whiskey with a cup of water straight from the river. The river water was thick and dark, and when poured into a tumbler it left a half inch of sediment. Rémi thought this was harmful but Mike explained that the sand in the water scoured out the bowels; the more you drank, the healthier you got. Plug, who was listening, agreed and added that the water was also very good for making a man potent and was a sure cure for the itch. Rémi thought that the water had a repulsive taste, but he conceded that it might be better with whiskey.

At first, Rémi thought the men suffered, working so hard, but all through the day Dirk Kettlehorn was playing his fiddle and singing, and they sang along with him.

> *Sun rose up, but we rows down*
> *All the way to Shawnee town,*
> *Pull away—pull away!*

The chanty Rémi liked best, was,

> *Oh! It's love was the 'casion of my downfall,*
> *I wish I hadn't never loved none at all!!*

Oh! It's love was the 'casion of my miseree,
Now I am bound but once I was free.

Sometimes Mike would take the lead, his big voice vibrating the
boat, the men singing back and forth with him:

The boatman is a lucky man,
No one can do as the boatman can,
The boatman dance and the boatman sing,
The boatman is up to everything.

Hi-o, away we go,
Floating down the river on the O-hi-o.

When the boatman goes on shore,
Look, old man, your sheep is gone,
He steals your sheep and steals your shote,
He puts 'em in a bag and totes 'em to the boat.

Hi-o, away we go,
Floating down the river on the O-hi-o.

When the boatman goes on shore,
He spends his money and works for more,
I never saw a girl in all my life,
But what she would be a boatman's wife.

At night, the boat either tied up, preferably where a fire for supper
could be started, or else, if the vegetation on the banks was too
dense, Dirk cooked on board while the men enjoyed still another
fillee.

Rémi found the food barely edible, usually burnt, and the biscuits
half-baked, but the crewmen ate it lustily. Occasionally Dirk cooked
a few of the chickens and that appealed to Rémi, but so far neither
the pigs nor the geese were served up. Occasionally the menu was
varied with the game that Mike brought down. He was a great shot
and Rémi was awed by his skill, especially the day he shot three
swans flying overhead, which Dirk made into a stew. Mike had a
prodigious knowledge of Mississippi birds. He shot down many spe-
cies just to show them to Rémi up close. Rémi, in turn, made a
collection of them: a dove, a red-headed woodpecker, a nighthawk,
a sandhill crane, a great white owl, a wild turkey, an ivory wood-

pecker, a great bat, a parakeet, a yellow titmouse, a ricebird, a red-
bird, a red starling, a crested bettern, a prairie hen, a tufted wood-
cock, and some birds that even Mike could not name. The prize
trophy was a white pelican. Rémi was impressed with the effortless
way in which Mike swivelled his gun, not bothering to take aim, and
boom!—the bird fell. He tried to teach Rémi who found it more
difficult than it looked. One morning the boat passed four canoes of
Choctaws headed for the Yazoo River. They had a hive of honey
they had found in the woods and Mike traded half the hive for a
white eagle he had shot, which the Indians prized because of its
showy, long feathers that could only be used by the chief for his
headdress.

After dinner, everyone rubbed themselves with smudge from the
fire to keep off the black flies, mosquitoes, and gnats. Some men
gambled and some danced. Almost every night there was a fight or
two, wrestling and punching, which the men rather enjoyed both as
spectators and participants. Dirk fiddled well and he was able to
keep the dancers going. The crewmen took turns dancing upon the
clear space on top of the cabin.

> *Dance, boatman, dance,*
> *Dance, away.*
> *Dance all night till broad daylight,*
> *And go home with the gal in the morning.*

Plug sometimes chimed in with the boat horn which somehow he
could convert into a musical sound. He claimed it scared off the
devil and brought good luck. The horn produced strange, sad, wailing notes, but it blended nicely with the fiddle, and the men had a
good time. It was a wonder to Rémi that they could dance and carry
on like that after a long hard day polling and cordelling, warping
and bushwhacking, but he concluded that the fillee kept them going,
the men dancing and singing, the smoke from their pipes curling up
in the light of the oil lamps, the fiddle sawing away against a moon-
lit sky. When the men got tired, they just flopped on the deck and
went to sleep until Mike would wake them with the horn at first
light and give them a fillee to start the day.

As for Tricot, the first days were pretty bad for him. Mike made
him eat from his own set of dishes, and the other men ate apart from
him. Not just the boatmen, but the other group of men, too. Rémi
was the only one who stayed near him. They did not use the word

nigger to address him, but talking among themselves they did. Rémi was getting angry about it, but Tricot said, "No, do not do anything; the way to fight fire is not with fire, but with water—that is what puts a fire out."

The second week on the river, the boat went aground on a hidden sandbar. The crew got into the water and tried to lift the boat off but it would not budge. Then they tried to dig a channel to float it off but that did not work either. Some of the men got into the skiff, tied a rope to the bow and tried to pull the boat off that way, with two men pushing from the stern but it still would not budge. Suddenly there was panic when one of the pushers slipped and fell into the current. Mike yelled, "Quicksand!" Tricot jumped in the water with a board and a length of rope that he threw to the crewman as he started to sink. He pulled him up and away from the sucking mud by putting the board down for the crewman to walk on. Tricot waded around to the front of the boat and maneuvered the board beneath the bow. He told the men to get out of the skiff and go to either side of the bow. At the count of three, they all lifted as Tricot took hold of the bow and pulled mightily. The boat moved slightly. Tricot called to Rémi to keep shifting the plank as the men lifted and he pulled. Slowly the boat began to slide forward on the board as the men lifted and Tricot, using his great strength, kept tugging until the boat came free at last, and was once more afloat.

That night something happened which, along with the boat incident, changed the men's attitude toward Tricot. Dirk was fiddling and the men were dancing when Tricot came on deck with ten glasses from the galley. He measured different levels of water into them from a pitcher; then with a knobbed stick, he began to strike the glasses, which gave off the notes of a melody that Tricot began to sing in a deep, mellow baritone. He sang Creole songs while accompanying himself with the music he created with the glasses. The men applauded and kept Tricot performing for over an hour. From that evening on, Tricot never again ate by himself.

Tricot was right: As he had said, water will put out fire.

VERSAILLES
REVISITED

Twenty-five

Guy arrived in France in a little under three months, the frigate *Piémontaise*, with double the sails of the *Gironde*, was more seaworthy. One of the ship's officers was going to Versailles to visit his mother, a lady-in-waiting to the queen, and he offered to share his carriage with Guy. Although the route was familiar, Guy nonetheless felt disoriented, as if this was strange, unexplored territory. And he had a certain apprehension about his reception at Versailles. He desperately hoped that his friend, Philippe de Lorraine, would be there, or else with whom would he stay? It was not likely that his manservant, Claude Reynaud, would still be around, and then, too, despite Grotesquieu's interpretation of his exclusion document, there was the possibility that the king, hearing about his reappearance, might take a dim view of it.

As the carriage swung through Versailles' massive gates and started to rumble across the cobblestones of the courtyard, Guy was struck by the magnitude of the palace, as if seeing it for the first time. Having now grown accustomed to the scale of the New Orleans mansions, Guy was awed by the majesty of Versailles, which he had for so many years taken for granted. But there was no feeling of homecoming or nostalgia for the familiar; in fact, quite the opposite was the case, a feeling that he was now liberated from this luxurious prison, from all the intrigue, backbiting, and gossip that swirled within.

Philippe de Lorraine was indeed in residence, and he was delighted to see Guy again. He had a commodious four-room apartment so there was no problem accommodating Guy for as long as he wanted to stay. On the first evening of Guy's arrival, at his request, they had dinner, just the two of them, in the apartment. Although Philippe understood Guy's uneasiness at being back in Versailles, he felt that Guy's concerns were groundless. "You are forgotten, dear Guy," he said. "The people of the court only care about today's intrigues and tomorrow's masked ball. There is no memory for recrimination."

Guy explained his fur-chartering mission and wanted to know about the disposition of the king and that of the new *maîtresse en titre*, Madame du Barry. "The King has changed somewhat since Pompadour died. If you ask me, the suffering of her last weeks deeply affected him. She had become such a pitiable creature, so agitated, so close to the edge of sanity. She could not sleep or eat properly, and was haunted by the fear she would suffocate. When I last spoke with her, she was completely distraught, almost raving. After her ghastly death, the King seemed more withdrawn from government than ever. He rose at eleven and led a self-absorbed life. He rarely met with his ministers, and when he did, he listlessly approved whatever they proposed. The very people who wanted to take advantage of him the most showed him the greatest attention. Pompadour once told me she knew every twist of the King's soul, and I am beginning to think that I have by now been around him long enough that I, too, know the twists of his soul. After Madame de Pompadour's death, His Highness had resolved never to have another *maîtresse en titre*, having had four, he said, and that was more than enough. But as you and I know, Guy, in the struggle between temptation and resolution, temptation always wins. And Madame du Barry—excuse me, *Comtesse* du Barry—was a temptation that easily melted his resolve."

"Is she the daughter of aristocrats?"

Philippe laughed. "If there is a muse of conniving and ambition, she is her daughter. Madame du Barry's mother, Anne Bécu, was an unmarried seamstress who supplemented her meager income by occasionally selling the favors of the voluptuous body nature had bestowed upon her. It is said that the most likely father was a monk named Gomard, known in their little community of Vaucouleurs as

Brother Angel, the local joke being that he had given her a bundle from heaven. With Brother Angel's help, little Jeanne Bécu, aged seven, was accepted in the Convent of Saint-Aure in Paris where she learned reading, writing, embroidery and housekeeping. Life there was austere—plain food, severe white serge uniforms with a coarse woolen hood. Jeanne stayed there until she was sixteen. When she left the convent, it was the first time in her life she was on her own. She was ravishingly lovely, as she is now, and so powerfully attractive that she aroused every man who laid eyes on her. Believe me, Guy, when you see her, you will feel a physical jolt."

"Philippe, please tell me as much about her as you can. If I am to get my fur charter, it will have to be through her, will it not? Is that not the province of the *maîtresse en titre?*"

"Yes, the King has relegated that kind of patronage to her."

"Well, I certainly cannot approach the King directly, feeling about me as he does, so if I am to succeed it must be through Madame du Barry. The more I know about her, the better."

"Well, she held a succession of jobs in Paris, apprentice to a hairdresser, companion to an old widow, salesgirl at the Maison Labille, a millinery shop on the rue Neuve-des-Petits-Champs. She was nineteen by then and made the acquaintance of gentlemen who frequented the shop to make purchases. Although Madame Labille locked up the sales girls every night in the dormitory above the shop, Mademoiselle Bécu invented ways to escape, and indulged herself with the raucous Paris nightlife. One of the places she frequented was a gambling house run by a man named de Duquenoy and it was there that she caught the attention of Comte Jean du Barry, a dapper, witty cardshark and wencher, brazenly unscrupulous, a polished conniver engaged in more questionable endeavours than a Pigalle pickpocket. I have met him on several occasions, each time with a different gorgeous young wench on his arm. The social world he inhabited referred to him simply as 'the Roué.' Although he did come from an old family, it was his brother who was the comte, not he, and the family château was a grubby place in remote Gascony. Du Barry's primary line of work was investments, and he invested in attractive women. He would come upon some seedy *grisette,* and after seducing her, he would teach her the manners, the speech, the carriage, the dance steps that libertines like the Duc de Nivernais would find irresistible. The Roué would then place the young lady with the customer at a substantial fee for himself, nothing for his disciple. I have seen the police reports on him—they are circulating around the palace, as is all this other information—and it says something like 'when he begins to weary of a woman he invariably sells her off, but it must be admitted that he is a connossieur and his merchandise is eminently saleable.'

"Well, he took one look at Jeanne Bécu, and he knew his fortune was made. After seducing her, he took her into his home and made her its hostess. That is where she met the crème de la crème of the Paris demimonde, princes of the most renowned houses in France: Lauzun, Fitzjames, Ligne, Richelieu. Here, Guy, is the police report about her, that we are all reading . . ."

"The Comte du Barry," Guy read, "exhibited his latest mistress in his box at the Comédie Italienne last Monday night, the demoiselle Bécu. She is a person nineteen years old, tall, well-made and of distinguished appearance with an extremely pretty face. No doubt he intends to dispose of her advantageously as he has with all his others."

"One evening she appeared at the Opéra Ball," Philippe continued, "unmasked and dressed entirely in white. The diarist d'Espinchal who writes for the *Paris Journal*, wrote this." Philippe picked up a newspaper clipping and read, " 'Never have I seen anyone more beautiful than this heavenly woman named Jeanne Bécu. She is tall, well-made, ravishingly pale, with an open forehead, fine eyes, beautiful lashes, an oval face with little moles upon her cheeks which only serve to enhance her beauty, a laughing mouth, and breasts most women would be wise to shun comparison.'

"At du Barry's house, Madamoiselle Bécu was the hostess of little supper parties where she entertained such high-level guests as Lord March, the future Duke of Queensbury and his companion, the Countess Larena, whose favors are reputed to cost him fifty thousand a year. Other exalted guests included the Duc de Duras, Lauzun, and Radix de Sainte-Foy, Treasurer of the Marine. The suppers were impeccably served, good conversation, fine wines, laughter, stringed music, and most of the time, the exquisite dessert was Jeanne Bécu herself.

"For four years, the future Comtesse du Barry presided over the Roué's house. All of the considerable income went to him with the rationale that she was serving an apprenticeship with much better things to come. Her years of apprenticeship refined her natural talents and instincts by bringing her together with many of France's most illustrious aristocrats; the Roué instilled in her the tastes and conventions by which these men judged a woman as desirable. He disciplined her to realize that an accomplished courtesan is one who can satisfy an aristocrat's image of the perfect woman, one who can alleviate boredom, amuse, beguile, and sympathize as well as arouse passion and satisfy it. Under du Barry's tutelage, Jeanne Bécu had become a formidable and valuable courtesan, and he was ready to cash in."

"He sold her to the King? How did he arrange that?"

"No, nothing so crass as that. He had the King *discover* her. You know how public it is here—the palace is always open to any farmer or shoemaker or tradesman who wants to wander around and watch the King eating or going to sleep or even watch the Queen in child-birth, all the crowds who gawk and gape at the procession of ministers and all that. Well, first du Barry ascertained the hour the King dined and what course he followed going from his quarters to the dining hall. Next, he alerted the King's first valet, Monsieur le Bel, who pimps for him. Then, two evenings in a row, du Barry had Jeanne Bécu place herself where she could be clearly seen as the King and his procession went to dinner. Le Bel had alerted the King. One look at Jeanne and His Highness was spellbound. He instructed le Bel to seek her out and invite her to the palace. The King had never experienced anyone like Jeanne—sexually, socially, intellectually, she dazzled him. All those intimate traits she had learned during her apprenticeship were paying off and in no time the King asked her to become his fifth *maîtresse en titre*.

"But there was yet another hurdle to jump—the King may only acquire a *maîtresse en titre* who is married. Since du Barry was already married to a woman he had not seen for ten years, he was desperate to quickly find a substitute, and that he did—his rather dim-witted brother, Guillaume du Barry, a clod who lived with his two sisters and aged mother in the backwoods of Lévignac. He was the one who legitimately bore the title of Comte, and in exchange for a modest sum of money, he participated in a church wedding with Jeanne Bécu who immediately left him at the portals of the church and departed for Versailles, never to see him again. But she was now officially the Comtesse du Barry.

"There was still one more crisis to overcome: In order to be officially received by the King, Comtesse du Barry had to be sponsored by a resident member of the court. None of the Versailles ladies was forthcoming, however, since du Barry's perceived reputation was that of a prostitute, and it was felt that any woman who presented her would bring disgrace upon herself. Finally the Duc du Richelieu, who was acquainted with Jeanne Bécu as a result of several visits to the Roué's house when she was hostess there, successfully prevailed upon the Comtesse Béarn whom he knew to be heavily in debt. In exchange for satisfying her creditors, the Comtesse de Béarn reluctantly agreed to present du Barry to the court.

"I was present in the King's Chamber when the assembly gathered to witness the presentation. The King was as nervous as a young groom at the altar while he awaited the arrival of the carriage that was bringing the Comtesses de Béarn and du Barry from Paris. They did not arrive at the appointed hour, and His Highness grew increasingly irritable. He was on the verge of dismissing the assembly when the clatter of horses' hooves in the courtyard presaged their arrival. There was an expectant silence as the two women were escorted up the *Escalier d'Honneur* and through the staterooms leading to the King's Chamber. A footman opened the doors and Richelieu triumphantly announced them.

"Everyone in the room seemed enlivened at the sight of this great beauty, her quite simple blue gown adorned with diamonds that the Roué had somehow inveigled for the occasion. She approached the King, her body lilting perfectly, and made a deep curtsy before him. Her hair was powdered to a snowy white that flattered the delicate rose color of her skin and the penetrating green of her partially closed, slanting eyes. The King invested her with his formal recognition and then she very coolly kicked back the long train of her dress, made three reverences, and deftly withdrew backwards from the room. Even her detractors had to admit she made a most impressive presentation."

"But how does she reveal herself now that she has the power of being the official mistress?"

"How do you mean?"

"As compared to Madame de Pompadour."

"Oh, she is much less ambitious, no comparison. To begin with, she is not at all political whereas Pompadour was more the King than the King himself. Who got us into the disastrous Seven Years' War? Pompadour. Who passed on all appointments to state office, especially the ministers? Pompadour. What wasn't she into? Raising taxes, building more and more palatial edifices—how many were there, sixteen? She was always raiding the Treasury to finance some grandiose scheme or other. Hers was a life of affairs, of intrigues, of negotiations, the maintenance of a political role, a public exercise of power, a commerce at all hours with Secretaries of State, with men of the sword, with men of money, with men of the robe, a control of the interests of the nation and of the will of the King, an influence on the destinies of France and, yes, of Europe. All of the King's mistresses must have been like that. Madame de Châteauroux, who preceded Pompadour, was made a duchesse, and in league with the Duc du Richelieu, who was probably her lover, also connived to control the affairs of state, including the military, as well as the intrigues and politics of Versailles. She died a violent and mysterious death when she was but twenty-seven years of age.

"But Madame du Barry is cast from a different mold than the previous greedy mistresses. It is true that out of gratitude she steered considerable compensation toward the Roué, but for the most part, she has cast herself in the traditional role of a mistress. Her day is devoted to the King to the exclusion of all else. The King has tea with her every day until his council meeting. While he is gone, du Barry gives audience to all petitioners—that is when you will present yourself. After that, she withdraws to prepare herself for the evening. She pays a great deal of attention to her clothing, jewelry, and cosmetics, and spends huge sums on them, knowing that her beauty gives the King enormous pleasure. Every evening she accompanies the King for a *souper* with a select group which invariably includes Madame de Mirepoix, Madame de Valentinois, Madame d'Aiguillon, the Duc de Cossé, the Duc de Duras, and the Prince de Soubise, all favorites of the King. Afterwards, this select group gambles at cards or dice, whichever the King prefers. Du Barry devotes herself entirely to keeping the King amused. At the slightest sign of boredom, she invents some new diversion. She is very clever at that and, of course, she also has an easy attraction at her disposal, her silky bed. As a matter of fact, the King has not visited the girls at the Parc aux Cerfs since du Barry arrived, and there is talk of closing it down. As a result the King has been rejuvenated and is in high good spirits. He greets those who pass him in the halls and is positively outgoing. Last week, at a dinner for his cousin, Charles III of Spain, I overheard the King telling him about du Barry: 'She makes me forget,' he said, 'that soon I will be sixty.' But it is not just sex that fascinates the King. Du Barry has an extraordinary library and she reads to him from it—*The Iliad*, Ovid's *Metamorphoses*, Shakespeare (she is quite a student), Voltaire, Pascal, and Montaigue. She also has an extensive collection of pornographic literature. One of her protegés is a man named Morlière who has written some of the most salacious stories you will ever read. The way she leads the King from Shakespeare to pornographic excess fascinates him."

"How do you think I should present myself?"

"Straightforward, no flattery or pomposity. You will find her gentle and attentive. Praise the King, be thankful for the opportunity he gave you to settle in Louisiana, talk about the theater, which she adores, admire the furnishings of her apartment, which are lavish and of which she is very proud. She is easy to talk to—*sympatique*."

"But do not forget she revoked my plantation charter and awarded it to Duroux."

"Yes, but we do not know what fabrication your Monsieur Duroux might have told her. Do you want her to restore your plantation? It is possible you could achieve that."

"No, I really think I am better off leaving New Orleans for a life up north. I am intrigued by the possibility of establishing a post for fur trading. My own place. My own business. I am not the same man who left here, Phillippe."

Three days later, Guy was able to arrange an appointment with the Comtesse du Barry. In the meantime, as Philippe had predicted, Guy was treated by the court regulars as if he had never left. Actually, most of them, concerned as they were by the social exigencies of the moment, had forgotten the gossip about him and the departed Madame de Pompadour. Out of sight was truly out of mind as far as Versailles society was concerned. But Guy had not yet been confronted by Louis XV and he continued to be concerned that the king might react vindictively when made aware that he had returned and was brazenly in residence at Versailles.

Guy's appointment was for ten o'clock. Madame du Barry's day had begun an hour earlier when, as usual, her personal maid came softly into her chamber and opened the heavy draperies, the daylight awakening Madame du Barry who slept cozily in a silk cocoon of pillows, laces and ribbons. Her four-columned bed, nestled in an alcove four steps above the floor level, was made of rare woods carved by several of the country's most eminent sculptors and gilded by a master gilder—Monsieur Clagny. The columns, entwined with carved myrtle and ivy with rose clusters at their apexes, upheld a baldachin of silk and gold. A white silk rug covered the steps that led to the bed. The bed itself was encased in silk curtains embroidered with a pattern of rose clusters, the same embroidery which embellished the window draperies and the room's thirteen chairs arranged in an arc at the foot of the bed. The boudoir was also adorned with a white satinwood commode inlaid with porcelain and a gold clock upheld by the figures of the Three Graces, while Eros, depicted on the clockface, pointed to the hour with a golden arrow. Doves and cupids in gold and crystal were everywhere around the room.

After awakening, Madame du Barry's ladies-in-waiting came quietly into the room, wrapped her in a peignoir, and accompanied her to the bath they had prepared for her—a bath redolent with elixirs and perfumes. While she luxuriated in her bath, her secretary read the mail to her; a potpourri of bills, invitations, letters asking favors, letters asking sponsorship, a stream of correspondence reflecting the influence of her position.

Following her bath, Madame du Barry, draped in a flowing robe of white silk, returned to her bedroom where her little Senegalese page, Zamore, was waiting to serve her coffee in her special gold cup. At the same time, her dressing table was placed at the window precisely where it would receive the strongest light. On the dresser's surface was an extensive collection of crystal bottles, porcelain jars, lacquered boxes, and silvered trays, each one with a special cream, liquid balm, or mysterious unguent that she would meticulously apply to her face, neck, and hair. The large dressing-table mirror, set in a solid gold frame, was the handiwork of the renowned artisan, Rottiers de la Tour, who had surmounted the frame with Comtesse du Barry's solid gold coronet. It was during this time-consuming process at the mirror when those awaiting interviews were ushered in.

Guy arrived precisely at ten o'clock, naively believing that the interview had been arranged especially for him. He was surprised to find that du Barry's lilac-and-gold antechamber was crowded with others, primarily merchants, who also had appointments. Since he was the last to arrive, Guy had ample time to study the surroundings. Through the open doors he had full view of the salon which had been designed and furnished by the prestigious decorators, Gabriel and Marigny, who had employed celebrated artists and craftsman from all over Europe to create what was patently the most sumptuous apartment in Versailles, including the king's. The lustrous ceiling of the main salon was covered with rock crystal. Two glorious commodes dominated the room, one richly lacquered with two gilded baboons in bas-relief; the other decorated with five plaques of priceless Sèvres porcelain. Aptly referred to as an "asylum of voluptuous pleasure," the salon presented remarkable treasures wherever anyone looked. Marbles, bronzes, porcelains, crystals, and lacquers of unprecedented beauty blended with the exquisite furniture. At one end of the room, a masterful piece of furniture contained the gambling paraphernalia so essential for the king's entertainment on the evenings he spent there. There was an ivory backgammon set built into a table of rosewood marquetry, four quadrille boxes in carved ivory, its counters, pegs, and markers inlaid with gold. Also dominant was a rosewood piano made by the Clicot company, inlaid with blue and white mosaics and decorated with fittings of bronze and gold. It was a setting like none other Guy had ever seen, and by comparison it made the apartment of Madame de Pompadour look like the concierge's loge.

The first to be summoned from the antechamber were the jewelers, Boehmer and Rouen, bearing the temptations of their trade: a dazzling array of rings, bracelets, necklaces, tiaras, pins, earrings, and clips. In addition, there were precious stones cut in intaglio, delicate cameos, and decorative hair combs of tortoise shell and diamonds. The jewelers also bore a velvet box containing several pairs of shoes encrusted with seed pearls. Madame du Barry made numerous selections, pointing to this one and that one, much as a child designates sweets at the counter of a candy shop.

After the jewelers departed, smiles of success on their faces, one after the other, the dressmakers, the couturiers, and the milliners were ushered in, bearing their creations. To have a dress or a purse selected by Madame du Barry was a great boon not just for the profit of the sale but primarily because Madame du Barry set the fashion that influenced European society. In fact, there were monthly dispatches of dolls, costumed in du Barry's latest gowns, sent from France to fashion centers all over Europe where the local couturiers eagerly copied these fashions for their clientele. The latest doll disbursed to the fashion centers replicated the white satin dress du Barry had worn at the wedding of the dauphin's youngest brother, the Comte d'Artois; the gown, embroidered with pale green and pink butterflies, the collar festooned with delicate little roses, had been created for du Barry by Pagelle, the most celebrated designer on the rue St.-Honoré.

On this particular morning, after the gowns had been selected, each costing the equivalent of three thousand dollars, and the couturiers and milliners dealt with, the next people summoned were Berline, the royal hairdresser, along with Viguier, the perfumer, who presented a new scent he had concocted for the comtesse who had challenged him to produce a perfume uniquely hers.

Now, finally, Guy was summoned. Madame du Barry offered her hand to him and explained that she was pressed for time, so would he mind if Berline continued to arrange her hair as they conversed.

"I regret, my dear Berline," she said to the hairdresser, "that I shall not be able to listen to your gossip today, but please remember the most scandalous items for tomorrow." At that, she gave her full attention to Guy.

For a moment, as he looked at her for the first time, Guy was shocked by her beauty, quite the most stunning woman he had ever seen. Her pure blond hair, now being coiffed by Berline, fell in a profusion to her shoulders. Her green eyes had an innocent, open quality as she kept them fixedly on Guy. She had a tiny nose, a very small mouth, and skin of alabaster whiteness. Her small hands, the curve of her throat, her luminous teeth, her whole being in harmonious perfection.

It was an effort for Guy to focus his attention on the purpose of his visit. "I thank you very much for consenting to see me on such short notice," he began. "Perhaps I should begin by telling you something of myself. I lived here at Versailles until recently when I went to New Orleans located in our Louisiana territory in the New World. I had been in possession of a plantation which the Crown has now assigned to someone else, leaving me without an undertaking of my own. What I would like to propose is a charter that would enable me to establish a fur post on the Mississippi up north where it joins the Missouri. That is where the skilled Indian trappers are concentrated. I understand France is in need of quality furs, and these, I assure you, Comtesse, are the finest furs in the world. I would ship them down the Mississippi to New Orleans where they would be processed and sent on to France. To accomplish this, I would need a Royal Charter granting me exclusive rights to that territory. I take note of your interest in fashion—you would have access to the finest furs of the lot—and I would establish, in the name of France, a post on the Mississippi that would become a fur center for the entire territory. It is my hope that you will look upon my request favorably and propose it to His Majesty. I can see from the magnificent accoutrements of your apartment, from your exquisite clothes, that you have a great appreciation for visual beauty, as you yourself personify, and certainly the luxurious furs of the fox, the beaver, the otter, and other exotic animals trapped so expertly by the Indians, would pique your interest."

Madame du Barry, who had been listening intently, now turned her eyes toward the mirror, and with a tiny golden knife began carefully to scrape away the slight excess of powder on her face. "Tell me, Monsieur Laroule, did you actually have an affair with Madame de Pompadour?"

Guy was taken aback by the abruptness of the question, but, without hesitation, answered, "No, Madame la Comtesse, I did not."

"It was generally perceived that you did."

"I'm aware of that, since we were indeed intimate friends who performed on the stage together, but that intimacy did not extend beyond the bounds of friendship. The Marquise was devoted to the King as his mistress, and I as his loyal and admiring subject."

"Your recent letter did not reflect admiration."

"What letter would that be?"

"The one you wrote renouncing your plantation and excoriating the King for having directed you to leave France."

"I assure you, Comtesse, I wrote no such letter. My plantation was successful, a source of joy for me, and I have never spoken nor written an excoriating word about the King."

"But I myself read the letter that was presented to me by Monsieur . . ." She looked toward her secretary who sat unobtrusively to one side. "Duroux," the secretary said, "Bernard Duroux."

"Do you have the letter?"

The secretary handed the letter to Guy.

I have asked my friend, Bernard Duroux, to present this letter on my behalf. Having been unjustly compelled by the Crown to leave Versailles, I am no longer willing to accept the primitive plantation assigned to me by His Majesty as compensation for having been banished from my native land. As a consequence, I renounce the charter granted to me for the Diderot Plantation in favor of M. Duroux, and I further renounce any future allegiance to His Majesty, Louis XV.

Guy Laroule (his seal)

Guy returned the letter to the secretary. "A forgery. I wrote no such letter. This is not my signature. Here, I will sign my name for you so that you can see for yourself. Duroux is an unprincipled, sadistic plantation owner who tortures his slaves and has no regard for the law. This letter was obviously a ruse by which he was able to force me off my plantation and claim it as his own."

"Would you like to reclaim it?"

"No, now I am committed to the fur project, but in all justice, I would like to see Duroux stripped of his ill-gotten charter and have the plantation ceded to an honest and deserving person."

"This Duroux, as I recall, also exerted some influence through the Duc de Richelieu."

"He knew Richelieu?"

"Perhaps. I am not clear as to just what the connection was. But since I pride myself on dealing honestly with people, I do not tolerate deceit, and if you will submit the name of someone in New Orleans whom you think better suited to the plantation, I shall make every effort to have the plantation transferred to him, with the understanding that a tithe of his income must be forwarded to the Crown. His Majesty is concerned about the huge costs of sustaining our presence in Louisiana. And the same tithe will apply to your fur trading post if we arrange it—is that agreed?"

"Yes."

"I cannot be sure that your request will be granted. Perhaps you should attend tomorrow night's *souper,* and afterwards entertain us with a few songs. We have a very gifted young singer, Madame Hélène de Lilane, who could join you in a duet."

"I have not sung in some time, and I do not have music."

"Perhaps you could rehearse with Madame de Lilane this afternoon. I am sure she has suitable music."

"May I be frank with you and mention something that is of concern to me?"

"Yes, of course."

"I wonder how the King will react to my presence. Perhaps he will be displeased that I have returned, briefly though it will be. I do not have royal permission to be here."

"Do not be concerned. I mentioned this appointment to him and he registered no disapproval."

"That is most reassuring."

"Now tell me about Madame de Pompadour. I never met her, and I have a great curiosity about her since she was my predecessor."

As Guy told her about the woman who had played such an important part in his life, the Comtesse continued to attend to her toilette, adding a touch of carmine to her lips, a trace of rose to her nails. For Guy, this peculiarly intimate yet impersonal businesslike interview was unsettling. Du Barry was so appealing, radiated such an aura of enticement that Guy felt an urge to touch her, as if to reassure himself that there was warm life beneath her cooly exquisite exterior. It was an urge he sometimes felt when viewing the portrait of a beautiful woman painted by a great artist. It was as if Boucher had painted du Barry in the gold frame of her mirror and captured her for posterity.

BATTLING THE
MISSISSIPPI

Twenty-six

For a time the *Espérance* made good, steady progress—twelve miles a day—against the Mississippi's current, even able to use the sails when the breeze was right. As Mike Fink said, "I ain't honey-fugglin' when I say we're goin' smoother than a baboon's sittin' area."

The big barges and flatboats going downriver fascinated Rémi. They carried great loads of commodities: whole barnyards of cows, horses, chickens, cats, turkeys, and geese; a forest of oak and walnut logs; carriages and dray horses, everything imaginable. The most amazing vessel was one that sported a huge paddle wheel on its side powered by eight horses on a treadmill, which, combined with the strong current, propelled the boat so fast that the patroon was hard-pressed to keep the tiller under control. A few of the big barges had little cottages built on them with brick fireplaces and a stable for animals. They had a complement of twenty-five boatmen, indicating that they were rich people determined to live on the water as they did back home.

The weather, however, soon turned ugly with strong headwinds and fog so thick you couldn't see from one end of the boat to the other. The gusts were so strong that some days they had to get close to shore and tie up to a stout tree to keep from being blown backwards. On those days, even the anchor couldn't hold the boat in place. When these dense mists blanketed the Mississippi, boatmen all over the Mississippi River started to sound their foghorns. It was exciting for Rémi to hear all that wild horn-blowing that seemingly came out of nowhere. It rained steadily and hard; after only one day and night of rain, the river had risen two feet. Despite the drenching, the boatmen did not bother to cover themselves and kept on working, soaking wet. Mike explained that when it rained that heavily, some of the mudbanks would slide into the river, so Mike avoided the shoreline if he could.

Occasionally, when Mike passed a flatboat that was tied up because the current was too strong, he was able to obtain supplies from them. One boat sold him a hundred pounds of bacon, and another, loaded to the gunwales with potatoes, sold him enough to last for two months.

Later, when the weather changed for the better, they passed a big barge with a large cabin anchored at an islet in the middle of the river. A white flag emblazoned with a green Christmas tree on it and the name "Annie" in red above it flapped atop a pole. When Mike saw the flag he called out, "Ahoy mates, here's Annie Christmas, but first man don't behave gets explatterated and explunctified!"

When he tied up alongside the barge, there came out of the cabin one of the biggest women Rémi had ever seen. In fact, *the* biggest. She must have been close to seven feet tall, but she had a pretty face and her body, big as it was, was very shapely. She was wearing a bright red dress with spangles on it that dipped so low in front you could see almost all of her breasts. Her cheeks were heavily rouged and her blond hair was down to her shoulders. "Mike! Mike Fink, you hell-raiser!" she yelled out in a voice as big as she was. "Hope your mule's got a kick to it, 'cause I ain't had a good customer for three days!" Mike hopped onto her barge as she wrapped her long arms around him and pulled him up off the ground. She kissed him ravenously. Behind her, girls poured out on deck, greeting the men as they came on the barge.

"You givin' me one on the house?" Mike asked Annie Christmas.

"You pay for two, the third one's free. That's house rules," Annie said.

"What about the fourth?" Mike asked.

"You get yourself up for number four, I'll pay you," Annie said, with a laugh that shook the very boards of the barge. She gave Mike a mighty shove that staggered him as, still laughing heartily, she pushed him into the cabin, followed by the other girls and all the other men.

"Girls, give them their money's worth," Annie yelled out to her charges who had already claimed their partners with whom they were disappearing into the cabin. Only Rémi and Tricot stayed on board.

Rémi asked Tricot why he did not go along. He said two reasons: One, he was not allowed since there was no black lady, and two, he does not believe in the kind of sex you pay for.

One day Mike gave Rémi a taste of the fillee of whiskey that the crew was drinking. Rémi said, "It tastes like the worst medicine I ever took and it burned my mouth, my throat, and my swallowing pipe all the way down to my stomach. With all the fillees they drink no wonder the men sing all day and dance at night."

The further north they went, the worse the weather got, incessant thunder, lightning, and fierce rains inundated them just as they had to cross roiling rapids that spun them around. The whole boat trembled. Rémi thought they were going under for sure. The downpour was implacable, three days steady, night and day; the river rose two feet every day, and entire sections of mudbanks crashed down into the river. Mike said if it did not let up, the river might rise so high that it would go over the top of its banks. He had seen it. They went through patches of stinging hail, and ice was beginning to form along the sides of the river. At one point, the *Espérance* barely avoided crashing into what appeared to be a floating island, but was in fact an enormous collection of trees and timber that had attached itself to the end of a real island, where it became tangled and matted together. These wooden islands were huge—this one covered a quarter of a mile—and it was particularly dangerous because the river was very deep, as much as sixty feet, and the current was extremely strong. All the men worked frantically to keep them from being dashed to pieces on its point.

One of the worst places they had to cross on the Mississippi was an underwater reef, called the Grand Chain of Rocks that extended across the entire river. The patroon had to know precisely where the openings in the rocks were or the boat would get torn to shreds. Just beyond that was a stupendous mass of rocks called the Grand Tower where the river suddenly turned to the left and in the next mile turned right again. Mike had to be on the lookout every foot of the way. Rémi kept watch up on the bow because Mike had said, "The floating island is teetotally twisted and I'm not honey-fugglin' you when I say young eyes catch on ahead of the hounds and kin keep us from windin' up worser'n a blind mule in a yaller jacket's nes'."

But the worst was yet to come. Toward the end of the month when the weather cleared but it was still cold, the sun broke through the cloud cover. The *Espérance* had been making good time with the sail catching some off-and-on breeze blowing behind it. Mike had maneuvered near the shore enabling the boatmen to reach the bottom with their poles and give good shoves to abet the wind. It was around four o'clock when Mike gave the order to tie up for the night and prepare for supper. Very dense brush kept the men aboard the boat, to indulge in the now-familiar ritual drinking fillees and dancing to Dirk's fiddle while waiting for the fire to catch on. A couple of men started a peculiar kind of jiglike dance with their legs kicking out and their arms waving over their heads, singing away and whooping while the others clapped hands and whistled. Still playing, Dirk, too, began to dance—he sort of shuffled his feet side to side and twirled around—when an arrow buried itself in his right eye. His arm shot up as the fiddle clattered to the deck, his right hand still holding the bow. Another arrow pierced his chest, toppling him backwards, blood spurting from his eye.

Arrows now came from all over as Mike yelled, "Ever'body down! Get your muskets!" Mike had briefed everyone on what to do if attacked, where to go, how to cover themselves, but trying to get to the muskets without being hit was a treacherous undertaking. In case of attack, Mike had instructed Rémi to get inside the cabin and lay down behind a mound of supplies, which Rémi managed to do. Indians on shore, a solid line of them, were blanketing the deck with their arrows one of which struck Plug Mackay in the arm, but he just yanked it out and opened fire with his musket. His first shot hit one of the braves who clutched at himself and pitched into the river. By now Mike and the others had stationed themselves behind the pile of lumber amidship and were firing too. They killed several of the Indians, but there were reserve ranks to take their places. The arrows fell thick as rain. Rémi grabbed a musket and began to load it just as an arrow with a tail of fire struck a wooden container of potatoes that burst into flames. One of the carpenters grabbed a pail of water and put out the fire as two of the crewmen who were in charge of the cannon fired a round at the Indians, but it went high over their heads. Mike had a musket in each hand, and each time he fired an Indian fell dead. Tricot was firing a shotgun from a place in the bow where there was an overhang he could use for protection.

Though arrows were all around him, he, too, was making every shot count. The cannon fired again, this time right on target; several Indians were struck, some toppling backwards, some thrown into the water which was turning blood red. Rémi was ready with his musket, prepared to leave the cabin to join the combat, when he saw two Indians coming up over the leeward side of the boat, brandishing tomahawks and knives. Rémi yelled for Mike and then fired his piece, striking the closest one who doubled over but kept coming at him as Rémi frantically tried to reload. The Indian had red and white stripes painted on his face and indigo smeared all over his naked chest and arms. There was a single white feather in his headband. A round of blood was spreading crimson over his indigo torso, but he continued to run at Rémi, holding onto his weapons. Trying desperately to get more powder in the muzzle, Rémi did everything Guy had taught him when they hunted together, but he was too slow. The Indian was almost upon him. The second warrior was right behind him. Mike seized one of the Indians who knifed him in the side, but Mike picked him up, hurled him onto the deck, and stomped on his head with his heavy boots. The Indian coming at Rémi was now only a few feet away from him. Rémi's back was up against the wall of the cabin. As the Indian raised his tomahawk, Rémi put up his arms in defense, but the Indian succumbed to his wound and fell dead at his feet. Rémi began to tremble from the brutality of the encounter.

Mike was on the leeward side where canoes were bringing Indians to board the boat from that side while the others were attacking from the shore. Mike couldn't use the cannon because it was only able to swivel from side to side, not up and down. Flaming arrows were peppering the deck. Two of the ship's men were dead, two others were wounded but continued fighting. The cannon on the starboard side was firing as fast as the men could reload, but it was missing more times than hitting. The deck was slippery with blood. Mike shouted a warning as canoes came alongside the *Espérance*. One was already tied up below with six braves in it. Rémi aimed down at them, holding his gun steady with both hands; his shot landed dead on, the Indians pitching into the water as the canoe sank to the bottom. But another canoe was already taking its place as Rémi desperately reloaded.

The Indians were getting the upper hand. Their flaming arrows had started little fires which the crewmen could not extinguish without exposing themselves to the steady stream of arrows. By now, the boat was completely surrounded with canoes. The Indians had grappling hooks tied to long ropes; one of them would twirl the rope around his head and let the hook end sail up onto the deck, embedding itself into the gunwale. Once solidly implanted, they would pull themselves up the rope to get on deck. By now, Mike was attacking the canoes by picking up the big oak logs on board and, one at a time, dropping them on the canoes. These logs were so heavy it had taken two men to carry them on deck, but Mike picked them up like matchsticks and hurled them down on the canoes. Rémi tried to loosen the hooks and drop them back in the water before the Indians could pull themselves up the ropes. But he had to be careful. Every time he rose up to loosen a hook a covey of arrows came at him. One of them went through the sleeve of his tunic and pinned him to the gunwale, but he tore himself away. Mike was yelling, "Stay down, lad, stay down, dammit!"

But there were too many of them to fend off. They were closing in on both sides. Rémi was terrified. He had heard many stories about how the Indians scalp you and leave you for dead with the top of your head missing. Plug Mackay was affixing a piece of white sail at the end of a pole ready to surrender, but Rémi's plan was to dive into the water and try to swim away, going under and holding his breath as long as he could. He was a good swimmer, so he figured his chances in the water were better than staying on board and getting scalped.

Plug hoisted the pole aloft. Rémi had started to take off his shoes, the better to swim, when there was a tremendous boom, the sound of fifty cannons going off. The boat suddenly pitched and shuddered, tossing Rémi down the deck and up against the cabin so hard his shoulder turned numb when it hit. Judgment Day, he thought, Judgment Day has come!

Everyone on board grabbed hold of something as the boat again was tossed up out of the water and came back down with a violent thump. The shore had completely disappeared, the entire bluff had collapsed into the water, taking all the Indians with it. The water of the river was roiling; all the canoes were wiped out, twisted uprooted trees fell into the river, slamming into other floating objects. Inhuman howling could be heard above the din.

Everywhere banks slid into the river, islands disappeared, logs boiled up from the river bottom creating a sea of logs, roots, scrubs, and great clots of mud so solid that the surface of the water was invisible.

Mike was yelling, "Quake! Quake!" Everyone was clinging to things as best they could. There were waves on the river that belonged in the ocean. The river bottom opened up, clearing a wide trough; everything that passed was sucked into its abyss. Even some of the canoes, along with the remains of wrecked boats, swirled to the bottom.

The rope holding the *Espérance*'s mooring cable snapped. Whole sections of the woods pushed forward, smashed together with a deafening crackling roar, all of it suddenly devoured by a voracious vortex. Everywhere the earth was splitting, throwing water, stones, and filthy fountains of slimy scum high up into the fetid air. Mike struggled vainly to control his boat. The whole world seemed to have turned upside down. The boat was rapidly spinning toward the whirlpool in the middle of the river. Mike had tied himself to the tiller and was trying to steer the boat away from its doom, but the water was much too savage. Everyone on board was holding on for their lives as the craft came nearer and nearer to disaster. Rémi prayed, prayed desperately, promising God everything he could think of to promise. Out loud he said his good-byes to his mother and to Guy, but the howling noise of the wind and the water obliterated his words.

The jolt threw Rémi clear across the deck where he hit his head hard against the bow. The boat had suddenly stopped stark still. *L'Espérance* was up out of the water on top of an erupted sandbar. Similar sandbars started appearing all around; islands submerged, with only the very top of their trees showing above the surface. Boat wrecks, parts of houses, sacks of supplies, endless cascades of barrels, entire sails, dead cattle and many other animals, crosses that must have washed away from a cemetery, coils of rope, boat horns, all kinds of tools and guns bobbed on the river's surface as far as the eye could see. When Rémi spotted a fiddle with its neck broken, he started to cry for Dirk Kettlehorn whom he would never see again and for those men who were dead, for the wrecked world around him, and for all the people, probably dead, who had lost these possessions, now merely flotsam on the river. He even cried because he had killed those Indians, especially the one he had shot in the chest who fell at his feet. Some of his blood was still on his shoes. Unable to cease sobbing, he asked God to forgive him.

Twenty-seven

FOR THREE WEEKS, Guy waited in vain for word from Comtesse du Barry about the fur charter. Guy had performed admirably at the musicale, his voice in surprisingly good form after not having sung for so long a time. At the conclusion of his performance, the king nodded to him approvingly before leaving with his entourage. But no word from Madame du Barry.

Guy constantly worried about Rémi going up the Mississippi in the company of those rough, unprincipled Kentuckians. How could he have sent a boy of twelve on such a mission? Guy also brooded about Marie-Thérèse with her pregnant baby. He thought about her all during each interminable day, and at night when he got into bed he yearned for her now-familiar but exciting body, her soft voice, her caressing hands. If God is willing that we reunite, Guy promised himself, I will never let us part again. I have become an alien here in my birthplace; wherever I am with her is my homeland. Some nights he would lay awake for hours, plotting life as it was destined to be with her and Rémi. It will happen, he declared, I promise them, I promise myself, I will make it happen. Then, too, he speculated about the baby stirring in her abdomen, his first child. Before Marie-Thérèse he had given no thought to having a child. The life he led at Versailles was thoroughly self-indulgent, a narcotic of events devoid of responsibility, of passion, of caring, pleasure for pleasure's sake.

To be back here now, was like being held a prisoner to the past he had so strenuously rejected. He could never again dwell in Sybaris.

To his surprise when he was finally summoned it was not to see Madame du Barry, but the king himself. Knowing the unpredictableness of palace politics, Guy was apprehensive as he approached the King's Chamber. And as he was escorted to the Throne Room, Guy's apprehension intensified when he saw his old nemesis, the Duc de Richelieu, standing beside the king who was not sitting on the throne but on a divan to the side. His Highness motioned Guy to a chair facing him.

"You were in very good voice, Laroule," the king said.

"Thank you, Your Majesty," Guy replied.

"The musicales have suffered from mediocrity lately."

"I am sorry to hear it."

"And my ears have been sorry to hear the onslaught of tenors to whom they have been subjected."

Richelieu smiled at the king's little joke. "And quite a few derelict sopranos," he added.

"Madame de Lilane excepted," the king said.

"It was a pleasure singing with her," Guy said.

"Comtesse du Barry has favorably presented your petition for a grant to establish a fur post in Louisiana with a tithe going to the Crown," the king said. "We are disposed to grant your request, but we wish to inform you of certain recent developments that may alter your thinking. Explain, Richelieu."

"His Majesty is referring to the fact that two years ago at Fontainebleau, in an undisclosed pact with his cousin, Charles III of Spain, His Highness ceded to Spain the Isle of Orléans and almost all of Louisiana Province. That transfer was made public last month when Spain sent a director general to New Orleans to take over the government and install Spanish officials."

"But the citizens are all French," Guy said.

"Yes, but they are all now subjects of Charles III, and will live under the laws of Spain."

"But why?"

The king answered, "For two reasons: it costs the Crown almost two million American dollars every year to support the colony which has never prospered. Also, Charles had been loyal to us during the battle with the British, a defeat which caused him to lose Manila, Havana, and Florida, so we gave him Louisiana as a gesture of our good will. We inform you of this because if you return you will be a subject of Spain, not France."

"Will all grants, therefore, become invalid?"

"No, under our pact all grants will be honored."

"Then if I had a Royal Grant it would be valid?"

"Yes," Richelieu said, "but subject to the rules and regulations promulgated by the Spanish Director General."

"During her last days, Madame de Pompadour spoke about you," the king said, "and convinced us that the edict pertaining to you should be rescinded. You shall be permitted to return to the Court if you desire."

"And if I prefer to establish the fur post?"

"It shall be granted."

"Then that is my preference, Your Majesty."

"So be it."

"May I please ask one additional favor of the Crown? It would be most advantageous to be permitted return passage on one of Your Majesty's warships."

"Arrange it, Richelieu. In return, Laroule, we would enjoy a farewell concert with Madame de Lilane."

"Of course, Your Highness. It would please me no end."

"On Comtesse du Barry's recommendation," Richelieu said, "you will also be given an edict ceding to you for your assigns the Plantation Diderot. I have instructed the authorities in New Orleans to interrogate this Duroux about the forgery which he presented to the Court. We do not suffer deceit without punishment."

"That is most gratifying," Guy said. "I do not know how to thank Your Majesty for such kindness."

"Do it with song," the king replied.

Twenty-eight

THE ESPÉRANCE LOST FIVE DAYS because of the earthquake. On the second day a significant aftershock caused the water to rise enabling the ship to float off the sandbar, but it was still much too dangerous to navigate. The river was choked with all manner of things uprooted by the earthquake. Afterward, there were a series of aftershocks, some sizeable, that stirred things up again; others rumbled like distant thunder, but were still ominous. For three days the boat was secured to a big oak tree on the bank.

There was much work to be done. First of all, the bodies of the four men who were killed had to be buried: two of Mike's boatmen, the two who manned the cannon, and two of Guy's men, a soldier and a carpenter. A party went ashore with shovels and dug six-foot graves for them. The remaining carpenter made crosses of wood, carved with the deceased's names, and placed them above each grave. Tricot read a psalm from his prayer book. Tricot included Dirk Kettlehorn in his psalm even though his body was never found. The men intoned the final amen and returned to their chores aboard.

There were many wounds. Some were not very serious, like Rémi's, just a bump on his head and some bruises, but others needed serious treatment. Plug Mackay had a very deep gash in his arm where he had pulled out the arrow; Mike had a cut on his side from the Indian's knife, but it was not serious. Three boatmen had glancing arrow wounds, and one boatman had burns on both hands from having put the fires out. The fur trapper and the cook had been wounded, but Mike told them it was nothing to worry about. Tricot had a deep cut across his forehead and another on his thigh. Mike treated all the wounds, including his own, in the same way: first he washed them clean with warm rum, and then bound them with poultices of hot bee honey. Only Plug's wound was cause for alarm.

In the pen where the animals were kept, all the fowl were dead; they smothered having huddled together in fright, but the two pigs and the lamb were all right.

It was necessary to do a lot of repairs and cleaning up, especially where the fires had been. Some of the supplies, primarily the logs and timber Mike had thrown at the braves, had been lost, and arrows had split some of the food bags, spilling flour, rice, and beans all over the deck.

A day after treating him, Mike examined Plug's wound and said that it was getting better; he could tell because it was beginning to form pus. Plug asked for his fillee and a smoke, which Mike said was a good sign.

With Dirk gone, Guy's cook took over the kitchen chores. Fortunately, everyone aboard was able to get to shore where a fire was built for the evening meal. A big argument erupted over whether or not it was safe to cook the dead chickens which were still in a heap in the pen. Mike said it was poison to eat dead chickens but the blacksmith, who said he was a cook himself, said Mike was crazy. Nobody ever cooks a live chicken, all chickens are dead before you cook them. What difference does it make whether you twist their necks or if they suffocate? Mike said the insides were the important thing, that you have to take out the guts right away but the suffocated chickens had not been cleaned for two days. The blacksmith said he would prove it, and he plucked the feathers from one of the dead chickens, slit it open and pulled out its insides. Mike gave it a sniff and said it stank more than two dozen dead skunks. They got into a terrible row about the chickens, yelling at each other and eventually they exchanged punches, and rolling all over the deck, they took turns knocking each other down. While they were trying to kill each other Rémi decided that anything that smelled as horrible as that chicken should not be eaten, so he threw the whole batch overboard thereby ending the argument.

Later that night, when Mike took the poultice off Plug's wound to change it and put on fresh honey, it looked much worse. It was swollen with pus which was not draining off. Mike asked him if he wanted his fillee but Plug just lay there as if he didn't hear him, with a vacant expression on his face. Tricot took Plug's pulse, felt his forehead, and told Mike that he thought he had lockjaw. Tricot said he once knew a hunter who had a gunshot wound like this when the pus did not drain. The man just stared and did not answer; he was dead of lockjaw inside a day or two.

That is precisely what happened to Plug. His entire body went rigid and by morning he was dead. He was buried ashore next to the others.

When the ship finally got underway, everyone was relieved to leave the vicinity of the tragedy, although navigating through the swirling debris on the Mississippi's surface was precarious. To replace the three men he had lost, Mike asked Tricot, the fur trapper, and the blacksmith to help him out with the poles and cordelling. After their fight, Mike and the blacksmith, whose name was Jacques Orlaud, became the best of friends. Rémi was once again stationed in the bow to warn Mike of obstacles in their path.

The first night, after supper, without Dirk and his fiddle and his dancing, the men just smoked and talked, a quiet and sad night. But then Tricot decided to liven things up. He started to sing to the music of his water glasses and the men responded; by the end of the evening everyone's spirits had lifted.

As the boat moved up the river, away from the earthquake area, life aboard became easier. Ice was forming in the water; each day it became colder, but Mike predicted they would get to where they were going before serious winter set in.

At this juncture, the boat was just passing the point where the Ohio River flowed into the Mississippi. Illinois was to the east, Missouri to the west. Most of the time, the boat was moving under sails and oars, the river being too deep to pole. The sail only helped slightly.

Just beyond the Ohio River confluence, Mike detected two men standing on shore holding a sign that said: DANGER AHEAD, WE ARE PILOTS. Mike asked Rémi what it said but when told he said the real danger was those goddamn pilots. He explained that the danger this sign referred to was a stretch of about eight miles which had three big obstacles in the river: Walker's Bar, Tower Rock, and Hurricane Island. These caused the river to narrow into a dangerous channel with bad currents, rocks, et cetera. It would be good to have a pilot for this stretch, Mike said, but this is pirate territory along here—you have to be very careful. Pilots were often in cahoots with them and would steer boats onto the rocks at a place where the pirates would be waiting to plunder a ship's cargo.

Mike knew most of the pirate tricks since he'd been working the river so long. He told about a Colonel Fluger ("Fluggy") who had a lieutenant called "Nine-Eyes," who stole onto boats at night, bored a hole in the bottom, and when the boat started to flounder Fluggy and his band of pirates came out in their skiffs pretending to save the cargo. Of course, what they did was row off with it since the captain could not follow them in his sinking boat; for this reason, a lookout had to be posted every night. Another favorite pirate ruse involved a man and woman yelling at you from shore beside a wrecked boat, pleading to be rescued. It was usually a pirate and his girlfriend, and as the vessel slowed to a halt, hidden brigands rushed the ship, looting everything aboard.

One day, as the boat was being poled, the men noticed a big sign on shore in front of a landing that said, WILSON'S LIQUOR VAULT AND HOUSE OF ENTERTAINMENT. Two attractive girls waved at the men as the boat passed by. Some of the men begged Mike to stop, but he just laughed at them. "You dumb bastards want to visit Jim Wilson's place, do you? You will get liquor and a girl, all right, but that's the last anyone will see of you, this boat, or its cargo. Jim Wilson, meanest pirate on the strip. Has one eye and only two fingers on his left hand and a peg leg, just like you read in the storybooks, but he does things inside that place of his that you're never gonna read in no storybook."

One afternoon as the crewmen poled around a big bend in the river they encountered a flotilla of fifty-one Indian bull boats, each one consisting of a large buffalo hide stretched over a willow framework and caulked with grease or tallow. Besides Indian men, there were women and children in the boats, three hundred of them. Mike stopped his boat and signaled a friendly greeting since it was likely that these Indian families were not hostile. In fact, an Indian, who was probably a young chief, paddled over and called out in English to ask where they were headed. Mike told him, then asked where they were going. The young Indian said they were crossing from Kentucky into Missouri to set up a winter camp on high ground. Asked what tribe they were, he replied that there were many: Delawares, Shawanese, Miamies, Potawotomas, Kickapaws, Poatowas, and Wyandots.

* * *

Every night since the Indian attack, Rémi was having terrible dreams, nightmares bathed in red, sometimes red animals with red fangs trying to kill him; often the red was blood, but Rémi could never determine where the blood was coming from. In one dream, he was about to drink a glass of water, but when it became blood he spit it out and it covered some unidentifiable animal at his feet. In another dream his feet were inundated with blood infested by white snakes trying to crawl up him, reminiscent of the red and white stripes on that Indian's face. Rémi also dreamt about Dirk and the manner in which he was killed; only in the dream Dirk had a long red tongue that reached up and pulled the arrow from his eye, whereupon he ate the arrow. One thing that was not a dream was the blood on Rémi's shoes. He scrubbed it diligently, but it had permeated the leather and would not come out. It remained a red dark stain that did not particularly look like blood but Rémi, of course, knew what it was. He hated the look of it because it reminded him that he had killed that young Indian. Mike told Rémi that the killing should not bother him, after all he was just an Indian, but an Indian bleeds same as me, Rémi had said, and it continued to bother him.

Rémi was dreaming one of those blood dreams on the night that had consequences as bad as those of the earthquake. He had heard voices shouting, but when he struggled to wake up, the shouting continued beyond his dream. Rémi finally realized there was a commotion on deck. He put on his pants and shoes and left the cabin to investigate. It was a very dark night, mist falling, neither moon nor stars.

Standing in the bow was a group of men holding torches in one hand and muskets in the other. They had boarded the ship without warning because the lookout had been tippling out of the fillee barrel and had fallen asleep. These men were pointing their muskets at the ship's men who had their arms raised high in the air, all except Mike Fink. A musket was pointed at his head by a huge man, even bigger than Mike; he was dressed in fancy, expensive clothes, and spoke in a quiet, cultivated voice. "Well, well," he was saying, "if it isn't Mike Fink."

"Samuel Mason," Mike said, "I thought you were pirating out of the Crow's Nest."

Samuel Mason said he liked it better at Cave-in-Rock. Then he pointed to a short thin man who looked like a pirate and said, "You remember Little Harpe, don't you?"

Mike nodded affirmatively. He remembered Little Harpe because they once had had a knife fight after Little Harpe pushed two women off a cliff.

"He cheats," Little Harpe said, "He's all bone on his sides."

"Well, he's not all bone in his head," Samuel Mason said. He kept his musket pointed at Mike's temple.

"Saw your brother last spring," Mike said to Little Harpe.

"Where?" asked Little Harpe.

"Not all of him," Mike continued, "but I was coming down the Ohio headed towards Cairo when there was Big Harpe's head stuck atop a pole on the river bank."

"That's where your head's going," Little Harpe retorted, and he pulled out his hunting knife and started toward Mike.

"Ease off," Samuel Mason said.

Rémi backed away, went to the cabin to get his Bible and returned.

"Now, then," Samuel Mason said to Mike, "who is the owner here?" Mike pointed to Rémi. "Don't joke with me," Samuel Mason said. Mike explained about Rémi and how Guy Laroule was going to meet the boat up north. Finally Samuel Mason was convinced. "So, lad," he said, "just turn over the boat's money and we'll take a few things and be on our way."

Rémi replied that he had no money, that Monsieur Laroule was to pay everyone when he arrived.

Samuel Mason said it was very bad for a lad to tell lies and told his men to search the cabin. Another pirate came over and searched Rémi. While he searched him, Rémi read out loud from his Bible: "Therefore all things whatsoever ye would that men should do to you, do ye even so to them: for this is the law of the prophets."

The pirates searched all over the boat but came up empty-handed. They began to take things from the boat and put them into their skiffs lashed alongside. They took all the ship's tools, most of the food, barrels of whiskey, the oars, the two cannons, most of the supplies meant for building houses, all the muskets, ammunition, knives and swords, clothes and blankets. They searched the crew, taking their money and tobacco. The only person they did not search was Mike Fink, perhaps because they were afraid if they got that close to him he would tear them apart. Four of the pirates kept loading the things onto their skiffs while the others stood guard over the men. They took the last of the animals, the sheep and the two loudly squealing pigs that they trussed up and tossed into one of the skiffs. It appeared that that was the end of it but they left their worst pilferage for last.

Samuel Mason looked at Tricot and said, "Tie up the slave. A big one like that would probably fetch two hundred dollars."

Tricot explained he was not a slave. He took out his paper as he always did and gave it to Samuel Mason to read. Mason took a look at it and then pretended it slipped from his fingers as it fell over the side and into the water.

"Tie the nigger up," Samuel Mason repeated.

Tricot suddenly grabbed Little Harpe by the throat, lifted him off the deck, ordering them all to get off the boat or Little Harpe was a dead man.

Little Harpe was making choking noises but Samuel Mason just laughed. Reaching over, he grabbed Rémi and said, "Nigger, put down Little Harpe or we take the boy." He was holding Rémi by the back of his neck where it hurt. Rémi told Tricot not to let Harpe go, but Tricot released him anyway. The pirates swiftly tied his hands behind him and pushed him onto the skiff. Mason let Rémi go, saying that a couple of days on the rack would make a good nigger out of Tricot.

"What's the reward on your head?" Mike asked Samuel Mason.

"Eleven hundred dollars" he announced, with pride, "I think I'm worth that, don't you?"

"And you, Little Harpe," Mike asked, "what they offering for you?"

"Nine hundred dollars," Little Harpe said, his voice constricted from the choking.

Mike said, "Well, you miserable bastards, one of these days I'm gonna be two thousand dollars richer."

Samuel Mason just laughed as they all got into their skiffs, and keeping their guns pointed at *L'Espérance*'s crew, they rode away with Tricot and all their booty.

Mike asked Rémi if they could have found the boat money. Rémi said he didn't think so. "Great," Mike said, "at least we got that. Where did you hide it?"

Rémi replied that he had best keep it secret, because "if we were boarded by other pirates and you were tortured, you might have to tell them." Rémi was secretly satisfied that he had outsmarted the pirates. While they were searching everywhere, all those gold sovereigns were right in front of their noses, hidden in a cache Rémi had hollowed out the back of his Bible.

After the pirates had disappeared into the night, Mike said, "Well, it could have been worse. Samuel Mason and Little Harpe were the cruelest pirates on the river and they could have torched our boat, which they sometimes do, and made us swim for shore. Now our only problem is to get replacements for the stuff they stole, especially the food, oars, tools, and muskets. "We are lucky," Mike said, "that Fort Chartres is just up the river. We could probably get everything there as long as we have the money to buy it."

"We have another problem," Rémi said. "We have to rescue Tricot."

"No," Mike said, "that's impossible since Samuel Mason and that gang of cutthroats are holed up at Cave-in-Rock." Mike had been there some years ago and described it as a cave in a long limestone bluff about forty feet above the Mississippi, almost two hundred feet long. "There's a rock shelf at the entrance," Mike said, "about fifty feet wide, and inside the cave is a good forty feet wide. Up there in that cave, with woods around and lookouts about, anyone trying to climb up and get in there would be shot dead in his tracks." Much as he liked Tricot, Mike insisted that there was no way to rescue him.

Rémi, enraged by Mike's attitude grabbed him and called him a coward. He said that since this was not a boat matter, he was in charge; that since he had their pay it was his order that they were not going to go one more foot upriver without Tricot on board. Rémi raised such hell that Mike said to ease up, exhorting him not to get so excited. "Alright," he said, "we will go to Fort Chartres, get our missing supplies, and try to find out how in hell we could possibly rescue Tricot."

All during the months at sea, feeling isolated from life as only the sea could make him, Guy spent hours pacing the deck of the big warship brooding about the immediate future. What had clouded his clear commitment to establish the fur post was the document bearing the king's imprimatur that gave him a choice of the fur venture or the Diderot Plantation. His musings revolved around Marie-Thérèse and the baby. Obviously, it would be more sensible to return to the comforts of the plantation and its economic security. He remembered the nostalgic serendipity of his life in the lovely home which he had built surrounded by bushropes, wild grapes, sarsaparilla, ginseng, and fan palms. On the opposite side of the river, callicarp, liquid amber, cedars, and Indian beards draped dreamily toward the water. Standing at the railing, facing the bleak, endless ocean, Guy could see in his mind's eye the hummingbirds, the butterflies, and the bees visiting the splendid chalices of the gordonia, the Indian fig, and the tulip trees. In contrast with that was the unknown; a primitive existence at best while seeking a new place to live.

It was questionable whether he could make peace with the Indians, some of whom were known to be hostile, and thereby establish a lucrative fur trade; if not, there would be no other means of support they could substitute. He had been warned about the perils of traveling the Natchez Trace on horseback, the only route one could take to the north; it followed a crude path from New Orleans to Nashville where the Wilderness Trail took over. He wondered whether Rémi and Tricot would be there when and if they finally arrived, or would some fatal disaster befall them before they got to their destination? On the first crossing from France, Guy had been indifferent about the time it took and about what lay in store for him once he got to Louisiana. Now, however, with Marie-Thérèse waiting for him, the slow passage of time on the endless ocean filled him with unbearable frustration.

We will resolve our future together, he told himself as he had many times before that all that mattered was being with Marie-Thérèse. His livelihood had nothing to do with it.

But still he could hear the high, crackling voice of Baron Vincent Huguenot, an octogenarian friend at Versailles who always had cliché-ridden advice for him: "Nothing ventured, nothing attained, Laroule. Do not wind up like me, weeping with regret over lost opportunities. Venture out of this soft cocoon, Laroule, risk ye and ye shall gain."

"Or lose," Guy had responded.

"No, no," the Baron had said, "even if you venture and lose, you gain something."

Yes, Guy told himself, when Marie came into my life I gained a loving, unexpected way of life. Until then he had only known ladies of the aristocracy, the artificial, self-absorbed, unscrupulous ladies of the court, who despite their royal marriages and their fashionable airs, were in essence courtesans—perhaps that is the origin of the word—upper-class prostitutes as were those powdered, wigged, bejeweled ladies of Louis XV's court, without values, without fidelity, without identity. Faceless women, all fashioned from the same sybaritic mold.

He despised their stilted, slouching movements, their inane flirting, gossiping behind their fans, scrupulously tending their faces, their coiffures, their gowns, their jewels, the thrust of their bodies, the measured protrusion of their derrières; watching them "perform" Guy reproached himself for having once been involved with these false women and their pretentious lifestyles.

His thoughts swung full circle back to Marie-Thérèse. Without artifice or pretension, she had come hesitantly and honestly into his existence and in so doing had brought him life. *I had no life before Marie,* Guy thought, *I had an existence but no life. She came to me, a shining ray that illuminated those dark morbid places within me that came to life. She is the mainstay of my existence now, bringing me riches.* "I love you, I love you, Marie," he said to the wind, hoping that it would carry the words to her.

Twenty-nine

The stump of Boustique's arm healed without complication, but the wound of his wife's defection to the man who had maimed him festered. Every night, after closing his bar, he would go back to his empty house. Drinking straight from the bottle, as he sat before the fire, he would give vent to his anger. He shouted obscene invectives threatening dire revenge. Wallowing in self-pity, he disconsolately addressed his handless stump, speaking to the ghost of his missing hand as if to a loved one who had died prematurely. Most nights his rage would reduce him to tears; finally, in a drunken stupor he would slump in his armchair where he slept until dawn.

Boustique derived some satisfaction when he heard that Laroule had been forced from his plantation and was living in a guest house belonging to his architect, but the fact that his wife and Rémi were also living there curdled his enjoyment. He had been to see a lawyer to determine if he could legally force his wife to return to him, but the lawyer could find no grounds for such an action.

As time passed, Boustique's angry frustration and his desire for revenge intensified, so when he found out one evening, overhearing bar gossip, that Guy had gone to France and Rémi was on a keelboat going up the Mississippi leaving Marie-Thérèse alone, he knew his time to strike back at them had come. After closing hours, he went home as usual, but this time, as he sat before the fire, guzzling rum, his spleen focused on Marie-Thérèse, who by leaving him to live with another man, had publicly ridiculed him. And the stump of his arm was also her doing. Was it not a battle over her? If he had succeeded in feeding Laroule to the alligator, she would have been forced to return to him. But she is still my wife, he thought, *my* wife, and I want her, this whore who services another man in his bed.

Flinging the empty bottle against the back of the fireplace, the glass exploding into the fire, Boustique staggered out to the stable, saddled up his horse and whipped it into the night. He was familiar with Grotesquieu's house and knew precisely where the guest house was situated.

The bedroom where Marie-Thérèse slept was located on the second floor at the top of a flight of stairs. No servants lived in the house itself. Not only was the house too small to accommodate servants' quarters, but, since the outbreak of yellow fever, Marie-Thérèse wanted to keep servants out of the house as much as possible. As a consequence, when Boustique reined in his lathered horse behind the house, he alerted no one. The rear door was unlocked and Boustique, sobered somewhat by his ride, entered slowly and noiselessly. Upstairs, Marie-Thérèse stirred but did not awaken. The door to her room was open. Boustique easily located her. In the hallway outside her door, he removed his boots and trousers, and half-naked pulled away her blanket and grabbed her, clamping his hand over her mouth to forestall her screams, barely perceptible against his hand. Awakening in terror, she dug her nails into him and tried to bite his hand, but had not yet identified her attacker; her violent resistance enraged Boustique, whose face was scalded by the raking of her nails. He pulled back his hand and hit her several times forcibly in the face, then grabbed her by the hair and, pulling her face up to his, his drunken breath repelling her, he said: "Listen to me, you whore of a wife, I am still your husband, and you are going to perform your wifely duties. You can spread your legs and receive me, or I can beat you like this until you do. You hear me, whore, do you hear me!"

"Please, Henri, please, I am pregnant, please, do not harm the baby." This revelation caused Boustique to intensify his grip on Marie-Thérèse's hair. "Pregnant now, are you? Let me see . . ."

He thrust his hand under her nightgown and ran it across the mound of her stomach. "Well, I'll be damned—so you are." He slid his hand down to her vagina. "Your baby is going to have a little visit from your rightful husband." Marie-Thérèse started to cry for help but Boustique jerked his hand from her nightgown and hit her hard across the mouth. She struggled frantically to get away from him, but she could not push him off her. He jammed the forearm of his stumped arm under her chin, ramming it against her throat, and again he struck her savagely in the face. "I am going to kill you, whore, if you resist me, you hear?" His forearm pressing against her throat made it difficult for her to breathe. Gasping for air, Marie-Thérèse was in danger of fainting.

Overcoming her feeble resistance, Boustique pulled her legs apart and forced himself into her, repeatedly pounding her, ramming her insides. Obsessed with the baby in her womb, he deliberately tried to harm it, to dislodge it, to rob her and that hated Laroule of this living thing they had created, this baby which should have been his; in his desire to bleed it out of her, he attempted to prolong his attack as long as he could, before orgasm could steal his weapon.

Marie-Thérèse lost consciousness before his assault ended, her face blue from lack of oxygen, her breathing so shallow as to be undetectable. When he finally climaxed with a wrathful explosion, a poisonous snake expectorating its venom, he expired inert, drained, the whiskey releasing him into a half-conscious state, bereft of rage or bravado. He recovered slowly. In his paroxysm, Boustique had paid no attention to Marie-Thérèse's condition, but now, as he looked down at her bloodless face, he was alarmed that perhaps he had gone too far and she was dead. There was no sign of breathing and his frantic fingers could not find a pulse beat. Her face was bruised and swollen; there was blood at one corner of her mouth and under her nostrils. Frantic now, Boustique quickly left the bed, put on his clothes and departed. He led his horse away from the house lest the sound of its hooves reveal his presence.

All right, I have killed her, he told himself, but she deserved it. If I cannot have her then neither shall he.

All the way back to his house he talked to himself, trying to allay his fears, but when he got into bed he could not sleep. Petty crime in New Orleans was tolerated, but he knew full well that the police did not tolerate murderers—murderers were swiftly dispatched by a public hanging in the Place d'Armes.

Despite her fears, Marie-Thérèse did not lose her baby. But the morning after Boustique's assault, she went to stay with the Ursuline nuns. They treated her abrasions which she attributed to a precipitous fall down the stairs in her house. One thing she knew for certain—she would not venture outside the walls of the convent until she was safely back with Guy.

She had decided not to tell him about Boustique's brutal assault. Guy would confront Boustique, but Guy was no match for him. Boustique was bigger, stronger, and as tough a brawler as any bar owner in New Orleans.

In the quiet isolation of the convent, seated on a bench in the meditation garden at twilight, Marie-Thérèse's thoughts reached out to Guy.

He had rescued her from a brutal and degrading marriage, and made her feel womanly in ways she had never felt before. Dominated by that sadistic bully she had married, she had been resigned to fearful subjugation, but with Guy, his gentleness, his love, his compassion, she had finally been able to surrender herself, to feel protected, to enjoy pleasing someone. He made her feel beautiful. For the first time, he brought true sexuality into her life; taught her what it means when two people who truly love each other can express that love in bed. For the first time in her life she had experienced orgasm. Her only wish was that she could make him as happy as he had made her.

He must never know what Boustique did to me, she thought. *Loving is so delicate, I do not want this beastly thing that happened to hurt Guy, or to make him think less of me. I could not prevent what Boustique did and I have suffered terribly, but if it now damages Guy's feelings for me, then I will suffer beyond my endurance.*

Thirty

FORT CHARTRES WAS SITUATED on four acres completely surrounded by eighteen-foot walls more than two feet thick. The walls were pierced with loopholes for guns, with two portholes for cannons in the faces and two in the flanks of each bastion. Mike Fink and Rémi entered the fort through a high, filigreed gate. At the bottom of the walls were banquettes three feet off the ground for the soldiers to stand on to fire their guns through the loopholes. Only Mike and Rémi went to the fort; the rest of the men stayed on the boat. Mike explained to the sentry on duty what had transpired on the river and asked to see the commandant. The sentry sent a sergeant to show them to the commandant's house.

Fort Chartres was not an ordinary military installation. There were two attractive barracks for the soldiers, made of stone and plastered over; elegant houses for the commisary; the *Corps de Guarde,* the supply depot; and an imposing house belonging to the commandant. Even the powder magazine was in an attractive building, as was the bakehouse, the prison, the chapel with special quarters for the chaplain, and even the stables were in a handsome building. All of the soldiers and officers wore attractive uniforms, and there were quite a few elegant women walking about who were their wives and daughters. Mike said it didn't look like these soldiers had been in much combat, and the sergeant told him that he had been stationed there for over a year and he had never fired a gun or even been outside the fort's walls. All supplies came up from New Orleans in keelboats, he said, mostly food, household things and clothing from Paris; almost no guns or ammunition or anything like that since none of the military supplies they had was ever used up. Mike asked if they had marches and gun practice. The guide said not during his time there, that life inside the fort was very peaceful, with frequent entertainments, formal balls, dinners, and musicales. Most of the officers and wives, he said, were of the nobility; the commandant, Captain Neyon de Villiers and his wife, Catherine, had once lived at Versailles. In fact, they bragged that they were responsible for transforming a crude Fort Chartres into a second Versailles.

The commandant was short, bald, and looked like he enjoyed eating. Not surprisingly, when Mike and Rémi were presented to him in his drawing room, he was having an afternoon tea with sandwiches, sausages, cheese, cakes, and tarts. Beside him was a woman he introduced as his wife. She was taller than he, heavily powdered and rouged. Her face displayed a prominent second chin and was well on its way to producing a third. The salon was decorated with exquisite copies of Versailles furnishings, crystal chandeliers included. Madame de Villiers was bedecked in voluminous swaths of silk and velvet bedecked with jeweled pendants and a triple-tiered necklace of diamonds and rubies. The captain was wearing a uniform grander than the one General Labuscière was wearing in the painting that hung in Monsieur Grotesquieu's office.

The captain proffered tea and cakes, a welcome treat for Rémi. Mike told the captain about the pilferage by Samuel Mason and his pirates, and Rémi told him about Tricot and asked if he would help. The captain called over the lieutenant by the door and told him to collect the items requested and have them put on board the *Espérance* the next day.

"What about Tricot?" Rémi asked. "Will you please send soldiers to help get him back?"

"You are asking me to send my soldiers to Cave-in-Rock," the incredulous captain said, "to risk their lives for a slave? If it were my own mother," the captain said, his mouth full of quince tart, "I would not risk my men against Samuel Mason in that cave. I am sorry, lad, but our mission here is to defend, not to attack."

"You mean," Rémi said, "you would only fight Samuel Mason and his pirates if they attacked you here?"

"Yes," the captain replied. "Or if Indians attacked us."

"But, Captain," Mike said, "Mason and his bunch are boarding river boats, stealing cargoes, killing crewmen, and raping the women."

"Unfortunately," the captain responded "the French government has assigned us to defend this fort. We are not expected to be the policemen of the river."

With that, the captain rose from his chair, brushed the crumbs off his elegant tunic and invited his guests to attend the evening's formal ball. The captain instructed the lieutenant to provide Mike with suitable clothes. Madame de Villiers told Rémi to come with her for a bath and proper attire. Rémi had not realized until she mentioned how dirty he was, how soiled his clothes were. He had tried to keep himself clean by bathing with river water but seeing his reflection in a mirror, he had to admit that he had failed miserably.

When Madame de Villiers entered her quarters, she was talking to Rémi almost faster than he could listen. "You poor little man, what you have been through!" She called him "little man" even though he was taller than she was. He had turned thirteen during the voyage, but he had not told anyone because he had seen one of the boatmen who had had a birthday pitched into the water. An old Indian custom, all boatmen observed it because it pleased Manitu, the god of the Mississippi who protected rivermen from Ohkononga, the evil god of the Mississippi, who brought on storms, floods, and black diarrhea. Rémi refused to believe that any really good god would want him dropped in that filthy river water full of dead animals and worse, so he did not mention his birthday.

In the middle of the room stood a copper bathtub that Madame de Villiers was filling up with hot water all the while jabbering away. Rémi anticipated the prospect of having a hot bath, but before he knew what was happening she was pulling off his clothes commenting on their lack of cleanliness in the process. In vain Rémi tried to protest, but she kept talking away and stripping Rémi who, once naked, immediately jumped into the water which was stinging hot but certainly felt good. No sooner was he in the tub than Madame de Villiers began to soap him all over and scrub him with a big sponge; she energetically washed his hair, getting soap in his eyes, and then rinsed him with a pail of fresh water poured over his head, talking the whole time. She was still talking as she dried him off.

"Oh, look at all those mosquito bites! I will massage you with balsam of copaiba and camomile, you poor little man." She pushed him down on the bed and began to spread her medicants all over him with her fat fingers digging into his skin.

All this time Rémi pondered how to get out of this predicament. He had never been naked in front of a woman before and besides he was convinced she was crazed the way she was kneading his flesh as though he were bread dough. The more she massaged, the faster she talked, getting louder and louder and crazier and crazier as she started to rub the balsam up and down on Rémi's privates—an area where he had no mosquito bites. Rémi tried to get up but she was suddenly on top of him, this ton of a woman. Rémi became aware of what she was doing to him, with her legs big as tree trunks clamped on his sides, but he could not move an inch. She had pinned down his shoulders with her fat hands. Astride him, she squirmed, making all manner of strange noises. Then with a huge heave, she suddenly collapsed on top of him; Rémi thought he would never breathe again. Her mountainous breasts covered the top of his face; he would have suffocated had he not been able to find a small breathing place somewhere between them. The problem was compounded by the fact that she had fallen sound asleep. Rémi tried to get her off, but his efforts were fruitless. He resigned himself to being immobilized there until someone came to his rescue. Mike is probably the only man around strong enough to pry me loose, Rémi thought, and if I am lucky he will come looking for me, but I do not really want him to see me like this. I guess it is a matter of pride or death.

He had survived a brutal stepfather, yellow fever, bloodthirsty Indians, pirates, and earthquakes, but he now faced the prospect of being crushed to death by a three-hundred-pound woman. He prayed no one would come to save him because he felt that if anyone discovered him like that, he would surely die of shame.

As it turned out, Madame de Villiers herself rescued him by suddenly waking up and chattering away as if nothing had happened. She went to an armoire and began to rummage through the drawers, taking out various items of men's clothing which she measured against him. Finally stacking a pile of them on the bed she left the room, still talking. Thank God she didn't try to dress me, Rémi thought. If she had, I think I would have choked her if I could have gotten my hands around her fat neck. Many times Rémi had fantacized about how it would be the first time he would lie with a woman, but nothing in his imagination had prepared him for how it actually happened.

At the captain's ball, Mike Fink was dressed in a fancy tunic much too small for him, a tight silk waistcoat embroidered with flowers, and silver-buckled shoes. He came up behind Rémi and said in his ear, "You laugh at me and I'll throw you through the window."

"I won't laugh at you if you don't laugh at me," Rémi said. Rémi had the opposite problem: all of his clothes were made for a man twice his size.

There was an enormous quantity to eat and drink, and Mike was more interested in stuffing himself and flirting with a pretty serving maid than in talking to Rémi who was trying to get his ear.

"What can we do to rescue Tricot now that the captain won't help us?" Rémi finally succeeded in asking him.

"Tomorrow," Mike said, "after we get all this new booty on the boat, I'll think of something."

Rémi had a few more questions, but Mike had gone back to the serving girl. By now, Rémi knew better than to bother Mike when he wanted to talk and devote his attentions to a member of the opposite sex.

Before they left the fort the following morning with a wagon full of supplies the soldiers were taking to the boat, Rémi again urged Mike Fink to think of a way to rescue Tricot. Infuriated, Mike replied testily. "Didn't you hear the captain say there was no way to get in that cave without getting killed?" Mike called Rémi pestifying, bear-brained, and a number of other Kaintuck expletives, but Rémi persisted.

"Mike, you like Tricot, don't you?"

"Yes, but not enough to wind up six feet under in a wood box," Mike said, "which is where they'll bury me if I storm that cave."

"But what if Samuel Mason and his men come out of the cave?"

"Sure," Mike said, "I'll just whistle and they'll come running."

"But what if you *force* them out?"

"How would I do that?"

"I don't know exactly," Rémi said, "but since they are all sealed up in there is there something you could throw in there, like a hundred skunks, maybe? That would send them scooting. And if you get your hands on Samuel Mason, eleven hundred dollars, and Little Harpe, nine hundred dollars, that is two thousand dollars. You could be a rich, rich man."

Mike gave Rémi a funny look, as if seeing him for the first time; lost in thought, he began to walk around in a circle. The wagon was just about loaded with even some live pigs and chickens, but Mike just kept walking around in a circle, thinking. When the sergeant in charge of the wagon came up to him to tell him that they were ready to go, Mike said, "Sergeant, there's a few more things I need—a length of soft rope, a barrel of gunpowder, a coil of cannon wick, and a bellows from the blacksmith."

A trifle dubiously, the sergeant said, "All right, but the blacksmith is an ornery fellow who may not part with one of his bellows."

"That's all right, sergeant, you get the other things, I'll take care of the blacksmith," Mike said.

When they got back to the boat and all the supplies from the fort were put aboard, Mike got everyone together. "Tonight we are going to pole upriver to the Cave-in-Rock and try to rescue Tricot," he said. "Them that are too cowardly to be with us can stay on the boat, but I warn you we got us some fresh barrels of fillee and those who go with us will get first dibs on rations, and we may run too short to include the ones who stay behind. Now who are the cowards that are staying behind?" Mike asked. No one stepped forward. "Good, then we'll go cut up some pirates and cook us up a stew."

All afternoon Mike practiced with the rope. He told the carpenter to stand on top of the deck while Mike tied a loop at one end of the rope and twirled it around his head trying to land it around the carpenter's neck.

"I used to be good at lassoing the steers," Mike explained, "but I got to get me back in practice." And he did. From forty feet away he got so he could twirl the rope around his head and lasso the carpenter's neck every time. That accomplished, he then revealed his plan and gave each person specific instructions as to what had to be done at the cave.

The men ate an early supper. As soon as it started to get dark they blacked up their faces with soot from the fire and began to pole along the shore. There was a moon shining through some high clouds so they were able to see where they were going. Mike kept a close watch on the bluffs above the banks until he saw what he was searching for. He ordered the men to tie up to trees and get out all the muskets and ammunition. He put two men in charge of the barrel of gunpowder, which they tied onto a plank they carried on their shoulders. He gave Rémi the coil of wick and the bellows to carry. Those who did not have muskets were armed with knives and stout clubs. No one was to make a sound; they were just to watch and follow Mike's hand gestures so they would know what to do next.

There was a long, steep path going from the edge of the river to the top of the bluff blanched by the moonlight. Mike led the way, moving in a low crouch so as not to be seen. When he got near the top of the path he held up his hand, and everyone stopped. Up ahead through the trees a man with a gun was discernible, the lookout guarding the entrance to the cave. White smoke rose from a cooking fire into the sky. From the smell of it, the pirates were probably eating the captured pigs for supper. Mike motioned for everyone to stay put.

With the lasso in his hand, he very stealthily started to move toward the guard, keeping behind him. Once or twice when the lookout moved, Mike froze, but then he would continue sneaking up on him. When he was close enough he loosened the lasso, gave it a good couple of twirls around his head, then let it sail up toward the lookout. The reata landed squarely around his neck and Mike yanked the noose tight before the lookout could utter a sound. Now Mike pulled him down from his perch and motioned the others to join him. By the time the men got there, the lookout was dead, still holding a gun which Mike took from him.

Mike nodded his head and his troop followed him single file up to the entrance to the cave. They could hear the voices of the pirates, laughing and singing. Mike opened the gunpowder barrel and quietly spilled a big pile of gunpowder inside the entrance and lit one end of the wick, which started to burn. Mike checked everyone to make sure they were in place and ready. Next he took hold of the bellows and began to pump as fast as he could, blowing the gunpowder into the cave. Rémi rolled the burning wick inside its entrance setting fire to the gunpowder. As the bellows blew the gunpowder deeper and deeper into the cave, it gave off a thick, black cloud of smoke which quickly filled the cave. The pirates began to yell and cough; some muskets were fired as they tried to find their way out of the cave through the dense smoke. Three of Mike's men were lying on their stomachs above the entrance, clubs raised above their heads; as the first pirates came staggering out of the cave Mike's crew clubbed them over their heads. Other men pulled the unconscious pirates away from the entrance to clear the way for the next surge of choking pirates who met the same fate. Soon there were too many stumbling out of the cave for the men on the roof to handle, and that is when the other men began to use their muskets, knives, and swords. The inside of the cave was now so black with smoke you couldn't see anything. Rémi wielded a club, using it to smash the pirates' knees. A few of them came running out of the cave and managed to escape, but Mike took off after them.

It was all over very quickly. Some of the pirates were dead, others were on the ground moaning with wounds. Rémi pulled the wick out of the cave, so it would stop burning. Mike's men began to truss those who were not dead. Mike returned with the one who had run away: it was Little Harpe.

"Almost had Samuel Mason," Mike said, "but this one's better'n nothin'." With that, he grabbed Little Harpe by the hair, bent his head over the empty gunpowder barrel and whacked it clean off with his machete as if he were killing a chicken in the barnyard. He put the head on top of the barrel to drain off the blood. The eyes and mouth were still twitching.

As soon as the smoke began to clear Mike and his men went in to look around the cave. At the rear was an enclosed area where the pirates had stored all their booty. Mike told his men to take whatever looked good back to the boat. Rémi looked everywhere for Tricot, but he was not in the cave. Distraught, he was convinced that the pirates must have killed Tricot on the way back, drowned him or buried him along the shore.

Mike stuck Little Harpe's head on top of a pole as the men started back to the boat, carrying as much loot as they could. As for the trussed pirates, Mike simply left them lying on the ground. "Mike," Rémi asked, "what if nobody finds them?"

"Then nobody finds them," he said in a way that Rémi knew was a final pronouncement.

Halfway back to the boat they heard a sound, a low moan, a sort of muffled cry rising up from the dense growth below. Rémi joined two men who went off the trail, pushing a path through the undergrowth in the direction of the sound which weakened and then stopped. They couldn't see anything through the scrub, but one of the men pointed and led the way to Tricot, who was tied to the trunk of a big tree, his head hanging forward onto his chest.

Rémi called out his name and Tricot raised his head a little and tried to smile at him, but his face was too mutilated to manage it. Both his eyes were swollen shut. He was naked and there were wounds and dried blood all over his body. One of his arms was crooked at the elbow and a gash of raw flesh ran from his cheek up to his scalp. The two crewmen cut the ropes that bound him, catching him before he fell. One of the crewmen took off his jacket and put it on Tricot. Two more crewmen, who had been following, appeared. They made a stretcher out of branches and vines and carried Tricot down the bluff to the boat. Rémi walked alongside and tried to talk to Tricot who did not respond. Occasionally he moaned whenever the stretcher bumped along the way.

Thirty-one

Baron de Bastrop, the Marquis de Maison Rouge, and André Grotesquieu had been meeting regularly at La Bagatelle ever since the announcement had been posted that His Majesty Louis XV had ceded to his cousin Charles III, Sovereign of Spain, "all right, title and interest in the Territory of Louisiana, together with the City of New Orleans and the island on which it stands." This concession was one of the stipulations in the Treaty of Paris which concluded the Seven Years' War, a conflict that had ended disastrously for the French. The treaty also gave to Canada all French possessions east of the Mississippi, and the Florida parishes owned by Spain went to Great Britain. To compensate for its loss of Florida, Manila and Havana, Spain was awarded all land belonging to France on the west side of the Mississippi. This ignominious surrender of what amounted to all her possessions in North America was a devastating blow to the pride the French had had in their military.

"Ulloa issued an edict today," the marquis was saying, "that no wine other than Spanish can be imported." He was referring to the recently installed Spanish governor, Don Antonio de Ulloa.

"What, no French wine?" the baron exclaimed. "Impossible!"

"No, very possible, my dear Baron," the marquis replied. "And why not? Spain now owns us, does it not? Our great King has stabbed us in the back but he does not bleed, we do. And what's more, we bleed Spanish wine." The men spoke in lowered voices.

"I think we have to view this rationally," Grotesquieu said, "to the detriment of our pride. Of course we are upset that His Majesty gave up Louisiana to his cousin Charles, but I invite you to examine the reasons why he had to do so. When the King was losing the war against the British he asked Charles to send troops to help him, which he did, but nonetheless they were defeated."

"How could that have happened?" the baron inquired. "The great French Army. Do not forget, I commanded a division in France until my disability."

"I remind you that the war began here in Pennsylvania," Grotesquieu said, "with our French Army fighting the Indians. We would have prevailed, too, except for the unexpected assault of that young British general, George Washington, who attacked us at Fort Duquesne and routed our soldiers. Our military was affronted that the British attacked us over the Indians, so we declared war on them. But the British overran the Plaines of Abraham and drove us out of Quebec and Montreal, and then when the war spread to Europe, they defeated us there also. Louis XV had no choice. When you lose a war, you compensate the victor. Giving up Louisiana is the spoils of war."

There were three rapid knocks on the door followed by a single rap. The baron unlocked the door and admitted the Comte and Comtesse de Villars du Breuil who apologized for their tardiness.

"We have been arguing," the comtesse said. "My husband, who is afraid of his shadow, trembles at the thought of provoking the Spaniards. It will not bother him in the least when the tricolor no longer flies over the Place d'Armes."

"Wha-what I s-say," the comte, who stuttered, replied, "really ma-makes no diff-difference if a Sp-Spaniard is in the Gov-Gov-Governor's Mansion so long as we live our lives without dis-disturbance."

"And are you content to drink that loathsome Spanish wine?" the marquis asked. "A notice has been posted today that only Spanish wine will be imported."

"F-f-f for me, it does not matter," the comte said. "M-m-my . . . my cellar is ample for many years."

"But it is the *principle,* dear Comte," the baron interjected. "Today it is the wine, tomorrow it may be all the foods we cherish—the cheeses, the foie gras, the preserves, and all the rest. And then they'll take our property, our slaves, our freedom. Where does it stop?"

"This Ulloa, this crass Spaniard who went to Balise to get married, and what manner of bride did he bring back?" the comtesse asked, her mouth reflecting her distaste, "a Peruvian. Peruvian! And when the finest ladies of our city went to the Governor's Mansion to present their respects, what did the Peruvian do? She refused to see them! Turned them away! And since her arrival, has Doña Ulloa invited one French person to her parties, suppers, theatricals, or balls—is that not the gravest affront, a direct cut like that? Duels have been fought over such an insult. But my brave husband is happy to sit at home with his precious bottles of wine while the whole of Creole New Orleans is ignored and insulted. I, a Comtesse, a true aristocrat by marriage and lineage, a woman of high breeding, I have yet to receive an invitation from this Peruvian whore."

"And what about his deputy, this Captain Luís Ostos," the marquis said, "that repulsive poppenjay who struts around with his chest full of medals? He also married a Peruvian, an Indian with skin the color of tobacco. Is this not an illegal mixture of the races, a flagrant violation of the Code Noir?"

Monsieur Grotesquieu held up his hand to command attention. "Venting our emotions may improve our dispositions but it will not solve our dilemma. If we are to act, it must be purposeful and clear-headed." He placed some papers on the table before them. "This is a recall petition. It was drawn up by Attorney General Nicolas Chauvin de la Frenière who, as you know, is leading our movement. He gave me this petition last week and I have had it signed by five-hundred and sixty people, more than enough to get Ulloa legally removed from the Governor's Mansion."

"But who will enforce it?" the baron asked. "Spanish judges sit on all the benches."

"It is not for the courts to decide," the marquis said. "We still control the Superior Council, you know. And do not lose sight of the fact that virtually all of New Orleans is French, and if they decide to take matters into their own hands . . ."

"Attorney General de la Frenière is helping that along," Grotesquieu said. "He had a meeting with many of the merchants and plantation owners, and tomorrow there will be a big protest in the Square."

"Why is la Frenière so involved?" the comtesse asked.

"Because he personally gets a tariff from every bottle of wine imported in from France and every slave smuggled in from the West Indies," Grotesquieu explained. "The plan is to force Ulloa out of New Orleans and set up a government of our own, with la Frenière in charge. I happen to know that he has sent an emissary to the British Governor of West Florida to see if he will back us in this. There is a company of soldiers stationed there."

"And if Ulloa doesn't leave, and Charles III sends troops, then what-what will we do?" the comte asked.

"We will all point the finger at you," the comtesse said, "and selfless person that you are, you will sacrifice yourself on our behalf."

"Perhaps you could sacrifice yourself on Ulloa's bed and s-save us the-the trouble," the comte said.

"No, I would not want to interfere with such a golden opportunity for you," the comtesse rejoined, a sweet smile on her lovely face.

The following day, groups of men began arriving from the plantations and nearby villages to join with the New Orleans men who were demanding the recall of Ulloa. Shouts of "Liberty!" and "Up with the wine of Bordeaux, down with the poison of Catalonia!" pierced the air as the ranks of the protesters gradually swelled into hundreds. These men spilled in and out of the taverns; the more they drank the louder they protested. Governor Ulloa, a timid, shy, scholarly man, became alarmed at the raucous disturbance in the streets; with most of the invective being directed at him, he decided to leave Governor's Mansion with his family and to take refuge on his boat anchored in the river.

When night fell, the rebellious crowd began to assemble in the Place d'Armes where they sang patriotic French songs while passing around bottles of their beloved Bordeaux. Toward midnight, Attorney General de la Frenière appeared, and with the Marquis de Maison Rouge, Baron de Bastrop, and Monsieur Grotesquieu beside him, exhorted the militant throng to capitalize on this moment of freedom, to throw off the Spanish yoke, and to let Ulloa, who was cowering on his boat, hear the fury of their protest.

The crowd roared its response. A group of them left the Place d'Armes and went up the quai to where Ulloa's boat was docked. Camouflaged by the moonless night, they cut the hawsers that tethered the boat to the levee. The swift Mississippi current immediately swept it downstream, eventually pitching it onto a sandbar. After spending an apprehensive night stranded on the sandbar, Governor Ulloa decided that it was no longer propitious for him to remain governor in the face of such hostility; he and his new bride set sail for Havana, never to return.

News of his departure set off a week of celebration. The baron, the marquis, Monsieur Grotesquieu, and the comte and comtesse were invited to Attorney General de la Frenière's house for a festive evening to savor their victory. Instead of appropriating the governorship for himself, however, la Frenière decided that he would have more freedom to exploit the situation commercially if someone else were to become governor. He therefore induced the commander of the small local French military detachment, Captain Charles Aubry, to take on the governorship.

"The rebellion succeeded beyond our wildest dreams," la Frenière announced. "We have driven the Spaniards and their revolting wine back to Spain; and it is reassuring that the New Orleans that was born French will remain French forevermore."

Thirty-two

Tricot did not move for five days. He lay on a bed of blankets in the cabin, covered with netting to keep the mosquitos off. Rémi talked to him many times a day but he exhibited no sign of life. He was breathing, but he was as still as a tree trunk fallen in the forest. Mike used his treatment on him, washing all his wounds with warm rum and then covering them with poultices of hot bee honey which he took from the hive he had obtained from the Indians. Mike also cut two thin, flat pieces of board that he bound on either side of Tricot's broken arm. Before he put the boards on, Mike manipulated Tricot's "teetotally twisted" arm to get it as straight as he could. Since Tricot did not respond to the pain in his arm, Mike said it meant that Tricot's "lambasting" had left him so badly off he might never come out of his coma. Rémi was angry with Mike for saying that but secretly he was afraid that perhaps Tricot would never wake up. But Rémi kept on talking to Tricot, as if the latter could hear him.

The crewmen were exhausted, having to work doubly hard to replace those who were killed; the extra men were trying to help out but they did not last very long on the running boards. Up north the Mississippi no longer twisted and turned with one corkscrew bend coming on top of the other as it did below, but it ran fairly straight and was best navigated with poles. The replacement men, although strong had not developed callouses where the poles rubbed their shoulders; this resulted in the formation of large blisters that forced them to stop. Painful blisters also appeared on their hands and feet, huge sacs which sometimes burst open. Mike's crewmen never blistered, having developed protective callouses. Rémi tried to pole just once, stooping down and running the pole along the narrow running board, but he lost his balance and toppled into the water. The men all had a good laugh as they fished him out. Rémi was humiliated and after that decided he would leave the poling to the crew.

Mike stuck the pole with Little Harpe's head on it in the bow of L'Espérance, a figurehead that made every passing boat aware of his nine-hundred-dollar prize. Some of the boats gave loud cheers and sounded their horns and bells when they recognized Little Harpe who had probably pirated their boats at one time or another. It had turned cold which helped preserve Little Harpe's head. The river was beginning to freeze and large chunks of ice banged against the sides of the boat.

Mike announced that since they were approaching the juncture of the Missouri and the Mississippi Rivers they should start looking for a place to set up the fur post. What Monsieur Laroule asked us to look for, Mike said, was high ground that would not be flooded when the Mississippi rose in the spring, thereby avoiding the problem that they have with the low levees of New Orleans. Mike put in at little villages along the way to get an idea of how they were situated. The first place he stopped was Kaskasia on the Illinois side of the river. Forty-five families lived in the village. There was one landowner with a big farm worked by twenty slaves, five Indians, the rest Negroes. It also had a church and a stone building inhabited by Jesuits. Most of the other houses were made of wood, however. The Jesuits had a herd of cattle.

Mike also put in at Ste. Geneviève on the Missouri side, and Prairie du Rocher which was about fourteen miles north of Kaskasia, a very small village of twelve houses and a little chapel. The people said it was hard living but they liked being there.

Up the line, Mike stopped at St. Phillippe which consisted of sixteen deserted houses, and a small church that needed repair. The only person there was the captain of the militia who had remained to try to sell the grist and sawmill. He said all the families had left to cross the river over to the French side and were now living in Herculaneum. All these little villages were above the river which gave

Mike hope that he would soon find the high ground where they could set up the post.

The next village, Cahokia, had been settled by several French Canadians driven out by the British. There were numerous dwellings and a half-completed church. A large section of cleared land was heavy with wheat. There were twenty cabins of Peoria Indians who worked the land for the white families.

About an hour's poling above Cahokia, as Mike followed a gentle curve in the Mississippi, he called out "Rest poles!" On the west side of the Mississippi he had spotted a rise of high ground that seemed to run along the river for a considerable distance. In order to cross the river, very broad here, Mike switched the crew to oars. The men were compelled to row very hard through the swift current. Mike, tied to and accompanied by Rémi, walked up the rising ground to the top where they could see a long way down the Mississippi.

"What do you think?" Mike asked. He said it in a way that indicated he had already made up his mind. Rémi said it looked good. They walked around. It was fine-looking land. "We won't do no better," Mike said.

They returned to the boat to start the process of bringing up all the supplies, but as they neared the boat they were startled to hear singing, and there was no doubt that it was Tricot's voice. He was sitting on top of the cabin singing one of his sea songs. As soon as Rémi saw him he ran over and hugged him.

"Where you been?" Tricot asked.

Rémi could tell from the way he asked it that Tricot had no memory of what had happened to him.

"You remember those pirates?" Rémi asked.

He did not know what Rémi was talking about. As far as he was concerned he had simply awakened that day as usual although he found it strange that he was sleeping on blankets in the cabin. And he was puzzled about his arm, which hurt. Mike and Rémi told him what had happened, but at first he did not believe them. When Mike showed him Little Harpe's head Tricot looked at it for a long while and then started to ask questions to convince himself that he was being told the truth. He had removed the boards from his arm but Mike convinced him to put them back in place until the arm healed.

"I guess I'd better thank everyone for my being here," he said.

"Thank him," Mike said, pointing to Rémi. "I said there was no way to get you away from those bastids, but he come at me like a ring-tailed roarer and jimber-jawed at me till we had to do it to clam him up."

Having arrived at his destination, Mike was in a hurry to leave. He had a cargo to pick up in Cairo, Illinois, to take down the Mississippi to New Orleans by flatboat for a "rip-roarin'" fee. Rémi had not expected Mike to leave immediately, with so much to be done, but having fulfilled his obligation, Rémi accepted his departure, and paid him and his men what was coming to them plus an extra sovereign for Mike. Rémi knew he was going to be hard-pressed without him. With Mike gone and Tricot in the condition he was in, it was solely up to Rémi to keep things going until Guy and his mother arrived. With winter approaching, the first order of business would be to build adequate shelter quickly, especially important because Rémi calculated that his mother would probably be having the baby soon after she arrived.

Rémi gave Mike a letter to deliver to his mother in New Orleans. The river current was very swift, and Mike figured he would get downstream in about two weeks, probably arriving before Guy returned from France. Four months for the trip upriver but only two weeks to return. He promised to leave the letter with Monsieur Grotesquieu. He would also leave Rémi's exact position on the Mississippi. Mike said that part of his deal was that he could take the keelboat with him and swap it for the flatboat in Cairo. He also planned to turn in Little Harpe's head and collect his nine hundred dollars at the military fort in Cairo.

Rémi and his men off-loaded everything except the barrels of whiskey and enough food to get Mike and his crew to Cairo. As a going-away present Mike gave Rémi his personal boat horn. It was silver with ships embossed on it, and it had a deep-throated sound that carried for miles. Mike said he got it back in the days when he did some pirating on the Ohio. "I was rambunctious in those days, and if I glommed a boat that was pernickety this sock dologer gave them a riproarous what-fer. But now I just do boating, so I got to obsquatulade on down to Cairo to fatten my poke."

Thirty-three

W<small>HEN THE</small> F<small>RENCH WARSHIP</small>, with Guy aboard, approached the harbor of New Orleans, it was confronted with an imposing flotilla of Spanish men-of-war, twenty-four in number, equipped with fifty pieces of artillery and forty-five hundred soldiers. Angered over the uprising that had driven Governor Ulloa out of New Orleans, Charles III had dispatched this armada in order to put down the rebellion and restore Spain's dominance over Louisiana. In command was a flamboyant soldier of fortune, Major General Don Alejandro O'Reilly, who had become a favorite of the king's.

In his youth, O'Reilly had fled from his native Ireland to avoid Britain's persecution of Catholics. After a series of military adventures in various countries he had enlisted in the Spanish Army and rapidly worked his way up the military ladder. He was known for his quick intelligence and efficiency, and for taking an occasional foolhardy risk that inevitably succeeded. All these qualities were displayed on the occasion when the life of the king had been threatened by an insurrectional assault on the palace which O'Reilly turned back, thus saving the king's life. Charles had gratefully elevated O'Reilly to the rank of major general, the highest military position in Spain, and afterwards entrusted him with the Crown's most important missions. His instructions now were to put down the New

Orleans sedition, re-establish Spanish rule, and put a functioning government in place.

Guy's warship had to bide time until all twenty-four of the Spanish ships moved through the harbor and moored at the levee. These vessels were gaily decorated in full dress and they presented as awesome a spectacle as New Orleans had ever witnessed. Guy's ship finally found a berth and Guy disembarked as soon as he could, intrigued and mystified by the imposing scene. As he stepped off the gangplank onto the levee he was swept along by crowds hurrying toward the Place d'Armes. The flagship's cannon set off a booming charge, a signal for the Spanish troops, in dress regalia and fully armed, to begin marching down the gangplanks in tight formations. As Guy reached the Place d'Armes, which was choked with what appeared to be the city's entire white population of fifteen hundred, the Spanish troops marched into the square. At one end, in front of the church, a small French garrison under Captain Aubry's command stood at attention. The Spanish soldiers ringed the other three sides, leaving a pathway to the flagpole in the center. The crowd was eerily silent, the only sound being that of the soldiers' marching feet.

A second cannon shot thundered from the flagship as all the troops, the French soldiers included, shouldered arms and fired skyward in salute to the new governor who now entered the square, preceded by a cadre of drummers and trumpeters, his staff and his personal guard. All wore distinctive uniforms of green velvet and gold brocade; the guards carried silver maces and the officers wore metal helmets and presented their ceremonial swords unsheathed.

O'Reilly positioned himself at the base of the flagpole where Captain Aubry awaited him with the keys to the city's gates. The flag of France which had flown over the Place d'Armes since 1718 was lowered and the Spanish flag raised in its place.

After a series of military maneuvers executed by the Spanish troops, they paraded in review past O'Reilly as they marched back to their ships. Then the major general preceded by his personal staff and accompanied by Captain Aubry, entered a government building next to the church where a large chandeliered reception room had been prepared for his arrival. It was at this point in the proceedings that Guy caught sight of the Baron de Bastrop, the Marquis de Maison Rouge, and Monsieur Grotesquieu as they were being escorted by soldiers into the building that O'Reilly had entered. Guy hurried after them and managed to maneuver himself into the reception room where a crowd of townspeople had already gathered. O'Reilly had positioned himself behind a desk at the far end of the room, his staff of officers arrayed behind him. He was a tall, broad-shouldered, handsome man with scars beside each of his eyes, one of which was slightly smaller than the other. He wore a tightly cropped wig and a devil's-head stickpin with ruby eyes in his jabot. He announced that he was abolishing the New Orleans Superior Council and that the city would henceforth be governed by the Cabildo comprised of the governor, six perpetual *regidors,* two *alcaldes,* an attorney general and a clerk. He also said that on behalf of Charles III, Sovereign of Spain, new special taxes would be levied on taverns, billiard tables, houses, butchers, and brandy.

Those matters out of the way, O'Reilly turned his attention to Captain Aubry. "Captain, sir, have you assembled those personages whose names appeared on the list I dispatched to you prior to my arrival?"

"Yes, General."

"Then bring them forward."

Two soldiers cleared the way for the baron, Grotesquieu, and the marquis; another soldier escorted the Comte and Comtesse de Villars du Breuil to a place in front of O'Reilly's desk. Aubry called off each one of their names. "Only Monsieur A. M. Braud is missing, General."

"And why is that?"

"He is in Natchez, but we are having him returned."

O'Reilly took his time studying the five people before him. "I have detailed information that all of you were instigators of the rebellion that took place here when the Honorable Don Antonio de Ulloa was Governor. Is that correct?"

"We were involved in an effort to preserve our city," the marquis responded.

"You knew that Louisiana had become Spanish property, did you not?"

"Yes, but an edict cannot make French people become Spanish people."

"You were allowed to live as you always lived, only the government was to change, not the people."

"We were required to drink Spanish wine," the baron protested. "French wine was prohibited."

"And so you started an insurrection over wine?"

"More than that," the comtesse said. "The Governor's wife refused to receive Creole ladies—a direct insult. I, a comtesse of the blood, snubbed by a Peruvian."

"May I point out, General," Grotesquieu said, "that although we admit participating in the protest, we did not violate any law of Spain since until your arrival today Spain had not legally annexed Louisiana. The French flag flew over the Place d'Armes and the Superior Council ran the city. How could there be an insurrection when no Spanish government existed in New Orleans? Only Governor Ulloa. We can assure you of our cooperation now that you have installed the Cabildo."

"Ma-ma-may I say for myself, Your Honor," the comte said, "tha-tha-that I was wholeheartedly against the protest and di-di-did everything in my power to dis-dis-dissuade these people from continuing."

O'Reilly sat back in his chair and again surveyed the group before him. Then he took his time reading a report which he had on his desk. "Monsieur Trémencourt, come forward, please."

Trémencourt strode up to the desk. One of his officers handed a Bible to O'Reilly. "Raise your right hand. Do you swear by God and the holiness of this Bible that each and every allegation in this report as it relates to the Marquis de Maison Rouge, the Baron de Bastrop, Monsieur André Grotesquieu, and the Comte and Comtesse de Villars du Breuil is true and exact?"

"I do, Your Grace."

"Let it further be noted that Monsieur A.M. Braud, Crown Printer of New Orleans by virtue of Royal Grant, aided and abetted the insurrection by printing this lengthy account of the grievances of the planters and merchants of New Orleans and vicinity, and did cause to have copies of this broadside distributed in this area and in Europe. Now, I say to you gentlemen, and to you, Comtesse, that there is no more serious crime than treason. To incite your fellow countrymen to rebel against their government and to drive out the authority placed here by order of His Majesty, Charles III—such insurrection cannot be tolerated. The King has charged me to find the instigators of this abomination and to mete out judicious punishment that will serve notice upon all others that such insubordination will not be tolerated. Accordingly, I hereby sentence each of you, including Monsieur Braud *in absentia,* to be executed by military firing squad upon the morrow. Furthermore, that properties of the condemned will be seized and forfeited to the Cabildo for redistribution."

The marquis was the first to recover from the impact of O'Reilly's pronouncement. "General, if you please, we request that the sentence be appealed to His Majesty, Charles III."

O'Reilly shook his head. "No, there can be no appeal, neither to the King nor to the courts. The power to investigate, sentence, and execute is solely mine. You may have secular visits this evening to prepare you for tomorrow."

Guy now frantically worked his way through the dense throng of spectators in order to address the general. "General O'Reilly," he called out, "may I be heard?"

"And who are you?"

"My name is Guy Laroule. I am a member of this community. I know all the accused and I wish to point out that they are among the leading citizens of our city. They are idealistic people who meant no harm to the Spanish Government, their aim being only to improve the lot of their fellow Creoles. We are a burgeoning city with a bright future. We can grow into an important port where most of the commerce of this country enters and leaves. We need these six people to help us grow. As we grow we become an ever-increasing asset to your country. For example, we are just beginning to harvest sugar cane in quantities that will impact the world. The same is true of other crops. We will be one of Spain's richest colonies, but we cannot succeed if you take away our leaders. Perhaps punishment is deserved but I implore you, sir, to sentence them less drastically so that at some future time they can again be a helpful force to this city."

O'Reilly leaned back in his chair and stared at Guy. "Were you involved with these people in this insurrection, Monsieur Laroule?"

"No, General, I was in France. My ship just made port an hour ago."

"Do you approve of what they did?"

"No, I do not, and if I had been here I would have counseled them against it."

"Then you can be thankful that I do not impose guilt by association. It is precisely because they are leaders that we wish to purge ourselves of this kind of reprehensible leadership. The sentences will be executed as directed. You may remand the prisoners to their confinement. We will now have an open house with refreshments to celebrate the occasion of our arrival."

* * *

Guy and Marie-Thérèse went to visit Madame Grotesquieu whose severe arthritis confined her to a wheelchair. The Grotesquieus' only child was a son who now lived in Philadelphia. Madame Grotesquieu was devastated by the terrible news which Guy brought her. "Perhaps if the General knew about my condition," she suggested. "What shall I do without André? Oh, he mustn't die! He mustn't! He has such a fine head, so talented, and his heart, such a big, beautiful heart he has. He meant no harm—he has never harmed anyone."

Guy and Marie-Thérèse consoled Madame Grotesquieu for several hours as best they could, then returned to their house. "If he does execute Grotesquieu," Marie-Thérèse said, "and they confiscate all his property, where will Madame Grotesquieu live? And all his slaves and the other people who worked for him? You and I will be leaving, but what will happen to the others who must stay here?"

"I cannot believe that Grotesquieu had no inkling that this would happen. He and the others must have heard that the Spanish were coming and they should have left the city. If only I had returned a day or two earlier. Perhaps O'Reilly has imposed this severe sentence just to scare them, and on the morrow he will reduce the sentence to a term of imprisonment. Let us hope."

O'Reilly did not change his mind. At three o'clock the following afternoon soldiers appeared at the jail to lead the condemned prisoners to the courtyard of the barracks. They had spent the night paralyzed with apprehension, especially Count de Villars du Breuil whose participation in the rebellion had been so reluctant. But now as the soldiers appeared and they were led through the barred door onto the street, the last shreds of hope fell from them, replaced by deadening resignation. Two priests joined the procession as it moved away from the old prison past the church on Chartres Street, then into the courtyard of the barracks where the executions were to occur. Guy had waited outside the prison all day for them. Now he followed the moving group but soldiers at their rear and their flank kept him at a distance. He did succeed, however, in calling to them and exchanging a few words.

The public was allowed in the courtyard and a sizable crowd had gathered. Crippled by his fright, the comte was only able to stay on his feet by leaning against the baron for support. The comtesse never looked more beautiful than in the slanted sunlight illuminating the wall against which they had been placed. Guy noted that she wore the same white dress she had worn that first day of rehearsal at her house. Grotesquieu walked very slowly, and stood looking down at the ground. Only the Marquis de Maison Rouge had an attitude of defiance. He stood straight and tall, his chest back and his chin raised, a look of challenge in his eyes. When an officer approached with his blindfold he pushed it aside. "I have many times faced death in the service of the King of France, my master, and I never once closed my eyes nor will I now." Then he turned to the others and said, "Let us die since we must die, but let us die bravely. Death brings no fear to me." The others also refused the blindfolds.

The priests now visited them, one after the other. Grotesquieu took a letter from his pocket, addressed to his wife, and asked the priest to give it to her. The previous night O'Reilly had refused their requests to be permitted visitors.

Now the six soldiers of the execution squad took their places. Grotesquieu asked for a pinch of snuff that one of the officers provided. "All of you are witnesses," Grotesquieu said forcefully, "that we died for wanting to be French. Yes, let it be known at my death that my heart is French, my allegiance is to the King of France, and I glory in the thought that my love of France is the cause of my death."

Unable to restrain himself, Guy called out, "Farewell, my friends—may God keep you all!"

On command, the soldiers shouldered their muskets. "Here are the wounds I suffered for France!" the marquis shouted as he tore open his shirt and revealed his chest scarred with war wounds. "What you do now is just another wound. Fire, executioners!"

The shots rang out in unison, each finding its mark. Captain Jacinto Panis, the officer in charge of the firing squad, gave a *coup de grâce* to each of the fallen forms. Two scarlet circles, like medals, adorned the comtesse's white silk bodice.

Thirty-four

By the time Guy returned, the vestiges of Boustique's beating had all but disappeared from Marie-Thérèse's face, but from the moment he took her in his arms, Guy sensed that something terrible had happened and was troubling her. He also noticed that despite the powder and rouge, there were faint underlying blemishes on her face. He sat her down and took her hands in his. "Tell me," he said. "I sense that something has occurred, I know not what. But you must tell me about it."

She started to tell him haltingly, painfully, but broke down and buried her head against his chest, giving tearful vent to the anguish and pain she had bravely kept contained until now. Guy's initial reaction was one of guilt for having left her unprotected, but then his reaction escalated into a murderous anger against this worthless, sadistic man who had brutalized a defenseless woman.

"Guy, promise me, promise me, you will not seek revenge for this. I beg of you. We will be leaving shortly, and we will never again participate in the life here. Boustique is a powerful, vicious fighter. I have seen what he has done to men in fights at the bar. You are no match for him. If you fight with him, there is a risk that you might be killed, or if you kill him there is the certainty that the police will punish you, despite the circumstances. After all, he is still my husband, and who you are will not arouse sympathy in a court. Promise me? Will you promise me?"

"There are some things in life, Marie, that transcend logic and promise. No matter what you have heard, justice is not evenhanded. In the unfair manner he attacked you, so will I attack him. I have learned that the life of honor and traditional fair play that prevailed at Versailles is not the way of life beyond its boundaries. Certainly not here. America is an unsettled, untamed place without traditions, making up its laws and customs as it goes along. It is a ruthless existence, and however you do it you must find a way to avoid the alligator pit. I am not complaining about life here. I prefer it. It is a hard challenge, but it is also opportunity. It is adventure. It is anything you want to make it. I could not go on living with myself if I did not confront Boustique who defiled the person I care about most in my life. I cannot erase what he did to you, but I can punish him for his transgression so that he will never demonize you or anyone else again."

To prepare for his confrontation with Boustique, Guy again called upon the ironmonger who had previously made the spikes for his tug-of-war shoes. It was a peculiar request, unlike any the ironmonger had previously encountered. Guy knew that he would have to have a significant advantage over Boustique's superior size, strength, and his experience as a vicious brawler. Guy knew that in his previous encounter with Boustique had he not had those spikes on his boots, he would have been the one fed to the alligator.

When we fight, as we certainly will, I will want to have the same advantage that Boustique had when he attacked Marie. I am no longer a proper nobleman of Versailles, following the traditional rituals of those court dilettantes. I am now a member of the new world order where no holds are barred. Where Indians pretend to be friends, but then maim, slaughter, and scalp the unsuspecting. Where in the midst of a sword duel, a secreted pistol is drawn and one duellist shoots the other. Where documents are forged, officials bribed, slaves stolen, bribes commonplace. Survival is the challenge here, and security a delusion. The only ethics are to do unto others before they do unto you. And that is how I will deal with Boustique. He will come at me with every dirty trick in the book, but thanks to the ironmonger I hope to destroy him with a dirty trick of my own. I am an American now, dispensing my own kind of justice. Some day we may be protected by laws and lawmen, but for now we must defend ourselves and the ones we love as best we can.

* * *

It was an hour before closing time when Guy sent a note to Boustique who was behind his bar, that he awaited him in the adjoining alley, the same alleyway where Guy had first seen Marie and Rémi being beaten by Boustique.

"So you are back," Boustique said standing in the doorway, "and you want to punish me for what I did to your whore." He laughed derisively as he came into the alleyway.

"Yes, that is right, Boustique, I am going to punish you, but I am going to do it fair and square. I have bound up my hand so that I have a stump, the same as yours." He held up his hand which was tightly bound with cloth in a manner that gave it the appearance of a stump. "You are an animal, Boustique, who doesn't deserve to be called a man."

"Let me see that stump of yours," Boustique said, coming towards Guy, but instead of inspecting Guy's hand which Guy extended for his inspection, Boustique unleashed several powerful blows to Guy's head. The sudden attack took Guy by surprise and sent him reeling backwards against the alley wall. Boustique threw himself at Guy, pounding him with his fist and forearm, knocking him to the ground, and kicking at him with his boot. Guy managed to roll away, regaining his feet as Boustique came at him again. But as Boustique's fist struck him Guy flung his arm at Boustique and stopped him in his tracks, hitting him a quick series of blows, not with his fists, but with the stump he had created. The side of Boustique's face began to run blood but he persevered in his attack, repeatedly hitting Guy, but the power of his blows had diminished. Guy stepped away from Boustique, circled him, and again smashed his stumped hand against Boustique's head, knocking him to the ground. Guy had now worked himself into a frenzy as he pulled Boustique to his feet and continued to batter him with prodigious blows; Boustique's face was rapidly becoming a bloody pulp.

As he beat him, Guy directed a steady stream of invective at Boustique, a mad torrent of outrage for what Boustique had done to Marie, culminating in a kick directed at Boustique's groin that again sent him sprawling on the ground, this time unconscious. Guy stood over him, his chest heaving, the cloth on his bound hand crimson with Boustique's blood. Then slowly he unwrapped the cloth and removed the metal casing which the ironmonger had fashioned to fit over his fist. He flung the casing down the alleyway. "I would spit on you," he said aloud, "but you are not worthy of my spit."

Boustique did not move. His bloody, broken face was not recognizable. As Guy left, he felt peculiarly unsatisfied. He did not suffer enough, he thought. I did it too fast, I should have prolonged it. I should have made him beg for mercy, the way Marie had begged him.

Thirty-five

THE BARMAN AT THE BAGATELLE told Guy, in response to his inquiry, that Monsieur Trémencourt came in every evening at six o'clock for a double whiskey before returning to his plantation. Two evenings after the executions when Trémencourt came into the club for his whiskey, Guy was sitting at one of the tables in the otherwise unoccupied room, waiting for him. Trémencourt greeted him pleasantly and joined him with his drink.

"So glad to see you, Laroule. Intended to look you up. What luck with the fur charter? Are we in business?"

I have to admire the man's gall, Guy thought, pretending that nothing happened but certainly knowing why I am here.

"What are you drinking? Henri, bring Monsieur Laroule a refresher. Yes, indeed, Laroule, I heard about the expedition with the boy and the nigger going up the Mississippi and I said to myself, now there's a man for a partner, knows how to get things done. If the king gave you a charter, my money is at your disposal. Just show me the charter and it's yours. The Spanish Government has just given me a monopoly on imports—you realize what that means? When the furs come in we set our own price. And whatever you need from here—supplies, workers, slaves—are yours for the asking."

"So that's your reward for killing your friends?"

"Now, just a minute, Laroule, you're not being fair. I simply stated the facts, I had nothing to do with the General's . . ."

"Trémencourt, shut your mouth."

"But I want you to know . . ."

"Shut your mouth and listen to me. Six of my friends are dead and I am their avenger."

"You are making a mistake, Laroule. I am well placed with General O'Reilly. One word from me . . ."

"You will not have the chance to utter that word because this is your last moment on this earth, and good riddance."

"It is preposterous for me to sit here in my own club and be threatened . . ." Trémencourt started to get up, but Guy clamped his hand around Trémencourt's wrist and abruptly pulled him back down; he continued to hold his wrist in a painful grasp.

"What is preposterous is that a worthless Judas like you can waste the lives of six fine people." Trémencourt nervously looked around the bar, hoping to find someone to help him, but it was deserted; even the barman had disappeared. "When the executioners fired their guns, your finger pulled every trigger. But I am going to give you an opportunity to survive, something you never gave them. We will duel with swords and that will give you a chance."

"I do not duel. I am not a swordsman." Trémencourt's voice was noticeably higher; the words seemed to stick in the dryness of his throat.

"You are now." Guy went to the bar where two identical foils had been placed on the counter. Trémencourt bolted for the door and frantically tried to get out.

"It is locked," Guy said, approaching him with the swords. "The barman is gone. Your only chance of survival is to defend yourself. You see, every member of the club knows what you did. I am their emissary as well as my own." Guy thrust the sword into his hand.

"But . . . but it is not a proper . . . proper place to duel, a bar, I protest, only in the woods or along the Tchoupitoulas Road . . ."

"En garde, you miserable informer. My sword itches to carve out your insides, first the liver, then a kidney, then the cavity where normal people have a backbone . . ."

Trémencourt made a sudden violent thrust with his sword hoping to catch Guy off guard but it was a clumsy effort. Guy flicked it away and then began to circle Trémencourt, pricking him with little thrusts that slit his clothes and adroitly nipped his skin, just enough to cause a few drops of blood to appear. Each time the point of his sword touched Trémencourt Guy would identify the sponsor, "this is for Monsieur Grotesquieu, this is for the Comtesse . . ." Trémencourt flailed at Guy, wielding his foil like a saber, all the time whimpering "It's not fair! It's not fair!"

When Guy felt he had inflicted all the preliminary torture Trémencourt deserved, he used the flat of his sword to pluck Trémencourt's foil from his hand and sent it hurtling across the room. "Do you wish a blindfold, Trémencourt? No?"

"Oh, please, Laroule, oh God, please, I beg you, spare me, I will make amends. I have money, please, please, oh God, oh God . . ."

Laroule whistled his sword through the air perilously close to Trémencourt's nose. "Any last words? A prayer? Did you pray for Grotesquieu before you turned him in?"

Trémencourt grabbed at Guy's sword with his hand, trying to wrench it from him, but all he accomplished was a deep gash across his palm. "I am bleeding, Laroule, look! For God's sake have mercy!" Trémencourt was desperately trying to use the tables and chairs of the bar as shields but Guy relentlessly pursued him, moving him from table to table until he was hopelessly trapped in a corner. "May God have mercy on your soul," Guy said. "No one else will." As Guy lined up his sword Trémencourt began to cry, wailing in high gasps as tears flooded his face. Then he pitched forward, throwing himself at Guy's feet, embracing his ankles, kissing his shoes, babbling incomprehensibly through his sniveling, his pants wet with urine, his face looking up at Guy for mercy, mucous running from his nostrils, blood from his hand smeared across his mouth, his clothes ripped from Guy's ripostes, his wig half off his sweat-soaked hair, spittle running his chin, and now a rush of vomit covering his tunic and running down his legs.

In disgust, Guy pushed him away with a kick of his boot. He picked up the fallen sword, unlocked the door, and departed, the cries of Trémencourt's cowardice following him.

After Monsieur Grotesquieu's funeral (a maximum of ten mourners permitted by the authorities), Marie-Thérèse and Guy accompanied Madame Grotesquieu to her house. She gave Guy a letter from Rémi and a position map which had been delivered to Grotesquieu by Mike Fink and given to her along with Grotesquieu's personal effects when the Spanish authorities shut his office the day after the execution. All the furnishings, the files, the trove of architectural drawings of houses he had created, were deemed property of the Government and therefore not returnable.

"My only solace," Madame Grotesquieu said as they were served tea in her parlor, "is that I received a letter from my son saying that he and his wife and their two little boys are returning to New Orleans. Thank God for that."

"Have the authorities done anything about your property?"

Madame Grotesquieu picked up a document from the table and handed it to Guy. "This came yesterday." The notice was brief and to the point: "As a consequence of his treasonous acts the property belonging to André Grotesquieu and all buildings on it will be confiscated by the Cabildo in the name of Charles III within ten days."

"Perhaps the Ursulines will take me in until my son arrives," Madame Grotesquieu said. "I do not know where else to go. Our friends are understandably frightened about associating themselves with me because of the taint on our name."

"Madame Grotesquieu," Guy said, "it is possible that a paper I have can be validated. I do not know. But if the Spanish authorities still recognize rights granted by Louis XV then perhaps there will be a place for you. But I do not want to get your hopes up until I go to see them."

It had occurred to Guy that if the order signed by the Louis XV redeeding Diderot Plantation to him was recognized as valid by the Spaniards, then Guy could transfer it to Madame Grotesquieu since the wording of the document granted ownership to him for his assigns.

It took two days to wind through the bureaucracy of the new government, but eventually the attorney general of the Cabildo looked at the charter and approved its validity. Guy went directly from the Cabildo's headquarters to the sheriff's office. The sheriff had not yet been replaced by a Spaniard; he was the same man, Claude Lèche, who had once served Guy with notice to vacate. He said he was glad to see that Guy had the charter again since he had no use for that "worthless Bernard Duroux. I have more complaints sworn out against him than all the other plantation owners combined. Many times he should have been jailed but through money, perjury and threats, he wins out. Yes, let us go now. It will be a pleasurable visit."

Turning onto the Diderot approach road Guy felt a surge of fondness and familiarity. He had not lived there long but it had inspired in him a deep affection for the land and the buildings, especially the exquisite manor house Grotesquieu had built. Guy's reverie was abruptly interrupted, however, by the sight of three naked slaves shackled to wooden posts in the punishing sun. All three had been caned and were covered with insects nourishing themselves on their open wounds. The sheriff made a sharp, guttural sound. He opened his tunic and slipped a pistol into his waistband.

As the carriage pulled up before the manor house, a large, scowling man came out. "Yes, what is it you want here?" he demanded.

The sheriff and Guy emerged from their carriage. The sheriff identified himself and asked for Monsieur Duroux.

"I handle everything for him," the man said. "What do you want?"

"As I told you, I want Duroux. My business is with him."

Without a word, the man went back into the house. Guy observed that the flower gardens were overgrown, that what he could see of the crops in the fields looked like they needed attention, and that, in general, the plantation had an air of neglect.

Duroux came out abruptly. "Yes, what do you want, Sheriff? I am very busy." He glanced at Guy but did not acknowledge his presence.

"I have here a duly executed document signed by His Majesty, Louis XV, revoking your deed to this plantation and awarding it to this gentleman here, Guy Laroule, the former owner who doubtless you remember."

Duroux snatched the instrument from the sheriff's hand and glanced at it. "Of what value is this?" he exclaimed. "We are now ruled by the Spanish Government. This needs the signature of Charles III, not Louis XV."

"Its validity has been attested to by the Attorney General of the Cabildo," the sheriff said. "On the bottom there you will see his stamp."

Duroux did not look at the paper. "Nonsense. I know the law. I will not budge from here unless I am presented with a Spanish document bearing King Charles' signature. Legally, this is my plantation. I have sold my former plantation, and I intend to remain here."

"Monsieur Duroux," the sheriff said calmly, "as Sheriff I am the enforcement officer of this city. Your defiance is ill advised. I intend to execute this directive from the King of France, and I advise you to abide by it. You have ten days to vacate the premises which now belong to Monsieur Laroule."

"Do not threaten me, Sheriff. We have tangled before and you may recall that in each instance my position won out over yours. Now be a good fellow and go back to your office and take this Versailles dandy with you."

"It may interest you to know that this Versailles dandy," Guy said, "has proved that the letter you gave Madame du Barry was a forgery and the Crown is considering filing criminal charges against you."

Duroux laughed. "So you got to that whore, du Barry, did you? Did she tell you about my visits when she was in the Roué's harem?"

"For the last time, Duroux," the sheriff said, "I am ordering you to comply with my orders given in accord with the directive contained in the document which you hold."

Duroux laughed again. "This is what I think of your precious document." Duroux ripped the paper in half and threw it on the ground.

"You are under arrest for destroying property of the Crown," the sheriff said. "Pick up that paper."

"Sheriff, you and the entire army could not force me to pick up that paper, which belongs in my toilet."

The sheriff drew his pistol from his waistband. "As Sheriff of New Orleans, I am ordering you to pick up that paper, which is the property of the Crown, and return it to me."

There was a slight movement on the steps of the house where Duroux's man was standing. He too had drawn a gun.

Duroux smiled at the sheriff. "Have you met my overseer, Arbois? He is a superb marksman. Now first let me summarize. I do not recognize the validity of this French document you have brought here. I will not vacate the premises. I will not pick up the two halves of this spurious document. If you were to be so foolish as to fire your pistol, Arbois would return fire. So Sheriff, you are entangled in an impasse. I advise you to put away your gun and to return to your carriage with your Versailles dandy, and get off my property before I charge both of you with trespass."

"Duroux, I do not think you realize the seriousness of your situation. You are challenging the authority of the Crown. I am sworn to enforce that authority and enforce it I will. I hereby inform you that you are under arrest. Put forth your hands to be manacled."

The sheriff took a pair of manacles from his pocket. Duroux laughed. "Did you hear that, Arbois? Put forth my hands, the Sheriff says. Show him what we think of his manacles."

Arbois fired his gun at the dangling manacles, knocking them from the sheriff's hand. The sheriff, in turn, shot Duroux in the chest. Arbois had withdrawn a second gun from his waist which he now pointed at the sheriff but before he could shoot he was felled by a shot that struck his head, spinning him around before he fell to the ground. The carriage driver, who now descended from his perch, held the gun that had shot Arbois.

"Thank you, Auguste," the sheriff said, then introduced him to Guy. "This is my deputy, not the first time he has been the saving gun."

"My God," Guy said. "I never expected it to come to this. Will there be trouble?"

"There will be rejoicing. Auguste, go cut those poor slaves loose and help them over to the slaves' quarters for attention." A delegation of five slaves approached. "Sheriff, Your Honor," one of them said, "we would like to feed them to the 'gators in the swamp. It would be the greatest of pleasures."

"No," the sheriff said, "but what you can do is hitch a mule to a cart and bring them to the coroner's office on Chartres Street."

"But what happen if the cart it get stuck in the swamp going over there?"

"If such an unfortunate thing occurs you come to me and we will fill out a report which you will sign."

"But, Your Honor, I can no write my name."

"I will teach you to make an X," the sheriff said.

Thirty-six

THE ONLY LAND ROUTE to the north consisted of a wagon trail to Natchez and then a perilous stretch of five-hundred and fifty miles to Nashville, the notorious Natchez Trace. Traveled mostly by Mississippi boatmen returning to their homes after leaving their boats in New Orleans, the Trace was feared for its rigorous travel demands, its diseases, and especially for the robbers, plunderers, and murderers who preyed on the unprotected travelers. There were no towns, forts, or settlements of any kind along the Trace, but once the traveler reached Nashville there were frequent towns and camps along the route from then on. Consequently, these land pirates confined their nefarious activities to the relatively easy pickings of the isolated Trace.

Guy had heard many stories about these Trace brigands and their cruel acts. The perilousness of his impending journey was on his mind when he visited the sheriff to sign assignment papers, confirming ownership of Diderot Plantation to Madame Grotesquieu.

"Yes, indeed, I know the Natchez Trace very well—too well," the sheriff said. "Most of the criminals we apprehend have committed crimes on the Trace. Just you and your wife? Very, very risky. To give you an idea, we hanged two fellows last month who killed a traveler on the Trace." The sheriff extracted a report from his desk drawer. "One of them made a confession—here, read it."

About noon, I had tired and stopped at a creek to get some water and rest a little. While I was sitting on a log and looking down the road the way I had come, a man came in sight riding a good-looking horse. The moment I saw him I was determined to have his horse if he was in the garb of a traveler. He rode up and I saw from his equipage that he was a traveler. I arose and drew a rifle pistol on him, and ordered him to dismount. He did so, and I took his horse by the bridle, pointed down the creek and ordered him to walk before me.

He went a few hundred yards, and stopped. I hitched his horse and then made him undress himself, everything down to his shirt and drawers, and ordered him to turn his back to me. He said "If you are determined to kill me let me have time to pray before I die." I told him I had no time to hear him pray. He turned around and dropped on his knees, and I shot him through the back of the head. I ripped open his belly and took out his entrails, and sank him in the creek. I then searched his pockets and found four hundred dollars and thirty-seven cents, and a number of papers that I did not take time to examine. I sank all his clothing and effects in the creek. His boots were brand-new, and fitted me genteelly, and I put them on and sank my old ones in the creek to atone for them. I mounted as fine a horse as I ever straddled, and directed my course for Natchez in much better style than I had been for five days. Myself and a fellow by the name of Crenshaw gathered four good horses and started for Georgia. We got in company with a young fellow from South Carolina just before we got to the Cumberland Mountains and Crenshaw soon knew all about his business. He had been to Tennessee to buy a drove of hogs. But when he got there pork was dearer than he had calculated and he declined purchasing. We concluded he was a prize.

Crenshaw winked at me. I understood his idea. He had traveled the road before. I never had. We had traveled several miles on the mountain road when we passed a great precipice. Just before passing it, Crenshaw asked me for my whip, which had a pound of lead in the butt. I handed it to him. He rode up alongside of the Carolinian and gave him a blow on the side of the head which tumbled him from his horse. We alit from our horses and fingered his pockets. We got $1,262.00.

Crenshaw said he knew a place to hide him. He gathered him by under his arms and I by his feet, and conveyed him to a deep crevice under the precipice and tumbled him into it and he went out of sight. We then threw in his saddle and took his horse, which was worth two hundred dollars, with us.

"As you can see by that account, there are some scurrilous scoundrels operating on the Trace. There was a man we were never able to catch named Joseph Hare, who murdered and robbed hundreds before they caught him and hanged him in Baltimore for robbing the mail. Another murderous bastard, still operating, is John Murrell, of Tennessee. Now, he's a peculiar one. His mother owns a tavern in Columbia, Tennessee that is a front for her brothel and thieves' market behind it. She lives with a man named Harry Crenshaw who taught her son, the John I referred to, how to operate as a highwayman and murderer. John has been at it since he was ten and now Murrell and Crenshaw along with confederates all along the Trace murder travelers for their money and their belongings which are then sold by John's mother in her thieves' market. Murrell is not your ordinary highwayman. He speaks in an educated way and often appears at camp meetings to deliver fiery sermons praising the ways of God and righteous living.

"So if you and your wife are going to attempt to travel the Trace, you would best take some precautions. You should travel the road from New Orleans to Natchez by wagon. I don't know of anyone ever being accosted there. But once on the Trace, your wife should wear men's clothes. Rape is always a possibility with these lowlifes. Also, you will have to travel the Trace by horseback since there are no roads, so you should take horses and pack mules with you when you leave New Orleans. Most importantly, you should have at least two men, professionals, to guard you to the end of the Trace."

"I would like to, but I know of no such men," Guy said. "Could you be of help?"

"Well, I have reserve deputies whom I would be willing to spare if they consent to go. Of course, you would have to compensate them. They know the Trace and they are trained in the use of firearms. But even this does not guarantee your safety—some of these robbers work in groups. However, it would be protection against culprits like the one whose confession you read. I suppose you realize that you will be riding over very rough terrain, hardly ideal for a pregnant lady."

"Yes, but she is determined to go. She is very anxious to be reunited with her son, and so am I."

The ride to Natchez was, as the sheriff had predicted, uneventful. The wagon was being driven by Madame Grotesquieu's gardener who would return with it to the Diderot Plantation afterward. There were numerous settlements along the way and the roadway itself was relatively smooth. The two deputies who the sheriff had provided rode horseback on either side of the wagon which had two stalwart horses and four mules bearing packs hitched to it. Marie-Thérèse was wearing a loose-fitting dress to accommodate her eight months of pregnancy, but she intended to disguise herself in men's clothing when they reached Natchez. Guy wore a holstered pistol and he had a rifle that he would attach to his saddle when they mounted their horses for the Natchez Trace. He was dressed in a riverman's outfit: brown overalls, a red shirt, brogans, and the broad-brimmed black hat favored by crewmen. Both deputies were heavily armed but since they were on a private mission, they were not permitted to wear uniforms, but they did wear their distinctive hats stripped of insignia. The object of their appearance would be to suggest that they were ordinary rivermen possessing nothing that would interest a highwayman. The presence of the horses and mules, however, might be enough to attract attention since almost all rivermen traversed the Trace on foot, not able to afford horses.

On the sheriff's advice, Guy had had secret money flaps sewn inside the canvas of the tent that they would pitch at night, so that if they were held up the robbers would only get the small amount of money that Guy was carrying. "They know all the usual tricks," the sheriff had warned, "money belts, sewing the money into clothing, hiding it in rifle butts that have been hollowed out—you have to be ingenious about it but don't tell anyone, not even the two deputies about the secret pocket in your tent. Money is the hardest temptation to resist."

They tarried in Natchez just long enough to prepare the horses and mules and take on food and water. For five-hundred and fifty miles there would be no sign of human life as they passed through flat, unhealthy country where there was no possibility of obtaining food. Although water was plentiful it was often what the sheriff referred to as "bad water that caused fevers, violent dysentery and bloody flux." He had also warned them that when they pitched their tent at night to be on the lookout for poisonous snakes, bears, panthers, and other wild animals. He instructed the deputies to alternate as lookouts, watching for predatory highwaymen, dangerous animals, and thieving Indians.

Marie-Thérèse wore clothes similar to Guy's, and from a distance they certainly appeared to be a couple of rivermen returning from

New Orleans. As they rode out of the city, they passed Natchez Under the Hill, a notorious two-block stretch located at the base of the bluff on which the city had been built. These two blocks, lined solidly with brothels, saloons, and gambling houses, were even more lawless than New Orleans' Swamp District. Robbing passers-by and killing them was commonplace and, just for the fun of it, roving gunmen often took aim at boats passing on the Mississippi. Both Marie-Thérèse and Guy felt relieved to be leaving these sordid excesses that the cities tolerated.

Once on the Trace, which followed a series of old Choctaw and Chickasaw trails, the two deputies rode fore and aft, their rifles across their laps. The path of the Trace was narrow but easy on the horses and the mules; sixty-two miles beyond Natchez, however, the travelers reached the Grindstone Ford on the Bayou Pierre, the last settlement before Nashville, five hundred miles away. The trail now ran along the ridge between the Yazoo and Tombigbee Rivers, and was so heavily obstructed with fallen trees, briars, and underbrush that the horses had to proceed in single file, picking their way very carefully over and around the obstructions. At night, Guy tried to find a deserted Indian camp which had a cleared area where he could pitch the tent while Marie-Thérèse cooked the evening's meal. The long day's ride did not affect Marie-Thérèse who said she enjoyed the activity after being so sedentary for those long months while Guy was away.

At the mouth of the Tombigbee was Big Town, a Chickasaw settlement, but the trail veered away from the town and the travelers did not encounter any Indians.

The next forty miles out of Big Town, the Trace became hilly and covered with wet marshland that made the footing of the horses precarious. This stretch of the Trace ended at the Tennessee River where the water was too swift and deep to be forded. The only way across was to take a ferry operated, with the help of several Indians, by a disagreeable half-breed named James Colbert who charged a dollar a head.

The stretch of the Trace from the Tennessee River to the Duck River, seventy-five miles away, was the most difficult terrain of the entire journey. Rock-strewn hills, impenetrable cane fields, and swamps of mucillaginous mud aptly called hellholes combined with swarms of mosquitoes to make this a challenging ordeal. It was during this stretch of the travelers' journey that they unexpectedly encountered two men who, as they came over a hill, blocked their path with guns pointed at them. For this stretch of the journey the two deputies had positioned themselves at the rear. When one of the robbers shouted "Stop! Dismount!" the deputies heard him and by stopping short of the hilltop, they did not reveal themselves. Instead, they maneuvered their horses off the trail and circled around the path of the Trace, eventually emerging behind the robbers.

In the meantime, the thieves, who wore bandanas across their faces, ordered Guy and Marie-Thérèse to dismount and lie face down on the ground while they searched the saddlebags on the mules. They took Guy's rifle and ammunition, most of the food, and several jugs of water that they loaded onto their own horses which stood beside the road.

Having done that they ordered Guy and Marie-Thérèse to stand up, one of the men pointing his rifle at them while the other started to search Guy. While he was on the ground, Guy had managed to shift his pistol from its holster to the back of his waistband where it could not be seen. The bandits were in the process of searching him when they both felt cold metal pressing into the back of their necks.

"Now just what do you think these fellows are up to?" one of the deputies asked the other.

"Why I do believe they are trying to rob these nice people," the other deputy said, as he reached around to relieve the robber of his rifle. Guy reached back for his pistol and pointed it at the two brigands.

"Well, I don't think it's polite of them to cover their faces, do you?" one deputy asked, as he bound their hands behind them.

"Definitely not," Guy responded, reaching forward and pulling down their bandanas.

"I know you, don't I?" one of the deputies said to the taller and fatter of the two robbers. "You are William Goodfellow of Natchez. Work for Murrell and Cranshaw, don't you? Trying to get a little merchandise for Mom Murrell to sell, eh? Well, let's just see what merchandise you fellows have with you."

The deputies emptied both men's pockets, and then went through the contents of the saddlebags on their horses. They found five drawstring chamois bags filled with silver dollars and another larger bag with an imposing collection of jewelry in it. They also reclaimed Guy's rifle and the other items the robbers had taken, along with a variety of valuable objects belonging to the robbers. Each deputy then took a coil of rope from his saddle bag, bound the robbers' feet around the ankles and tied the end of the ropes around their horses saddles. They slapped the horses across their rumps, sending them galloping down the path in the opposite direction. The two robbers, jerked off their feet, violently bounced along the ground in the horses' wake. It would be a *slow* execution.

After fording the Duck River, the road to the Cumberland River became very sandy with washboard hilliness. The horses' pace slackened as they sloughed through the deep, heavy sand. It was along this stretch that the only other encounter with Trace brigands occurred. At a point where the narrow, grumous path took an abrupt turn and descent, four ominous-looking armed men formed a shoulder-to-shoulder barricade. They carried their weapons at their sides and simply stared at the lead deputy who was forced to come to a halt. He raised his rifle from his lap with the muzzle pointed skyward. The rear deputy joined him and the two sides faced each other in a wordless confrontation. Guy had removed his rifle from its saddle holster and held it in the crook of his arm. For a full three minutes the tableau stayed frozen in place, no one moving or uttering a word. Then, very slowly, the deputies' horses started to move forward as the deputies kept sharp eyes on the men blocking their path. As the horses began to press against the men in the path they were forced to give ground slowly, grudgingly, backing to the sides of the road as the horses now forced a path for themselves with Guy, Marie-Thérèse and their caravan of mules following closely. After the mules passed one of the deputies doubled back and again faced the barricaders until his group had gone a considerable way down the Trace at which time he wheeled around and caught up with them. During the entire episode not a single word had been spoken.

They arrived in Nashville seventeen days after their departure from New Orleans. Despite the frightening encounter with the Trace robbers, Marie-Thérèse had sustained the often bumpy eight-hundred-mile journey surprisingly well; even her morning malaise had subsided. Since the Trace ended in Nashville and the route beyond was reputed to be free of marauders, the deputies terminated their protection and headed back to New Orleans, the confiscated booty secure in their saddlebags. Guy was sorry to see them go because it was an unknown road he would now travel; he would have welcomed their familiarity with the terrain.

Marie-Thérèse shed her riverman costume, but Guy felt comfortable traveling in his. They replenished their supplies of food and water, and Guy consulted a local cartographer to plan a route that would take them to the northwest. The plan that evolved took them across the barrens to Danville, a dense rather desolate area, but from there the road to Paducah was well defined with numerous settlements along the way. Out of Paducah there was a rather primitive road which wound up in Cairo, Illinois, on the east side of the Mississippi. From there they would have to find a path running north that paralleled the river.

The second day traversing the barrens, they came upon an Indian camp situated along the road, a camp with established cabins and a look of permanence about it. Several of the Indian men came to the roadside to observe them as they passed, displaying neither hostility nor friendliness. Their stolid presence, however, had a chilling effect on both Marie-Thérèse and Guy whose memory was still seared by what the Choctaws had done to Diderot Plantation and its occupants.

Until now the weather had been cold but dry, with some sun on most days, but now after an extended overture of thunder, a veritable monsoon fell out of the sky. The combination of driving wind and torrential rain made further travel impossible. Guy hobbled the horses, hitched the mules to a tree, and pitched the tent under some sheltering pines.

The horrendous weather continued unabated through the night, drumming thunderously on their quaking tent. Guy and Marie-Thérèse slept huddled together on a pallet Guy had elevated by mounting brush on top of supporting stones. During the night, Marie-Thérèse awoke but after an hour of trying not to awaken Guy, she reluctantly disturbed him. "I have contractions," she said, "at regular intervals."

Still groggy from a fitful sleep, Guy did not at first comprehend the meaning of what Marie-Thérèse had said.

"We have some time," Marie-Thérèse continued, "but I think it will be within a few hours."

"Oh, my God, Danville is two days away! What will we do?"

"Well, darling, we have no choice, do we? We will have to have the baby here."

"Here! In this wet, muddy tent? What chance will it have? And what about you? No, no, the risk . . ."

She put two fingertips over his lips. "Now there is nothing to get so alarmed about. We have water and you have a knife to cut the cord."

"But I have heard that the water should be hot . . ."

"We will build a fire."

"In this rain?"

"Under the tarpaulin."

"There is no dry wood."

"Then we will use cold water. Books are full of stories about women having babies in open fields, on rivers, in the most unlikely places."

"They are fictional ladies in novels. Do you personally know any woman who has had a baby in a muddy field in the rain?"

"No, not personally."

"Well, there you are."

"Although a friend of mine went into labor while riding in her carriage."

"But she had the baby in her bed with a proper midwife, didn't she?"

"Yes, I suppose so. But you and I are going to have our baby here. Don't forget I have had the benefit of one previous maternity. Besides the water and the knife, we will need some towels and those extra blankets in the saddlebags. I only hope you don't faint. Do you think you might faint, darling?"

"Wait . . . hold on . . ."

"What is it?"

"Of course!"

"Of course what?"

"It's worth a try!"

"What is?"

"That Indian camp we passed."

"What about it?"

"We will go there."

"I should say not! They will scalp us and kill the baby."

"Not all Indians are as mean as the Choctaws. Franchmastabbia was one of the sweetest, gentlest men I ever met, a Chickasaw."

"But we don't know what tribe that is, do we? Did you see the cold look those savages gave us as we passed? I would rather take my chances here."

"Marie-Thérèse, listen to me. Be sensible. This tent is covered with mud. Everything is wet and filthy. Water is dripping through the canvas. We are not prepared for any of this. The Indians know midwifery and how to take care of a newborn. I have a good feeling that they will help us. I have some things in my saddlebag that I can offer as gifts. Some trinkets, things like that. I'm going to saddle my horse and you will ride my saddle with me. But we must hurry."

"But, Guy, there is the risk . . ."

"Yes, yes, of course, the risk. There is no such thing as a safe risk. I'll be right back."

Guy saddled up his horse and took their raincapes from the pocket of his saddlebag. Marie-Thérèse was up and ready when he returned to the tent.

"How are the contractions?"

"Speeding up a little."

"Then so must we."

The Indian camp showed no signs of life when they rode onto the grounds in the punishing rain. Guy reached into his saddlebag and extracted the small curved horn the sheriff had given him to sound in case of emergency. He blew it now, its shrill cry resounding through the camp. After a short interval, he blew it again. This time there was stirring; several torches flared revealing forms moving toward them. Guy dismounted and then carefully assisted Marie-Thérèse to the ground as a group of men, holding torches, approached them.

"Anyone speak French?" Guy asked. "English? German?"

The Indians spoke to each other in their own tongue. Guy resorted to pantomine, pulling back Marie-Thérèse's raincape to reveal her swollen belly, cradling his arms, and even mimicking a baby's cry. "Please," he said. "Help us."

The Indians conversed more animatedly but they kept their distance. A burly Indian in the forefront of the group was speaking angrily and gesturing toward Marie-Thérèse in what appeared to be an unfriendly manner. She pulled her raincape more tightly around her. The contractions were more persistent. She looked at Guy with fear in her eyes, but he frowned at her. The discussion, mostly a harangue by the burly man who shouted down the others, seemed to go on interminably; suddenly, the man came forward to face them.

"Go back," he said in English. "We no want white faces here."

"But it is a baby, a baby!" Guy exclaimed.

"White baby. No want white baby. Go!" He took a menacing step forward, and they both instinctively backed up. The wind-driven rain was dripping from their faces, ground water up to their ankles. A sharp peal of angry thunder shook the sky. "Guy, Guy,"

Marie-Thérèse whispered, "my . . . my . . . we must hurry." She gripped his arm for support. There was a stirring in back of the men as three robust Indian women abruptly pushed the men aside and came forward. One of the women spoke authoritatively to the Indian who had been the spokesman, chastising him. The women circled Marie-Thérèse and shepherded her toward the interior of the camp. Guy tethered his horse and followed them.

The cabin that the women entered was warm and dry. The stove in the corner gave off a good wood smell. The women unceremoniously pushed two men who were in the cabin out the door. They also covered the two cabin windows with blankets when the men crowded around them to watch.

The wooden bed in the corner of the room was covered with fur skins. The women helped Marie-Thérèse out of her wet clothes and replaced them with a loose-fitting robe before assisting her into the bed. She was already far along in her labor. The women moved with the expertise of having assisted in many childbirths. Hot water was on the stove. Clean towels were on the bed. They spoke soothingly to Marie-Thérèse who was now in the final, painful contractions of her labor. Although she could not understand the words, she found their compassion reassuring.

Guy had attempted to follow the women into the cabin but had been rebuffed. With the windows covered, there was no way for him to know how Marie-Thérèse was being treated. He stood with his back against the wall of the cabin, his eyes closed, the rain swirling around him, drenching him, dripping off his nose, the thunder assailing him, thunder without lightning. I would pray, he thought, but I am not religious enough to merit divine intervention. It is in the hands of these women and I must trust them not to lose my baby or my wife. I believe in you, women, I believe in you, he kept repeating to himself, willing his declaration of support to somehow reach them through the cabin's wall.

The baby was born exactly one hour later. She was healthy and rosy, and at the sound of her first cries Guy rushed into the room. The cord had been cut and one of the women was already washing the newborn. Guy took Marie-Thérèse in his arms and put her sweated cheek against his; relieved of their ordeal, they both wept. One of the women brought the baby, now wrapped in a small blanket, over to the bed and placed her in Marie-Thérèse's arms. The infant had hazel eyes and a tuft of blond hair on the top of her head. Marie-Thérèse and Guy folded the baby into their embrace.

"I would like to call her Pélagie, after my grandmother," Marie-Thérèse said.

"Then that will be her name," Guy said. He looked intently at the child and touched her cheek with his fingertips. "Pélagie Laroule," he said, "welcome."

Marie-Thérèse and Guy stayed with the Indians, who were Miskogis, for five days. The Indian woman who had taken charge of Marie-Thérèse was the widow of the tribe's recently deceased chief. Since the Miskogi was a matrilineal tribe, by custom the chief's powers had vested in his wife, and it was at her insistence that Marie-Thérèse and the baby remained with them for a few days before continuing their journey.

Each evening there was a feast or a ceremony: to celebrate the baby's birth; to give thanks to the gods for the harvesting of their crops; to bless the construction of a new cabin (the cabins were made of logs chinked with mud, the roofs thatched); to celebrate a wedding; and on the eve of the departure of their guests, an elaborate ceremony to purge any evil spirits that might be lurking along their path.

The chief's widow, who had five daughters, had assigned one of them, fourteen-year-old Filonea, who had the beatific features and mien of a Limoges angel, to be the baby's nurse. Filonea had attended a school in Danville and spoke English quite well. She came to Marie-Thérèse during the last evening's ceremony while the medicine men were planting feathers in the sand, which they burned during their incantations, and explained that her mother had instructed her to accompany Marie-Thérèse on the trip to help care for the baby. Also, if Marie-Thérèse desired, once she reached her destination, Filonea was to stay with her for as long as she wished.

"Is this something you would like to do, or is it just to please your mother?" Marie-Thérèse asked.

"It would be my dream," Filonea answered.

So now there were four of them on the trail with Filonea riding a Pinto pony given to her by her uncle. Both she and Marie-Thérèse had been provided with papoose slings, and they took turns carrying Pélagie on their backs.

The paths and roadways from Danville to Paducah and then over hilly terrain to Cairo were relatively easy to navigate, and the lush scenery illuminated the journey. The Miskogis had packed the mules' saddlebags with fresh vegetables from their fields: maize, beans, cane-millet, Jerusalem artichokes, and small pumpkins which Filonea cooked for their dinners. Along the way, Guy hunted and was able to complement their meals with rabbits, squirrels, and pheasants.

Baby Pélagie prospered.

Once they reached Cairo, Illinois, Guy knew from the map Rémi had drawn for him that it was necessary to cross the Mississippi to reach Rémi's place on the western side of the river. After making inquiries, Guy found a bargeman who was willing to ferry them across for five silver dollars. It would be necessary, however, the bargeman explained, to start upriver because the current would be carrying them downstream during the crossing. The barge had strong stanchions for securing the horses and mules, and the bargeman had four slaves aboard to work the oars while he navigated with the tiller. During the crossing there was a moment of panic when one of the mules got loose and almost bolted over the side, saddlebags and all, but Guy just managed to catch his bridle and get him under control.

Once on the Missouri side, they began to feel a mounting excitement as they moved ever closer to the point on the map that Rémi had marked with a big X. But to follow the marked route that took them through Ste. Geneviève and then Herculaneum, they had to thread their way along terrain that presented no discernable path. Several times Guy had to dismount and cut through dense undergrowth that had brought them to a standstill. They had hoped to reach Rémi's outpost on that day but the going was too slow; reluctantly, as night closed in on them, they pitched camp for what they hoped would be the final time.

After dinner they sat around the fire, Marie-Thérèse breast-feeding Pélagie while they speculated about Rémi and Tricot and what kind of place they had created.

"I expect we will find that Rémi has grown up a lot," Marie-Thérèse said. "Do you think he has, you know, become a man—I mean, boatmen are always finding women . . ."

Guy pulled her to him. "How I love you, mother of Pélagie."

"Don't change the subject."

"The subject is love and it will never change."

"Hear that, Pélagie? Guy loves you and I love you, and he loves me and I love him, and we all love Rémi. And it will never change."

"Never," Guy said.

ST. LOUIS, 1763

Thirty-seven

As THEY CAME UP over a densely-vegetated rise, the clearing was suddenly before them, a gently sloping plateau terminating in a rocky bluff safely above the river's floodline. A break in the bluff afforded easy access to the river. The timber of felled trees was neatly stacked at the clearing's edges. They saw the two log cabins, smoke curling from their chimneys, that had been built already. On land near the water, men were at work on the foundation of what would be a large house.

As the horses cantered up to the workers, Rémi straightened up and faced them. What he saw were three people on horseback, one of them carrying a baby, a train of mules behind them. What Guy and Marie-Thérèse saw was a tall young man dressed in weathered buckskin and wearing boots of buffalo hide, his long hair bound in an eelskin bag secured with a colored handkerchief. At first neither recognized the other.

"Rémi?" Guy inquired as he dismounted.

"Guy . . . ?" quizzically, then with a cry of recognition, "Guy!" as Rémi rushed forward to meet him.

"Rémi!" Marie-Thérèse called to him as she approached on her horse.

"The baby!" Rémi exclaimed. "You've had the baby!"

Marie-Thérèse handed Pélagie to Filonea as she swung off her horse and embraced Rémi who had grown taller than she in the months they had been apart.

"This is your sister, Pélagie, and this is our lovely helper, Filonea." Marie-Thérèse handed the baby to Rémi who held her carefully and awkwardly. Pélagie reached up and grasped his forefinger as a gurgling smile lit up her face; it was a bonding moment that Rémi would never forget.

"How grown up you are, Rémi," Marie-Thérèse said.

"I did not recognize you," Guy said. "You look to be ten years older. The Mississippi has made a man of you."

"I see you've already built two cabins," Marie-Thérèse said.

"Yes, the big one is for you."

"What are you starting here?"

"This will be your real house, which will not be a log cabin. We will use limestone from the bluff that fronts the water." The men who had been working on the foundation now approached. Rémi introduced them: "Vincent Beccé, our carpenter; Jacques Orlaud, our blacksmith; Leon Thibault, who served in the Army under Captain Aubry in New Orleans; our scout, Tico Verdoux . . ."

"Scout?"

"He knows the Indian tribes up here—when you start to acquire fur pelts . . ."

"Oh, yes, of course."

". . . and this is Gilbert Antoine who is an experienced trapper, and our cook, Emil Lefèvre."

"I see you have three slaves at work," Guy said.

"Yes, runaways."

"Are they branded?"

"No, no marks on them. They want to stay here. But we need more. Twenty, thirty more. And we need people to live here."

"In due time. Do not concern yourself. We have a fur monopoly for eight years, and we will be sought after."

"Mother, I suppose you and the baby would like to go to your cabin where it is warm, and you can bathe. Vincent made the furniture and the bed out of forest cedar. Jacques fashioned a tub out of metal. Gilbert will bring you river water to heat over the fire for your bath. Tico, help the slaves unload the mule's packs and carry the things into the house."

Marie-Thérèse was impressed with the easy command that her son exercised over these men. It was difficult for her to reconcile this self-assured young man with the boy who had departed New Orleans just a short while ago.

Guy had crossed the cleared area and now he stood at the edge of the bluff, looking down at the river below. From his vantage point, off to his left he could see gently rolling uplands sweeping all the way to the horizon, alternately prairie and open woodland, covered with high, luxuriant grass. Along the banks of the river were perpendicular cliffs separating the uplands from the bottoms, but there were also discernible places where gradually, almost imperceptibly, the uplands rolled gently towards the lowlands which were covered with towering forests. Along the hillsides Guy could see gushing springs snaking their way into the river. The verdancy and majesty of the terrain were overpowering.

"What do you think of the land I chose?" Rémi asked as he joined Guy.

"Spectacular. More than I had bargained for," Guy replied. "What shall we call our little village? 'God's Choice?' "

"Perhaps for the King. Sieur de la Salle named Louisiana as a tribute to Louis XIV."

"Why not name it for His Majesty's patron saint, Louis IX, whom Pope Boniface canonized?"

"Then it would be 'St. Louis'?"

"Precisely. 'St. Louis.' A good name, that. And I'm sure it will please the King."

That evening's supper was a joyous affair. Emil Lefèvre produced a Creole dish, West Indian gumbo, popular in New Orleans, a spicy concoction of fricasseed possum (chicken in New Orleans), catfish (substituted for New Orleans crayfish), okra, tomatoes, lima beans, and various herbs and condiments. There was also a side of spit-roasted venison and two plump pheasants decorated with their plumage. Claret, whiskey, and a bottle of prized Madeira, all preserved for the occasion by Rémi from the keelboat supplies, were also on the table. Rémi explained that he obtained vegetables by bartering with Missouri Indians who had an encampment on the Missouri River, which emptied into the Mississippi a few miles to the north, and who came down the Mississippi in bull boats to trade their foodstuffs for mirrors, combs, and other trinkets.

After dinner, by the light of the candles, Guy sketched the layout of the future village. The gridiron pattern which he penciled on the paper spread out on the table was modeled after New Orleans. There was a market place situated above the boat landing. The Place d'Armes was placed at the riverfront but protected from the river by limestone ledges. Running parallel to the river were three lengthy streets: rue Royale, rue de l'Eglise and rue des Granges. Bisecting these streets were narrower, shorter streets: rue Bonhomme, rue de la Tour, and rue Missouri. Guy divided each block of streets into small lots which would be given to families without charge providing, however, that the property would be forfeited unless improved within a year and a day. Altogether forty-nine such blocks were indicated on the plan. At the rear of these streets, Guy sketched an area to be used as a common field on which to grow crops.

"And do you really think people will come here to build on these lots?" Rémi asked.

"Of course," Guy replied.

"But Kaskaskia and Ste. Geneviève are so near, and they are excellent villages with churches and schools—why would anyone come here?"

"For the furs," Guy replied confidently. "Yes, Ste. Geneviève is established with a good population of four or five hundred, but what do they do? They mine lead and ore, but no one will ever get rich from that. But fur is like gold. And we have a monopoly on trapping and shipping them to New Orleans where the boats will take them to England and France and Germany where customers eagerly await their arrival. We shall assemble here Creoles of breeding with whom we can enjoy a cultured and civilized existence. Now that the Treaty of Paris has been signed—two years it took—the British will take over the east side of the Mississippi and we will be able to offer refuge to those French at Fort Chartres who do not want to remain under British rule. I shall go there and try to persuade proper families to come here rather than return to New Orleans."

"But how are you going to obtain the furs? You see how vast the land is and how difficult the terrain."

"We will send out however many trappers come to us, but mostly we will deal with the Indians."

"You will need a great many men to reach all the Indian tribes in this area that trap furs."

"Yes, true, but what if they all come here?"

"The Indians? Here?"

"Yes, why not? The chiefs and their council of warriors could come together in a fur powwow."

"But many of these tribes are hostile to each other."

"Do not worry, Rémi, if the prizes are tempting enough, they'll come. At least that's my theory."

"And if you are wrong?"

"Then we will think of something else, won't we?"

By the time they were ready for bed, Vincent had made a simple cradle for Pélagie to sleep in.

The following day, Guy, Rémi and Marie-Thérèse mounted horses and toured the area that the new village would occupy. Just north of what would be the common ground where each family would plant its crops, they came upon a huge mound of earth, as tall as a cathedral, surrounded by clusters of smaller mounds, all of them so smoothly constructed they could not possibly have been made by animals.

The men working on the new house came with their picks and shovels and began to dig an opening into the large, central mound. A half-day of digging earned them access into the mound's interior which to their amazement proved to be an elaborate burial chamber of an ancient tribal chief who had been laid to rest with many rich possessions. From the look of the contents, the burial mound was probably several centuries old. The smaller mounds contained warriors who had been entombed with their spears and arrows, possibly while alive, to protect the chief on his voyage to the hereafter.

It was while Guy, Rémi and Marie-Thérèse were examining the contents of the burial mound that Tricot appeared. His hair was long and matted, he had a full beard, and he was wearing a thick, ground-length coat of buffalo fur. He was emaciated. His left arm hung uselessly at his side. In his right hand he carried a spear with the remains of a small animal embedded on it. He walked with a severe limp.

Knowing that Guy and Marie-Thérèse would not recognize him, Rémi said, "Guy, this is Tricot."

Guy looked at Tricot uncomprehendingly.

"I'm sorry, Guy, I should have warned you," Rémi said.

Tricot stared at Guy but said nothing.

"There are a few times when he seems to remember some things, but mostly his mind is gone. He lives in the woods there. We set out food for him, but sometimes we don't see him for days. He was tortured and badly abused by pirates who kidnapped him. We rescued him, but we could not undo what terrible things they did to him. He was all right for a while, but then his mind got worse and worse. He began to act very strangely. Now I cannot tell if he knows any of us. He never talks." Tricot continued to stare at Guy; he stepped very close to him, peering intently at his face. It appeared that he was trying to identify him.

"Tricot," Guy said, "I'm Monsieur Laroule. Laroule. New Orleans. Diderot Plantation. Tricot . . ."

Tricot stepped back keeping his eyes on Guy.

"Tricot," Guy said, "do you not know me?"

After one last look, Tricot turned and limped away toward the forest.

It was decided that priority should be given to the construction of log cabins. Unlike the American system of laying the logs horizontally and notching them at the corners, the carpenter, Vincent, used the French method which was to set the cedar logs perpendicularly, bore holes near the end of the logs, and hang them over a sheeting. Plaster made from powdering the limestone was used to fill the cracks. A long overhang of the roof on all four sides protected the limestone from the rain and would also serve as a buffer against the blistering heat of the summer. The kitchen, which had a wide, deep fireplace to cook in, was in a separate cabin.

Everyone worked on the cabin which went up in short order, with only one significant delay. One morning while busily at work, Tico Verdoux, the scout, who had been at the edge of the forest supervising the slaves and selecting the logs, came running to the construction site shouting, "Indians coming! Indians!" No sooner had he given his warning than a mass of Indians, painted and armed, approached, led by an elderly chieftain who wore an elaborate headdress of eagle feathers which hung down his back. The warriors, close to a hundred in number, arrayed themselves behind their leader. Fortunately, Filonea understood their dialect and could translate the chief's message.

They were Missouris. Word had reached them that the white man had broken into the sacred burial mounds of their ancestors, and they had come to drive out these white devils and occupy the sacred area with some of their own people to protect it. The Missouris are a peace-loving tribe, the chief said, not given to warring and hostility, but they will not tolerate evil behavior by white devils who disturb the souls of their ancestors. Therefore you must pack and be gone within the hour if you wish to avoid the wrath of our spears. The warriors brandished their weapons and shouted their approval of the chief's words.

Guy bowed his head to the chief in a show of respect and invited him into his cabin to discuss the situation. The chief motioned to the four braves who were his lieutenants, and the five of them followed Guy and Rémi into the main cabin. Guy spread blankets on the floor and they all sat in a circle. Marie-Thérèse handed Guy a bottle of whiskey which was passed from man to man around the circle in the manner of a peace pipe. The bottle came to rest with the chief who would occasionally sip from it.

"Most honored chieftain," Guy said, "your people are perfectly right to be upset that we dug into a sacred burial mound. But we did not know what it was, and now we will show it the respect it deserves. But please do not force us to leave. We are here to do good things. We will purchase from you all the pelts you trap in exchange for treasures that I am sure will please you—vermilion and verdigris for your ceremonial paints, awls and other tools for working deerskins, tobacco, colored beads, mirrors . . ."

"Whiskey?" the chief inquired.

"Yes, and taffia."

"Gunpowder?"

"Yes, and a special gun as befits a chief."

Marie-Thérèse put a musket, the stock inlaid with mother-of-pearl, on the blanket.

The chief took a long pull from the bottle but did not pass it along. Rémi opened a box in the corner and took out a high hat ornamented with colored glass and plumes which towered above its crown. It was one of the hats Dirk, the fiddler on the keelboat, had worn when he performed.

"This hat," Rémi said, proffering it to the chief, "belonged to the King of Paris, who wore it on important occasions." The hat generated an animated response from the chief, who immediately removed his headdress and replaced it with the hat which made him look like a street entertainer.

"Also, if you wish, we will employ some of your men to help with the houses we are building."

The chief rose, feeling uplifted by the important hat on his head and the whiskey inside him. Without speaking he left the cabin and strode back to his warriors, still carrying the whiskey bottle in his hand. He spoke a few words to them. They turned around and started to leave.

"Then you will send us pelts?" Guy asked.

"Yes," the chief replied. "Beaver and fox."

"And will some of your men come to work?"

"No, Indian men do not do such work. We will send our women."

With that, they returned to their canoes and began paddling up the river.

Thirty-eight

By the time the four keelboats arrived from New Orleans, bearing all of Guy's household goods plus large supplies of building materials, tools, food, livestock, liquor and wine, all the necessities Guy and Marie-Thérèse could think of before their departure, eight cabins had been built. The Indian women, helped by their children, had dug the foundation and half-finished the construction of the limestone house that Guy, Marie-Thérèse, Rémi, Pélagie, and Filonea would occupy.

After unloading, Guy assembled the four keelboat patroons and inquired whether they had return cargoes for their boats and crews. Two of the patroons said they were engaged to carry flatboat loads from Ste. Geneviève to New Orleans but the other two patroons were at liberty.

"Then I have a proposition for you," Guy said. "We are starting a fur-trading post here. We have an exclusive grant for eight years that covers all the territory up here in northern Louisiana, all the way up to the Great Lakes and the territory west of the Mississippi. I would like to hire you to go up the Missouri and Mississippi Rivers and invite the Indian tribes to sell their pelts to us. One of you will go in the direction of the Miamis and the other tribes in the Wabash River region. There are three tribes in the St. Joseph area along the Illinois rivers. There are five along the upper Mississippi including the

Sioux, the Sauks, and the Panimahas from the Missouri Valley. And four tribes from the Straits of Mackinac. The other boat will go up the Missouri and contact the Mandans and Hidatsans, the Omahas, the Cheyennes, the Gros Dentres, Chippawas, Winnebagos, and Menominees. I have a map here I procured in New Orleans from a trapper who worked for the Hudson's Bay Company. It shows the Arikara villages, the plains where the Comanche live, and the locations of the Assiniboin, the Cree and the Kiowa-Apache. And here on this bend of the Missouri are the Osages, the Otoes, and the Padoucas. These tribes are all along the river route you would take."

"But we know nothing about fur trading," one patroon said.

"Not necessary since you will not trade for furs. You will simply give a few presents to the chiefs and invite them to come here to St. Louis for a big fur powwow next spring where we will have many more presents for them. It is my plan to have the tribes bring furs to us rather than the other way around. It is not the custom now, but I am the only fur trader. It would be an advantage if the furs came to us."

By the end of the day, Guy had signed up the patroons of both keelboats as his traveling salesmen.

After rejecting "Laroule Fur Traders," "The Louisiana Company," and "Furs of France" as names for the fur company, Rémi came up with the one name that appealed to all of them: "The American Fur Trading Company." "We are in this country to stay," Rémi reasoned, "so we best call ourselves by our rightful name."

Guy divided up their duties: Since Marie-Thérèse was best with figures and bookkeeping, she would be in charge of the business side of the venture; Rémi would supervise St. Louis itself—construction, dealing with prospective inhabitants, the slave trade, et cetera; and Guy would attend to the acquisition and shipping of the furs. Even Filonea was assigned a responsibility—attending Pélagie and supervising the preparation of meals.

Rémi and Filonea became fast friends. They were strikingly handsome together, looking much more mature than their ages. They went on excursions into the woods where Filonea taught Rémi to distinguish between good and bad mushrooms, desirable and undesirable berries, edible and inedible nuts. She taught him, as her father had taught her, how to make simple snares to catch hares, raccoon, possum, and other small game. They found honey hives and sweet wild fruit to bring back to the table.

Among the effects that the keelboats brought from New Orleans were Guy's books, a hundred and fifty volumes that covered a wide range of subjects and authors: history, politics, commerce, geography, science, math, agriculture, law, and even anatomy and surgery by such authors as Locke, Descartes, Petronius, Began, and Corneille. With these books in hand, Guy and Marie-Thérèse took turns tutoring Rémi and Filonea. At first Rémi protested that he was beyond schooling, but once into the books he became absorbed with their contents.

The keelboats' cargoes also included quantities of presents for the Indians: blankets, knives, kettles, tin cups, scarlet cloth, beads, earrings, brooches, bracelets, and bolts of strouding, a cloth the Indians coveted for breech clouts.

Guy went hunting with Rémi whenever they could find time. They had discovered that coon and deerskins were in general use as barter currency, so they concentrated on these animals, but they also hunted for their dinner table. Wild turkeys and pheasants were plentiful, as were large fat bears who roamed the nearby forests. When butchered properly, bear hams were tastier than those of the hogs. Guy and Rémi were also on the lookout for buffalo although they appeared infrequently. The meat in the buffalo hump was far superior to beef, and the skins were good cover for the dirt floors in the cabins.

Fully stocked with supplies and presents, the two keelboats departed on their missions, with Tico, the scout, in charge of one boat, and the ex-soldier, Léon Thibault, in charge of the other. At the same time, Guy and Rémi went downriver to Fort Chartres to see if they could recruit families to live in St. Louis. "Our only hope of getting them," Guy had reasoned, "is because the Treaty of Paris has given Fort Chartres and all that territory to the British, but I'm sure that Frenchmen will not be happy living under British rule."

"But would they not prefer to return to New Orleans," Rémi asked, "rather than come here where all we have is a little cleared land and promises?"

"Yes, I suppose most of them will, but perhaps a few families prefer this region and would like to stay here. We have to be damn good salesmen, Rémi—seduce them with fur and how rich they can get. The French love fur. It would be nice to get some of the aristocrat families to move here. It would be so civilized. A little taste of

New Orleans, of Paris. We could have fancy dress balls and proper weddings and maybe a musicale or two."

"I would like to watch you perform. Mother says you have a wonderful voice. Why don't you sing for us?"

"Perhaps I shall now that our spinet is here for accompaniment. I'll tell you what, Rémi, your mother and I both have our thirtieth birthdays approaching. We will have a festive dinner with some of the good champagne we brought, followed by entertainment. I am told that Filonea dances beautifully, and I shall sing a song to your mother. And what can you do?"

"I can applaud. I am very good at that."

Thirty-nine

Guy WAS CORRECT in surmising that with the British on their way to take over command of Fort Chartres and the territory around it, most of the French, who despised the British, having just been defeated by them in the Seven Years' War, would not wish to stay on. Twelve families in all committed themselves to move to St. Louis with the understanding that they would be given a plot of cleared land, building timbers, and other supplies if they pledged to construct their houses within a year and a day.

Having seen the attractive contents of their houses, Guy and Rémi knew that when the Fort Chartres families moved to St. Louis their dwellings would be elegantly furnished. The plan was to give these families large, contiguous plots in choice locations thereby creating an elite district similar to the district in New Orleans that surrounded the Governor's Mansion. There would be a secondary area where cabins would house craftsmen and traders. And then a third district in the least desirable area where boatmen, laborers, hunters and trappers would be accommodated, thereby providing St. Louis with the same three-tiered society that existed in France and New Orleans.

Guy was especially pleased that the fort's adjutant, Lieutenant St. Ange de Belle-Rive and his family were among those who decided to move to St. Louis. And Rémi breathed a sigh of relief when he learned on their arrival at Fort Chartres that Captain Neyon de Villiers and his corpulent wife had already departed for New Orleans.

In addition to securing the dozen families for his fledgling village, Guy was able to purchase eighty Negro slaves from families who did not want to ship them to New Orleans. He was also offered six Indian slaves but Rémi, sensitive to Filonea's presence, convinced Guy not to buy them. But Guy did enthusiastically purchase quantities of building materials, foodstuffs, livestock, books, gunpowder, kitchenware, garden tools including two much-needed plows, oxen, several Indian-Spanish Opelousas horses, Bibles, bridle bits, tinware, playing cards, flint, panes of glass, earthen jars, iron kettles, boots and shoes, jugs, bear's oil, beeswax, ginseng, and candy.

Guy also purchased several keelboats and flatboats that the slaves had been taught to operate. These boats would provide him with a ready means of transport for humans and cargo. "Can't you see these flatboats piled high with furs," he said to Rémi as they inspected them at the shoreline, "flying the American Fur Trading flag, a line of them riding the middle current of the Mississippi, the pelts on their way to the markets of the world? How amusing it is to contemplate that the furs we gather will be coveted by those vain ladies I used to know at Versailles. Perhaps I should write to them and take their orders."

"I do believe you should send some silver foxes as a gift to Madame du Barry," Rémi suggested, "considering that she is our sponsor."

"Yes, Rémi, fine idea. And what can we send the King?"

They both gave the matter some serious thought. Finally Rémi said, "The blacksmith has a standing, snarling grizzly in his smithy, realistically preserved by a taxidermist—perhaps Mr. Grizzly might amuse His Majesty."

"Splendid, Rémi, splendid! It would go very well in the royal hunting lodge at Fontainebleau where Mr. Grizzly could join the stags and moose that the King has on the walls."

"How shall we keep the smithy, whose temperament matches the grizzly's, from taking it with him to New Orleans?"

"Does the blacksmith know how to read?"

"No, nor write."

"Then we shall show him this ordinance that prohibits the importation of stuffed animals into New Orleans under penalty of a heavy fine and jail."

"And we offer him a silver dollar to take it off his hands?"
"Precisely. Then we build a box for it and send it with our compliments to the King."

By the end of 1765, the first year of its existence, St. Louis had a population of sixty; the Laroules' stone house was completed as were six other dwellings built by the newcomers from Fort Chartres; the fur trade with the Indians was under way; independent French Canadian fur trappers were arriving to sell or barter their pelts; the common field had been plowed and planted; and Marie-Thérèse was pregnant again.

Despite their pledges, only six of the Fort Chartres families actually arrived, but there remained the possibility that a few more might show up when the British forces under Captain John Sterling, a strict disciplinarian, actually took command. There were inspections by curious inhabitants from the Illinois towns of Kaskaskia and Cahokia, and some of the fur traders who lived there contemplated moving their families to St. Louis and doing business with Guy.

The limestone for the Laroule house, which covered six lots and had gardens on three sides, was quarried with crowbar and sledgehammer from the river bluffs in front of the village. The entire house and gardens were enclosed by a solid stone wall two feet thick and ten feet high with portholes every ten feet to be used to fire on Indians in case of an attack. The walls of the house itself, two stories high, were also of solid limestone two-and-a-half feet thick. The house was surrounded by a large portico about fourteen feet wide, supported by pillars in front and at both ends. The floors of the house were made of black walnut and were kept finely polished to a mirror-like shine.

The newcomers from Fort Chartres built commodious houses of wood with generous porticos and ornate railings in the mode of New Orleans. There was the possibility, however, that future houses might be constructed of brick, for Jacques Orlaud, the blacksmith, had built an oven and was producing bricks which, though a trifle soft, would have an advantage over wood in the severely fluctuating St. Louis climate. Each owner was required to enclose his property with *pieux debout,* upright stakes of rot-resistant cedar or mulberry, about seven feet high and sharpened to a point at the top.

Using the two old plows and the oxen purchased by Guy, the

slaves were able to sow the common field with its first vegetable
seeds, some brought by Guy's keelboats, others provided by the Fort
Chartres families. Slave quarters were built adjacent to the common
field; four slaves were allotted to each new dwelling, but Marie-
Thérèse had claimed ten for the Laroule family.

The fur powwow exceeded Guy's expectations. Not all of the tribes
responded but a total of fifteen chiefs arrived with their entourages,
pitched their tents, and for three days it was a roiling, boisterous,
threatening gathering. Each chief tried to outdo the others with
flamboyant costumes, fancy plumed military hats, white buffalo
coats decorated with painted porcupine quills, ornate medals, mul-
tifeathered headdresses, gaudy tunics sequinned with bits of mirrors,
capes of white fox fur, colorful sashes, jeweled leggings. Chief
Wabasha was carried on a throne chair by a group of his Sante Sioux
warriors; Chief Matchekewis of the Chippawas wore an elaborate
dress uniform traded to him for twenty beaver pelts by a retired
British general of the Hudson's Bay Company; the Omaha chieftain,
Blackbird, covered with elaborate body paint and coiffed by a gold
diadem; Chief White Hair of the Osages wore a face mask decorated
with precious jewels and carried a silver mace.

Befitting the occasion, Guy wore his finest Versailles costume replete with ceremonial sword at his waist. Rémi, too, was impres-
sively dressed in some of Guy's silks and brocades; Marie-Thérèse,
however, did not dress up in deference to the low esteem in which
most of the tribes held women. But she had prepared deerskin
pouches which contained an array of presents for each of the chieftains, and these were ceremoniously presented by Guy.

Chief White Hair rose to his feet, however, and stated that British
and Canadian fur traders also plied them with presents; was there
not something special that would induce them to deal exclusively
with the American Fur Trading Company? Guy and Rémi were
stumped by this request, only able to make promises in generalities,
but Marie-Thérèse came to their rescue. While Guy and Rémi had
been trying to recruit families in Fort Chartres, a trader had appeared in a keelboat with a cargo of sugar, one of the scarcest commodities in the entire Louisiana Territory. Marie-Thérèse noticed
that the trader was nervous about his cargo, probably because he
had not come by it legitimately, and as a consequence she was able
to acquire all the sugar in exchange for a pig, several panes of glass,

a bottle of whiskey, a container of gunpowder, and a barrel of molasses. Surmising that since the Indians were so fond of whiskey they must also have a collective sweet tooth (all the drinkers she knew also liked sweets), she had two of the slaves fill a cart with some of the sugar and pull it over to the meeting area. Its appearance drew an immediate, enthusiastic response from the chiefs whose tribes were chronically short of salt and sugar. A small quantity of the sugar was apportioned to each chief as a sample of larger amounts when pelts arrived. The sugar proved to be the deciding factor. After a brief powwow, the chiefs committed their furs exclusively to the American Fur Trading Company in a document signed by all of them:

> *We send greetings to all mankind. Be it known unto all nations that the most ancient, most illustrious, and most numerous tribes of the redskins, lords of the soil, from the banks of the great waters unto the tops of the mountains upon which the heavens rest, have entered into a solemn league and covenant to make, preserve and cherish a firm and lasting pact with The American Fur Trading Company, that, as long as the water runs and the grass grows, they may hail each other as brethren and smoke the calumet in peace and friendship. Be it known that in the year 1766, the powerful and distinguished nation of fifteen blood Indian tribes by their Chiefs appeared at St. Louis, near the spot where the Missouri River unites its current with the Mississippi, and in the abode of the President of the American Fur Trading Company, Guy Laroule, conforming to all ancient customs and ceremonies, and observing due mystical signs, enjoined by the Great Medicine Man, the Treaty of Friendship and Commerce was entered into by the said high contracting parties, and it is testified by their hands and seals hereunto annexed, hereafter and forever to live as brethren of one, large, united and happy family; and may the Great Spirit who watches over us all, approve our conduct and teach us to trust one another in the exchange of animal pelts for compensation.*
>
> *Done, executed, ratified and confirmed at St Louis, on the day and year first written, in the presence of all parties to this agreement.*

Forty

THE SECOND YEAR of St. Louis' existence, 1766, the Spanish Government of New Orleans dispatched an official named Francisco Cruzat to be the governor of the Upper Louisiana Territory. He and his retinue of men stopped in St. Louis on their way to where they intended to establish their headquarters north of St. Louis, a few miles from where the Missouri joined the Mississippi. Guy had appointed St. Ange de Belle-Rive as chief political administrator to deal with the Spanish authorities. Along with St. Ange, Guy had appointed a council to govern St. Louis. The council consisting of himself, Marie-Thérèse and Rémi. Thus it was St. Ange who officially greeted Cruzat on his arrival. Among Cruzat's party was a tall angular man whom Guy recognized but did not immediately identify.

"Claude Lèche," the man said, introducing himself to Guy. "I was Sheriff. . ."

"Oh, of course, of course! Without your uniform. . ."

"I have been replaced by a Spanish officer, but Governor Cruzat has appointed me to his staff as liaison with French officials up here."

"Tell me, Monsieur Lèche, were there any repercussions over the shooting of Duroux?"

"Duroux? Why would there be repercussions when a loathsome

man and his equally loathsome assistant are attacked and devoured by alligators?"

"So the slaves, really did feed them to the gators on the way to the coroner?"

"A most unfortunate accident. But remarkably, after his death, there was not a single inquiry about Duroux. Isn't that extraordinary? Not one person gave a damn about him. The consequence of being despised by everyone."

"And how is Madame Grotesquieu doing at the plantation, do you know?"

"I heard that her son was managing it very well."

"That's good to know."

Dinner was being prepared for the visitors, with Marie-Thérèse supervising the preparations. Lèche looked at her quizzically. "Is that lady your wife?"

"She is Madame Marie-Thérèse Boustique. She lives here, but she is not my wife."

"Boustique . . . there was a tavern keeper named Boustique . . ."

"Her husband."

"But she lives here . . . ?"

"They are separated."

"I thought I recognized her from the tavern . . ." Lèche hesitated for a moment before continuing. "Will you introduce me?"

"Madame Boustique," Lèche said after the introduction, "I presume you know about your husband?"

"What about him?"

"He was killed in a fight at his bar."

Marie-Thérèse sucked in her breath, her fingers covering her lips. "Boustique? Dead? My God!"

"We had responded to many of his fights, his opponents always severely beaten. This time someone turned the tables on him. He was found dead in the alleyway next to his bar."

Guy was shocked but did not show it. It had not occurred to him that the beating he had given Boustique would be fatal. He had long ago ceased thinking about it.

"I must tell Rémi," Marie-Thérèse said.

Rémi's reaction was unexpected: "Now you can marry Guy."

"What?"

"Is that not permitted by the Church, that a widow can remarry?"

"Yes, I suppose so."

Overhearing this exchange, Guy said, without feeling any guilt for Boustique's death, "I was thinking the same thing. Now we can marry, Marie-Thérèse."

"Well, my condition . . . a blushing bride who is six months pregnant."

"And you can hold Pélagie during the ceremony."

"Oh, yes, very amusing. The bride has one in her arms and one on the way. You must admit it is rather embarrassing."

"We will be the first couple to get married in St. Louis."

"I hope my condition will not set a precedent."

"May I be the best man?" Rémi inquired.

"I should say not!"

"Oh, let him be best man," Guy said. "What do we care? Let's just have fun and a damn fine wedding. Husband and wife, you and me. What an unexpected prize."

The wedding was set for two weeks hence, the sixteenth of June. Since the village had no church, a makeshift altar was erected at a spot that commanded a sweeping view of meadows blanketed with wildflowers. Marie-Thérèse wore the fullest dress she owned, but it did not mask her pregnancy. Guy, resplendent in his finest tunic, looked as if he had just arrived from a court function at Versailles. Rémi had severely outgrown his best clothes, so Guy outfitted him from his wardrobe. Filonea borrowed a dress from Marie-Thérèse, preferring not to wear her Indian clothes for the occasion. She wove a garland of flowers into Marie-Thérèse's hair, the colors arched like a rainbow across her head, and she made a nosegay of violets for Marie-Thérèse to carry. Although Guy and Marie-Thérèse were indeed a handsome pair, dressed in their finery, while awaiting the arrival of the justice of the peace from Ste. Geneviève, it was Rémi and Filonea who looked more the part of a wedding couple, partly because of their youth, but also because of their open fondness for each other, a tentative but irrepressible intimacy.

The justice of the peace was delayed because the Mississippi current was running stronger than usual. The food for the banquet would suffer from the delay but with the quantity of champagne and wine on hand, the overcooked dishes would doubtless be forgiven. Finally, three hours late, the justice of the peace arrived, flustered, somewhat dishevelled, and definitely under the influence of several bottles of claret he had imbibed to ease the frustration of his journey.

The judge was as tall and thin as the mast on his keelboat. His long, naked neck which dominated the narrow shoulders of his short torso and his skeletally-thin, spindly legs gave him the appearance of the crane the Indians called Fly-Over-the-Creek. His small head was haloed by ice-grey hair, thick spikes stuck out in all directions like that of a boar. Through his gold-rimmed glasses, perched on his falcon's-beak nose, carried by a pair of ears which stood out from his head and extended and retracted as he spoke, stared a pair of grey, sharp, unsettled eyes. A long, thin-lipped mouth with tobacco-tinted teeth and a sharp protruding chin completed his physiognomy. He was clothed from head to foot in black; even his shirt front and standing collar were hidden by his atlas vest and a wide, high cravat in such a way that only a thin, white strip was visible.

The wedding began as soon as the judge, a French Canadian named Hannibal Ditois, was guided to his station behind the make-shift altar. Marie-Thérèse and Guy stood before him with Rémi and Filonea at their sides. (After much discussion, it had been decided not to bring Pélagie to the ceremony.)

For a minute or two the judge dazedly studied the group before him, trying to get his bearings. A decidedly pregnant woman and a handsome man, nicely dressed as if for an occasion, and two attractive young people staring at him.

"Now what can I do for you?" the judge inquired, his speech slurred.

"You can marry us as quickly as you can," Guy said testily. "The marriage feast is suffering, and we are tired of waiting."

"Marriage? Oh, yes, marriage," the judge intoned. "Well, now, we have a complication . . ."

"Which is?"

"I seem to have forgotten my book which contains the ceremony, all those vows—sickness, health, poverty, wealth, those things."

"I will run down to your boat and fetch it," Rémi said, starting to leave.

"Problem is," the judge said, "I forgot to bring it from Ste. Geneviève. But it will be all right. Worry not. Married you will be. But I wonder if I may have a tot of whiskey to unparch my throat."

Fortified with a significant swallow of the whiskey, Judge Ditois launched the ceremony. "We are gathered here to celebrate the union of these two nice people who from the look of the bride seem to have already enjoyed one union, but this will be their spiritual union under Almighty God." Another swallow of whiskey. "This is a serious business, marriage, and it can have serious conse . . .

consequesh . . . consequences." Swallow of whiskey. "Now, then, do you two love each other?"

"Yes," said Marie-Thérèse.

"Yes," said Guy.

"Do you promise to God not to fool around with anyone else?"

"Yes," said Marie-Thérèse.

"Yes," said Guy.

Swallow of whiskey. "Love is all you need. I had a wife when I lived in Canada, but she was ugly and didn't love me so I left her. Love is the glue that keeps two people from falling apart. Truth is, I didn't love her either. She smelled of onions. Permanent smell of onions. Lady, do you take this man for your husband? Gentleman, do you take this woman for your wife? Good. I drink to you." Long swallow of whiskey. "Anyone have a ring?"

Rémi produced the ring and handed it to Guy who put it on Marie-Thérèse's finger.

The judge nodded his approval solemnly. "I now pro-ownce, er, perouse. . . pronounce you man and wife. Give the bride a little kiss. So will I."

The wedding party went on all through the night. Guy sang love songs to Marie-Thérèse as promised, his rich baritone reverberating through the night air; Filonea danced like a gossamer angel; the keelboat men sang river songs, and the townspeople danced minuets. Rémi surprised everyone by appearing in a clown's costume that had belonged to Dirk, and performed juggling routines Dirk had taught him: three, four, then five balls in the air; a cane supporting a spinning plate balanced on his chin; then colored hoops simultaneously rotating on his wrists, ankles, and around his neck; finally, concluding his torchlit performance Rémi, the clown juggler, nimbly balanced a chair on his chin.

Later in the evening, Guy drew Rémi to one side to have a chat with him. "Now that your mother and I are married, I would like to formally adopt you. I would be proud to have you bear my name. I love you, Rémi, I admire you, and I want you to feel that you are as much my son as Pélagie is my daughter."

"That is wonderful to hear, Guy. As far as I am concerned, you are everything I could possibly want in a father. And I do feel I am part of this family. But I have this feeling that I want to keep my name to honor my father. It is the name I was born with, and I will bear it as best I can. Would it really matter to you that I take your name? It will not affect my affection for you, but if it is important to you, of course I will do it, although I would prefer to go on being Rémi Riveau."

"I understand, Rémi, and I admire your loyalty. No, by all means, keep your name. I only care that your heart is with us."

"It is. And it always will be."

The baby was born in September. A boy. The midwife came across the river from Kaskaskia, a copious, jolly woman who had been birthing babies for twenty-five years. It was an easy delivery, without complication, in stark contrast to Pélagie's birth.

By October enough pelts had been received from the Indian tribes to fill a flatboat. The pelts were stored in a large shed that had been built for the purpose and now in a ritual that would be repeated thousands of times in the coming years, the pelts were loaded onto carts and transported to the flatboat that had "American Fur Trading Company" prominently lettered on its side. The fur was compacted and loaded amidship, then securely covered with oilskins for protection.

As a defense against piracy, it was Rémi's idea to have one keelboat precede the flatboat, another to follow it, both crews heavily armed. In addition, the flatboat had three mounted maneuverable cannons. If the ships succeeded in reaching the New Orleans market, the high-quality furs would probably generate enough profit for the citizenry of St. Louis to live comfortably for the remainder of the year. By now the population, exclusively French, had risen to eighty-three, all of them engaged in the fur trade in one capacity or another. Once the furs started arriving, the flow was irrepressible: beaver, otter, fox, buffalo, muskrat, deer, and other pelts streamed into St. Louis like a mountain brook rushing into the Mississippi.

Forty-one

By THE TIME Guy reached the end of his eight-year fur monopoly in 1773, his sources were so well ensconced that he lost few of his suppliers to competitive traders. The secret of his success lay in the originality and copiousness of the presents he bestowed upon the Indian tribes with whom he traded. Considering the significant growth of its trade, however, the population of St. Louis had not kept pace. A census conducted in December counted four hundred forty-four whites, of whom two hundred eighty-five were men, one hundred fifty-nine were women, and one hundred ninety-three were slaves.

The slow growth of the village was mostly attributable to Guy's insistence that there be no commercial establishments—neither shops nor trade other than that related to the business of the American Fur Trading Company was allowed. Itinerant boats would tie up and sell their wares from the dock, but there were no permanent shops in the village which was so constantly in short supply of necessities and food, especially flour, which had to be obtained from Ste. Geneviève, that outsiders commonly called it *Pain Court* ("Short of Bread") rather than St. Louis. There was neither judge nor priest, teacher nor doctor. The only medicines obtainable were those offered by self-designated doctors who occasionally visited in their so-called medicine boats. These doctors would charge fifty cents a visit plus the cost of the patent medicine they prescribed, such as the "Celebrated Stomachic Elixir of Health" and "Infallible Worm-Destroying Lozenges." One of the most popular medicines was "Dr. Lee's Billious Pills" which, according to a printed form contained in each box, had been "Successfully Administered for Intermittent, Remittent, Billious, Inflammatory and Yellow Fevers, Jaundice, Colic, Indigestion, Dropsy, Gout, Rheumatism, Pleurisy, Chlorosis, Dysentery, Worms, Billious Vomitings, Convulsions and Epileptic Fits, Asthmas, Coughs and Colds, Accompanied with Costiveness Foul Stomach, Scurvy, Sore Throat, Hypochondria, Hysterical Affections, et cetera."

A dentist, Dr. D. M. Pritchitt, who made regular stops, had a sign on his boat announcing that he would "Extract, Plug, Clean, and Strengthen Teeth" in his office on the boat. Of course, there were no diplomas on his wall attesting to any source of preparedness for his profession or who had commissioned him a doctor of dentistry.

For its first four years the village had no church. When the services of a priest were required, a tent was pitched on Church Street and Father Sebastian Meurin, pastor at Ste. Geneviève, came up the river for the occasion. His first visit was to baptize the new arrival, Marc Pierre Laroule, and two-year-old Pélagie. Eventually, as the need for a church increased, Guy built a small log chapel. It was dedicated by Father Pierre Gibault from Kaskaskia, pastor to the two thousand Catholics of British Illinois, who thereafter visited on a regular schedule to conduct masses and officiate at baptisms, marriages, and funerals; one of those baptisms was performed for the Laroules' third baby, Rosalind.

Every Sunday, after Mass, the citizenry indulged in the New Orleans credo that everyone should be happy on his day of rest. To that end, Sunday was devoted to dancing, performing music, playing billiards, ninepins, dice, cards, roulette, shuffleboard, quarter-racing, and other such activities. The Laroules had open house with a copious bar; many homes gave informal parties that featured sumptuous meals, followed by singing profane songs and playing cards for money stakes. Guy's philosophy was that a Creole Sunday of merriment served to bind the community, and that it pleased the Creator far more than a gloomy and stiff Sunday which did nothing to prepare the church-goer for the hard work and stress of the week to come. Guy also encouraged the villagers to stay after Mass to exchange or acquire land, buy and sell slaves, barter merchandise, or otherwise indulge in deals and negotiations which, since they took place in the pastor's presence, were considered binding.

The slaves also congregated in an open space allocated to them where they danced and drank, often to excess. Some slaves, however, worked on Sunday, the one day they were permitted to earn the money that eventually, when they had earned enough, could buy them their freedom.

During those eight years, the Spanish Government in New Orleans replaced the governor of Upper Louisiana seven times, which meant that Spanish authority was never really organized; the governors themselves were mostly ceremonial. This situation allowed Guy to be autonomous and operate his village without much interference. He was certainly succeeding in his determination to preserve St. Louis as a bastion of French aristocracy, in contrast to the villages the British controlled across the river. "Here we defy the English," Guy had explained to Marie-Thérèse. "We have an elite group of Frenchmen—Pierre de Volsay, Joseph Labuscière, Sylvestre Labbadie, André Condé, Antoine Hubert, Jean Baptiste Martigny, Eugene Pouré—men of elegance, breeding, taste, and education with beautiful, fashionably dressed wives. We bring a civilized society to this primitive territory."

"All well and good," Marie-Thérèse had responded, "but commerce must come before everything else. Just remember that it is our workmen, trappers, boatmen, tanners, scouts, Indian go-betweens, and slaves, who are our lifeblood. Commerce, Guy, do not overlook it. It is well and good to have fine families of style and breeding, but the prettiest sight I see is when our flatboat leaves for New Orleans piled high with our furs."

Marie-Thérèse had run the business very well. Fur purchases had been generous, but nevertheless profits were considerable. She had negotiated high profits on the New Orleans market and had shrewdly manipulated the amount of furs being shipped at any one time. "To be financially desirable, the beaver has to be a little less accessible than the demand. Once they are easy to obtain, our prices will suffer. The white fox must be as rare as a black diamond."

Marie-Thérèse had also devised a way sometimes to use money instead of barter. If the amount involved in purchasing a pelt was less than a dollar, Marie-Thérèse would take a Spanish silver dollar and have it cut into four bits, each bit then representing twenty-five cents. Her invention quickly spread to other villages in Upper Louisiana.

* * *

When Rémi turned eighteen, he came to Marie-Thérèse and Guy and asked permission to marry Filonea. "I know that it is customary for parents to arrange a marriage," he said, "but we love each other more than I can say, and I hope you will give us your blessing."

"We love Filonea also," Marie-Thérèse said.

"She is like a daughter," Guy added.

"We are certainly aware of how happy you are with each other, and we are happy for you."

"Then we have your permission . . . ?"

Guy put his arm around Rémi's shoulders. "Come sit down, Rémi. This is a difficult, but important moment, and we must be honest with each other. Marriage is something that deeply affects the rest of your life, and what we must determine now is not the life you have at the moment, but how you will live down the long road of the future. That is why parents arrange marriages—because they have the experience of knowing what is best for their children."

"Let us be very frank with you, Rémi," Marie-Thérèse said. "Filonea is a lovely girl, lovely to look at, with a lovely disposition. But she is an Indian . . ."

"I knew you were going to bring that up!"

"It is not of our doing," Guy said, "Filonea lives here as one of us. We love her. But you know very well how people react to mixed marriages. It is true that some of our trappers are married to Indian women, but they are with their own kind—illiterate people who live in crude surroundings and have no manners or ambition. But in the civilized society in which we live, intermarriage with an Indian or a black is unthinkable. You would have no social life. Who would invite an Indian wife to their home to be treated as an equal? You would be completely ostracized, and it would destroy you professionally. I can see that someday when the Spaniards are gone—and believe me they will not last very long because Louisiana is a constant drain on their money just as it was for Louis XV—you could rise to high office, perhaps even a governor of the entire Louisiana Territory. You can be rich and powerful, but not if you have a wife who is an Indian. Even as lovely a wife as Filonea."

"All that does not matter to me. I do not want to be a governor. Nor do I want to be rich and powerful. I just want to have a happy life with Filonea."

"But, darling, that is just the point," Marie-Thérèse said. "You will *not* have a happy life, and your children, mixed breeds, will not be happy either. Indian children will make fun of them, and so will white children. I have seen this and so have you. Their parents will not let them mix with your children. Please do not resent us and turn on us for being honest with you. We cannot give our consent to something we know will hurt you."

"One other thing, Rémi," Guy said. "Eighteen is really too young to marry—not for a girl—they mature much more quickly, but you should have a few more years of unmarried freedom before tying yourself to a marriage."

"Which the two of you will arrange for me, of course," Rémi said, bitterly.

"Yes, when the time comes," Guy replied. "Until then, you and Filonea can enjoy your life together."

"And when I marry, what happens to Filonea?"

"Why, she will marry one of her own kind," Marie-Thérèse said.

"And to hell with love?" Fighting back his anger, Rémi abruptly turned his back on them and quickly left the house.

After a pause, Guy said, "He is angry now but Rémi is too intelligent not to know that we are right."

"He deserves a good marriage, Guy."

"And he will have one. I promise you."

"Have you given it some thought?"

"Yes."

"Someone in particular?"

"Yes, St. Ange's daughter, Emelie. What do you think?"

"She is only twelve."

"In five or six years when Rémi is ready for marriage she will be just the right age. St. Ange was a Chevalier of the Court, and his wife comes from royal lineage that goes back to Henry III. She was Madame Delphine de Liasou, you know."

"I do not like imposing ourselves on Rémi. It will break his heart to have to give up Filonea."

"His heart will mend."

"I hope so. I hate to cause him pain."

"Better a little pain now than endless pain later."

That night, his anger unabated, Rémi decided that he and Filonea should discuss their future together, which they never had before. They had many times declared their love for one another, but not a word had ever passed between them about where that love would take them. Now, for the first time, Rémi told her that he wanted to make her his wife, but that his parents had objected on the grounds that a mixed marriage such as theirs would be doomed to ostracism as would their progeny.

"But I do not care about approval," he said, his anger steeping his words. "If need be, we will keep to ourselves, not here. Not with all these taboos. But somewhere else, a place where we can create our own existence, where people will accept us for who we are, as human beings, not for our ancestors and our skin color. It will be a struggle at first, but we will manage—I know we will."

Filonea did not respond. They were sitting on the dock at the river's edge; she intently watched the ripples roll up against the shore and thought about their being husband and wife. Finally she said, "My parents would say the same things to me. The Indian world would also reject us and our children."

"Then we will live alone somewhere. In the woods. At sea. We will reject them."

"And how will we live in the woods?"

"I will be a trapper and take my pelts to market."

"No, sweet Rémi, you could not be a trapper. Or a fisherman. Or a woodsman."

"But everyone here accepts us being together. They know we are . . . are intimate."

"But we are not married."

"I hate all these stupid rules we live by."

"I am so happy with you, my Rémi. Let us enjoy ourselves as we are."

"Why can they not understand?"

She took his angry face in her hands and pressed her lips lightly against his. "I love you," she whispered. "Forever."

Forty-two

IT WAS FATHER PIERRE GIBAULT, making his monthly visit to the log church, who brought the sad news about Louis XV and Madame du Barry. "Died of small pox," Father Pierre reported as he had tea with Marie-Thérèse and Guy after the afternoon's baptisms. "One of my parishioners, whose father is on the King's Council, just returned from a visit to Versailles. He told me there are all sorts of rumors as to how His Highness contracted it: having sex with a pretty girl of sixteen at a debauched party at the Trianon; from a little dairy maid who had been washed, combed, perfumed and put in the King's bed despite the fact that her brother was dying of the disease; from the daughter of Montvallier, Madame du Barry's secretary, on and on—all sorts of rumors. But dead he is of the black pox, buried in a double lead-lined coffin to guard against the smell and the contagion. I personally don't think it was contracted from sex since there is an epidemic of small pox running through Versailles. It doubtless got to him just like to everyone else. He was certainly vulnerable, well over sixty, and not in the best of health. But His Majesty had such a reputation for debauchery, all those young women he kept at the Parc-aux-Cerfs, that I suppose his Versailles enemies easily spread these stories of sexual contamination. The body of the King was rushed out of Versailles to St. Denis in a hunting coach escorted by forty of his bodyguards and pages carrying torches.

"My informant tells me that Madame du Barry acted admirably during his illness, keeping a vigil at his bedside despite the high risk of infection. What was her reward? On the very night of the funeral she was deemed a prisoner of the State, seized by the constabulary and taken to the Abbey of Pont-aux-Dames. My informant was told by du Barry's lady-in-waiting who accompanied her in the carriage that she cried like a child all the way there and, as she crossed the threshold of the dilapidated monastery, she looked at the high, looming walls, saying: 'What a wretched place to which to condemn me.' The severe, haughty abbess, Madame de la Roche Fontenilles, surrounded by the sisters, awaited the prisoner in the parlor. The young nuns did not at first dare to look directly at her, but examined her in a mirror. They were all surprised not to find the features of the devil, as they had probably anticipated, but the most beautiful and distressed of women. There were thirty ladies of the choir and twenty lay sisters; each wore the white robe and stomacher of the Bernardines, with a black veil and long scapular reaching to the feet. The Contesse du Barry was taken to a small austere room in the most remote corner of the convent and placed in solitude. And so it is that on the plea of 'political necessity' she remains there in closest imprisonment."

Guy was surprised at how deeply touched he was at the cruelty of du Barry's predicament. A woman of such radiant beauty who had been so fair with him. He was even more moved by her fate, alone in a dank cell within a forbidding monastery, still more than by the suffering death of the king at the hands of the Black Plague. And yet he had known her for only an hour, whereas he had known the king for as long as he had known his own father.

When he was twenty, Rémi again spoke to Guy about marrying Filonea. Alone in the woods hunting pheasant and turkey, they had taken a brief respite and were sitting on a fallen tree trunk eating cheese and sharing a goatskin of wine.

"What I do not understand, Guy, is why it is acceptable for me to be with Filonea—dance with her, eat with her, sleep with her—but if we marry, then we are condemned. What difference does that silly ceremony make? We are married now as much as any couple in the village."

"But until you are joined in the Church and take your vows, you are not married in the eyes of God. At the ceremony you call silly, your union is consecrated and your children blessed."

"But consider how many children are fathered by white men who have had mulatto concubines. The children endure nicely without the Church's approval."

"Yes, they endure. But they are besmirched all their lives as mixed breeds. Their futures are tainted. We live by laws, Rémi, by rules of behavior. It is permissible for gentlemen to maintain concubines, just as it is permissible for His Majesty to have a *maîtresse en titre*. Filonea is your *maîtresse en titre*. But the King cannot marry his mistress, just as the Church will not allow you to marry Filonea."

"And why not?"

"Because God has decreed that we shall not marry outside of our race—whites must marry whites, Negroes must marry Negroes, Indians must marry Indians. It is God's will, and His will must be done. Not to obey Him is sacrilegious."

"If that be God's will, then He lacks compassion. How can that be the will of God when He tells us to 'love thy neighbor?' "

"Rémi, there are many discriminations in this world: Between the rich and the poor, the intelligent and the dim-witted, royalty and bourgeoisie, men and women, healthy and crippled, slaves and freemen, the sighted and the blind, tall and short, heroes and cowards, and on, and on—God discriminates among His children. He must have devised these discrepancies with a purpose; perhaps diversity is a form of strength; whatever His reason we are here on earth to serve His will. So it is that you and I have to accept the roles assigned to us. As a young man enjoying the indolent life I had at Versailles, I never dreamed that one day I would wind up in a different world with the mission of starting a new city in a new land. And now you, who came into my life by an incident engineered by God, must assume your God-given role, and that is to succeed me."

"But you have your son, Marc, to succeed you."

"You are also my son, Rémi, just as much as Marc is. You have shared this adventure with me, and you shall inherit the life which we created together."

Guy opened his knapsack and withdrew a pen, inkwell, and paper. He started to write:

I, Guy Laroule, being of sound mind and of my free volition do hereby declare this my Last Will and Testament. Upon my death, I do give and bequeath my house and all my worldly goods therein to my wife, Marie-Thérèse. All my assets, now contained in my strongbox are hereby bequeathed to my wife with the proviso that she is to administer them on behalf of my children, Pélagie, Marc and Rosalind.

As for my stepson, Rémi, I unconditionally bequeath to him the American Fur Trading Company of which I am the sole owner. I instruct him to operate the company to the best of his ability and I further instruct him to share fairly the company's profits with his mother, his half-sisters and half-brother. However, before such distribution of profits, he shall first pay all my outstanding debts, if any, and expenses of my funeral and burial.

To which I set my hand this fourteenth day of October, 1771.

Guy Laroule

On the way back to the village, their gamebags filled with pheasant and grouse (no wild turkeys had been sighted), they came upon a bower of interwoven branches in the midst of a dense coppice of white birch. As they approached the bower a repugnant odor assailed their nostrils, the unmistakable smell of death. They approached the bower cautiously. Curiously, the tightly woven shelter was solid on all four sides and its roof, without any indication of an entry point.

"Whoever built this," Rémi observed, "imprisoned himself inside it."

With his hunting knife, Guy gouged an opening and they slid inside the bower. A funeral bier, five feet high, had been constructed of branches interlaced with leaves. On top of the bier, his arms crossed across his chest, a pleasant look on his face, was Tricot.

"My God," Guy said, "he just laid down here to die."

"He even built a canopy," Rémi observed. "That is why the birds have not eaten his face."

"This is Choctaw custom. I have seen it. They do not bury their dead. We must come back another time, after the flesh has putrified and slipped off the bones. We will then bury the flesh and put the bones in an urn. I am sure that is what Tricot would want us to do. What a sad moment for me. Tricot meant so much to me when I first came to New Orleans. I do not think I could have found my way without him."

"It was that evil bastard, Little Harpe—all his doing. I am glad Mike Fink cut off his head."

"We should say a prayer for Tricot's soul. He was a fine man."

They closed their eyes and Guy began to pray: "Our Father in

heaven, please look down upon this fine man. We beg Thee to free
his soul still imprisoned in his body and allow it to rise up to heaven
to be nurtured in Thy safekeeping. We are grateful to Thee, O Lord,
for all Thy bounties. Amen."

They crossed themselves, repaired the opening they had made,
and slowly trudged back through the woods to the village without
speaking.

Rémi's marriage to Emelie de Belle-Rive took place on the very day
in 1776 when word reached St. Louis that the colonists had risen in
rebellion against the British. Lieutenant St. Ange de Belle-Rive and
his wife, Delphine, were unstinting in the preparation of an elaborate wedding for their daughter. It took place in the stone cathedral
recently erected in the same place where there had once been the log
cabin church. Marc, now ten, was best man for Rémi, who had just
turned twenty-five. Five-year-old Rosalind was the flower girl, and
Pélagie, who at twelve had developed a remarkable voice, sang a
ballad by Guillaume de Machaut at the start of the ceremony to the
accompaniment of musicians who had arrived from Ste. Geneviève
the night before. Emelie's three sisters were her bridesmaids. After
Father Pierre concluded the marriage ritual and blessed the couple,
there was a feast and a ball lasting well into the night. It was the
most festive event in the young life of the village.

That night, after returning from the wedding celebration, Guy said,
"Marie-Thérèse, hearing the marriage vows today I got to thinking
of my own vows to you. In a busy life there is little time to pause and
count one's blessings. We are likely to take them for granted, likely
to assume that happiness and well-being are automatic birthrights.
But sitting there in the church beside you, I thought how much I love
you."

They were sitting in front of the fire which had become a deep bed
of glowing embers. Guy gently pulled Marie-Thérèse against him,
his arms around her waist. "I love the way you look, all of you,
everything in harmony with everything else. Your lovely face, the
lines of your neck, the sheen of your hair, the daintiness of your
hands and feet. I love the way you are when we make love, comply-
ing and demanding, and giving and wanting, and when you climax,
how your entire body responds to me. I love how sensible you are

with just a soupçon of perversity. I love the way you purse your lips when you are annoyed with me. Then again, how inviting your lips are when you tiptoe up and kiss me. I love the way you look at me, the way you still take my hand in yours under the table. I love how you are with our children, how much of you is in them. I love the way you lecture me when I am extravagant. I love how jealous you are when I spend time talking to an attractive lady at a social gathering. I love the way you boast about me, most times unjustifiably. I love the gracefulness of your dancing and the way your body sways to mine. I love the little presents you give me for no reason at all. I love the way you defend me when I am criticized, and the way you deflate me when my ego is overexpansive. I love the enthusiasm for nature you have when we walk in the woods, and I love your compassion for all our animals. I love to listen to you when you tell stories to the children. I love the formal way you speak English and the exotic way you speak French. I love the way you canter a horse. I wish I could capture your laughter in a bottle and release it a little at a time when I am downhearted. I wish I could marry you over and over just to experience again the rapture that was mine when first we were married."

They sat silently for a moment, listening to the whispers of the embers. "You know, Guy, every time I think I could not possibly love you more, you make me love you more. But for all that, do you realize you have never sung for me?"

"Of course I have."

She turned to face him and held him at arm's length. "I mean for me alone. Just for me. Not on a stage or for a social group but just for me, your most devoted audience."

"It is with infinite pleasure, madame, that I oblige."

Holding her close, his voice modulated to intimacy, he sang to her:

> *Speak to me softly,*
> *Speak to me true,*
> *Is this love that is a-borning,*
> *Is this true love you?*
>
> *Tell me in whispers,*
> *Close to my ear,*
> *These sweet words I am hearing,*
> *Are they truly sincere?*

Listen my lovely,
Listen my dear,
I will love you forever,
Forever and a year.

The euphoria of the wedding was muted by the discovery, the following morning, of a letter which Filonea left on her pillow:

"My dear family Laroule:
By the time you receive this letter I shall be well on my way back to my tribal village. I leave with a heavy heart for I love all of you so dearly. Pélagie is more my sister than the sisters I will soon be with. I cannot even picture life without all of you. But I also cannot be true to my heart by staying in St. Louis now that my beloved Rémi has married another. She is a lovely girl and I wish them great happiness. During these past six months when Rémi and I have no longer stayed together, I had tried to prepare myself for staying on after the wedding, but to no avail. As I watched them being united by Father Pierre, I knew my time had come to depart. As I write this I can hear the wedding revelry outside my window and tears are running down my cheeks. I have saddled my horse and filled the sidebags for the long, sad journey home. But I do not regret for one moment the wonderful life I have had with all of you.
                                    Affectionately, Filonea."

Pélagie covered her face to hide the rush of her tears and Marc, who was given to impulsiveness, vowed that he would go find her and bring her back. Pélagie suddenly turned her tear-drenched face on her father. "Why didn't you let Rémi marry her? You have broken her heart—and mine! You are horrid! Horrid!" She ran from the room, up the stairs, locked her door, and flung herself on her bed, not emerging until the following day. Marc, too, angrily went to his room, slammed the door, and did not appear for supper.

"Sometimes it is difficult to be right and popular," Guy said to Marie-Thérèse as they dined alone.

"But it is not difficult to be wrong and unpopular," Marie-Thérèse rejoined.

Guy's face clouded over. "Do you really think we did the wrong thing? I do not want to lose Filonea any more than you do."

"Losing Filonea is certainly a drastic price to pay for doing the right thing, if in fact we did the right thing—but how do we know? What is wrong and what is right—can we really tell?"

"No. We cannot."

The rebellion of the colonists against the British did not come as a surprise. The discontent on the Illinois side of the river which was under British domination, had been reflected in the number of people who were moving across to St. Louis. For the past year, Guy had surreptitiously been sending contributions to a French friend of his who was now living in Virginia and working with the revolutionists. Guy envied those warring on the British. He yearned for the day when the autocratic Spanish authorities would be overthrown and he would be in control of his own affairs, when he would be free to make his own rules and not be answerable to inferior men whose morals were commensurate with the size of their bribes.

"There must be government, of course," he said to Marie-Thé-rèse, "I am not proposing anarchy. But we who live here and work here should have a say in the government, just as the colonists are trying to rid themselves of the tyrants who govern them from afar who only care about the taxes and products they receive."

"Do you think they will win?"

"I do not know. But whoever wins, it will take a long time and many dollars and lives."

"Why do you not follow their lead and begin a revolution against the Spanish?"

"Because having seen what happened to my dear friend, Grotes-quieu, and the others when they tried to rebel, I am too much of a coward to risk it."

"No, Guy, you are not a coward. But you are also not a martyr. A martyr is a brave man who wants to die for his cause. A brave man who knows how to operate within the limits of fatal risk is the only one who can help his cause. A dead man, martyr or not, cannot stop the enemy. Do not ever call yourself a coward, not the Guy Laroule I married."

Forty-three

THE MYSTERIOUS KEELBOAT that pulled up at the St. Louis levee, painted black with red trim, had the word *Entdecker* painted on its bow, German for *Discoverer*. It had been navigating the river for three months on its way up from the Côtes des Allemands, a German enclave situated eight hours north of New Orleans. The stocky man who stepped ashore wore a jaunty sea captain's hat which complemented his luxurious moustache and goatee. He inquired of the dock foreman where he might find Monsieur Guy Laroule; the foreman dispatched a slave, who was working on the dock, to show him the way to Laroule's house.

Guy was busy taking inventory of the pelts in the warehouse but the visitor patiently waited until he returned, two hours later. "I appreciate that you see me," the visitor said, speaking ungrammatical French with a German accent. "My name is Hugo Brockmeir. I have arrived to here by boat with mine family from the Côtes des Allemands which probably you know . . . ?"

"Yes, of course. Perhaps it would be best if we spoke German—I am quite fluent," Guy said.

"Yes, thank you. Well, then, word reached us of your new village here, St. Louis, where you give a plot of land to newcomers, and also there is a common field for growing crops. It is for this that I have come here with my family, to join your new city."

"How many in your party, Herr Brockmeir?"

"My wife, my three children, my four workers and their families. We made the journey on our own, without a crew. It was quite an experience. You have come up the river, no doubt."

"No, I came on the Trace."

"*Ach*, the river, so unexpected, so savage . . ."

"What is it that you and your workers do?"

"Soap, Monsieur Laroule. We will make soap. This is what I did at Côte des Allemands. It is a very fine soap I make at a modest price. Do you have someone to make soap?"

"No. People make it in their houses."

"*Ach*, fine! So we will make your soap and also sell the soap to those villages we passed on the way here, both sides of the Mississippi. And we will build a good house on our lot—we Germans are very good builders."

"Tell me, Herr Brockmeir, why did you leave Côtes des Allemands?"

"Why? Why does anyone leave one place for another? To better ourselves, to live better. Do you know Côtes des Allemands, Monsieur Laroule?"

"No. I have heard of it, of course, but I have never been there."

"It is a strange place. We are all Germans, but we are also Creoles. It is next to impossible to be both. Some Germans who want to be Creoles change their names—Katzenberger becomes Casbergue, Kissinger is Quisingre, but then there are Germans who want to stay German, so we have schools which strictly teach in German. It traces back to how the city began. Years ago there was this Englishman, John Law, who formed a company to sell land in Louisiana. He printed up fancy pamphlets full of descriptions of how wonderful the land was, how all kinds of minerals and jewels, including diamonds, could easily be found all over. For the price of his land the buyer would get a supply of farm animals, plows, tools, clothing, and a year's supply of food. This Law fellow sent his representatives all over Germany where the poor people who had no land were only too eager to give up their meager savings for all those promises."

Guy was reminded of how, during the crossing from France, Trémencourt had naively described how John Law had promised the flowers that produced diamonds.

"Thousands of Germans were caught up in the scheme," Brockmeir was saying. "Of course, it was all lies, all those promises, just a ruse to get hold of the people's money. Those who did leave

Germany were packed into foul, filthy, rat-ridden boats. Masses of them died during the ocean voyage, and many of those who lived through it were so weakened by the crossing that they succumbed to the heat and primitive conditions encountered in Louisiana. Only the strongest and hardiest survived, but even for those few John Law's company never produced the land they had promised; and those Germans who remained, my father among them, finally floated on the Mississippi on rafts that wound up near New Orleans on a stretch of land given to them by the government of New Orleans. It is crowded, and the town of Des Allemands, where we lived, was victimized by rowdy rivermen, not an attractive place to live and raise a family. There are two other soapmakers there, and it is very hard to make a living. So we come here for a fresh start. To build our own house. To be the only soapmaker. To be far away from the rowdies who came off the boats and terrorized the town with their drinking, fighting, whoring, which often led to robbery, rapes, and murder."

"Frankly, Herr Brockmeir, I think you would be better off in Ste. Geneviève which is just a few miles below here. You see, I have dispersed all the lots here in St. Louis. There are no more. We have had a rush of families from the British side of the river. As for your soap company, we do not have any commerce here. It is our policy. We are only fur traders. Some of our needs are imported from New Orleans, and other things we buy from itinerant merchants who visit our docks. So if you came up from Ste. Geneviève, let us say, selling soap from your boat, you would very likely get customers here. One more thing: We are all French, and unlike you Germans of the Côtes des Allemands, we have no ambivalence—we want this to be a French town. Only French is spoken. Jean Baptiste Trudeau, our schoolteacher, only teaches his boys in French with French books just as Madame Marie Rigauche teaches the girls she tutors at their homes. Our whole existence is French. Father Pierre conducts services in French. Our cooking is classic French and Creole. Our songs, our games, our whole way of life would be foreign to you. St. Louis would not be a satisfactory place for you and your family."

"But, Monsieur Laroule, if all you desire is to be French, then why did you and the others leave France?"

"Primarily for the opportunity. The land here is so vast and beautiful. Waters that have never been fished. Soil that has never been turned. Game that has never been hunted. We could not trap these beautiful furs in France. Also we have boundless freedom here. We live as we want. There are no soldiers or police to deal with. No rules or regulations save those we set for ourselves. But now my lots are filled with the right kind of French people, the American Fur Trading Company prospers, and we are enjoying the kind of life we invented for ourselves. We think of ourselves as French-Americans with the accent on the French."

"We all speak French, my family better than I, and we often dine on French dishes . . ."

"Your staying is not open to discussion, Herr Brockmeir. We cannot accommodate you."

"May I ask, sir, if you are the declared owner of the land you call St. Louis?"

"Yes, to the boundaries of the cleared land. If you find a similar site somewhere, perhaps you could lay claim to it."

"Yes, perhaps." Brockmeir lingered for a moment more, thinking about the consequences of this rebuff. "Thank you," he said finally. "I appreciate the time you have given me."

Guy was sorry to have had to turn Brockmeir away. It was the first such incident. Everyone before seemed to understand that this was to be a French village and no one but the French had applied, which included Creoles and French Canadians. But Germans! Not only would it be a foreign group that would defile the French purity but it would be *Germans,* a people more at odds with the French than any other country in Europe. What is more, there was a noticeable touch of Teutonic arrogance about Brockmeir—the jaunty captain's hat, the immaculately trimmed goatee and moustache, the determined stride to his walk, the ramrod posture, the powerful voice, definitely a challenge best avoided.

The following day, Vincent, the carpenter, interrupted the Laroules at breakfast. "I am sorry to disturb you," he said, standing in the doorway, hat in hand, "but there is activity in the forest to the south of us that merits your attention."

Guy and Rémi saddled their horses and followed Vincent who led them to the south end of the village where the cleared area met the adjacent woods. They dismounted and proceeded by foot into the woods where several men with axes and two-handed saws were felling the trees. One of the men was Hugo Brockmeir.

"Herr Brockmeir," Guy said in an even voice, "may I inquire as to just what you are doing?"

Brockmeir put down his long-handled axe and leaned his hands on it. "We are felling trees."

"Obviously, but to what purpose?"

"The purpose being to clear the land."

"And the purpose of that?"

"To build houses on it."

"I thought I made it clear in our discussion yesterday that you were not welcome to build here."

"Yes, but you also suggested that I find a tract of my own on which to build. So I have."

"But not here."

"I asked you what your land claim area was, and you said the area that had been cleared. This is beyond the clearing. I claim it and will build on it."

"What I meant was for you to find an area removed from us."

"This is removed from you, Monsieur Laroule. We will leave a line of trees to mark the border between St. Louis and South St. Louis."

"You plan to call it South St. Louis?"

"It's as good a name as any."

"I'm afraid I shall have to refer the matter to Governor Gálvez in New Orleans. Perhaps you should wait for a ruling."

"No, that would take months, perhaps years. We will take our chances."

"I warn you that no one in St. Louis will buy your bloody soap."

"I understand they now buy from Ste. Geneviève . . ."

"Yes, and we make our own."

"Only in the spring when there are ashes left over from the winter with which to make lye. Our soap will be better and cheaper than what you now buy in Ste. Geneviève."

"No matter, sir, there will be no market here for your soap."

"Then we will sell it elsewhere."

"And how will you get it to market? You will not have access to our levee . . ."

"We will make one of our own."

"The bluffs are very high here as you can see."

"Whatever we have to do, Monsieur Laroule, we will do. Thank you for your concern, and good-day."

Brockmeir resumed swinging his axe into the substantial trunk of a hickory tree. Around him, falling trees thumped onto the moist, soft soil. Even Brockmeir's beautiful wife, Trudi, was working one end of a two-handed tree saw. Guy and Rémi looked at each other, knowing that force was the only way to deter Brockmeir. For the time being there was nothing further they could do.

"This afternoon," Guy said as they returned to their horses, "I shall go to see Governor Francisco Cruzat. He adores whiskey and I have a rare bottle I have been saving."

But that afternoon when Guy went to the governor's house, bearing his prize whiskey, he discovered to his dismay that Governor Cruzat had been recalled to New Orleans. Pending the arrival of a replacement, there was no one in authority.

"What does it really matter, Guy?" Marie-Thérèse asked at dinner that evening. "The man is creating his own village and if truth be told, it would be a pleasure to have a bar of decent soap considering the abrasive stuff we have been getting from Ste. Geneviève."

"You do not seem to understand, Marie-Thérèse, these are *Germans*. They will be right on top of us, eating sauerkraut and wearing lederhosen. The very same Germans who attacked the armies of Louis XIV and raided our villages."

"Then all we need to do," Rémi said, "is to post guards at our border and make sure they stay on their side of the line."

"Did you see his wife?" Marie-Thérèse said.

"She is blonde and quite beautiful."

"Yes," Marie-Thérèse said, "we must post guards."

In the weeks that followed, while they lived in tents, Brockmeir and his people cleared enough land to accommodate six cabins, four for his workers, one larger cabin for himself, and a cabin for making soap. An area beyond the cabins was cleared for the crops and livestock they had brought on their keelboat. In the livestock enclosure was a cow, a horse, chickens, geese, goats, pairs of swine, and sheep. The vegetable garden was planted with seed and plants brought from the Brockmeir's garden in Des Allemands. Particular care was given to the barley and hops essential for the beer the Brockmeirs would brew for their table.

It did not take long for soap production to begin. The wood ashes from the daily fires had been saved and stored in a large wooden container. By pouring water over the ashes Brockmeir was able to drain off a residue of lye. The lye was then placed in a large iron kettle and put over a fire; then Brockmeir added grease, bacon scraps, and fat that he had accumulated from butchers in Des Allemands. After a certain period of boiling, the contents were allowed to cool, then cut up into cakes of soap. Steps were built going down to the water and a suspended rope slide was erected for transporting the boxed soap down to the boat.

The first runs to Kaskaskia, Kohokia, and Ste. Geneviève resulted, disappointingly, in only a few barter sales for such things as cooking oil, gun powder, and tools, for the townspeople were somewhat suspicious of the Germans, since none existed in the north, and, in addition, most of the locals made their own soap.

"We must not be easily discouraged," Brockmeir said to his family. "They will get to know us, and those who use our soap will tell others how good it is."

"It is very lonely here," said his daughter, Maria, who was eighteen.

"Yes, I'm afraid it is," her mother said, "but there will be more families coming . . ."

"The Faberhagens and the Reinhauses said they might follow us," Brockmeir said. "And I hear some Germans are beginning to come to America."

"It is not so bad for Rudolf and Brigette," Maria persisted, referring to her brother, age nine, and her sister, age six, "because there are these other children their age here, but for me . . ."

"Would you like to go away to school?" Brockmeir asked.

"Where to school?"

"Back to Germany. We still have family in Wiesbaden. There's a university there."

"No, I don't think so. I would be a stranger there, and I have no real interest in more academics. I learned enough in Des Allemands. Perhaps I could go back and work there."

"Doing what?"

"At the school, to help teach."

"Be patient, my darling," her mother said. "We have only just arrived. Give it a little time."

"I am tired of soap," Maria said.

"So am I," Rudolf said.

"Me, too," Brigette said.

Not long thereafter, a young voyager named Willibald Valtz arrived in his keelboat at the St. Louis dock. On board were six slaves, one of whom was Willi's personal slave; the other five runaways had been captured in the woods by Willi as a hunter captures game, and these were now up for sale. Willi was twenty-five years old, six feet tall, the muscled torso of a keelboatman, which he had been, possessed of a brash, indestructible personality that got him both into and out of trouble. He began working on keelboats out of the Côtes des Allemands when he was fourteen. He had had no formal schooling—both his parents had been scalped during a vicious Chickasaw raid when he was nine—but he had taught himself to read and write in both English and French, although, curiously, not in German although he spoke it fluently. From boyhood on, he had yearned to escape from Des Allemands, and the keelboats were the most accessible way out. He thrived on the hard, rough river work, saved his money, eventually bought a keelboat of his own, and became the youngest and most belligerent patroon on the Mississippi. His pugnacious reputation even had the salubrious effect of discouraging pirate raids on his boat, *Willi's Own*. The one pirate crew that did attack Willi's boat wound up with five dead in the water and the others swimming for their lives.

Tiring of the arduous hauls up the Mississippi, Willi decided to remain in Upper Louisiana and enter the lucrative slave trade. Assisted by his slave, Cheramond, he combed the countryside for runaway slaves in the vicinity of villages. He returned the branded ones to their owners and collected a reward. But the unbranded slaves were the ones he prized for he could sell them for whatever price he could cajole from eager buyers. He was excellent at cajoling.

On a previous visit to St. Louis, Willi had sold ten slaves to Guy for a substantial price, and now he hoped to market these on board just as favorably. From Willi's point of view, the most attractive aspect of the runaway slave trade was that the product cost nothing to acquire, therefore the sale itself was pure profit.

Guy and Rémi came down to the levee to inspect the five male slaves whose virtues Willi vigorously extolled, turning them this way and that, showing their healthy teeth, their flexed muscles, but after conferring, Guy and Rémi decided they had enough slaves at present and besides, this group seemed a bit undernourished. Willi accepted their refusal cheerfully, thanking them for their time, and hoping they would be more kindly disposed toward his next crop of runaways.

"On the way here," Willi said, "I noticed a new clearing next to yours . . ."

"Yes, soap people—I doubt they have money for slaves. I would not bother if I were you."

But Willi tied up at the Brockmeir landing anyway; you never knew who might be in the market for a slave or two. He had sold three that morning to a passing flatboat for a good price, and he would have liked to unload at least two or three more before the day ended.

As it turned out, Brockmeir was indeed interested in the slaves and in Willi himself. "These people who buy slaves from you, would they buy soap, if it was a really good soap, better than any they could make?"

"Soap, eh? Soap . . ."

"I do not have the men who know how to travel in a keelboat and sell—we have made one effort and did not do well—but the slaves I buy could power your boat, and you could reach a lot of customers. And another thing, there is much money to be made in soap, which costs very little to produce."

"Yes, perhaps there is, but I do what I do for the freedom. I am my own boss. I go where I want, when I want, no one to tell me what to do, understand? If I worked for you, you would want me to go here and there, do this and that, but I would do as I pleased and you would get mad at me. To hunt slaves hiding in the forest is one thing, selling soap is another. No, I do not think soap is the thing for me."

"But we are a *gemütlich* little German group. More will come. Does that not appeal to you, to be among your own people? I would like you to meet my family before you make up your mind. Perhaps at dinner tonight. Will you stay?"

Just before dinner that evening, Willi was introduced to Hugo's family, first to Trudi, then to Rudolf and Brigette, and finally to Maria whose candescent face smiled at him, her blue eyes looking directly into his, her soft blond hair loosely falling around her graceful neck, the stark white of her teeth glimpsed between the perfect symmetry of her lips. At that moment, Willibald Valtz felt a constriction in his chest that made it difficult for him to breathe. He had heard the expression to take one's breath away; Maria had indeed robbed him of his. Although this encounter had barely taken a few moments, he instinctively knew that he must capture this girl as surely as he captured a prize runaway in the forest. The uncommitted, peregrinating Willibald Valtz, who had pledged that he would never tie himself to anyone or anything that would interfere with his wanderlust, was now sitting here at this crude pine dinner table trying to eat, impassioned by the extraordinary girl across from him who looked at him with amused eyes and made a mockery of all his vows.

For her part, Maria certainly felt the impact of Willi's presence, the intensity of his pull toward her. Young as she was, she had never before experienced this emotion, this projection of desire. Nor had she experienced anyone quite like Willi. The way he looked at her, she had never before been looked at like that. She liked it. It made her feel fulfilled, as if being this openly attractive to a man enhanced her burgeoning womanhood.

"In appreciation of this wonderful dinner," Willi said, "may I entertain you with my horn?"

Rudolf and Brigette clapped their hands in approval as Willi opened the scruffed instrument case he had carried from his boat.

"A flügelhorn!" Brockmeir exclaimed, laughing. "Where is the rest of your band? Should we get up and march?"

After a few warm-up notes, Willi began to play a Bach fugue with a delicacy not associated with the flügelhorn, but more akin to the flow and nuances of a pianist. It was a far cry from the sound of an instrument usually associated with the oom-pa-pa music of beer-gardens. The capricious music warmed the room, brought smiles to his listeners' faces, and, to Maria's bewilderment, touched her sexually, as if with the pliant music emanating from his horn Willi was caressing her.

At their enthusiastic insistence, Willi played an encore, a lullaby, sweet, slow, sentimental music that emerged from the horn's bright brass mouth as soothingly as if it were played on the violin.

Forty-four

IT WAS GUY'S STRATEGY to discourage the Germans by the use of hostile silence. Wherever encountered, on the water fishing or hunting in the woods, no matter how cheerfully they were greeted, St. Louisans were instructed not to reply. "Treat them as if they do not exist," Guy said. "Never look at them, never speak to them. Go right past them as if they weren't there. Needless to say, we must neither barter with nor buy from them."

The villagers cooperated and the policy of hostile silence worked very well with a few exceptions. On one occasion, the five-year-old son of one of Brockmeir's workers wandered away from his cabin, crossed the treeline, and entered St. Louis territory. At a nearby cabin there were two children about his age playing hopscotch. When the German boy approached, they gestured for him to join in, which is how his frantic mother found him, an hour later, playing hopscotch in forbidden territory. The St. Louis mother emerged from her house and the two women attempted conversation but quickly surrendered to the impasse of their languages. They were cordial to each other, however, and the German woman profusely thanked the St. Louis woman for having looked after her son.

The incident was observed by a neighbor and reported to Guy who cautioned the St. Louis woman. "But a little five-year-old boy, am I not to look after him?"

"Yes, of course, but do not socialize with the mother. Give her the child and go back into your house."

"I am sorry," the woman said, "but that is inhumane. Mothers must support each other. The woman had been frantically searching for her little boy, and she needed my sympathy."

Willi's first soap run across the Mississippi to Cahokia was a success; he sold and bartered his entire supply in half a day and was back in South St. Louis before dark. The slaves had cleared a plot of ground for him, and he planned to live on his boat while his cabin was being built. The day after his return from Cahokia, Brockmeir again invited him to dinner, pointedly suggesting that he bring along his flügelhorn. This time, after dinner, Willi played a Handel concerto with a dexterity that belied the fact that he could not read music but had been able to learn this piece, as he learned all the others, from hearing them played.

"Now we shall entertain you, Willi," Brockmeir said. "Get your guitar, Maria."

"Oh, but I do not think that Willi wants to hear . . ."

"Yes, I do, Maria. It is your turn."

Maria's guitar was a rosewood five-stringed instrument that had been given to her by a girlfriend who had attended her school in Des Allemands, whose father was the Spanish vice-consul. Maria played three Spanish dances she had learned from her Spanish friend, at first with stiff, self-conscious fingers, but then, warming to the music, the music began to soar as her nimble fingers danced over the strings.

"What do you think, Willi" Brockmeir said after Maria finished to applause, "can a flügelhorn and a guitar play a duet?"

"Why not? It has probably never been done, but Maria and I will practice and see what happens."

All the way down to his boat, Willi thought of nothing but Maria just as she had occupied his mind all day long. He never stopped thinking of her, seeing her face, her lithe body, hearing her voice, her laugh. This obsession startled him, because he had known many beautiful women, but none had ever consumed his thoughts like Maria.

It was a glorious evening, and the full moon glinted across the waters of the Mississippi. He was sitting on deck, smoking his pipe and listening to the sounds of the river—the cadence of nightbirds calling and the muted cries of nearby animals—when he heard steps approaching. Maria stood on the shore, holding her guitar.

"I thought we might practice a little," she said in a constricted voice. "I mean, it is such a lovely night to play music."

He took her hand and helped her aboard. For an awestruck moment, not releasing her hand, he was frozen by her moon-enhanced beauty, then slowly they moved together, and wordlessly embraced. Tentatively their bodies touched, her lips on his, her diaphanous hair against his cheeks, her firm breasts pressed against his chest, his hands gently pulling her towards him, their breaths quickening. Suddenly she pulled away, turning her back on him, confused, startled by her boldness, suffused with her desire. They stood for an instant, reconnoitering. Nervously she ran her fingers across the strings of the guitar, random chords, marking time. In some far-off forest an animal sent a piercing cry into the night. Willi moved toward her and put his arms around her, pulling her back against him as his hands enfolded her breasts. She put her free hand on top of one of his. She had never been touched like this before. She closed her eyes and tilted back her head, her hair covering his face. As he lightly brushed his lips against the nape of her neck, her hand dug into his. All these new senses, this sensuality, wanting to give but wanting to restrain herself, resenting her desire yet victimized by it, ever since she first laid eyes on him.

"I love you, Maria," he said.

She pulled his hands away from her breasts and quickly stepped off the boat onto the dock.

"I should not have come here," she said.

"But you did."

"I could not help myself."

"Come back."

"I should not have come."

"Please."

As she slung her guitar over her shoulder and started to move away, a huge ball of fire roared into the night from above followed by an explosion that painted the black sky red, and bathed the moon in smoky flames.

They ran up the steps as fast as they could. The soap cabin had turned into a bonfire, an acrid black smoke emanating from the putrid-smelling soap as it dissolved in the flames. A sudden plume of brighter flame shot up within the outer flame as the wooden bin filled with animal fat ignited. Pots of lye exploded. All of the special equipment for draining the lye from the ashes went up in flames. The iron kettle melted along with the stove that provided its heat.

In response to the cries of distress, everyone came running, eager to help put out the fire, only to be rebuffed by the intense heat, helplessly watching the thatched roof cave in and the burning walls pitch into the sepulcher of their soap business. The fire burned until dawn, and when the last hot embers had died there was nothing left, nothing at all, only the smoking ashes of their dreams.

The day after the fire, the bell on the roof of the St. Louis cathedral summoned the townspeople to the church. As they assembled, they found Guy impatiently awaiting them. He stood alone on the altar dais, acknowledging no one, his face grim, his eyes scrutinizing the face of each arrival, searching for an expression, a downward cast of eyes, a furtive glance that might be a clue.

"I suppose all of you know by now that last night the Germans' cabin where soap was made burned to the ground. I have made no secret of my displeasure at having them so close to us, and I have been trying to find a way to induce them to move, but never, never would I approve of this kind of vandalism. Of course, we do not know for sure how the fire started, but when green logs burn that fast and furiously it indicates that something highly flammable was involved. I watched the conflagration; there is no doubt in my mind that the fire was deliberately set. I do not believe the Germans would set fire to their own means of livelihood. Is there someone here who will step forward and admit to this deed, someone who was well-intentioned but misguided?"

No one responded.

"I thought not. Any man who commits such an act is usually too cowardly to admit it. And it just may be that the fire was not inflicted by someone here. But I want it understood that our policy of strict segregation from the Germans means we are also segregated from any hostile acts toward them. We St. Louisans are civilized, fair-minded people, and we must not destroy that which isn't ours. We will continue to discourage all contact with the Germans, hoping that that will induce them to move away, but that must be the extent of our hostility toward them. Any questions? No? Then, that will be all."

* * *

"They were hostile, yes, but I never thought they would go this far," Brockmeir said as he surveyed the destruction. "To replace the cabin is nothing, but except for a bucket of lye, all my soap-making equipment is destroyed—the cooling boxes, the trays for draining the lye from the ashes, the kettles and firestalls, all those things—how will I replace them? They are not things we can make here. The only way we can replace them is to return to Des Allemands and hope to find replacements. But to go downriver and come back up would take four months. How would we live in the interim?"

"It looks like the French have won out," Trudi said. "I guess we should not have stayed here. They warned us."

"The hell with them!" Willi interjected. "I can go back to capturing runaways until we get the soap cabin going again."

"Thank you," Brockmeir said to Willi, "that is very kind of you, but impractical, I'm afraid."

"May I say something?" Maria asked. "Why not wait a few days while we think all this over? Why should we rush into doing something so quickly? Maybe we can find a way . . ."

"Like what?" her father said. "I do not wait for miracles."

"But they would have the satisfaction of making us quit," Maria said. "Do you want to give in so quickly?"

"I agree with Maria," Willi said, motivated more by his desire to stay near her than to help Brockmeir's plight. "I know that this is your affair, Herr Brockmeir, and I should keep my nose out of it, but you can get along for a while, can't you? There is enough to eat, you have crops growing, you make your own beer, why give up these nice cabins and all this work? We can have a guard on duty every night. Let's take turns."

The discussion continued throughout the day; in the end it was decided to stay on for the time being while trying to find a way to replace the soap-making equipment.

It was also agreed that every night one of them would stand guard.

It was discovered on the morning of the second day after the fire, that a quantity of pelts in the fur storage shed, awaiting tanning and shipment to New Orleans, had been damaged during the night. The furs affected were those on the top layers of the piles; they had mysterious, irregular holes in them, not knife cuts nor damage caused by gnawing animals. At first, Guy and Rémi were unable to

identify what had caused these strange holes and erosions but a
single word uttered by Marie-Thérèse in the form of a question
helped solve the mystery: "Revenge?"

"Of course," Rémi said, "revenge! When you make soap, you use
lye, and lye poured across the pelts . . ."

In all, forty beaver pelts had been ruined by the lye.

"Guy," Marie-Thérèse said, "I hope you will not undertake another assault on them . . ."

"I did not burn their cabin," Guy said.

"We must put an end to this right now before we all fear for our
lives."

"And how do we do that?"

"With a meeting."

"What?"

"An agreement. You must meet with them."

"Why me? Let them contact us."

"May I arrange this?" Marie-Thérèse asked.

"Arrange what?"

"The meeting."

"It all depends . . . I am not going to them."

"This is a dangerous situation, Guy—will you leave it up to me?"

"But I want to know . . ."

"Guy . . ."

"Oh, all right."

Forty-five

OVERCOMING HIS APPREHENSION, Willi decided to be bold and bring up his love for Maria while he and Hugo Brockmeir were engaged in brewing a batch of beer. For the past few days they had hunted together and had brought back a variety of game they had now hung to age: hares, raccoons, opossum, squirrels, partridges, ducks, a fat brown bear, and two deer. The hunting camaraderie between them emboldened Willi to speak about Maria. While the water the slaves had brought up from the Mississippi was boiling in a large copper over a wood fire, Willi and Brockmeir were mashing dried barley malt between stones.

"Herr Brockmeir, I have wanted to tell you . . . well . . . I . . . I have grown very fond of your daughter, Maria."

"Ah, yes, Maria."

"We have been practicing . . ."

"Maybe tonight you will make your debut?" He began to add the pulverized malt to another vat, also filled with water, to induce mashing.

"We like each other very much . . ." Willi caught one of his fingers between the stones and swore. "I know we have not known each other for very long . . ."

Brockmeir was pouring hot water into the mash vat and seemed not to be listening.

"But some things happen to you that change your life. If the truth be told, Herr Brockmeir, Maria has changed my life."

Brockmeir was drawing wort from the bottom of the malt vat and began stirring the malt with a long-handled wooden paddle.

"I never thought it would happen," Willi continued, "but I no longer want to be on my own, roaming around, no cares or worries. I used to thrive on adventure—no more. I just want to be with Maria."

Brockmeir was gradually adding a scoop of hops to the mixture. "Are you telling me you have seduced my daughter?"

"No, sir, I have not—not yet. But we are . . . we are so inclined, and that is why I am talking to you." This time Willi nervously caught two fingers in the stones, but this time he paid no attention to the pain. "If I seduce her, you will be outraged, as a father should be. You will challenge me to a duel which, of course, I would have to accept. We will shoot at each other or thrust swords at each other. If I seduce Maria we each have a fifty-fifty chance of being killed."

Brockmeir was slicing pieces of yeast from a large block he had brought from Des Allemands; he added the yeast to the mixture. "Then the solution is simple, Willi—do not seduce her."

"If you do not mind me saying, Herr Brockmeir, there is another solution."

"Which is?"

"To marry her."

Brockmeir sipped a taste of the brew from a ladle, decided it needed more hops which he added. "That comes later. First do not seduce her. She is still too young to marry."

"She is eighteen."

"Too young."

"How old was Frau Brockmeir when you married?"

"Those were different times."

"But how old was she?"

"Seventeen."

"And you had Maria when she was eighteen?"

Brockmeir added two more pieces of yeast. The fire was turning to embers. He spread cloths over the steaming copper to keep the heat in.

"How old are you, Willi?"

"Twenty-five."

"And do you plan to support Maria by going all over the territory hunting for runaway slaves while she waits patiently back home?"

"No, sir, I have other plans."

"Which is?"

"The Brockmeir-Valtz Beer Company."

"What?"

"I had been thinking of this, even before the soap cabin burned. In fact, that very first night you had me to dinner—your beer is delicious, Herr Brockmeir—better than anything we used to get at the taverns in Des Allemands. The yeast you have, the barley plants, these hops you grow yourself. Beer, Herr Brockmeir, beer, is much easier to sell than soap. Anyone can make soap in the kitchen, but not beer. And there are no brewhouses in Upper Louisiana. I know—I have been all over. We would have it all to ourselves. Beer is for everyone. The ancient Egyptians, the Babylonians before Christ. I know about beer. God knows I have drunk all kinds: beer made with persimmons and molasses, beer with coriander seed, caraway, and hartshorn shavings. Beer made from corn stalks. Even drank an English beer that had ginger and cinnamon in it. Oh, I know about beer all right, and yours is the best, Herr Brockmeir. We will build us a brewhouse and plant more barley and hops. The Brockmeir-Valtz Beer Company, you and your son-in-law."

"Wait now, hold your horses, how can we sell beer—in what?"

"Bottles."

"And just where will we get the bottles?"

"From Monsieur DeMarcy, the glassblower in Cahokia. Not long ago I sold him four slaves. He would make us all the bottles we want. We will barter beer for bottles. And he also has a stockpile of good cork bark. I have given this a lot of thought—'Brockmeir-Valtz Beer cools you in the heat of summer, warms your blood in the winter, and allows a man to drink long hours without getting too drunk.'"

Marie-Thérèse's solution to the nettlesome problem with the Germans was to handle it herself. "I am going to send word to Frau Brockmeir to suggest that we meet about this."

"You two women?" Guy asked incredulously.

"Precisely. When men become so destructive it is time for women to take over."

"It will not happen. You overlook the fact that Brockmeir is Teutonic—the German male will never let a woman invade his authority."

"Ah, Guy, my darling, when will you understand that what authority the husband has is determined by what the wife does not want to do."

"Oh, yes? Like what?"

"We do not want to punish the children, so we give you that authority. Husbands refer to themselves as 'head of the house,' but everything about the house is controlled by the wife: the furniture, the kitchen, the servants, the entertaining, the children—their studies, when they bathe, what they wear, where they go, but wives are only too content to have the husbands pay the bills, argue with the creditors and debtors, supervise repairs, and do all the things women dislike doing. But you see, my love, settling this situation with the Germans is something I *want* to do, and husbands who tend to argue and shake their fists at each other are not very good at it, so I will meet with Frau Brockmeir, who, I assure you, will convince her husband just as I am convincing you."

As Marie-Thérèse predicted, Trudi Brockmeir met with her. She came by boat to the St. Louis levee, accompanied by Maria, and the two wives pledged that henceforth there would be no untoward acts between the two communities.

And there weren't.

Except for the one incident involving Rémi and Willi. It occurred on a path that ran through the nearby forest, a path that at one point became very narrow and twisting. Both Willi and Rémi were on horseback and confronted each other head-on as they came around a sharp turn in the path. The brambled vegetation was dense on either side, permitting only one horse in the path. At first there was a wordless stand-off, each man trying to stare down the other, the horses skittishly brushing noses, then Willi started forward striving to push Rémi backwards but Rémi's horse was just as determined as Willi's and stood his ground, responding willingly to the tightening of his reins. It was head to head now, each animal straining at the other, the riders growing more and more demanding but neither horse giving ground. Willi and Rémi still said nothing, only the exertions of the horses piercing the forest's stillness as they skirmished and snorted at each other. The confrontation was becoming brutal, both horses suffering cuts and bruises, their heads butting together, rearing, their flanks scratched to bleeding by the sharp brambles. Then suddenly, in deference to the exhausted horses, as if an agreement had been reached between them, both men reined in. One last hostile look at each other as they started to back away, withdrawing down the path.

That was the only belligerent incident.

The Brockmeir-Valtz Beer Company got off to a good start. After a convincing visit from Willi, the Cahokia glassblower made special bottles and brought them across the river on a barge, receiving several barrels of Edelweiss Beer in exchange. As Willi had predicted, the nearby villages welcomed the new product, necessitating the construction of a large new brewhouse with additional equipment that Brockmeir's workers were able to make. A few bottles of Edelweiss were even smuggled into houses of certain St. Louisans who had a predilection for beer.

Willi Valtz wed Maria Brockmeir at a traditional ceremony presided over by Father Pierre Gibault who had maintained a stubborn impartiality in the Laroule-Brockmeir dispute, presiding over services in each village when he came up from his Ste Geneviève parish. After the wedding, Willi and Maria finally made their musical debut; the guests were astonished that the peculiar combination of the flügelhorn and the guitar could produce such satisfying music. And nine months to the day after their marriage, Maria gave birth to a daughter whom they christened Christiana Valtz.

Rémi and his pretty but bland wife also became parents, producing twin boys whom they playfully named Jean Christophe and Christophe Jean. Rémi promptly built a house of his own adjacent to that of his parents. The American Fur Trading Company grew more prosperous with each passing month although St. Louis was still without shops or any other commerce, which accounted for its slow increase in population.

It was a curious coincidence that both companies adopted the bald eagle as the symbol of its product; the fur company's eagle majestically intertwined with the "A" of the American Fur Trading Company while the beer company's eagle soared, one wing extended through the top loop of the letter "B."

Forty-six

In its beginning years, the Revolutionary War was confined to the states and territories east of the Mississippi, ignoring St. Louis and all the other villages west of the river. However, in 1780 word reached Guy, through one of his trappers, that General Frederick Haldimand, resentful of the financial aid that St. Louis had been giving to Virginia, had ordered the commanding officer of Fort Michilimackinac, Patrick Sinclair, to mount an attack on St. Louis. Sinclair appointed Emmanuel Hesse, a British officer who was an experienced fur trader, to head up the attack. As compensation, Hesse and his officers were promised the fur trade that then belonged to the American Fur Trading Company. It was no secret that for many years the British had coveted the remunerative trade along the Missouri that Guy had monopolized.

Hesse's forces were composed of Indians from the Great Lakes region who were friendly to the British as a result of having regularly received gifts from them, particularly whiskey. Two hundred Santee Sioux warriors, a group of Chippawas, and sizeable recruitments of Winnebagos and Menominees comprised most of the contingent. To lead the Indians under Hesse's direction, Wabasha, chief of the Sioux, and Chief Matchekewis of the Chippawas were outfitted with ornate British uniforms and medals and commissioned as generals.

When Guy received several reports from trappers returning from the area that Hesse's army was on the move, he immediately consulted St. Ange who had been a lieutenant at Fort Chartres prior to leaving the military. Rémi and Marie-Thérèse also attended the meeting. They were faced with the fact that St. Louis had no fortifications and could not even attempt to resist a large attacking force like that being assembled by Hesse. The current Spanish governor, Don Fernando de Leyba, who had established his headquarters thirty miles to the north with a small garrison of soldiers, had shown very little interest in establishing any military defenses along the Mississippi coast. But now faced with the prospect of the village they had worked so hard to create being obliterated and its occupants slaughtered, it was imperative for the Laroules to do whatever they could to protect themselves. It was regrettable that this crisis was occurring at the height of the trapping season when fully two-thirds of the village's men were away, either trapping or acquiring pelts from the Indians. The scout, Tico Verdoux, was dispatched to inform Governor de Leyba about the attack and request immediate aid.

Since St. Ange was the only person with military experience, he was put in command of the operation. The fortification plan he evolved was to build immediately four stone towers at each corner of the village equipping them with the cannons once mounted on their boats to fend off pirate attacks while en route on the Mississippi. It was decided that the west side of the village was the most vulnerable, so work on the first tower was begun there. The thirty-five foot tower with a thirty-foot diameter was to be constructed of stone and mortar with apertures for firing guns. The slaves were diverted from other labor and all able-bodied villagers, women and children included, pitched in. By the time the tower was completed, a group of returning hunters warned Guy that Hesse's contingent was already on flatboats and had reached the mouth of the Des Moines River. Obviously, there was not enough time to build any more of the towers; an alternate plan was devised to dig a series of overlapping trenches around the exposed front of the village.

De Leyba's response to Guy's request for assistance was to send three four-pounder and two six-pounder cannons from his compound, and a small contingent of men who were endorsed as "good shots." De Leyba's cannons were mounted in the tower, and the ones from the boats were set up at strategic points along the mile of entrenchments that had been dug.

As Hesse moved toward the Mississippi, he lavished gifts on the

Indians he encountered thereby inducing a sizeable number of war-riors to join his forces, including some two hundred and fifty turn-coat Sauk and Fox warriors who had been regularly receiving presents from the American Fur Trading Company. Guy again dis-patched Tico Verdoux to Governor de Leyba, this time to urge him to send more men but the governor tersely replied that what he had sent was all he could spare. Guy also sent Léon Thibault down to Ste. Geneviève to deliver a plea of desperation to the authorities there; unlike the governor, they responded by dispatching Lieuten-ant Francisco de Cartabone with a detachment of sixty militiamen. Of the two hundred and ninety males who lived in St. Louis, how-ever, only eighty were actually in the village; as a result, adding the detachment sent by Ste. Geneviève to the number of de Leyba's men put the total force at St. Ange's command at only one hundred sixty men, many of whom had no military training. Hesse's band, on the other hand, numbered close to a thousand as his barges swept into the Mississippi and proceeded downriver toward St. Louis.

Guy also sent a runner to South St. Louis with a note warning Brockmeir of the impending attack.

In the early afternoon of May 26, the second day of the Feast of Corpus Christi, numerous people were in the fields, mostly women and children, picking wild strawberries and flowers when Hesse gave the signal to attack. At the same time he sent three hundred of his Indian troops to capture the village of Cahokia. In the vanguard of the St. Louis attack were the Sioux and Winnebagos who came streaming down from the north with shrill war cries and a barrage of gunfire. Not aware of the last-minute emergency preparations, Hesse had informed the Indians that according to his informants St. Louis was defenseless, so they charged the village head-on with ab-solute abandon. As soon as he spotted the Indians, the guard who St. Ange had posted in the tower sounded an alarm which sent mili-tiamen scurrying into the trenches and the gunners dashing to their stations in the tower.

As they neared the village, expecting no resistance, the attackers were startled by the cannon shots and musket fire directed at them from the tower and the trenches. Despite the volleys, the Sioux and the Winnebagos kept advancing, although more warily. But the Saulks and Foxes, who were some distance behind them, cautiously slowed down; the rear echelon, comprised of Canadians com-manded by Hesse, never advanced at all, but observed the action from a stationary position on a hilltop. The Sioux and Winnebagos overran most of the men, women and children in the strawberry field, slaughtering all of them.

For two hours Chief Wabasha tried to manoeuver his Sioux to entice the militiamen out of the trenches, even going so far as to collect the corpses of the women and children, brutally disembowelling them in full view of the militia trenches, but St. Ange and Guy were able to restrain their men from leaving the safety of the trenches and to continue firing. Actually their muskets were not very effective beyond one hundred yards—the Indians did not come that close—but the musket fire augmented by the thunderous blasts of the cannons inhibited the Indians from advancing any farther.

Finally, Chief Wabasha and Chief Matchekewis realized that the Saulks and Foxes, afraid of the cannons, were at a standstill and that Hesse and his Canadians were in cowardly retreat; so the enfuriated chieftains vented their wrath by inciting their warriors to pillage and destroy as much as they could in the area outside the village. For the next hour they swept through the surroundings, wiping out crops, leveling and burning outbuildings, slaughtering cows, sheep, horses, pigs and other domestic animals, even killing dogs and cats. The slaves they encountered were either scalped or captured, to be traded to the British for whiskey and trinkets.

At a signal from the chiefs, the pillaging Indians quickly disappeared. Since the attack on Cahokia had also failed, there was great satisfaction in having prevented the British from conquering the villages, but it was a joyless victory considering the loss of life and property. The fields were red with blood. Sixty villagers had been killed along with thirteen slaves, and an additional nineteen slaves had been abducted. The livestock pens were covered with mutilated carcasses. An entire season of crops had been trampled and slashed; barns and silos, hen houses and toolsheds, the village's only water tank, carriages, the tannery, the storage shed laden with pelts, all had been smashed and some of them set on fire. It would take a long time to recover from this onslaught.

South St. Louis, on the other hand, was unscathed. Upon receiving Guy's note of warning, Brockmeir had ordered a massive camouflaging operation. Everyone who was physically able was put to work cutting down heavily leafed branches, and these were used to cover all the cabins and other buildings in the settlement. When completed, the entire village was under foliage and looked like part of the forest.

The sixty St. Louis whites who had been killed were buried in a cemetery that was created beyond the planting fields. Working around the clock, it took three days for Vincent Beccé and a group of volunteers to make all the coffins. The attacking Indians had only suffered four dead and four wounded; it was suspected that most of those had not been hit by St. Louis fire, but by the Foxes and Saulks who were firing from their rear.

On the day of the St. Louis funerals, Father Pierre came up from Ste. Geneviève to conduct the services, and a boatload of flowers had arrived from the people of Cahokia to place on the graves.

Just before the start of the service, which was held in the open because the church was too small to accommodate all the coffins and mourners, the Brockmeirs arrived dressed properly in black and bearing flowers. Guy saw them approaching and confronted them.

"Why are you here, Herr Brockmeir?"

"We have come to pay our respects. Such sorrow should be shared."

"You should have paid your respects the day of the attack."

"How do you mean?"

"I mean we were under a vicious attack—surely you heard what was happening—that is what you should have shared."

"Nothing was asked of us."

"You saved your own hide while our people were being killed. You knew what was happening here, did you not?"

"Monsieur Laroule, you banished us from your midst and now you attempt to blame us for not having been here when you needed us. You cannot have it both ways. We do have compassion for the people here, however, and we have come to express our sympathy for the tragedy that occurred."

"Well, sir, you are not welcome. We prefer to grieve without your mock sympathy."

"Our sympathy is sincere. We would like to be good neighbors."

"A good neighbor would have helped us. You Germans are no better neighbors here than you are in Europe. Good-day, sir. Those who did not fight with us are not welcome to grieve with us."

Guy abruptly withdrew and left the four Brockmeirs standing awkwardly by themselves. They were angry and embarrassed; there was nothing to do but leave. Trudi and Maria gently placed their flowers on the ground; wordlessly the four of them turned away and walked back to their village. The service began as two violins started to play. Guy felt badly for having turned the Brockmeirs away, but it was best that the French bury their own dead without the presence

of outsiders, no matter how well-meaning. He picked up their flowers and placed them on the altar.

The strawberry-field massacre created tragic consequences for many
St. Louis families. Among those killed was one of Guy's most trusted
traders, Jean-Marie Cardinal who had led the American Fur Trading
Company's first expedition up the Missouri to contact the Indian
tribes. He was married to a Pawnee named Careche-Caranche who
had mothered seven daughters and a son who now, along with other
children who suffered the loss of a father or mother, became wards
of the village. Even worse off were the children of two families who
lost both parents in the massacre; these children were adopted by
two childless couples.

As the problems created by the attack escalated in its aftermath,
Guy became increasingly bitter towards Brockmeir and his camouflaged neutrality, and toward Governor de Leyba for having refused
to send more soldiers or other aid. Guy's animosity toward de Leyba
was short-lived, however, because not long after the infamous attack
the body of the governor was discovered on the floor of his bedroom. A drunken, avaricious, preening man, disliked by everyone,
de Leyba's death was attributed to suicide by poison, but it was
obviously not suicide since there was no vestige of poison in the
room. In fact, the blisters on his skin were ample proof that the
poison had come from the manzanilla, a tree with beautiful oval
leaves and saw-like teeth, whose stalk encapsulates a sac filled with a
milky, deadly sap. It is this sap with which the Indians poisoned the
tips of their arrows, and someone, somehow, had used it to finish off
the repugnant de Leyba.

There was no such resolution of Guy's animosity toward
Brockmeir. The more Guy inventoried his losses—the mutilated
pelts, the slaughtered animals, the eradicated crops, the destroyed
cabins and sheds, the shambles of his dream village—the more his
condemnation of Brockmeir escalated.

"Guy, you are being unreasonable," Marie-Thérèse said. "Herr
Brockmeir was under no obligation to us. You forget we rejected
him. He did what was best for his own people."

"Yes, of course, saved his own skin while our people were being
butchered."

"And why not? The camouflage probably saved all of them from
being slaughtered. Guy, you have allowed your inbred prejudice

against Germans to turn into a fixation, like water added to stone dust hardens into mortar."

"Marie-Thérèse, I would sooner trust a copperhead in my boot than trust a German."

Forty-seven

On Pélagie's nineteenth birthday, she was married to the twenty-three-year-old son of the aristocrat, Jean-Baptiste Marigny, who had come to St. Louis among the first wave of settlers. The wedding ceremony was conducted by Father Bernard de Limpach, a Capuchin who had recently been installed as the village's first resident priest. Monsieur Marigny built a large, limestone house for the newlyweds, furnished it with fine French furniture, linens and draperies that keelboats had transported from New Orleans, and staffed it with twelve slaves he bought from an itinerant slave trader. Pélagie was not particularly interested in getting married and didn't know Marigny's son very well, but Guy had entered this nuptial covenant on her behalf and she did not want to disappoint him, beset as he was with all the problems he faced as a result of the Indian attack. It was difficult to find replacement livestock, to prepare ruined fields and replant them with seeds and plants difficult to come by, to find materials with which to rebuild the sheds and barns, and to hurriedly replace the destroyed furs which had been on order from companies in England and France.

In addition, grim news from France settled upon Guy like a black mantle: most of his Versailles friends had been executed by the Revolutionary Tribunal, even Louis XVI himself. Guy hoped against hope that his dear friend, Philippe de Lorraine, had somehow escaped the executioner's blade, but word eventually reached Guy that Philippe, too, had been guillotined. As had Madame du Barry. Accused by the Tribunal of having conspired against the Republic although she had had nothing to do with matters of state and politics, she had been summarily condemned to death and immediately guillotined before a jeering crowd in the Place de la Concorde.

"The irony of it," Guy remarked to Marie-Thérèse. "At the time I left France I felt I was being banished to my death but instead I live and the favored ones have all had their heads chopped off. If it had not been for my misfortune, I, too, would now have my head in the executioner's basket."

As the American Fur Trading Company stumbled, trying to recover from its losses, the fledgling Brockmeir-Valtz Beer Company was quickly gathering momentum despite Hugo's cautious nature. Although he tried to suppress Willi's impetuous enthusiasms, Brockmeir was simply no match for his son-in-law, who was respectful but not to be deterred, driven by some goading force that seemed to have anointed him the apostle of beer. Quite by accident, Willi discovered huge caverns deep under the village where it was very cool even in the intense heat of the summer. It was a perfect place to store the beer until ready for transport. In the winter, when the Mississippi froze over, slaves were sent out on the ice to saw large blocks which were taken down into the caves and wrapped in heavy burlap to preserve them. In the summer, the boats transporting the beer would cover it with the burlapped ice thus preserving it for the longer voyages.

Since Willi knew many of the keelboat patroons from his days on the Mississippi, he was able to enlist some of them as distributors of Lorelei, "the Prince of Beers." Willi knew that most of the keelboats had to return to New Orleans without cargo since shippers preferred flatboats which had the capacity to carry more cargo down river. It was relatively inexpensive to ship beer on keelboats and distribute it to villages all the way down to New Orleans. In fact, Willi even found a distributor in New Orleans who was willing to introduce Lorelei beer into shops and taverns.

Ten years after the attack on St. Louis, the Brockmeir-Valtz Beer Company and the American Fur Trading Company had become the most successful firms in Upper Louisiana. At the time, South St. Louis had a population of three hundred and eighty, singularly devoted to beer, and St. Louis' had risen to five hundred and seventy, all of them affiliated with the fur company. But both were subjected to harassing inspections from the Spanish authorities who made them abide by autocratic rules and regulations, imposing a tax of fifteen percent on all their products shipped on the Mississippi which was under the total control of Spain.

When Washington was sworn in as the first president of the United States in 1789, Guy openly envied the freedom the colonists had attained. Rémi, however, was skeptical of this newfangled government that allowed the people to make their own laws; Guy, however, yearned to be on the other side of the river where avaricious, overbearing Spaniards did not control the lives of the people who lived there.

As for the relations between the two St. Louis villages, they had finally reached a peaceful accommodation, coexisting without encroachment, each village self-sufficient but wary of the other. By 1785, South St. Louis had its own school teachers and a German pastor for its church, but there was only one doctor, Arnold Flaubert, who had settled in St. Louis, and he serviced both villages.

As business increased, Brockmeir had had to keep adding to his brewhouses; now, five large brewhouses worked full time to keep pace with the demand for bottles of Lorelei. The American Fur Trading Company also had had to double its tannery operation and its pelt storage sheds in order to meet its demands. The two villages accounted for more than half of all commerce in Upper Louisiana as the Spanish authorities kept close watch on their sales in order to extract their full 15% tariff.

Guy and Hugo had not spoken to each other since their encounter at the funeral services, but their hostile relationship would eventually be affected by what occurred on the fateful day that Guy's grandson, Jean-Christophe, went out to catch catfish on the Mississippi.

Forty-eight

JEAN-CHRISTOPHE RIVEAU was a dead ringer for his father, Rémi; the same lean build, deep-set eyes, sandy hair, and the same prominent, slightly cleft chin. But there the similarity ended. Now twenty-three, Jean-Christophe was the only member of the Laroule-Riveau family who was not involved in the fur business. Rémi had done everything he could to induce him into some phase of their operation—he was sent on expeditions with the best trappers; he visited Indian tribes on the Missouri with whom the company traded; he spent several months working in the tannery, learning how to cure the furs; he voyaged down the Mississippi with the crew of a pelt-laden flatboat; he took part in the selling of the pelts on the New Orleans fur market—but none of these activities interested Jean-Christophe. He was a dreamer, a poet, a musician who composed music that he performed on the piano. His twin brother, Christophe-Jean, industriously worked for the company but as far as Rémi was concerned that did not compensate for the fact that he had failed to involve Jean-Christophe in the fur business.

But Guy felt differently about his grandson. Guy's own talent for singing and performing identified him with Jean-Christophe's artistic personality, the songs he composed on the spinet, the quality of his voice, the soulfulness of his poetry. Jean-Christophe was Guy's favorite grandchild and, to the annoyance of Rémi and his wife, Guy encouraged Jean-Christophe in his endeavours.

One of Jean-Christophe's passions was fishing; he loved to anchor his boat on the Mississippi and set his pole for catfish while he read Shakespeare aloud or composed his own stanzas of poetry. On this particular day, he sat there on his bobbing boat, the swift middle current swirling around him. His fishing pole baited with a large earthworm, Jean-Christophe was reciting *As You Like It,* enjoying the lilting words as they rolled across his tongue, declaiming the verse to the breeze that gently stirred the treetops on the neighboring shore:

> *Sweet are the uses of adversity;*
> *Which, like the toad, ugly and venomous,*
> *Wears yet a precious jewel in his head;*
> *And this our life, exempt from public haunt,*
> *Finds tongues in trees, books in the running brooks,*
> *Sermons in stones . . .*

The boats collided with such force that the impact violently pitched Jean-Christophe's boat, almost capsizing it. A flatboat with full cargo, riding the swift Mississippi current, had struck the Cahokia ferry amidship, sundering it and catapulting its passengers into the water. The flatboat, tiller smashed and out of control, was bearing down on Jean-Christophe's boat. The passengers thrashing in the deep, muddy water, some hurt and bleeding, were crying out for help as they struggled against the churning current, its flow enhanced by the disgorging Missouri.

To avoid the threatening flatboat, Jean-Christophe dove over the side and, in an effort to try to help them, started to swim toward the people who were being swept downriver by the current. He made a grab for the wrist of one woman who was drowning, her eyes wide with horror, but an eddy sucked her under before he could get a good grip on her. Still another body, that of a young woman, was propelled into him, hitting him forcibly as he reached for her; he succeeded in getting his left arm around her waist. The unconscious woman had a deep gash across her forehead, and blood was running down her face. With his free arm, Jean-Christophe tried to swim to shore but the current was too strong for him, and he was losing his grip on the woman. He decided to hold her with both arms, pin her tight against his body, and ride with the current while trying to kick his legs in the direction of the shore. The woman is probably dead, he thought, but I cannot desert her. He was a good enough swimmer to know that if he had both arms free he could have swum to the shore and rescued himself.

The woman was small and slight so it was relatively easy for Jean-Christophe to stay on the surface, but having been raised on the Mississippi he knew he would have to be on constant alert for floating logs and debris, for planters and sawyers, and for the dangerous outcroppings that suddenly surfaced on the river. The water was very cold. The day was waning fast, which meant that river boats would be putting in for the night. Jean-Christophe spotted a large branch with foliage on it floating in their path. Freeing one arm, he guided them alongside the branch and girdled it with his free arm, locking onto it, providing them with a float to relieve his fatigued legs. There were a few keelboats passing along the opposite shore, slowly bushwhacking their way up the Mississippi, but the river was too wide for them to see the two people clinging onto the passing branch. Jean-Christophe called out to the keelboats, but cold and fatigue had affected his voice which in any case could not have been heard at that distance. Putting his fingers on the young woman's wrist, Jean-Christophe was relieved to locate a faint pulse, but other than that she displayed no sign of life. The wound on her forehead had stopped bleeding. Jean-Christophe was beginning to shiver from the cold, and the arm holding the branch was starting to pain him. But he knew he must hold on because by now he didn't have enough strength to keep them afloat on his own.

Night fell in a sudden curtain. A thin slice of moon gave no illumination. Once or twice as water filled his nostrils, Jean-Christophe was roused from falling asleep. He had no idea how far downriver they had floated, but he knew that it was imperative for them to get out of the water. They could not possibly last the night. The arm around the branch was now causing him such pain that he decided to try to change arms without losing his hold on the branch or the woman; that is when, with a violent jolt, they struck a small river island, which patroons called the Toadstool. Releasing the branch, Jean-Christophe grabbed at the island's vegetation and with great effort succeeded in pulling them out of the water.

It was getting colder, and their wet clothes intensified the chill wind blowing across the Mississippi. The woman, who appeared to be around twenty years of age, remained unconscious. Jean-Christophe explored the tiny island which was nothing more than a knoll of earth, dry leaves, vines, and scrub. He knew that wet as they were, it was imperative to get shelter from the cutting wind. He broke off a branch from one of the gnarled scrub bushes and began to dig down into the sandy, black soil. Before long, he had excavated a trench approximately three feet deep, seven feet long, and four feet wide. He gathered up armfuls of dry leaves and lined the bottom of it with them, and then stacked a mound of leaves and branches beside the dugout.

He picked up the woman and carried her over to the hole. Her wet blond hair cascaded over his arm. "Whoever you are, wake up!" Jean-Christophe exhorted. "Please, please!" He desperately wanted to rouse the woman to keep her from succumbing to the cold. She was wearing a badly ripped wool dress, but she had lost her shoes and probably a cape or coat as well when she was pitched over-board. Jean-Christophe carefully lowered the woman into the trench and got in beside her. He reached up and blanketed them with the leaves and branches he had placed there. He pulled the girl against him and wrapped his arms around her. Sheltered now from the wind with the cover of leaves, it was Jean-Christophe's hope that his body heat might keep her alive until morning.

She woke with a startled cry and a violent attempt to free herself from his grasp. He spoke to her calmly, finally quieted her, and explained what had happened and where they were. Hours had passed but their clothes were still soaked despite the protection of the dugout. The woman listened to Jean-Christophe without saying a word, then she pushed away from him and raised herself up out of the dugout. She walked to the edge of the knoll which was no more than twenty feet in diameter, and inspected her surroundings. Jean-Christophe stood beside her. The wind was sharp.

"Who are you?" she asked.

"My name is Jean-Christophe. And you?"

"Christiana. It is freezing here. We are better off in the place you made."

They returned to the dugout and covered themselves with the leaves, but they did not hold one another as they squeezed in side by side. The girl said her head ached badly but she would try to sleep. In that way, they passed the night, sleeping fitfully.

Jean-Christophe awakened as dawn striated the sky. In the quickening light, for the first time, he could clearly see the sleeping woman's face, and he was startled by her beauty. Her long blond hair, now almost dry, fell gracefully along her shoulders. Despite the nasty forehead cut, flecked with dried blood, despite the dabs of mud on her face and neck, despite her bedraggled clothes, she was easily the most beautiful woman he had ever seen. As he stared at her, transfixed, his face only a few inches from hers, she opened her eyes. They were green, a vivid green.

"I'm so cold," she said, turning to him. "Do you mind? I'm so very cold."

As he held her, he could feel the tremors of her body begin to abate. "You saved my life, didn't you?"

"That sounds too grand. I just kept you afloat."

"I have no memory . . ."

"The blow to your head . . ."

"I have forgotten your name . . ."

"Jean-Christophe."

As they lay there exchanging the warmth of their bodies, the full dawn brought first a sprinkle then a steady downpour of rain; a mist of fog rose from the surface of the water, obscuring the surroundings.

"What do you do?"

"I write poetry and music."

"Oh, how wonderful! I've never known anyone who wrote poetry."

"I'm afraid it's not very good."

"Would you recite some for me?"

"Oh, I don't think I'm ready . . ."

"Please. It will take our minds off the rain."

So to pass the time Jean-Christophe recited his poetry, and the girl, Christiana, was thrilled by them: poems about love, about heroism, sacrifice, nature, fear, rapture, sleep, death, and the joy of living. He even sang some of his songs, obviously showing off for this unexpected beauty lying in his arms in a mudhole on the Mississippi.

The rain fell unabated all day long. By evening they were thirsty and hungry but neither dared drink the river water even though it was commonly drunk by slaves and trappers. By dark they had both fallen asleep and thirst was not a problem. They slept peacefully in each other's arms, the thick covering of leaves and scrub giving surprisingly good shelter from the rain.

In the night they both awoke, their faces close together, and they kissed.

"It will sound silly," Jean-Christophe said, "since we have only just met, but the truth is, I think I am in love with you."

Christiana laughed. "That's what my father said the day he met my mother."

"Then it runs in the family." He kissed her again.

"Yes, my father says the Valtzs are known for being impetuous about love—that my grandfather declared his love eight hours after meeting my grandmother."

"Valtz? Did you say Valtz?"

"Yes. Willibald Valtz—do you know him?"

"My God!"

"What?"

"Oh, my God!"

"What's wrong?"

"You are from South St. Louis, aren't you?"

"Yes."

"My father is Rémi Riveau."

"It can't be."

"My grandfather is Guy Laroule."

"And you have kissed a dreaded German."

"Do you think it matters to me? Because they are stupid doesn't make me stupid." He pulled her tightly against him and kissed her again. "I love you, Christiana—does it matter to you that I am a loathed Frenchman?"

Christiana laughed. She was even more beautiful than her mother. "Won't they be surprised?"

"We won't tell them for a while."

"Do you like German cooking?"

"Oh, yes."

"Well, I don't. If you love me for my German cooking then you may as well . . ."

There was a sudden commotion of voices, a bell ringing. Christiana and Jean Christophe shouted and scrambled out of the mud hole. A boat had pulled alongside. A man in rain gear stood on the deck. "Hello," he said. "We're searching for people from the ferryboat accident . . ."

"Yes! Yes!" Christiana said.

"And you?" the man asked Jean-Christophe.

"I . . . I lost my boat. Can you give me a ride?"

* * *

In the weeks that followed, Christiana and Jean-Christophe met every day. They met in various clandestine places: in the forest, on the shore at night, in an empty shed, until they decided the time had come to announce their plans to get married.

Surprisingly, both sets of grandparents were not as disturbed as Willi and Rémi, who absolutely forbade their children ever to see one another again.

"I'm twenty-three," Jean-Christophe said, "and I can marry a woman I love."

"I'm twenty," Christiana said, "and Jean-Christophe is going to be my husband."

However old you are, the fathers said, having hated each other since their long-ago encounter in the forest, we will not tolerate that person in our family. The grandmothers tried to mediate, but their sons politely told them to stay out of it, that this was a matter that had to be settled between parent and child.

"I can promise you," Willi said, "that if you marry this Frenchman and come to live in South St. Louis your life here will be miserable. I will never speak to him and he will not be welcome in my house."

"You listen to me," Rémi said, "I've indulged you, Mr. Poet, while all the rest of us worked hard, including your brother, but I won't indulge you if you marry Fraülein Sauerkraut. You understand? I will have nothing to do with her."

Guy was bemused by Rémi's hostile attitude toward Jean-Christophe's professed desire to marry Christiana. "Need I remind you," Guy said, "of the time, when you were Jean-Christophe's age, that you came to me burning with desire to marry Filonea. How you hated your mother and me for denying you permission! Now here you are doing the same thing to Jean-Christophe. You disapprove of her because she is German, and we rejected Filonea because she was an Indian. What say you?"

"I say you are right. I was immature and romantic, but as you said, we would have been ostracized, as would our children. It is for that reason that parental approval is necessary. We parents have the experience of having lived through our children's years. Loving them and knowing them as we do, we know what is best for them."

"And what is best for you, Rémi? You do not want the German

Willi as your in-law, so it is for that selfish reason and not for Jean-Christophe's well-being."

Rémi was being goaded into anger. "Where would they live? Not with us, I will not have a German—especially a Brockmeier German—under my roof nor will the Germans tolerate Jean-Christophe. Is that not looking out for Jean-Christophe? For a brief time he may manage a blissful indifference to his problems, but one day he will realize what he has lost."

"Tell me something honestly, Rémi," Guy said gently, "honestly, now, just between us—never to be revealed—do you ever think about Filonea? Does she ever enter your mind?"

Rémi took a long time answering. "Yes," he said, "I sometimes wonder how she is, what became of her."

"You still love her, do you not?"

"I . . . I do not know."

"I know you love your wife, of course, but have you ever felt as close to her as you were to Filonea?"

"To be honest—no. Filonea touched something in me that . . . well, I suppose after losing her I walled off that part of me."

"And walled her up inside it."

"Why are you asking me?"

"Because I too sometimes think of Filonea and wonder if we did not make a mistake in forbidding your marriage."

"You do? Why?"

"Because after she left I never again witnessed the exuberant, loving Rémi you were when you were with her. You had a vibrancy, an openness . . ."

"I wanted to elope with her."

"It is no different from Jean-Christophe."

"Oh, yes it is! Filonea was an innocent, the Germans are connivers, manipulators, for all I know they are using Christiana as a means of infiltrating our family and scheming to take over American Fur."

"Oh, Rémi, Rémi—your anger has robbed you of your reason."

"Better robbed of my reason than robbed of my fur company."

The only person who knew about Jean-Christophe's plan to elope with Christiana was Christophe-Jean. Despite the differences in their personalities, conformist and nonconformist, the twins were closely allied and had always shared their secrets, their complaints, their heartaches, and their dreams. Christophe had tried to dissuade Jean from running away, but soon realized that Jean's love for Christiana was pervasive. No amount of reasoning would change his mind. So when Christiana and Jean-Christophe met secretly at dawn down by the shore to elope across the river, Christophe-Jean was the only person there to see them off.

"My only reluctance in leaving to do what I feel I must do, is having to leave you," Jean-Christophe told his brother. "Try to sneak across to see us if you can. Our plan is to settle down in Cahokia, just across the river."

Christophe-Jean kissed both of them and wished them godspeed. He watched as Jean-Christophe rowed across the Mississippi to Cahokia on the Illinois side. When they disappeared in the early morning fog, he finally left the levee with a heavy heart.

Christiana and Jean-Christophe were married before the justice of the peace. They rented a room in the house of the widow Le Nôtre, who took in boarders. Jean-Christophe gave music lessons and Christiana designed clothes for the Cahokia ladies. After a while, they were able to build their own cabin. They made no attempt to get in touch with their families, and neither Willi nor Rémi made an effort to contact them.

"Christiana is a traitor, and I never want to hear her name again," Willi pronounced.

"I only have one son," Rémi said. "I once had a second, but he no longer exists."

As time passed the fifteen percent tax imposed by the Spanish authorities became increasingly onerous. Not only did it severely affect profits, but it was a symbol of subservience to the Spaniards whom the French regarded as exploiters who had contributed nothing to the development of their commerce. Finally, goaded by the audacious demands of the tax collectors, Guy, Rémi and Christophe-Jean went to New Orleans to meet with the Cabildo. As spokesman, Rémi forcefully lodged their complaints, and surprisingly, Christophe-Jean spoke up even more aggressively, but the members of the Cabido were arrogant military men who were not disposed to tolerate any interference with their authority. The fifteen percent tax generated a considerable amount of revenue much of which they secreted in their personal bank accounts. So when Rémi, who knew of their graft, informed them that copies of their tax payments would in the future be directly sent to the authorities in Spain, they responded angrily and ordered them to leave the chamber.

"Now they know," Rémi later said, "that unless they reduce the tax, they may lose their honey pot altogether."

"I am always wary of arrogant men. When challenged," Guy said, "their usual reaction is not to compromise but to fuel their arrogance with more arrogance."

AMERICA, 1800

Forty-nine

On June 28, 1800, Guy and Marie-Thérèse jointly celebrated their sixty-fifth birthdays. One hundred guests were invited to the Laroule compound for the party, which began at noon and lasted until the morning of the following day. Surrounded by Pélagie, Rémi, Rosalind, Marc, and their nine grandchildren, the birthday couple basked in the glory of their family. Although they did not mention it, they both felt remorse over the long absence of Jean-Christophe. Father Pierre attended, as did the chiefs of the Chippewas, the Missouris and the Osages in full regalia. There were fireworks, music, dancing, and singing. Performers from a traveling circus juggled, ate fire, did magic feats, clowned, and put a dancing bear and other animals through their paces. The food had been three days in preparation: great spits of venison, buffalo, boar, and hogs were rotated by slaves over open fires; tables were heaped with fruits and vegetables; sidebars displayed a variety of fish, snails, mussels, crabs, and other delicacies; there was a steady popping of corks being pulled from bottles of claret; carts were laden with pastries, puddings, and other succulent desserts. Giant torches lit the night which also benefitted from a full moon and a plethora of stars.

As the party began to break up on the following morning, one of the governor's boats, bearing the Spanish colors, tied up at the dock and three men went ashore to seek out Guy. One of the men was

Claude Lèche, the former sheriff now on the governor's staff. Guy was surprised to see him.

"I'm sorry to intrude," Lèche said.

"You are still on the Governor's staff?"

"Yes, governors come and go but I stay on because none of them can speak French."

"May I offer you and your fellows some refreshments?"

"That is kind of you, Monsieur Laroule, but I'd best attend to the purpose of our visit. The Governor has asked me to serve you with this notice." He handed a document to Guy.

> *Know all men by these presents that effective as of this date, the Port of New Orleans will be closed to all boat traffic except to vessels of certified Spanish ownership. Any boat entering Mississippi waters within ten miles of the port of New Orleans will be interdicted and turned back. This edict will remain in effect until further notice.*
>
> *Dated: June 26, 1800*
>
> ---
>
> *Bernardo de Gálvez, Governor*

Guy read the document a second time, to assimilate its implications. Finally he looked up at Lèche, a disbelieving expression on his face. "The port is closed?"

"Yes. I'm sorry to be the messenger of such . . ."

"I can't use my boats?"

"That's correct."

"But there are no Spanish boats . . ."

"The orders came from Spain."

"How will I get my furs to market in New Orleans?"

"Perhaps by land."

"How? There are no trails big enough . . . Why are they doing this to us?"

"I have been given no information other than . . ."

"And how will supplies come up to us from New Orleans?"

"Please, Monsieur Laroule . . ."

"I shall go to see the Governor."

"It will be of no help. He has no authority in this. This edict comes directly from the King. I do know it has something to do with the situation with Napoleon. You know that last year he tried to conquer New Orleans, do you not?"

"Bonaparte?"

"Yes. He dispatched an army of thirty thousand men to the Caribbean under the command of Charles LeClerc, his brother-in-law, to attack and occupy Santo Domingo. His plan was to use Santo Domingo as a base in order to conquer the Spanish in New Orleans, gaining control of all the shipping in the entire Louisiana Territory, therefore enabling him to establish what he hoped would be a French empire. Although LeClerc did succeed in capturing the Haitian leader, Toussaint, his soldiers loyally fought Napoleon's troops from the jungle which, of course, gave them a great advantage. The French soldiers fell prey to a ferocious epidemic of yellow fever and they began dropping like flies. When LeClerc's army had shrunk to less than four thousand men he retreated, boarded his ships, and returned to France. As you might expect, Napoleon was furious over the defeat and still has designs on Louisiana. So I suppose closing the port is a way of protecting it from a surprise invasion from the north. Mind you, I'm only surmising. I do hear many references to Napoleon, but I am not privy to the important meetings behind closed doors."

"Is there no way that I could get permission to send one last shipment of pelts into New Orleans? As you can see, our fur sheds are full, and in this heat if there is any delay in shipping they will begin to mildew and rot."

"I have no such authority. But I will put your request to the Governor. I'm afraid that he, in turn, will have to forward your request to New Orleans—all of which will take considerable time."

"Yes, and in the meantime my furs will rot."

"I'll certainly see what I can do."

"Thank you."

"But don't get your hopes up. There is this anti-Napoleon feeling right now, and since you are French . . ."

Claude Lèche also visited South St. Louis and served Hugo Brockmeir with a similar notice, but as Willi pointed out, closing the port of New Orleans would have little effect on the Brockmeir-Valtz Beer Company other than denying them the few accounts they had there. Yes, it would be an inconvenience not receiving certain European goods, but none of it was essential to their business or to everyday life in their village.

For Guy and Rémi, just the opposite was true. The New Orleans port was as essential to their lives as the furs themselves. They evaluated alternate means of transport but concluded that the only feasi-

ble land route was the Trace; even if they shipped the furs by flatboat to a harbor near the Trace, it was not a feasible means of
transportation since it had long, narrow stretches which could
barely accommodate a single horse, much less a wagon full of furs.
Lastly, of course, there were the bands of pirates yearning for just
such prize booty.

As the weeks passed, with no reply from New Orleans to Guy's
request for a variance, just as he had predicted the pelts began to
fester and decay in the unrelenting July heat. The tanning process
did not sufficiently immunize the pelts; the stench from the putre-
fying skins was overpowering, permeating the entire village. When it
became unbearable, Guy and Rémi reluctantly ordered the slaves to
cart away all the furs and bury them in the woods. Trappers were
also hurriedly dispatched to contact the Indians along the Missouri
River who had been bringing their pelts to the St. Louis market. The
chieftains were asked to delay sending any more pelts, but trinkets
and whiskey were nevertheless distributed to them in order to sustain their allegiance.

Having exhausted all peaceful means of overcoming the Spanish
blockade, Guy decided to invite representatives from all the nearby
villages on both sides of the Mississippi to consider the serious dilemma they all faced.

After three days of meetings, it was decided that the only way they
could re-enter the port was by force. The villages could muster a
sizable flotilla of cannon-bearing boats and men equipped with muskets and rifles, but St. Ange warned that a frontal attack on the
highly garrisoned fort at the mouth of the New Orleans harbor
would be extremely dangerous; furthermore the vessels of the Spanish navy patrolling the waters around the port were heavily armed.

"But even if you could overcome the patrol boats," St. Ange
warned, "you could only hope to prevail against the fort if French
sympathizers in New Orleans would rise up and attack from the rear
thereby catching the Spaniards in the crossfire. There is most probably some clandestine group already in place—wherever there is an
occupying force there is bound to be some patriots who exist secretly plotting against them—but it may be difficult to make contact
with them."

The problem was that those present at the meeting had all left
New Orleans long ago, so that they had lost contact with the people

they knew well enough to trust. The mayor of Ste. Geneviève volunteered to return to New Orleans with two of his aides to see if he could find any old friends who might lead him to a clandestine group, if indeed one existed.

The meeting ended with hollow speeches of brave hope that could not belie the deeper mood of despair. As a matter of fact, after returning to their villages, the various leaders did little or nothing about organizing attacking forces, perhaps out of fear that their heretical behavior might be revealed to the Spanish authorities who would inflict punishing reprisals.

Without fur to barter, Guy was increasingly forced to spend his treasury of silver dollars to the point that Marie-Thérèse warned, "We are at our limits, Guy. We can no longer draw on the dollars to purchase food and supplies."

"But then how do we make purchases?"

"We don't."

"What! Marie-Thérèse, have you lost your mind? We have a population of over six hundred people . . ."

"Who have been prosperous."

"That's right."

"Well, for now, we will all have to give up the kind of life we were used to leading. What we grow is what we eat. The eggs we gather, the pigs we slaughter, the wine we make from wild grapes, the game we hunt down, the fish we catch, that will be what is on the table. The wood we cut will heat our houses, and bear oil will light our lanterns."

"And the gifts and whiskey for the Indians?"

"We will have to ration them. You don't have to worry about your competitors since they can't get to the New Orleans port any more than you can."

"We will begin losing our best citizens. They will move to other villages not dependant on the New Orleans port."

"The ones who leave are not our best citizens—the ones who stick it out are our best citizens."

Guy shook his head despairingly. "We are back to our beginnings, living off the land, trying to get started."

"Look at it as a renewal, Guy. Like after the harvest, one plants new crops in the spring."

*   *   *

Guy never did get a reply from New Orleans, but it really didn't matter since all the pelts he had had on hand were long since buried in the ground. Some families did pack up and move. The supply of trinkets and whiskey finally gave out, and the Indians no longer came to St. Louis. Because there was no mail delivered from New Orleans, the villagers had no way of knowing what was happening beyond their confines.

Despite his predicament with those Indian tribes that had been supplying him with pelts, Guy did receive a message of support from Chief White Hair of the Osages:

> Friend and Brother,
> This Comes to Let you no that I am well and hope this will find you in the Same This is to Let you no that I am a man of a Strate hart and one talk and dont want to tell you lyes nor to hid any talk from you—I Believe in you and you Believe in me Our acquaincence is Small but the Chaine of our Friendship is Grate We are bound to hid no bad talks from Each other. You can be sure I will waite fatefully until agin we can resoom our commerse wen the grate river waters will wunce more be open to us all.
>   Osage Chief White Hair

The St. Louisans had been relying on their crops to produce the food to sustain them during this bleak period when no supply boats arrived from New Orleans, but the weather turned relentlessly hot, no rain fell, and the planted crops shriveled and died, browning the once verdant fields.

At the same time, a flotilla of canoes unexpectedly arrived from tribes far up the Missouri who had not received notice of the embargo. The pelts they bore were of the highest quality and this one load, if it reached market, would have produced income sufficient to sustain St. Louis for the remainder of the year.

"We must find a way to market them," Rémi said. "Our existence is in the balance."

They studied the feasibility of moving the pelts to the ports of New York or Philadelphia, but that represented a distance of more than a thousand miles over difficult terrain, fraught with brigands. Then, too, there was the barrier of the Mississippi itself. Barges would have to be built capable of moving wagons across the river, even if there were vehicles sturdy enough to move the heavy peltloads over the challenging trails. Rugged wagons that could with-

stand such a voyage would have to be built, a time-consuming process endangering the survival of the pelts in the oppressive heat.

Desperate now, the discussion turned toward the feasibility of
trying to run the gauntlet of Spanish warships and patrol vessels
ringing the New Orleans harbor entrance. Any plan that involved
combat was immediately dismissed as impractical to the point of
being suicidal. "I have been thinking of a plan," Christophe-Jean
said, "that might work because we wouldn't be using boats. My idea
is this: Along with the pelts, we mount a load of logs that have been
scalloped out with an opening that we can seal. When we get close
to New Orleans, we put ashore, pack all the pelts inside the logs and
seal them in. We attach ropes to the front of the logs, and we put our
best swimmers in the water to tow the logs past the warships. We do
this on a night when there is no moon. We know that ever since the
embargo, the French ship, *Estragon,* has been tied up way past New
Orleans in the East Bay harbor. Once we get the logs alongside, we
can pull them up on deck and unload the furs which have been
wrapped in oilskin. There are many of us who are good swimmers.
What do you think? The worst that can happen is that we lose the
pelts—the logs get loose or get confiscated—but we are going to lose
them anyway if they stay here and rot in the heat."

"But there is risk to the swimmers," Guy said. "If they are caught,
the penalty will be severe."

"Yes, but if anything happens, all the swimmer has to do is to
escape under water."

The discussion dragged on for several hours, but Christophe-
Jean's plan was eventually considered worthy of the risk.

The following day, he rode across to Cahokia to tell Jean-Christophe about his plan and to try to enlist him in the undertaking. "It
is time we asserted ourselves," Christophe-Jean said. "Younger gen-
erations everywhere are changing things. What the colonists have
done here, rising up against the British, and in France, getting rid of
the monarchy. We are the ones who should be in charge here in
Louisiana. It is our country. Father and grandfather created the village of St. Louis out of wilderness, with their own sweat and ingenu-
ity. Why should the Spaniards now come in and tell us what we can
and cannot do? Our land. Our people. We were born here, you and
I. We should protect it as ours. And the Mississippi is our river, not
theirs—not these interlopers who think that a piece of paper gives
them the right to run our lives. It does not work like that anymore.
Not in France, not in England, not in New York, not here on the

Mississippi. You are the best swimmer we have, Jean-Christophe. Will you lead the formation?"

"I agree with what you say, Christophe, but I am not a part of your fur world. I am against the slaughtering of those animals just to decorate some decadent ladies. There will come the proper time to rise up for a cause that matters."

"We have the right cause, Jean. What does it matter if it is about pelts or indigo or what books to read—it is our freedom that is at stake here. I am talking about freedom of the river, freedom to write what we please, freedom from the fifteen percent tariff imposed on us. Look what the colonists did to the British in Boston when they taxed their tea. They dumped it in the river! The furs are just a symbol, and we should not let the Spaniards get the better of us."

"I must be truthful, Christophe. Now that I live here on the American side of the river, I feel less a part of that Louisiana world. If you do succeed in getting rid of Spain, you will simply revert to the French. What you propose is a dangerous mission, and I am not willing to risk my life for France."

Four barges left St. Louis with two swimmers, a patroon, and three crewmen on each one. Three of them carried pelts and supplies, one of which had a stove and a cook. The fourth barge carried eight large hollowed-out logs lashed to its deck. The barges only traveled under cover of night. During the daylight hours, they hid under a camouflage of trees and vines. The Mississippi's current was at its swiftest, enabling the barges to cover the distance to New Orleans in less than two weeks.

When they were within a half day of the port, they put into shore where a little inlet shielded them from view. The pelts were securely wrapped and tied in layers of oilskin and placed inside the logs which, when filled, were sealed with wax and capped with the section of the log that had been removed. A stout rope, dyed black, was affixed to a grout on the end of the log.

When darkness fell, Christophe-Jean and the seven other swimmers covered their bodies with bear grease and fitted snug goggles over their eyes. The starless night was as black as the calendar had promised. When the silhouettes of the brilliantly painted Spanish warships appeared in the distance, the logs were rolled quietly over the side of the barge, and each swimmer entered the water with his logs. Christophe-Jean was the lead swimmer. He kept his head beneath the surface, only breaking the surface with his mouth to gulp air when needed. As he neared the warships he became aware of the quickening of the pulse in his throat. He knew that the warships would have watchmen on their bows, and he tried to stay submerged as long as he could. The logs floated easily on the current as they passed quickly down the canyon formed by the two huge ships. The clang of the ship's bell startled Christophe-Jean and momentarily alarmed him, but it was only the changing of the watch. The swimmers kept their logs well apart from each other, giving the impression that they were just strays that would end up at one end of the dock.

Christophe-Jean had been informed that small patrol boats would be in the area but not this night. It was with great relief that the swimmers maneuvered their logs past the last of the galleons and reached the deserted portion of the river leading to the East Bay harbor. It was all right to breathe frequently now that the blockade had been penetrated.

The *Estragon* was the only ship at the dock. East Bay was the farthest point of the peninsula and as a result not used frequently. Christophe-Jean led the swimmers to the portside of the boat where a rope ladder hung over the side. A thick rope with a hook on the end was being lowered as Christophe-Jean approached. He attached his log to the hook which immediately hoisted the log on board. As the other swimmers reached the ship, their logs also were lifted onto the deck.

When the last of the logs had been pulled aboard, Christophe-Jean and the others went up the ladder to the deck, prepared to celebrate their dangerous achievement. But the ship's captain who greeted them was wearing a Spanish naval uniform as were the first mate and the other seamen behind him.

"Good evening, gentlemen," the captain said in Spanish. "I presume you expected this to be the French frigate *Estragon,* but unfortunately it was expelled from the harbor for unfriendly activity and the *Santa Rosa* replaced it. Oh yes, we did display the *Estragon* name because we thought it would make you feel more at home. The first mate leaned over the bow and removed the *Estragon* panel that had been placed over the name *Santa Rosa.* "I am sure that you gentlemen are aware that goods can only be transported on the Mississippi by Spanish ships," the captain continued, "which means that you are in serious contravention of the sovereign law of the Cabildo. Since your crime occurred on water, admiralty law will prevail.

Smuggling contraband on the seas is a capital offense, and you are
all hereby adjudged guilty."

"Captain," Christophe-Jean said, "I admit that we have tried to
run your blockade and deliver our skins to market, but we are desperate because our people have lost their income and they have run
out of food. If this shipment goes through, the income would serve
our needs for an entire year. We ask your compassion."

The other swimmers had bunched together behind Christophe-
Jean.

"You do indeed have our compassion," the captain said, as his
seamen stepped forward and fired pointblank at Christophe-Jean
and his group, instantly killing them.

Their bodies were unceremoniously dumped over the side of the
ship into the gulf. The executioners then put down their guns, filled
their buckets, and washed all the blood off the deck.

Life in South St. Louis was booming. Lorelei, the "Prince of Beers,"
was fast becoming the most popular beer on the Mississippi.
Brockmeir and Willi had constantly improved their brewing pro-
cesses, adding such measuring devices as a thermometer, a hydrome-
ter (to measure strength), and an attemperator (to control the temperature of brews in progress). They promoted Lorelei beer by
distributing cigars to tavern owners with the Brockmeir-Valtz eagle
embossed on the band. (The cigars were acquired by bartering beer
with a cigar-maker in Herculaneum.) In the summer, they gave away
Brockmeir-Valtz hand fans.

"Our poor neighbors," Trudi said to Brockmeir, "I have heard
how devastated they are by the blockade. Isn't it time you let
bygones be bygones and have a talk with Monsieur Laroule?"

"What kind of talk?"

"To offer to help out until they can ship their furs again."

"It is his place to ask *me*—then we can discuss aid."

"But he is too proud . . ."

"And so am I. Don't forget he ordered me off his land. I shall not
put foot on it again unless he invites me."

"You are being petty."

"Call it what you will, Trudi. If the French are as superior to us as
they pretend to be, then they should be able to solve their own
problems."

*   *   *

The dreadful news that their eight young men had been executed was slow making its way back up the Mississippi to St. Louis, but when it did a pall descended on the village akin to the aftermath of the attack by the Sioux and Winnebagos who massacred so many, desecrating crops, razing buildings, and killing animals. The Laroules reacted with anger, vowing retribution, but after days of mourning and a very emotional memorial service they began to view their future more calmly, reassessing possible ways to deal with their predicament.

The one Laroule who was not able to shake Christophe-Jean's death from his conscious was his twin brother. Jean-Christophe was consumed with guilt for having refused to accompany his brother on the mission. Christiana tried to console him, telling him that he had no obligation to participate, and that if he had gone the result would have been nine corpses instead of eight.

"Not necessarily. Perhaps I would have seen something that they missed and kept Christophe from that deadly ambush. He so wanted me to go. He needed me, but I rejected him and sent him off to his death. There is no denying it." Jean-Christophe broke down and wept.

The day after the memorial service, Rémi had a private talk with his mother. "We must put this terrible tragedy aside. If we become obsessed with it we will not pay attention to the potentially devastating position in which we find ourselves. I have lost a son I cherished, and my longing for him will never abate, but survival is our immediate necessity. Farfetched though it may seem, I have been considering a bold move that might work out for us. A desperate move, I admit, but we are desperate, are we not? To sit back hoping and praying as we have been doing, will only lead to our ultimate destruction."

"Yes, I agree that action, however desperate, is better than waiting for Spain to have a change of heart."

"I can understand why we are in such a predicament," Rémi said. "After all, this is now Spanish territory and we have become French interlopers, but the American side of the river has also been hurt by the ban, and they are not interlopers."

"Well, the Americans are allowed to use the river all they want with the exception of entering New Orleans now owned by Spain, and they have a right to prohibit our boats if they want to," his mother said.

"But the rest of the New Orleans port is opened to all vessels, only the Mississippi side is closed. Now what I was thinking is since the American villages are suffering as much as we are, do you think President Jefferson knows about this hardship to the people of Illinois and Kentucky and all the other colonies that need to ship their products through New Orleans?"

"Of course. He must know."

"Maybe not. He has not been President very long, and I would think there are a great many things on his mind."

"So how do you propose bringing our problem to the attention of the President of the United States?" his mother asked.

"By presenting it to him."

"Oh, sure—he is waiting anxiously for Rémi Riveau of the village of St. Louis to show up in Washington and tell him what to do."

"I read that President Jefferson has open house every morning. Any citizen can come to the White House and ask to meet him."

"Don't tell me that you . . ."

"Why not? Guy and I could go. Mr. Jefferson spent several years in France. He likes the French. Why not?"

To Marie-Thérèse's surprise, Guy was receptive to Rémi's suggestion. "When you are as desperate as we are, then any action should be considered, however bold."

"Well, this is bold all right," Marie-Thérèse said.

"As President, Jefferson could use the military to attack the Spaniards."

"And you and Rémi are going to persuade him to go to war with Spain so that you can get your furs into New Orleans?"

"Be as sarcastic as you please, Marie-Thérèse, but have you any other plan for saving us?"

"No, but that doesn't mean that I can't stop you from making fools of yourselves."

Two days later, a visit from Claude Lèche made the purported trip to Washington seem less foolish. On horseback, Lèche had ridden alone along a difficult trail from the north.

"I have come upon information that I think may be useful to you," Lèche said when he and Guy were by themselves. "There were dispatches in the last pouch that arrived—marked "confidential" but the Governor who is fond of sherry absentmindedly leaves letters and documents all over the place—there were these confidential dispatches from the Crown I happened to see, complaining about what a financial drain the Louisiana Territory was to Spain, how much it cost to support it—all about money, saying that the Spanish treasury was low, and what a burden Louisiana was, and maybe it could be traded—those kinds of comments—and I thought, well, if the Laroules knew about all this maybe it might help them to think of some way to get out of the fix they are in."

"How can money be a problem for the King of Spain?"

"Money and Napoleon."

"Napoleon seems to be everywhere."

"I copied the financial figures from the Crown's report," Lèche said, taking a sheet of paper from his pocket. "Last year Louisiana cost Spain nearly eight hundred thousand dollars but only received sixty-eight thousand from customs revenue. There were other figures that involved a payment to Spain from Mexico, but even so Spain lost of hundreds of thousands of dollars. Apparently things are not going too well in Madrid and the Crown is in need of funds, so the King is not pleased about having to pay out all this money to maintain Louisiana."

"May I have that sheet of paper?" Guy asked.

"Yes, but do not make it known that it came from me."

"Of course. I would like to show it to the President."

"And what makes you think the President doesn't know all this?" Marie-Théèse asked.

"He may not, ma'am," Lèche replied. "It is a confidential communiqué from the Spanish Crown to the Governor. The American Government may not be privy to such information."

"At the very least," Guy said, "it will get us in to see Mr. Jefferson."

Fifty

As the stagecoach rounded a sharp bend in the narrow road, it came upon a wide, sprawling expanse harboring a few houses widely separated by swamps and uncultivated fields. In the distance was a stretch of forest, but there were no trees and little vegetation in the cleared area. The dyspeptic, fleshy traveler who shared the carriage with Guy and Rémi remarked sourly, "There you have it— Washington City, a paragon of beauty, to rival Paris and London, a fitting tribute to this wonderful new republic." He spoke with the broad accent of an upper-class Englishman. The road they jolted down was muddy and rutted as were the few other discernible trails and cowpaths that crisscrossed the fields.

"My God," Guy said to Rémi in a low voice, "St. Louis is ten times more beautiful—and civilized."

"Where are the streets?" Rémi inquired.

"Why, there they are, young man," said their companion. "That muddy path there is Bond Street, and that tangle of weeds and scrub is Regents Park. Washington City is a capital of magnificent distances. Where are you gentlemen staying?"

"We will have to find an inn or a hotel."

"Not in Washington City, you won't. Boarding houses are all they offer, and you'll be lucky to find one not full up with Congressmen. I am headed to Mrs. Conrad's Boarding House—would you like me to put in a word for you? I am a desired resident."

"Yes, please—if you will. And can you point out the President's Palace to us?"

"No longer called the President's Palace."

"But I thought President Washington and President Adams. . ."

"Yes, but the name was too grand for Mr. Jefferson, so he changed it to the President's House—and there it is."

Guy and Rémi looked out the window of the stagecoach and saw a large, plain, sandstone building, painted white, with no decoration other than four frontal columns. It was surrounded by crude fields devoid of trees, grass, or vegetation.

"Twenty-three rooms it has," the English passenger was saying, "big enough for two emperors, one pope, and the Dalai Lama in the bargain, but only Mr. T. Jefferson lives there, all alone, sans wife, sans children, sans friends. Gives him plenty of time for his hobbies. Imagine—he can speak six languages, calculate an eclipse, survey an estate, dance a minuet, tie an artery, plan an edifice, break a horse, write the Declaration of Independence, and play duets on the violin with Patrick Henry. No wonder he can't find time to pay America's debt to England."

"Where is his wife?"

"Died some years back. He has married daughters who live elsewhere."

As the coach turned along the Potomac, the desolate landscape was suddenly relieved by a profusion of trees and shrubs along its banks—the tulip poplar, magnolia, azalea, and hawthorne with a luxurious wild grapevine connecting the trees.

Mrs. Conrad's Boarding House was a short distance away from the President's House, and thanks to the intercession of the dyspeptic Englishman, rooms were provided for Guy and Rémi. Dinner was served at one sitting for all of the boarders, including five Senators and twelve Congressmen, around a large table that accommodated thirty of them. After the evening meal, the Englishman invited Guy and Rémi to the Union Tavern where they were seated by a hearth before a roaring wood fire and served wine by slave women. By evening's end the talkative Briton had provided the newcomers with a detailed overview of the capital, the Congressmen, the President, the Supreme Court judges and the women of Washington with special emphasis on which ambassadors' wives were promiscuous.

*   *   *

Guy and Rémi walked up the muddy path to the President's home with trepidation. There was no gatehouse nor anyone stationed in front of the building itself. The untended grounds were covered with weeds and brush. In front of the house was a man on his knees with a trowel planting seeds.

"Excuse me," Guy said to the gardener, "but can you please tell me the procedure for meeting the President?"

The gardener turned his head, looked at them, and smiled. "I am the President," he said, getting to his feet. Guy and Rémi were dumbfounded as Thomas Jefferson put forth his hand.

"The Congress refused to appropriate any money for landscaping so it is up to me to try to beautify these miserable grounds. So far the only funds I have been able to wrest from them were used to plant Lombard poplars along Pennsylvania Avenue, but I shall replace them with willow oaks when the landscape appropriation bill passes—if it ever does. And you are?"

"I am Guy Laroule, and this is my stepson, Rémi Riveau. We have traveled here from the village of St. Louis in the Louisiana Territory to speak to you about an important matter."

"From your accent, you are both French."

"Yes, Your Excellency."

"Please—that is a form of address I do not favor."

"But I thought that President Washington. . ."

"Yes, he liked vestiges of monarchy. I do not, although I spent five years as American Ambassador to France, a country I am very fond of. Even now, I have a French steward, a French chef, and I brought my valet, Petit, back with me when I returned from Paris."

"I was once a member of the court of Louis XV," Guy said.

"Then you must tell me about those times. I arrived in 1785. Now, then, I've only one more row to plant and then we shall go into the house to discuss the purpose of your visit. Poor, dear house. Do you see how it suffers? The roof is too heavy. As you can see, the walls are bulging out like they are going to pop, so we have had to wrap these huge iron bands around the house, like a big bale of cotton, to keep them from popping out altogether."

"What will you do about it?"

"They're about to remove the roof and replace it with a lighter one, so they can straighten the walls. But that's not the least of it. There is trouble getting rid of the rats. Also Mr. Adams forgot to build a staircase up to the bedroom, so I have to climb a ladder to go to bed."

His planting finished, Jefferson mounted the rickety wooden steps leading up to the front door. When the warped door didn't respond to a turn of the handle, he opened it with a brisk kick and led Guy and Rémi into the house. The lofty entrance hall was bare and freezing cold. They passed the deserted East Room, which was empty and still under construction, and along a corridor that afforded a glimpse of rooms that were also scantily furnished with damask furniture formerly used by President Washington in Philadelphia.

Eventually Jefferson reached the cabinet he had appropriated as his private quarters. It was a spacious room, its walls lined with maps, charts, books, architectural drawings, portraits, and other memorabilia. In the center of the room was a long table with drawers on each side that contained, among other things, carpenter's tools, lighting equipment, and small garden tools. The window recesses were filled with flowers and plants; suspended in front of one window was a birdcage housing a sleek mockingbird that Jefferson immediately released. The bird flew around the room a few times before alighting on Jefferson's shoulder. The President took a grape from the bowl of fruit on the table and put it between his lips. The bird immediately plucked the grape from his lips and swallowed it.

"He is my Chief of Staff," Jefferson said, as the bird began to warble.

Guy quickly and concisely described the situation on the Mississippi and what harm it was causing to villagers on both sides of the river with emphasis, of course, on how the blockade had destroyed his fur business. He handed the President the financial sheet that Lèche had provided.

"I am, of course, aware of the situation on the Mississippi," Jefferson said, "but we have not seen this information relating to Spain's financial concerns. I am very glad to see these figures because they help explain the retrocession to France. Now as you appear to be conscientious gentlemen of discretion, I would like to let you in on the latest development relating to the Louisiana Territory. My secretary, Mr. Merriweather Lewis, has recently brought me disturbing rumors which we have now confirmed that in the Treaty of Ildefonso, secretly signed sometime last year, Spain retroceded the Louisiana Territory to France. These figures you show me help explain why they did it. The fact is, it was Napoleon who ordered the closing of the Mississippi port at New Orleans."

"What? France has regained the entire Louisiana Territory?"

"Yes, I am afraid so. I make no bones about the fact that I detest Napoleon and his violent ambitions. Despite the fact that he was roundly defeated at Santo Domingo, I suspect he still nourishes an ambition to establish a colonial empire from the West Indies all the way up the Mississippi Valley to Canada. This being the case, I am making military preparations for our defense. I have moved officers, troops, and supplies to strategic points on the Mississippi. I have asked Congress for legislation to strengthen our Western Militia so that they can march on a moment's notice. And we have established a United States Military Academy at West Point in New York to train more officers. I fully appreciate what hardships the embargo has brought to companies like yours. I realize that time is running short for your people. A group of hotheaded Kaintucks, for instance, marched in here last week with two proposals: they will storm down the Mississippi and seize New Orleans in the name of the United States or, if we don't approve, they will secede from the union and conquer New Orleans on their own. My friend, James Madison, has further inflamed the situation by sending a threatening dispatch to Napoleon telling him that Americans are men of action who have been aroused enough to start a war."

"How much did Napoleon pay for the Territory?" Rémi asked.

"He bullied more than paid. No money passed hands, only Napoleon's promise to carve out a kingdom in Italy for Charles IV's son-in-law. He also promised not to sell Louisiana to any other country without first giving Spain the right to repurchase the Territory by matching the sum involved. But since the promise is based on Napoleon's word it is worthless."

"Those of us in St. Louis, and I think I speak for Cahokia, Kaskaskia, Ste. Geneviève and other Mississippi villages, would certainly join in any military action against New Orleans."

"Last resort, Mister Laroule, last resort. First we must try peaceful means. . ."

"Why not offer to buy *all* of Louisiana, not just New Orleans?" Rémi interposed.

"All that land? It would be an astronomical sum. As it is, Congress has still not approved the offer of two million I made for New Orleans itself. These eastern Congressmen do not approve of westward advancement. But let us explore, let us explore. My friend, a fellow Virginian, James Monroe, is coming to dinner tonight to discuss this very situation. I have appointed him to be Minister Plenipotentiary and Extraordinary to France and Spain, and he will be leaving within a few days. This Louisiana situation has the highest priority on his list. He should be made aware of the assets of the Territory. Will you gentlemen do me the honor of joining us? I shall have to write a pass for you since at night there is a guard at the door—when he remembers to show up."

Jefferson placed a sheet of paper under the copy machine he had invented. As he wrote with one pen there was another affixed to it in such a way that it wrote an identical copy. The bird hopped from his shoulder onto the arm that connected the two pens and seemed to enjoy the motion. Jefferson handed the two passes to Guy and Rémi. He then escorted Guy and Rémi to the front door, which again opened with difficulty. As they stepped outside, a strange, growling noise assailed them. "My grizzlies," Jefferson said as he stood on the stoop and pointed to a walled section at the back of the house. "As a gift, Merriweather Lewis brought back four grizzlies from his expedition to the West, and I am raising them as pets."

"Grizzlies as pets?"

"Oh, yes—actually, they have very nice manners."

Fifty-one

THE FOUR OF THEM, President Jefferson, James Monroe, Guy and
Rémi, dined at a round table in the small oval dining room. From
the start of the meal to the finish, no servants entered the room.
Alongside each of the men was a dumbwaiter, also a Jefferson invention, containing everything necessary for the meal; food was served
on circular shelves built into the wall, which, when a spring was
touched, turned into the room laden with dishes placed on them by
servants on the other side. Empty dishes were removed in the same
manner.

"You gentlemen will never dine at another table like this the
world over," James Monroe said.

"I contrived it so that conversation couldn't be either overheard
or interrupted," Jefferson said. "We dine at our own pace, with no
one to summon, and no one to listen."

"I did not mean it as criticism, Thomas," Monroe said. "I admire
your inventions, especially the rack that automatically rotates your
clothes out of the closet—I would gladly install one in my own
closet."

"And your comments about the food I serve, are they not critical?"

"Now, Thomas, you know I like French . . ."

"You have called me a man who is 'unfaithful to his native vict-uals.' "

"In jest, Thomas. What succulent dishes have we this evening?" he asked, changing the subject.

"A *capilotade* of chicken, but also, to demonstrate my faithfulness to native victuals, a casserole of macaroni and cheese."

As the shelves spun into the room, bearing various courses, the President steered the conversation toward the situation in Louisiana, explaining the disaster Guy, Rémi and many others in the Territory were facing.

"Now you and I have been discussing the possibility of buying New Orleans from Napoleon for two million dollars," Jefferson said to Monroe. "But Mister Laroule here has made a much grander suggestion."

"We feel very strongly that you should try to acquire *all* of the Louisiana Territory, not just New Orleans," Guy said.

"What, *all* of it? My dear fellow, I know Louisiana very well and what you refer to is an area of approximately one million square miles, five times the size of your native France. Do you realize that the Louisiana Territory equals in size the entire United States as it now exists? If we acquire Louisiana we would double the size of this country. If Napoleon did agree to sell it—and it is rumored that he is hurting for money to finance his wars—Napoleon would want a fortune for that much land, far beyond the means of the Treasury of the United States. Besides, what will we do with all that land? Is it suitable for settlement by our citizens? Southern Louisiana, with New Orleans as its centerpiece, would be a good buy, but the vast empty part to the north?" Monroe shook his head. "My friend, Hugh Murray, the geographer, has said that all that land east of the Rockies, what he calls the vast Arkansas desert, is entirely unsuitable to civilization. And Congressman Griffen of Louisiana has stated on the floor of the House that the area would prove to be a cemetery for our citizenry."

"I can only say that in the light of their statements neither of these gentlemen really know the land," Guy said. "The soil is of a richness unequaled in this world, the forests thick with a variety and an over-abundance of tall timber. There are deep lodes of coal, ores and minerals lying just beneath the surface, and even, as in the case of Missouri lead, right on the surface in full view. A desert you say? Why, it is the most verdant, the most inviting place on earth. The game and fowl that populate the forests, the fish of the rivers, the

fruit trees, the berry bushes, the majesty of the mountains, the bil-
lowing grain in the fields, the wildflowers that grace the meadows, I
promise you, sir, if indeed you obtain this vast territory, it will not
be the cemetery the Congressman fears, but a domain with a life-
giving force that will bring prosperity and happiness to any citizen
of this country who goes to live there."

"And it will allow those of us who now live there," Rémi added,
"who are presently without identity to join the people of your country and become Americans."

"Do not underestimate the opposition there is in Congress,"
Monroe said to Jefferson. "One group wants to use military might—
James Ross of Pennsylvania makes speeches on the floor of Congress
calling upon us to seize New Orleans, maintaining that paper agree-
ments are too feeble to be relied upon. Another Congressman speaks
against purchase, describing it as a mean and degrading mode of
acquiring territory—that war is the only honorable means. The Senators Timothy Pickering of Massachusetts and Roger Griswold of
Connecticut want to create a separate New England republic and
deal with Napoleon on their own."

"James," the President said, "we cannot be concerned about petty
politicians. The New England Federalists oppose everything I do.
We must do what is best for the country and not worry about the
ranting and railing of politically motivated Congressmen. I do believe that Mister Laroule has made a valuable suggestion. I don't
think that Napoleon has the resources or the resolve to attempt
another campaign to invade the West Indies and Louisiana. And I do
think he needs money to feed his ravenous troops, especially now
with a new war brewing with the British. Let us offer him a large
sum—ten million let us say—for all of Louisiana plus West Florida."

"And what about his debts?" Monroe asked.

"You refer to the claims of American merchants for spoliations by
French cruisers? How much can that be?"

"Well over three million."

"Then also offer to assume those payments."

"But, Tom, Congress will never approve."

"I don't need their approval. I will call this a treaty—a President
can act unilaterally."

"And if the United States runs out of money? From what the
Secretary of the Treasury tells me you have less than twenty million
in the Federal coffers—can you afford to deplete the Treasury of the
United States to such an extent?"

"What is our alternative? To have unfriendly governments as our neighbors—Spain in the Floridas, France all along the Mississippi, the British to the north? No, it is a financial risk we are forced to take if we are going to hold our own, much less prosper."

"There will be hell to pay in the Congress, Tom. The Secessionists will be hollering for impeachment."

"I have a homily for that, James: the noisy wind of politicians barely ruffles the sails of the ship of state."

"Mr. President," Guy said, "we will gladly try to raise funds in our territory. Of course, many of us are without any money, but there are many who prosper . . ."

"Thank you kindly, Mister Laroule, but this is a sober matter of great import. A government must be able to advance its own cause. Do not be concerned. If money will lure Napoleon, then we shall pay out the line until we hook our prize."

The shelves swung into the room, bearing dishes of ice cream. Both Guy and Rémi were mystified by the strange, cold substance and gently probed at it inquiringly with their spoons. Monroe laughed. "Another invention of our President—ice cream, although Dolly Madison claims it to be hers."

"It is neither hers nor mine. It is simply a question of which one of us first brought back the recipe from Paris. I have relinquished my claim in her favor. One always relinquishes to Dolly."

Guy and Rémi tasted the new concoction with equal approval.

"Ice cream," Jefferson said, "is but one of the many blessings the United States Government is going to bring into your lives. May I thank you again for your visit. I have made you privy to matters which I trust you will keep in strictest confidence. I feel it is important to involve citizens in their government, and it has been my experience that those who have not taken an oath of office are more trustworthy than those who have."

Fifty-two

On March 9, 1804, boats gaily decorated with brightly colored pennants and flags flying from their masts began arriving at the St. Louis levee before dawn. After the docking space filled, late-arriving boats lashed onto them until they formed a bridge ten rows deep, a considerable distance into the Mississippi. This was the day that the United States was to take formal possession of Upper Louisiana, and St. Louis had been designated by President Jefferson as the site of the ceremony. A similar ceremony commemorating the United States's acquisition of Lower Louisiana had previously occurred in New Orleans. All the villages of the upper Territory had been invited to attend; many of them pitched decorated tents in the Place d'Armes and filled them with tables of food and drink. Guy's St. Louis tent featured a variety of French dishes and wines, and an intriguing device that dispensed a new confection called ice cream. It was a great day for Guy, a realization of his dream that one day his fur village would emerge as a meaningful place on the map. Disregarding fashion, he was dressed in his Versailles clothes, replete with a sash once presented to him by Louis XV. With his inlaid silver sword sheathed at his waist, he was the definitive portrait of a French nobleman. Surrounded by his children and grandchildren, with Rémi at his side, who was gradually taking over for Guy now that age was taking its toll on him. Guy was exhilarated by the enthusiastic crowd and by the fact that after the embargo had been lifted the business of the American Fur Trading Company had become stronger than ever. None of the Indian tribes had defected; the chieftains were still eager to haul their loads of skins and furs, compressed into tight bundles, into St. Louis and resume receiving their supply of sugar, salt, beans, mirrors, gunpowder, and whiskey. Marie-Thérèse, dressed in a silk gown of royal blue, also felt a sense of pride over their accomplishment in having turned this expanse of wilderness into a place which was now the focus of the entire region. She felt the comfort and uplift of her handsome, healthy family that was now busily serving wine and French delicacies to the joyful people visiting their tent.

Brockmeir's tent had tables laden with wursts, *Leberkasen,* and streudels, plus barrels of Lorelei beer. The grandchildren wore lederhosen and dirndls; Brockmeir, Willi, and Rudolf were decked out in green Alpine jackets with gold buttons, and peaked hats decorated with colored feathers in their bands. Trudi and Brigitte wore silk dirndls embroidered with a profusion of flowers. The beer flowed freely from the kegs and the interior of their tent had the air of a *Wirtshaus* on the Rhine. Although outwardly radiating good fellowship, Brockmeir was actually ambivalent about this day; on the one hand, he was pleased with his business success and with the loving family around him, but on the other hand, he was still an outsider, still isolated—a German enclave on the outside looking in.

By noon the square was packed solid with hundreds of villagers, many of whom had had to pole and bushwhack their way upriver for days. A dozen Spanish troops in dress uniforms were present, as were token United States troops under the command of Captain Amos Stoddard, the official representative of the United States Government. Military bands of both countries took turns playing for the crowd. A small French contingent was also in attendance but it was diplomatic, not military. The flags of both Spain and France flew from the flagpole.

In Paris, after days of tense negotiations, James Monroe had bought all this land for $11,250,000. He had also assumed the cost of paying all claims of United States citizens against France, a sum that came to $3,750,000, making $15,000,000 the total purchase price for the 900,000 square miles, about four cents an acre. The purchased land extended to the west as far as the Rio Grande. Somewhat surprisingly, Jefferson had prevailed with his insistence that

West Florida was part of Louisiana, a claim Spain objected to vehemently, but her protests were ignored.

As predicted, the Louisiana Purchase set off a firestorm of denunciation in Congress by the New England Federalists who claimed that the Constitution did not authorize the purchase of territory, and, besides, that Napoleon had no legal right to sell Louisiana without first offering it to Spain as he had promised. But Jefferson calmly and confidently rode out this storm, and eventually the Senate confirmed the treaty.

At a signal from Captain Stoddard, a bugler sounded a clarion call to order and a salvo of rifle shots quieted the crowd amassed in front of a bunted dais erected at the far end of the square. Lieutenant Governor de Lassus was the first to speak. He spoke fondly of the many years that France and Spain had enjoyed their command of this area, and he bade the United States godspeed in its new acquisition, promising to cooperate in every way to facilitate the transition. Then facing Captain Stoddard he announced: "By the authority vested in me and according to the treaty dated April 30, 1803, signed by Napoleon Bonaparte, Emperor of France and Thomas Jefferson, President of the United States, I hereby transfer all right, title and interest to this Louisiana Territory to the United States of America."

As the band struck up a spirited march while the colors of Spain and France slowly descended, de Lassus signed the transfer instrument and handed it to Captain Stoddard who affixed his signature. The crowd cheered and applauded as Captain Stoddard faced them from the dais.

"This is a fruitful and fulfilling day for the United States," he said in a loud, forceful voice. "We have doubled our size and added all you exemplary citizens to our population. The treaty of cession requires the incorporation of Louisiana into the Union and . . ." (here Captain Stoddard read from the document itself), " '. . . the admission of its inhabitants as soon as possible, according to the principles of the Federal Constitution, to the enjoyment of all the rights, advantages and immunities of citizens of the United States.' On behalf of President Thomas Jefferson, I welcome Louisiana and all of you assembled here to the American family."

This time it was the United States band that played as the United States Color Guard slowly raised the American flag up the flagpole to its summit. Dancers in gay costumes materialized on stage to entertain the crowd, as did musicians and acrobats, magicians and jugglers, in a spontaneous celebration of Louisiana's rite of passage.

But at a particular moment when there was a break in the succession of entertainers, a young man appeared alone on the stage, put up his arms and asked to be heard.

"My name is Jean-Christophe Laroule," he called out, "and even though I am not a designated speaker, I beg your indulgence to listen to what I have to say." He waited until a wave of silence slowly rolled backwards across the crowd. "Today, like all of you, I received the precious gift of becoming an American, a gift I find particularly welcome because although I was born here in St. Louis and my wife, Christiana, was born in South St. Louis, neither of us had an identity. I was born to a French family, she was born to a German family, but I do not consider myself French and she does not look upon herself as German—we are native Americans. I am an outcast from my family, however, and she is an outcast from hers, because we committed the sin of falling in love, a French man and a German woman. As we heard Captain Stoddard say, today we all have been granted the enjoyment of all the rights, advantages and immunities of citizens of the United States. But how can we partake of this enjoyment if we still cling to other allegiances? The French Creoles among us only speak French, rigidly follow their French customs, and look down upon those of any other persuasion. The Germans speak only German—their whole way of life from food to clothes to school is exclusively German. The Kaintucks speak their own dialect and steadfastly adhere to their own customs. The same goes for the Canadians who have come to live here, but who keep their own particular identity. The Spaniards living here strictly confine themselves to their way of life and their language to the point where today, when the Spanish flag was lowered, the Spaniards among us shed tears. They showed no sign of approval when the red, white, and blue of the United States was raised atop the flagpole. Look around you—every person here from Ste. Geneviève to Cahokia to Hannibal is set apart from the others; there is little or no tolerance for those who are different. And yet Captain Stoddard tells us, as of today, we are all the same—Americans. But are we? I love my father. My heart is here in St. Louis with him and my family, but I am banished because fifty years ago the French and the Germans fought a war over their boundaries in Europe. It seems that the hate in my father's heart is greater than his love for me. I have made this plea very personal because all deeply felt emotion is very personal. If we are truly going to be bound by a common identity, then we must cleanse the hatred from our souls. My twin brother, Christophe-Jean, a wonderful young man whom I loved as much as I have ever loved anyone, gave his life believing that this land where we were born was ours; that we are all one family, and that we should not knuckle under to those who would destroy us. Americans must accept Americans, and prejudice must be purged or this young, tottering nation taking its first unsure steps, will never survive. The artificial barriers we have erected between us, reprehensible barriers of bigotry, suspicion, hate and revenge, must be eradicated so that we can all freely enjoy this new country of ours. If we do that then it will never happen that a son who loves his father loses him because a blindfold has obstructed the father's view. Let us all speak the same language, observe the same holidays, respect each other's religious beliefs, help each other in order to embrace this new and different life. An ancient poet once wrote:

I tell thee love is Nature's second son,
Causing a spring of virtues where he shines.

"I have not seen my father, my mother, my brothers and sisters for years now. They have never met my lovely wife, or known the joy of my existence. Why? Because love lost to prejudice, hatred's cousin. It is my hope and prayer that on this day when all of us have, in a sense, been reborn, we can reclaim those precious things we lost, that we can find strength and friendship in the people we once blindly rejected. I am not a Frenchman. I am not a Louisianan. I am an American. We are *all* Americans."

As Jean-Christophe walked off the dais, there was, for a moment, an undisturbed silence but then, imperceptibly, the applause rose to a crescendo in a roar of approbation. And the cry went up: "Americans! We are all Americans!"

Guy had listened to his grandson's speech from the St. Louis tent. He unashamedly took his handkerchief from his sleeve and dried his tears. Marie-Thérèse, coping with tears of her own, came over to comfort him. Those in the crowd who knew Guy were looking in his direction. As he left his tent and started to walk to the opposite side of the Place d'Armes, the crowd made a path for him as if sensing his mission. He walked determinedly, finally reaching the tent that proclaimed South St. Louis on its sign. Guy entered the tent, picked up an empty beer stein from a table and placed it under the spout of a keg. Brockmeir pushed down on the spigot's handle, releasing a rush of the amber, foaming liquid; then he filled a glass for himself. Both men drank, not toasting, not even looking at each other, but standing side by side they drained their glasses.

In the morning the stand of trees that once separated them would be felled, and rue Royale, soon renamed Main Street, would run directly from the American Fur Trading Company building to the Brockmeir-Valtz brewery.

A.E. Hotchner has written extensively for the theater, as well as authoring several acclaimed books including *Papa Hemingway*, the best-selling biography; *Blown Away*, an account of the Rolling Stones musical group; and *King of the Hill*, a memoir of his youth in St. Louis which was made into a feature film in 1993. A graduate of Washington University in St. Louis, Mr. Hotchner is also Paul Newman's partner in Newman's Own and the charity which receives its profits. Mr. Hotchner divides his time between Manhattan and Connecticut.